Night

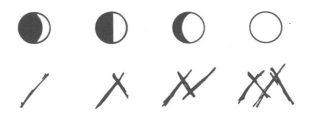

First published in Great Britain 2024

Copyright © 2024 by Zelda Rhiando,

The moral right of the author has been asserted

Ampersand Press, Brixton, London SW2

A CIP catalogue record for this book is available from the
British Library

ISBN: 978-0-9572203-4-8

Printed in Great Britain by Copytech UK Ltd, Peterborough

http://www.badzelda.com

Night Shift

Zelda Rhiando

Ampersand Press

For Mum, who tried to fill the void with love.

Yen's sorry,
twee's morry,
three's a wedding,
fower's death,
five's hivin,
six is hell,
and sivin's the
Deel's aan sel.

Contents

Part 1

Hello Charlie!
Kenneth
A statistical anomaly
Harvesting
The night shift
Just the two of us
Distraction
More of the same old
Cheese night
Following
All hands on deck
The path not taken
A teabag
Coming home

Part 2

Raking over the past
Temper, temper
Seven for a secret
Finding the way
The dark net closes
Four for a boy
Holed up
The first challenge
My girl lollipop
Making the pact

Five for silver
A place of safety
Night time warning
The investigation stalls
Dover crossing
Mortuary tour
Lunch with Mother
Brockley Cemetery

Part 3

Sav
Cutting
Closing in
Ronald
I am in blood stepped in so far
A new arrival
Doc returns
Cog in the machine
Ritual
Honesty is the best policy
Losing the Midas touch
A visit to the nick
Good as gold
Marks in an almanac
The calling bird
A snare is set
End game

Part 1

I was never loyal

Except to my own pleasure zone

I'm forever black-eyed

A product of a broken home

Placebo, Black-Eyed

Hello Charlie!

Fuck me this bus is crawling. I guess it's always been this bad, and I just forgot after six weeks off. It's years since I've been away from work that long. I miss it so bad it hurts. I just need some dead bodies to cut up.

Not going to happen sadly. Even if I do manage to field the oh-so-predictable jokes about where I've been, my desk will still be knee-deep in 'essential' paperwork. And that's before I get to what will almost certainly be a lengthy stock-take of mortuary supplies. I probably won't feel the weight of a knife in my hand until tomorrow at the earliest.

Don't get me wrong. I'm not some kind of nutjob. I've spent years honing these skills. I'm good at what I do. Sitting at home in my jammies watching the box might be alright for a Bank Holiday, but it's not me.

It's hard to explain how much I miss my work. Not only is there the thrill of it, the satisfaction of discovering the specific cause of death for each person whose body crosses my domain; there's also the pride I take in having a perfectly orderly department.

I wouldn't change it for the world. I can't see myself doing anything else. We're a family here – we look out for each other. Every single one of my work colleagues is also a trusted friend.

The phone buzzes with a message from my girl.

- Darling, I've woken to find an empty space beside me.

I thumb out a quick reply.

- Already missin u 2 babe...day cant pass fast enough :(

It was murder leaving that soft, warm nest at 5.30 am – but duty calls. I need to get back into the swing of things. With the best will in the world the temporary locums won't have been able to keep up with the clients coming in without me there to organise them. They just don't get it. I pinned photographs of how each work area should look at the end of the day on the walls for reference, but the quick visit I made last week wasn't encouraging. There were bloodstains on the floor, tools scattered at random on the worktables, and the cupboards are in need of some serious restocking.

The fridges are so stacked that I'll probably need to put them on a one-in, one-out policy. Only hitch is with only one technician working, it's more than likely that the one-out won't happen nearly as fast as it needs to. Yes, it's fair to say that despite leaving a frankly luscious babe in my bed, I'm looking forward to getting back to work.

The bus shudders to a halt and I peer through the hole I made, already misting over again.

Imperial War Museum – nearly there now. Old Bedlam eh...things were a bit different back in the day, when it was an insane asylum – marble slabs for cutting them, not the stainless steel trolleys that we use nowadays. They must have had a mortuary...mad people die too. Not that everyone in the old Bedlam was mad – in those days I would probably have been locked up for being a lesbian.

The lights change, and the bus bumps its way past Lambeth North station and under the curve of the railway bridge. As I jump up and head for the stairs the driver slams on the brakes. I reach out to grab a pole, with the wrong, broken hand – the right one of course. I've not got used to being left-handed whilst the bones knit. The pain is intense, but at least the hand is starting to build strength again. You need that with the size of some of the clients we get in. I've never bothered going to the gym – I might be skinny, but I'm strong as fuck. Once you've got the hang of moving an eighteen-stone body, weightlifting seems a little pointless.

The lights change again, and the bus lurches towards my stop. The rain is still falling heavily, so I sprint across to the underpass that takes you down under the hospital. As usual it stinks of piss, dank in the way that only a place that never gets the sun can be. Fresh tags overlay older ones, a meaningless semaphore. They don't hide the rotten concrete.

The loading bays are busy with ambulances, and I dodge them with long practice as I fumble in my pocket for keys. The entrance to the mortuary isn't signposted – except for a discreet laminated notice, directing funeral home staff to park elsewhere. I slip through the door, which clangs heavily behind me. There's no one in the family room, so I nip straight through into the tiny cubbyhole that serves me and my senior as an office.

Fran looks up from her laptop – her face up-lit by the screen - and raises both hands in an ironic cheer.

"The wanderer returns! Life and soul of the mortuary. Place hasn't been the same without you."

As usual towering piles of paperwork surround her. Several days' worth of lunch wrappers, a variety of cuddly toys, and an amusing selection of snapshots also decorate her desk. In contrast, mine is satisfyingly clear apart from a giant pile of papers in my in tray. I like to keep an empty desk – clutter distracts me. The pinboard above my desk is covered with photos of work mates, thank-you notes, and get-well-soon cards. Opening my wallet I take out a passport-sized photo of Eva and tack it right in the middle of the board. I smile once at the photo, then spin round and give it back to Fran.

"Alright slim – how the fuck are you? I missed you."

Fran sighs and starts ticking items off on her fingers.

"Missed you too bitch. We're totally stacked – they're six deep in the fridges. First thing we need to work through the backlog of babies. Fridge one is completely full, and four's on the blink – seals are leaking. We need to clear six spaces ASAP."

I raise an eyebrow.

"That could be tricky. Any specials?"

"No, just the usual for now."

"I'd better get busy then!"

I go through to the prep area and put on overalls, boots, gloves, mask and hood. Two of the stations are occupied, but my favourite one is free. It's in a right state though. I needle around collecting the tools I'll need: knives, scissors, forceps, scalpels, rib shears and needles, probes and picks. I mentally catalogue which supplies haven't been restocked since my last inspection. The cupboards are just shocking. Supplies scattered here and there, with packaging half-open and surgical gloves spilling out onto the floor. Must resist the urge to start sorting them out right now. I take my supplies back to my station and arrange them neatly in order of use. Deep breath and through to the cold store. A quick glance across the indicators at the top of each polished steel door tells me all the fridges are in order, apart from the aforementioned number four.

Fran hadn't been lying. There are indeed a lot of babies – every single shelf is occupied – tiny bodies wrapped in white cloth, each with a soft toy or a blanket to keep them company as they wait for their final rest. Even after all these years in the job the babies don't get any easier. Stillbirths. Every one will need a full autopsy – a confirmed cause of death for the coroner's report.

I wheel the disconcertingly light gurney back to my station and start unwrapping the first client of the day.

* * *

The canteen is packed with porters, nurses, orderlies and admin staff queuing up for their institutional grub. I join the queue and check my phone as it inches forward. There's another message from Eva:

- Hope work isn't too chaotic. On shift @ 2 today so won't see you till late. Keep the bed warm for me xxx

Still a few people ahead of me in the queue. I tap out a reply.

- Stacked 2 the rafters here – avin a quick bite o lunch & then back 2 it. L8rs lvly xxx

Just then I feel a tap on my shoulder and spin round, to be confronted by Arcadioz, one of the hospital porters, who regularly pitches up at the Annie Nightingale for a Friday-night drink.

"Charlie – where you been? For weeks I not see you. I ask myself 'where is Charlie?'"

No need to go into the details.

"Alright Arc – I've been off sick."

"Sick? Are you OK? What kind of sick?"

Bless him, he looks genuinely worried.

"I broke my hand."

I hold up the hand in question. It was a bad break that didn't look pretty after two bouts of surgery, and to be perfectly honest I've not been that good at looking after it since. My misshapen knuckles are not exactly enhanced by the livid scar that crosses them, with plenty of stitch-marks for good measure.

"Ah, shit Charlie! I bet the other guy looks more worse."

"It wasn't a fight actually. I rather stupidly hit a concrete wall. Not recommended!"

"So. Wall,one, Charlie, nil. I'm thinking hitting wall is not such good idea."

"Yeah, yeah. How's tricks anyway? Busy, busy?"

We've nearly reached the front of the queue. I reach out and grab a tray from the pile. Beside me Arcadioz slumps, like a man with a lot on his mind.

"Really, I'm a bit worry. Maybe my hours cut. Not so much work for me."

"Want me to have a word? You're the only porter in this gaff with an actual clue. Leave it with me. Who's your manager?"

"Mr Temple."

"Should have known. Temple's just winding you up. I'll sort it for you."

Arcadioz visibly brightens, and pats me gently on the back, which I allow, this once.

"Thanks you so very much Charlie. Is so very good you back. Maybe you let me buy you beer at pub?"

"No problem Arc. Happy to do it."

And I was happy. That kind of shit pisses me off, and Temple is a twat, but unfortunately the kind of twat who gets ahead. What little power he has amassed in life he uses to oppress people. That's hospital hierarchy for you. There's always someone on the next level up shitting on your head.

"Excuse me, I'm up. Bangers and mash for me today please darling."

This last is addressed to Pat, the dinner lady. Like all the canteen staff she's been working here for donkeys, and knows better than to give me any peas with that. I take my plate and look around for somewhere to sit. The long hall is filled with round tables, each seating four or five people. It's one of the few remnants of the original hospital, and not being client-facing, it hasn't felt the touch of the modernisers for many decades. It still features formica table-tops and a slightly sticky lino floor. Murky ceiling-level windows bring light in from outside, dappled with the trees that grow above them. I avoid eye contact and choose an empty table at the far end of the hall. I don't have time to chew the fat, and I'm definitely not up for explaining all over again what happened to my hand (or more to the point, dodging the question). I take a seat and dig into my lunch, After four straight hours of neonatal post-mortems, I'm genuinely fucking starving.

As I eat I think about Eva, and about how I really broke my hand. I wasn't completely open with Arcadioz. I did punch a wall – that much is true, but I should probably explain why. Like all our arguments, it happened on a comedown. We'd had a heavy weekend, starting on Friday, and by Sunday lunchtime after two days of solid partying, had been reduced to the state where we were gurning at each other like old men. One by one the friends we'd spent the weekend with made their excuses and left, and finally it was just the two of us. Theoretically that should have been perfect. It's Sunday night, I've work in the morning, and it's still a novelty to snuggle up with someone I'm actually going out with, but Eva is restless, pacing the confines of my studio flat.

"Is there somewhere else you need to be Eva? Don't mind me if you'd rather not hang out."

I hate that nagging tone in my voice - when did that arrive?

She looks so distant. Like she would buy and sell you.

"Well? Penny for them?"

"Penny for what?"

"For your thoughts?"

She looks at me blankly.

"It's a thing! So, what's on your mind?"

Eva glides across the room, languid as a python. She slides down next to me.

"Sorry Charlie – I'm a bit on edge. It's not you. Maybe we should watch something together? It's been such a busy time. We've hardly had a minute to stop for breath."

She opens her arms and I relax into the length of her; fitting hip to curve, neck to chin. The obvious next move is to grab the remote and pull up the latest digital offering. The go-to Sunday menu; I've got work tomorrow. But even through the ease and comfort of Eva's embrace something feels off. Like I'm looking at her through a mirror. I can't forget the missing days. The many excuses. Where has she been?

Eva won't meet my eyes. I pull away. I need to bridge the gap. I reach out, grab her chin in my hand, wrenching it upwards so she is forced to look at me. I'm shaking. The walls hurt; the lies hurt. The feeling of being shut out, of things being hidden. Now it's my turn to pace the room.

"What are you hiding from me, Eva? Where do you go? Is there someone else?"

Still, she doesn't answer, just sits there with her head downcast. I feel anger rising, the same rage that sent me rampaging in my teens, breaking windows, people. I want to smash Eva. I take a step towards her. I need to do something with all that rage, with all the power and the anger that's in me. Eva looks up at me and pulls into herself, protectively - as if she knows what's coming; as if she's experienced it before. My right hand balls into a fist. Just one more move and I'll punch her. But I've never hit her. I can't hit her now.

I can't do that.

And still Eva is silent. She doesn't react, or look at me. It makes me even angrier. I still don't believe in it. It's an act.

"Answer me for fuck's sake Eva."

The balled fist has a life of it's own. It wants to hit her. I know I have to get rid of the energy somehow or I'll crack. And then there will be no way back. Another step takes me to the door – but I can't just leave. I'm worn out. This is the last of me.

I turn my back and punch the wall behind me as hard as I can, I feel the second the bones snap; feel the hot indescribability of fracturing ulna; the pain so strong I can barely speak. I fall to my knees, cradling the hand. Behind me I hear Eva stand; hear the rustle as she grabs her bag, her coat; feel the breeze as she brushes past me on the way to the door, which closes behind her with a snick as the lock catches.

Kenneth

As usual, Eva was early for her appointment with the client. Ahead of her she spotted one of them. She didn't think it had seen her, but then it whirled and landed in her path.

"Good morning, Mister Magpie, and how are your wife and children?"

The magpie ignored her and she turned to see what it was eyeing so fixedly over her shoulder. An elderly man was observing her watching the magpie, from the crossing on the other side of the road. Their eyes met.

Eva broke contact first. The magpie scolded her and shook its head, then took flight. The lights changed and the man crossed towards her. He was in his seventies, at a guess, tall once, but a little stooped now. His corduroy trousers were worn, but scrupulously pressed, as was the jacket he carried folded over one arm. He gained the near curb, and went to pass Eva, but she stopped him. She had her instructions.

"Excuse me – do you know Wilkie House?"

"As a matter of fact I do," he replied – a cut-glass accent that reminded Eva of the old BBC broadcasts which had formed part of their English lessons at school back home in Brasov.

"It's just down the road on Cureton Street – the first block along. I'm going that way myself, if you'd like me to accompany you?"

"Thank you - if you're sure it's not too much trouble?"

Eva worried, as they walked slowly along the tree-lined street, about the magpie. Checking up on her no doubt. There was no sign of it now, and her attention switched to the man at her side. She could sense him watching her, surreptitiously. He was obviously too polite to ask what brought her to Pimlico on a Tuesday afternoon, and she could hardly tell him the truth. Even if client confidentiality allowed it, he'd surely be shocked if she turned around, and apropos of nothing, said 'I'm here to beat the shit out of a naughty little boy that didn't get enough cuddles from his mother,' which, if not too simplistic an interpretation, was probably the prime driver behind her client's wish to be dominated. Anyway, that was for later. The magpie had been sent as a messenger. They had plans for this man.

"It's very kind of you to help me find my way – are you local?"

"Yes – I live in Wilkie House in fact. Frightfully convenient for town, and of course the Tate is just outside my back door. I've lived here for 30 years now."

"You must have seen many changes in your time here."

"Oh, it never changes much in this street – but when I take a walk up to Vauxhall Bridge the skyline is unrecognizable. And people in the streets – they walk about absorbed in their phones with never a glance at the passer-by. It's nice to meet someone who actually asks for directions for a change."

His tone was chipper, but Eva could sense loneliness behind his words – an anachronism in his own lifetime. Her own phone was a comforting weight in her pocket, but nevertheless it contained the potential to betray her. She discreetly powered it off, and stopping, turned to face him.

"I couldn't agree more – human contact is so rare now! My name's Anna – I should have introduced myself before now. And you are?"

"Kenneth. Very pleased to make your acquaintance Anna."

A statistical anomaly

The first case of the day is an older gent – sixty-plus and trim. Apparent cause of death: asphyxiation. The ligature is neatly coiled in a plastic bag beside his head: a piece of nylon rope, slightly frayed, the kind of rope you might use for tying something on top of an old car.

I do a head-to-toe visual check, looking for bruises or abrasions. Fingertip examination next. Armpits. Groin. Something? Through the thin latex gloves that barely limit sensation, I feel some slight, regular grooves. I part his legs slightly and see fresh cuts, roughly done - maybe with a thin blade:

Now that is unexpected. Ritual scarring?

I make a quick sketch on the whiteboard next to my station, and continue my examination down the backs of his thighs. No pinpricks or other wounds; mild varicose veins. Stripes on the palms of his hands – like they'd been hit with something hard, maybe a cane or a belt.

More cane marks across his back. They could have been inflicted by someone else – and not too long before the hanging or they would have faded. Some kind of kinky game?

Lateral inspection complete, I flip the body over.

There are no marks on the front, and no clue in the slack features as to whether the strange cuts are connected to the stripes on his back and the palms of his hands. Still, the body has ways to reveal its secrets, and I am the mistress of them.

I start with a 'T' incision. You never know what else might

be masked by an apparently simple case of asphyxiation. All sorts of chemicals injurious to the human body turn up in people's livers when the blood work comes back. From the tips of both shoulders I carve deep lines across the collarbones to his sternum. A single vertical cut down to the pelvis completes the incision. I crack open the rib cage with a pair of wide-angled shears and force open his torso, revealing the organ cavity.

From a quick glance all looks perfect. Obviously Ronald was not a smoker - those gloriously white-globed lungs are like an advert for clean living. Kidneys and liver, immaculate. Removing each organ in turn, I take tissue samples for the lab - several centimetre-square blocks from each organ, that will be hardened with wax and then thinly sliced to be mounted on slides. I add more notes to the PM board and move onto the head.

My next incision curves over the top of the skull from ear to ear, allowing me to peel his scalp away in two flaps – one covering his face, and the other hanging down over his nape. I swap the scapula for a circular saw and neatly cut him a tonsure, which comes away easily to expose his brain. Then I snip through the spinal cord and lift it out: again, it looks and feels healthy, with no signs of aneurism or growths. The final sample is taken with a corer. The brain joins the other organs in a bucket of formalin next to me. That will do for now. He'll have to go back into the freezer until the results of the tests come back, and the coroner is satisfied. That could take quite a few weeks, what with the backlog. Then I carefully stitch him back up, taking pride, as ever, in leaving seams that won't show when he is in his coffin.

But that's for later: now I have a stack of other cases to get onto, and it's nearly lunchtime. Best not to neglect the admin. I add a quick note alongside my earlier sketch:

"Unusual markings found on upper anterior thigh, perhaps with scalpel or similar, within 48 hours of death.

Capillary damage and bruising on palms, consistent with impact of a narrow blunt object such as a cane or belt."

I wheel the body back towards the fridges, and check the next case on the list: drowning. Brilliant. Looks like it's going to be that kind of day. Hopefully the body was recovered quickly. They're never pleasant when they've been under too long.

***

It's nearly nine by the time I finish up and leave the post-mortem room as I expect to find it. Standards have definitely slipped in my absence. Now that I'm back I'll be making sure the usual tight-ship regime is adhered to. I've processed so many clients today that the details are blurred – except for that strange mark. A mark that shouldn't have been there. I change out of my scrubs, and dig out my handwritten notes. Should I write up the incident report now, or wait until the morning? The last thing I feel like doing now is a lot of extra paperwork, but in my experience, anything you put off reporting comes back to haunt you – and when it's busy things start slipping through the cracks if you don't get on them right away.

The mortuary is deserted and the rest of the staff long gone. I'm knackered, and my hand is aching again, but who knows what could come in during the night. Better get it over with.

I grab the PM sheet, listing the patient numbers of the day's cases. In my small office everything is dark, save for the standby lights on various devices. I pull my chair out and fire up my computer. As usual it takes an age to turn on, and a further age to log in. I think about making myself tea whilst it warms up. It has been known to take that long. I'll have to ask Laurence, the IT guy, if he can try and speed it up again for me. The man with the magic touch.

Is that the door of the mortuary opening?

"Hello?"

"Ah! Hello Charlie."

I recognise that voice. It's Doc. Thank fuck – he's exactly who I need to speak to right now. It's lucky he's still here. The consultants are normally done and dusted by 3 pm.

"I'm in here."

He comes through the door, rumpled in a linen jacket and chinos.

"What are you doing here so late Charlie?"

"I've got a lot of catching up to do. Man it's good to see you. Zoe's done her best but..."

"Place hasn't been the same without you. I didn't realise what a tight ship you ran until you weren't here. How's the hand?"

I give an experimental flex of my fingers. The pinkie doesn't quite curl as it did before.

"Getting there. I don't think I'll be a candidate for hand modelling any time soon, but I can hold a scalpel."

"Good to hear it. Sounds like a bad break...I never did hear how it happened?"

He's probing but I don't give an inch. Of course Doc knows why I've been off, but he's not a party to the detail of how the injury happened and this is very definitely not the venue to start opening up about my current relationship. We've always kept it pretty professional, and that suits me just fine. Doc's known me since I was a trainee. There were quite a few missed shifts, but no mistakes on the job. In return, he kept the faith through the wild years when I worked the Hoot bar between shifts, and partied for days, until the inevitable crash and burn kept me off work. He knows I need to work hard, and play hard. He sees the core of me. If there's one thing that's guaranteed, it's that he'll listen. He might not always agree, but he'll hear you out. Then of course you get the riot act. I'm most definitely not in the mood for that now.

"Yeah, well luckily the NHS was able to patch me up proper. Back to it – and not a moment too soon – paperwork won't do itself, and I've been flat out all day. It will keep for now though, Something weird turned up earlier. Would be good to get your take on it?"

"Oh?"

"Ligature case – older man – all vitals within range, except for a strange set of cuts on his inner thigh. Some bruising that may suggest beating or caning. Given last year's ritual magic case…"

I watch him clasp his hands round his belly. His eyes, peering out from beneath a halo of white hair are half closed as he considers this information.

"Cuts you say? How about I take a quick look..?"

I consider this. Maybe I'm not in the best state to complete the job now, and the paperwork will still be here in the morning.

"I'm not going to argue with you, given I've been here since before 7 am. Here's the PM list – it's number 8 – the one with a red dot next to the name, and the body is in fridge 23."

"Go home and get some rest. I'll take care of it."

I hand Doc the sheet and grab my keys off the desk.

"Thanks Doc."

"It's nothing, Charlie. I'll lock up afterwards."

***

Laurence flipped to camera 27 and spotted a beloved figure on the screen; the capture cycle creating a jerky freeze frame progress that robbed her of grace. Six weeks without Charlie. Something had changed. She looked so fragile – she had always been slight – barely seven stone, with dark shadows under her eyes and hair cut sharp and pixie-style. She reached the end of the corridor and he switched to camera 25.

She must be working late tonight. Catching up. A bonus for him. He could watch her all day. He'd missed her so much in the weeks she'd been away. He had just been going through the motions until she got back. She turned a final corner and camera 14 filmed her exit from the hospital. When she reached the street she was hidden from his many eyes.

He sat back and opened another can of Red Bull.

Five foot in his socks, a balding junk food addict, with an IT maintenance job he lived for – he was hardly a catch, nor was he under any illusions that Charlie would suddenly turn straight and fall for him. That didn't matter to Laurence. She didn't judge him. When she looked at him, he felt seen. She was real, and she respected him. That was enough for him. As long as he could see her regularly, could hear her laugh and enjoy her smile, he was happy.

In between he marked time by playfully hacking into enterprise systems and planting little Easter eggs. Never anything harmful of course – he wasn't a criminal. He did it as a warning to the systems guys that they really ought to tighten up their security. Most systems guys were pretty lazy when it came right down to it. Almost the first thing he'd done on the job was to hack into the central CCTV feed – now every camera in the hospital was an extension of his eyes: his own personal panopticon. One of his screens was devoted to this constantly cycling mosaic.

Much as he loved his work, the reason he turned up every day was Charlie. When he had first met her, six years before, she had been a young trainee, and he had barely dared to glance in her direction. Although he could access footage from anywhere in the hospital, the mortuary was the one dead spot. His all-seeing eye couldn't follow her there.

Then one day he had a brainwave. Soon enough the support call came in. All of the workstations in the mortuary were frozen. Could an IT bod come and check them out as soon as possible?

Laurence had been able to fix them in double-quick time and as a bonus he got to interview all the mortuary staff about how they'd been using their computers. He saved Charlie to last and lingered over the fix whilst she got busy with paper and pens – too nice to even show he was holding her up. That had been the first time, and Charlie being Charlie, she had given him a nod and a smile whenever their paths crossed. Charlie's computer was now running like a dream.

Harvesting

Doc powered on the lights in the cold store area. The mortuary was dead quiet despite the busy ambulance bay outside. Unless there was an extraordinary case, where a PM needed to be done as a matter of urgency, or a major disaster, he was safe.

The same technology that allows the transplantation of critical organs also enables the far more common transplantation of tissue: bone can be used to repair fractures; veins harvested for heart bypass surgery, and tendons and ligaments can restore mobility. There's always a shortage of suitable donors to meet the demand for tissue, so the profit from one body can reach six figures. And that's before you get into the corneas, or the thymus gland. The chances of them checking for these once the body has been autopsied and signed off are slim. No one would miss a few here or there.

He had sample boxes ready to go; had already consulted the patient records for these particular specimens; he knew exactly what he was after, and exactly how much it would fetch in the right market. He had come prepared with scalpel, and blades, and gloves of course – not that there would be any blood. He donned the gloves, unsheathed his scalpel, and had the samples in three minutes flat.

Doc pocketed the boxes, re-sheathed the scalpel, slipped it in his pocket, and peeled off the gloves, which went into another pocket. Nothing to see here. He looked around. He'd made a tidy job of it, and everything was as it had been; he was pretty sure of that.

On a high shelf, a bag full of belts and ropes reminded him he was meant to be looking into Charlie's case; the old man with the strange marks who had hung himself. Charlie was very young, and newly in a senior post, and he had watched her grow from an angry and chaotic teenager into the role she held now. She would always do it by the book – that was Charlie – it was how she had escaped her past, and it was what made her good at her job. Probably best not to file the report. He didn't want people interfering with his plans. He stepped out of the alcove and stopped, listening. Silence.

He crossed over to the scrub area, where the boots and overalls were kept, and powered the lights down again. He was abruptly in darkness, with only the outline of the fire-escape sign gradually clarifying from the gloom, for orientation. He let his eyes adjust to the dimness and turned into the small office, snapped the desk-light on and took a chair.

Her desk, of course, was spotless. Upcoming cases neatly stacked in her in tray, ready to be reviewed and triaged, as appropriate. He pulled them towards him, and one by one reviewed them meticulously, making many notes in a small black book.

Shortly he had everything he needed, and a pretty good idea of where his next batch of samples was coming from, and when they'd be ready for harvesting. He put the files back in order, making sure the corners were lined up, exactly an inch back from the front of the tray. In a matter of minutes he was back in his office.

The night shift

Laurence was idly watching the cameras cycle through on the banks of screens around him. Kind of like the Starship Enterprise, except that he alone was lord of all he surveyed. Or so it seemed, in the dead of night, when he was alone in the Sanctum Sanctorum. Here he could forget his line manager Nigel, who patronised him, and the other drones on the IT team.

With its threshold monitors, HUD arrays for every server, generator, circuit; blinking lights monitoring data traffic, this place could very justifiably be described as the brain of the hospital. Here lived the records of every procedure, every patient, every staff member, each requisition. Here lived every email and instant message. Communications with the outside world had to get past this firewall.

And of course, it worked both ways. Nothing could get in either. Here lived the lists of approved websites – and banned ones. Here lived the intranets and email servers. The lists of blocked attachments and approved senders.

Laurence saw it as a sacred trust – it would be terribly easy to abuse. There were many safeguards.

In reality, no systems are impregnable to anyone with a little bit of knowledge and determination. It was his job to keep them safe.

He was fundamentally a good guy, but had spent his life under a cloud. He grew up in Watford – but it wouldn't really have mattered where he came from. He'd never fitted in anywhere. He lived his real life online. He could get lost in code, be the master of the game.

He was a rape suspect. Mistaken identity, but even if you're innocent that kind of thing sticks. Your face in the local paper. Especially when you had a face like Laurence. Even he had to admit he looked like a nonce. It was immaterial that he was cleared after the DNA test turned out to match someone else's profile. The Watford Enquirer published a retraction. In ten-point type. On page 10. The damage was done by then. He moved south of the river. At least in a place like Newington Butts it was easy to be anonymous.

And he could walk to work.

He truly loved his job at the hospital, and for the first time in forever felt that he fitted in. He had a place. And a smile from Charlie when he was able to fix her computer was the cherry on top.

He was worried about Charlie. She often came to work late, and recently he had noticed that her cheekbone was outlined by a dark bruise, stark against her pale skin. Laurence hadn't quizzed her on it at the time, but he was sure it was Eva that had inflicted it. The effects of the mental wounds were subtler. Charlie was almost snappish, her usually limitless patience in short supply. As well as arriving late, she would get calls, and abruptly vanish. She was perpetually broke. Something wrong was going on with that girl, and Laurence made it his business to find out what it was.

He considered what he would need to do to get hold of Eva's data. In theory, both smartphones and old-school handsets could be hacked, with varying degrees of success and difficulty. Easier by far to gain cloud access to her social graph – with the right passwords and usernames all of her data would be his. He wanted to know what she had been doing with that old man, outside the Tate. He wanted to be able to listen to her voicemails, to read her emails, her texts, her WhatsApp messages, her Facebook posts.

He needed the entire digital footprint.

A flicker of movement on an upper monitor. Visiting hours were long over and the corridors were deserted; the wards darkened down for the night. The upper floors were quiet too – only, wasn't that Doc on his way to his office on the 7th floor?

Must be working late again.

As a consultant pathologist, Doc had every right to be in the hospital late at night. His work wasn't shift-based. Perhaps he'd left something in his office? It was out of character though. Doc was usually gone by 4 pm. Laurence downloaded a time-stamped screen shot and added it to Doc's file. When you spent more time watching people than interacting with them you noticed small changes in their behaviour, People think that data sets can be anonymised. Laurence thought those people were dumb. If you've got enough data sets you can overlay them, and de-anonymise anything. Laurence had always been good at spotting patterns, sorting the signal from the noise. With enough data he could work magic.

Just the two of us

Later that afternoon I get a text from Eva.

- Meet you after work? 4.30? xxx

I'm more than ready to knock off on time for a change. I make my way to the garden where Eva is waiting for me. I see her before she sees me, sitting alone and watching something in the trees. The garden is quiet. There are the usual patients, with crutches, or walking frames, or chairs – sneaking clandestine cigarettes; coughing their guts up whilst they drag on their fag like it was their last hope. Outside the hospital grounds tourists stroll up and down the riverbank. Stately pleasure boats pass.

"Where shall we go? Are you hungry?" – Eva is all solicitation.

"No – I had the somewhat dubious pleasure of canteen lunch today."

Used to be I would be at the Hootananny every day after work – either fitting in an extra shift to top up those band 2 wages, or on my off-days, just playing pool and hanging with my crew. Used to be...

"We could head up North and see what Francesca's up to? She'll be finished work soon... "

Eva shakes her head impatiently.

"Not today please. It would be so nice to just spend some time with you together. I've got a good idea. I know a nice little Baltic place, not so far away. Shall we go there for a couple of drinks, and see where we are then? It's just near Southwark Station. It's a nice walk from here."

I consider this for a split second.

"OK – you're on. Down the Cut, is it?"

"Yes – you don't mind a walk?"

"Of course not – at least it's not raining for a change."

The Cut is one of those streets that has semi-gentrified and then paused. Like a street preserved in aspic, the same strange mix of businesses, from 1930's vintage, to silverware, to specialist musical instruments. Even the model shop and the military surplus place are still here. You can't say that about many high streets in London any more. We pass Southwark College, where the students are spilling out, and Eva squeezes my hand. We've arrived.

As we take a window table a waitress appears to take our order. She doesn't seem particularly Baltic, and I find myself wondering what exactly that would seem like. She does have dark hair, and dark eyes, and a charming manner. If Eva notices me noticing this she doesn't comment. She orders without even looking at the menu.

Small dishes start to arrive – caviar, pickles, cucumber salad, rolls of salmon wrapped around herby sour cream centres. Finger food. She feeds me delicately curated morsels while we talk about my work, about an upcoming conference in Blackpool. Whether we should go to Brighton Pride.

I realise I am doing most of the talking.

"You're not very chatty today Eva – is something up?"

Eva takes my hand in hers.

"Sometimes I like to just listen to you. The energy of you; the way you tell stories. It doesn't mean anything if I'm quiet. You mustn't worry about me. I think it's a good idea to go to Brighton. We should definitely do that. I had a really wonderful time the last time we went – it wasn't so very long since we had met. You know – soon it will be a whole year we are together. Imagine! I could not have thought it when we first spoke in the Candy Bar."

I smile and my eyes go a little misty as I remember another of London's lost gems; part of a gay-friendly Soho that is fast disappearing forever, demolished to make way for the dreaded Crossrail.

The Candy Bar was a kitschy place, and Soho's only

dedicated lesbian bar. Quite apart from its other charms, the
floor was illuminated, and cycled through a rainbow of pastel
colours. We used to meet there regularly for bingo, cocktails
and a cracking soundtrack. It can be a bit of a meat-market
on the weekends, but the C U Next Tuesday club used to
gather there for a couple of years. You might even say it was
an institution. I met Eva over a full house. She was there by
herself, but quickly latched onto our crew and asked us to
explain the rules of bingo.

"What's your name?"

Her eyes wandered.

"Eva," she said after a moment's pause.

"Are you sure?" I'm teasing her.

"You don't sound sure. Maybe you need another drink..."

And that first Tuesday I took Eva's number and we met
again at the Candy Bar the next week, and the week after that
we disappeared under a duvet together, and things just grew
from there.

"It's been a while since the CUNTs met."

"I suppose that's partly my fault. You'd probably still be
going there every week, if you hadn't met me."

"Don't blame yourself Eva; we've all moved on. I've
certainly got a lot more on my plate now, work-wise. A lot
has changed in the last year – not just us getting together.
Being a senior APT was not easy. Running the mortuary is
a whole different level of pain. Even if the Candy Bar hadn't
suffered an unfortunate demise at the hands of developers, I
wouldn't be down there every Tuesday any more. Anyway,
this is nice: us, outside Brixton, eating and drinking....

What are these called anyway?"

"Blinis" – Eva supplies, with a smile.

"I didn't think I was hungry, but they're soaking up the
vodkas nicely."

"I'm glad you like it. A...friend from work recommended

it. Baltic food isn't so easy to come by in London – and it's so close to your work. It's nice to have a taste of home sometimes. Let's try the black bread and herring next."

Eva discreetly signals to the waiter. She doesn't look out of place here, amidst the white-clothed tables, laid with crystal; the blond-wood furniture. I try to picture her in her natural environment. A waiter glides over and Eva places our order.

"Where did you live when you were growing up Eva? Was it in the city?"

Eva's face shuts down, momentarily. As fast as a blink she is composed again. It's so quick I wonder if I imagined it.

"I lived in a village near the mountains. I left a very long time ago. What made you ask about that now?"

"I was just curious. It's this place. Is this the kind of food you grew up with?"

"Not really. This is more typically Russian. We had a lot more stews. Everything with potatoes! I don't miss that food to be honest. It's nice to have a bit more choice. There's a couple of things - pickled mushrooms, *pelmeni*, home-made damson jam. Of course in London they're probably available if you know where to look."

"Would you like to go back? We could go there for a holiday. Is it pretty?"

"God no! You wouldn't like it. It's a very boring place. It's not set up for tourists. They don't like strangers there."

"I guess we wouldn't exactly be tourists, if you're from there..."

"Not any more."

The finality in her tone suggests I'd better not press any further. It's not the first time this has happened. All attempts to find out more about Eva's background have been similarly rebuffed. It's probably best to leave it; perhaps it's wise to live in the now.

Eva pulls her phone out of her pocket, her forehead

creasing as she scans the screen.

"Shit. I've got to go. I'm so sorry Charlie."

"What's up?"

"I need to cover a shift at work. Someone fainted. So sorry – there's no one else. I can come to yours after?"

Eva is already gathering up her stuff.

"Of course darling. Mi casa, tu casa. A shame to cut our evening short, but I guess it can't be helped. What about the black bread and herring?"

"They'll pack it for you if you don't feel like eating it now. I'll pay on the way out. Don't worry about it – and sorry again. I really can't get out of it. Bye!"

She leans in and kisses me, briefly but deeply, a hand grasping each shoulder as if she wants to hold me forever, and then she is gone, in a rustle of perfume and silk. That woman! I look at the remains of our supper and sigh, then down both sets of vodka. I might as well hit the road too.

★★★

From across the road Laurence saw Eva stand up and give Charlie a quick kiss, before leaving the restaurant. It seemed their date night had been cut short.

He shrank back into the wall as she passed on the other side of the street. She paused and pulled out her phone. Answering a call? She tucked the phone back in her bag, and stared at nothing. Then she seemed to pull herself together. Out came a mirror and she gave herself a quick once-over: a smear of lipstick, quick dab of powder, shoulders back.

Her pace quickened down Union Street, heels clicking. She didn't look back.

It made her easy to follow.

Union Street was relatively busy, so Laurence pulled his beanie down low and kept several pedestrians between them.

She came to a corner, and turned down a narrow street,

that twisted and turned. He felt horribly exposed and kept to the other side of the street. Eventually they came to the Tate, with its spindly trees, and a lone magpie, who seemed to heckle them with its harsh cry. Eva stopped and looked around with a fearful expression until she located it. She quickened her pace.

It was harder to remain hidden here. Luckily a litter of large recycling bins gave a good view of the benches, and he watched as Eva strolled up to one of them, and sat next to a suited man. They spoke briefly, and then seemed to come to an arrangement. Eva took the lead, and he followed her submissively, as she led him around the side of the building. Laurence scurried to catch up. He made it as far as the corner, only to see Eva flag a black cab at the rank. The pair of them climbed in, and then they were gone. Laurence sat on one of the stone benches to think about what he had seen.

Distraction

Midweek at the Hootananny, and the usual crop of regulars prop up the bar and clog up the three pool tables. You have to look sharp to get a game, and watch your penny like the proverbial hawk or some chancer will slip in there and you'll have to start all over again. It pays to watch the table and win your first game if you want a realistic chance of staying on. After that it'll be plain sailing for minimum five games, sometimes even ten. Those are the best times. Eva doesn't like the vibe of the Hootananny and the random friendly nutters sharing their life stories in the garden. However, the night is young and I'm not expecting Eva back till late, which leaves a good few hours for sipping cider and kicking some arse on the table. The perfect antidote to a crazy Thursday.

It's a while since I've had a good pool session. Everton is on top form, and there are even a couple of usable cues that haven't been broken in a fit of rage by some punter pissed off that he's missed the black. Tonight the force is flowing and I soon see Everton off with a sneaky double.

Tall Paul is up next: you have to watch him. Master of the manoeuvre, he arranges the balls in temptingly pot-able positions, only to pull a demon snooker on you at the last minute and clean up in the resultant two-ball bonanza. I play it cool and get him with his own trick; appearing to just miss the pockets until he starts potting out of sheer boredom. It's a tactic that can easily misfire with a real pro; they'll happily stalemate till the cows come home. Takes Paul down nicely though.

Right. Next victim. Another pint of Strongbow. Strong-arm Keith – he can be tricky. Deadly accurate unless you force him to shoot from the centre of the table, putting the full weight of the cue on his single wrist. I feel bad about using that tactic, but ultimately it prevails.

Next, a new face on the scene. The first thing I notice is the ink snaking up her neck from under a high collar. She smiles and sticks out her hand - and just like that I'm dragged out of my pool daze and into the present.

"Hello, I'm Chloe. I'm up next I think? Am I playing you?"

I take my baccy out of my pocket and start rolling.

"Sure – OK if I pop out for a fag whilst you rack 'em up?"

"Of course...Don't be too long!"

I'm already heading for the door. It's a damp, chilly evening; the brief spring warmth has fled from the air and a light drizzle is falling. A few people crowd around the nearest table, and the doorway is already thick with smoke and huddled bodies. I feel my pockets and realise I've nothing to light my fag with. I spot someone I know, an Algerian, always a natty dresser, who deals a nice bit of hash on the side.

"Got a light mister?"

"For you my darling, of course."

He produces said light and as I draw continues.

"How you been Charlie? You don't come around here no more? I never see you."

"I've been busy at work mate – it's like a madhouse in there."

"And with that lady of yours, non? She's so hot. You know I would make love to her like that, all night long."

You've got to hand it to him - he's consistent. I grin.

"Easy mate...I don't think you're quite her type."

You could say that again. Eva recently described him as 'one of the more repulsive of your Hootananny friends'. It was one of those moments when I took off the goggles for a second, had a reality check, and wondered what she really sees in me.

"Hah! Any woman, she get to know me, she is my type.

You'll see."

"Yes dear. We'll all see. I know. I'd better get back inside mate. I only popped out for a fag."

"Ah – I see that girl you're playing with. She's so hot too. Is she a friend of yours?"

"Never met her before. I'll let you know."

Back inside Chloe has the balls racked up nice and tight. I grab my cue from where I'd stashed it by the window.

"All the Hoot cues are knackered. Shall we share?"

"Sure – on you go."

"Winner breaks, two shots carry, anywhere behind the line, and one on the black. Alright by you?"

"House rules."

I take up position and let fly with a wicked break. Two yellows down. It works that way sometimes – after a few games played against the same old faces a new person comes along and creates the extra edge.

I pot one more and my third shot leaves two more yellows over the pockets – looking good.

"I think that just about does it for now. You're reds. "

Chloe doesn't seem phased. She circles the table like a cat, balancing the various angles. Reds don't look promising – one tricky shot that won't leave anything on; several pockets covered by my yellows. I get a chance to study her more closely.

As she leans over the table, I spot more ink below the cuffs of her rolled-up jeans. She plays a tricky double neatly into the corner pocket and follows with a cushion shot. A red ball rolls down and slots itself neatly behind my yellow into another pocket. Straight on for the middle. Just like that, we are even. Then, unexpectedly, the false tap of a miscue: two shots to me.

"No fair! You didn't deserve that!

"I can take my medicine. Live by the sword, die by the

sword! Here - you might need some chalk on this."

She smiles right into my eyes as she hands me the cue, and I wonder if Chloe is sharking on more than one level. I'm a little surprised. Seems like my usually infallible Gaydar has let me down. I don't exactly wear my sexuality on my sleeve, but I do have short hair and dress like a boy – always have, since I can remember. Damn she is good though! And hot! Note to self: do not play this woman for money. Time to up my game.

The third pint of cider has made everything a bit fuzzy. I take a moment and rest my eyes. Give myself a stiff talking-to – something I've been doing ever since I could remember – five or six at least, round about the time I realised I'd have to look out for myself in this world since all the grown ups were too crazy and messed up to rely on.

"I'm going for the double on the yellow into the middle pocket...doubt it's going in, but you never know."

All or nothing. I bop up and down to the sound of the Skatalites booming out from the empty band-room next door, and slam the cue hard into the ball. Double off the cushion, and the yellow drops! Fist pump. Chloe claps her hands together. Irony or celebration? Never mind that now. I'm down to the black, and Chloe's still got one red on the table.

I'd better take it easy. I don't want to risk potting the white. I play it safe, and tuck the white awkwardly behind the black. Chloe is looking intently at the table, clearly relishing a good challenge. I've been acquainted with a few too many fuck-ups in my life to take to people immediately. As Chloe squares up and leans in to take her shot, the high neck and baggy jeans fail to conceal a long and lean body. I try and fail to concentrate on the game.

Somehow she MacGyvers the red into the far corner. Without missing a beat she goes straight in for the black, which misses the pocket, bounces, and rolls to a stop an inch away.

"Sorry" I say, sincerely. "I can play a double?"

"No, just pot it. I can take my medicine."

I tap the black down and the locals lose interest and go back to chatting amongst themselves. Charlie winning is standard fare for a Thursday night. Nothing to see here.

"Nice one!"

She gives me a firm shake and smiles right into my eyes. Not just hot, and sharky, but also a good loser. A nice change from beating the lads.

"That was quite a game. Seems like I underestimated you."

"I know my way round a pool table. Terrible upbringing don't you know. I used to go down the snooker hall in North Finchley with my brothers. "

"North Finchley eh? Quite a way to come for a game of pool. What brings you to Brixton?"

"I live down here now. Medical student, for my sins – I'm actually seconded to St Thomas at the moment for my second year training."

"Tommy's eh? I'm NHS too as it happens. I mostly work below stairs. Head APT in the mortuary - that's Anatomical Pathology Technician in human. I'm happiest with a scalpel in my hand and an interesting case on the table."

"I'm surprised I've not seen you around the hospital? I'd definitely remember you."

She gives me a cheeky smile. She's definitely flirting with me.

"Well, the mortuary is pretty hidden away. Officially it's the Pathology department, but you can only really find it if you know where to look. It even has it's own entrance."

Chloe picks up her empty glass and gestures in my direction.

"Fancy another drink?"

We go back inside to find Rory on shift. A bmx-er with waist-length dreads that never seem to tangle in his wheels, he's broken most of the bones in his body, but always seems to bounce back. He's looking a bit less perky than usual today.

"You alright mate?"

"Knackered. I'haven't slept in two days, and I don't finish till three tonight."

He does look tired. He can't be more than 22 and he's got dark shadows under his eyes and crows feet beginning to form at the corners.

"Sounds like you need a Sambuca. Are you doing local's specials today?"

"I reckon I can do you three for a fiver."

"Nice one - and a Strongbow chaser for me. Chloe?"

"I'd love to offer, but I'm afraid funds are tight at the moment..."

I wave a crisp tenner at her.

"Don't worry about it - I'm good for it!"

Chloe sizes me up for a moment before answering.

"Go on then - and a Guinness for me. Are you sure you're not trying to get me pissed? That's one way of getting to know each other better."

I nearly blush but manage to conceal it.

"You're not that easy are you?"

Chloe lifts the shot glass gingerly, careful not to spill a drop of the dark, sticky liquid.

"To pool!"

I slam the drink back and chase it with a glug of cider.

"Right now - where were we? "

We head back to the table with our drinks.

I'm feeling fuzzy and pliantly merry by now. Work is a distant memory of stress, and the Hootananny is looking pretty good. As is Chloe. I'm usually pretty reserved with new people, but there's something about this frank, funny, and let's face it, attractive girl that's breaking down my barriers. It feels good to be out, and, if I'm honest, it feels good to be out without Eva. Chloe's casual down-at-heel scruffiness couldn't be more of a contrast to Eva's studied elegance.

Speaking of Eva, I haven't checked my phone for hours. 11:30! Early doors in the Hootananny, but late enough on a Thursday when I need to be up for work by 6 am tomorrow. Shit. Time to hit the road.

"Is that the time? Looks like I'm about to make like a pumpkin and vamoose. Early start tomorrow and all that."

"Shame! We've been having so much fun! Be nice to bump into you again sometime?"

I wonder if it would be creepy to grab her number.

Why do I want it anyway? Play it cool, Charlie.

"I'm sure you'll find me here or Tommy's - it's a small world after all. I spend half my waking life in the mortuary, and the other in my local. God that makes me sound sad."

"Not at all. I'm so interested in the mortuary. I should pop in for a tour. Any chance you'd be up for that?"

Some people would find a request like that weird. It just makes me think she's my kind of woman.

"Sure - if we're not too busy. Best to call ahead. You'll find me on the index under Charlie Tuesday."

I grab my bag and coat and wrap my scarf tightly against the chill. My flat is only a couple of streets from the Hootananny, or a short stumble as I like to say. Chloe is wrapping up too; layers hiding the ink that I belatedly realised I hadn't got round to asking about. She snaps the final button shut and smiles at me.

"This is a great pub. It's very friendly - definitely full of my kind of people."

"It's a bit of a shit-hole, but we like it."

"Well it's my local too now. Catch you soon!"

I watch her back retreating down Effra road, and turn my steps towards home. I'm more wasted than I thought. No messages from Eva. All the way down Brixton Water Lane I think about Chloe. She's cool and funny with no sub-text. I could do with more of that in my life.

* * *

"So, how was the wonderful Hootananny?"

Her voice is calm, level, but her eyes and body tell a different story. Suppressed rage. I realise I've been holding myself tense, fight or flight kicking in, pure instinct triggered by a sixth sense warning me that the person facing me is unstable. I've been there, with my step-mum, Georgie, balanced on a knife edge whilst I unwrapped a many-layered Christmas present containing used syringes, razor blades, broken glass. I was eight. Snap back to the present.

"Same as ever – the usual care-in-the-community regulars. I won a few games of pool, lost some. I'm well ready for bed now."

I don't mention Chloe. Eva can be the jealous type, although we've never actually said we're exclusive.

I'm down to my vest and undies in double-quick time, and on with some jogging pants. Not the sexiest, but warm at this time of year – a bonus in a studio flat with no central heating and crap insulation. It would have been even colder if it weren't so tiny.

"Did you feed Thug?"

Thug's a sixty-four varieties moggy that I somehow acquired when I moved into this flat. I hadn't realised I was a cat person until he arrived.

"He hasn't been around. I've only been here myself for a short time."

"No doubt he'll be in soon, shouting for his dinner. I'd better leave some out for him or there'll be claws."

With the final chore of the day done, I take a flying leap

from the wardrobe, and land on the bed next to Eva, who grabs me tight, as if she hasn't seen me for months; as if she's drowning and needs me to save her. I notice she's trembling slightly.

"Is everything OK, love?"

"Just tired dear. Let's go to sleep."

We kiss, briefly, like a long-married couple, once on the lips, and then spoon, back to front, with the lights off. I feel myself drifting to sleep, as at my back I feel the long warm length of Eva, breathing deep and evenly as though she's already asleep. Maybe she can do that. I've never been able to – my busy mind takes time to munch through the events of the day and sort them into their proper compartments... Drifting, now.

* * *

Eva concentrated on keeping her breathing even as she felt Charlie drifting off, her body gradually relaxing, and one arm flung up over the pillows. She'd seen them together at the bar of the Hootananny, through the window that looked onto Brixton Water lane. She considered going in, when she saw Charlie there, but stopped herself. The body language hadn't looked good. The way they were laughing and doing shots together. Compare that to a quick peck on the cheek and a spoon. Maybe her hold was slipping. It happened that way with clients...of course it did; they got bored. That didn't make her angry though; that was just money. They weren't even people to her – just assignments, to be researched and treated the right way to keep them needing more. She hadn't felt the draining, paralysing, incandescent rage of jealousy for a while; not until she'd seen Charlie's casual touch of a woman she could sense was a threat to her. Of course she had lied to Charlie today. It didn't occur to Eva to test the logic of being angry that Charlie hadn't told her about a girl she'd met whilst she lied every day about everything she did.

Charlie's little studio flat had become a bolt hole for Eva over the months that they had been seeing each other. Charlie had given her a key after a couple of weeks – a gesture of trust that had surprised Eva. They had got close fast. Or as close as Eva would allow herself to get to someone. There was never any question of telling Charlie everything.

This moment. In this bed. By this woman. In this room. That was all she needed now. Eva lay back down again and tried to calm her busy brain. Tonight had been rough; a hard session that had ended with a long walk in unsuitable shoes instead of the promised limo. Shoes that would now have to be re-heeled. Silly to think about that now. Better to think about that now than the other. Think about the nice cobbler in the little arcade off the high street – a tiny enclave that he ruled supreme amidst his humming and whirring machines. He always told her off for being so hard on such beautiful shoes.

Try as she might she couldn't drive out the fear. How many magpies had she seen that day? There was always at least one watching. One for sorrow...two for joy...three for a girl...Was it a message?

She made one last, desperate effort to fall asleep without those thoughts in her head; to drive away the inevitable nightmares, but they were already massing, like the troops of the dark, at the door to sleep.

Cheese night

Four slashes that form an M.

It's my last PM of the day. The client an older guy, no next of kin. Found two weeks after hanging himself with the belt of his dressing gown. Nice.

The intervening days have not been kind to him. Gravity has forced his blood to the lower parts of his body, and hypostasis has coloured his legs with livid reddish purple stains. Decomposition is already advanced, causing parts of his skin to swell away from the underlying tissue. Yet despite this, the marks are clear, the pale lines sharp against his corned-beef thigh.

I check again, in case there's anything I've missed, but this body is nothing like as well-preserved as the others. If there's any other marks that shouldn't be there I can't see them. And it's already 5 pm. Normally I'm long done by now – and this isn't the kind of thing you can rush. I decide to put the client back on ice, and do a full PM in the morning. It might push back a couple of cases, but unless anything urgent turns up that shouldn't cause too much bother. It's time for a well-earned pint.

Every Friday night from five we hit the Annie Nightingale armed with BabyBel, Edam, Gouda, and a variety of smoked and preserved meats – the more plastic the better. Like a Scooby-snack, except there's no greens and no carbs. Just layer a few slices of whatever you fancy between two pieces of plastic dairy, and you've made a cheese-wich – which must of course be liberally washed down with cider and black. And that's Cheese Night!

The mortuary crew are already at the pub – Zoe, Lara, the two trainees, Jake, our mortuary assistant, and Fran, the queen of admin – wedged together on the inside of the long outdoor table. Laurence has his back to me, but I'd recognise his bad posture and stumpy form anywhere. There's a woman across from him, and I realise with a shock it's that girl from the Hoot – Chloe.

I nod hello to the crew, I slot myself in on the end of the bench next to Laurence.

"Hi Charlie - we're just chewing the fat with Chloe here. Chloe, this is our head APT."

"Actually we've met. Turns out Chloe's a bit of a pool shark. Are you sure Chloe needs to know our dirty secrets?"

As soon as she hears my voice her head turns in my direction; eyes widen. Genuine joy.

"Charlie!"

"Fancy seeing you here. As you were, Lara."

Lara's continues, waving her arms whilst nibbling on a sandwich constructed out of Edam and Dover ham.

"Every week I get some random punter turning up to 'collect' someone without bringing any ID at all. The funeral directors' people know about it, and always turn up with the right paperwork – time is money after all – but the bereaved aren't always so clued up. Every week I have to tell them the same thing. You can't check a body out of the mortuary, or even view one, unless you can present your passport and that of the deceased – which should of course have the corner cut off to show that it's been invalidated. That doesn't stop people from trying though. They think it's like a funeral home, where you can just pitch up and arrange a viewing. That's Fran's department."

Fran rolls her eyes.

"You wouldn't believe the hours I spend trying to get people to understand basic regulations. Then there are the calls I have to make to the dead persons' relatives – to tell them that the body is ready to be released. One time it was so hectic in the mortuary that I called up the family and accidentally asked for the deceased by name. A quick-thinking 'Sorry – have you been mis-sold PPI?' reduced the embarrassment factor on that one."

"You need to be a bit weird to do this job – but not too peculiar. They never advertise, and it's a tiny community – just 900 APTs in the UK. It's a small club, and most people know each other – even if just from conference. You'd get all kinds of nutters applying if you put a job in the paper – reading between the lines it's all 'I want to touch dead bodies'. I can't explain why I wanted to do it. I just did."

Lara cuts in.

"I just love doing post mortems. The clients don't ask awkward questions, try and get around the rules, or get impatient. PMs are bloody hard work, but they don't play on your heartstrings like the cries of the bereaved. Some people seem to take death quietly, but you can see the pain in their eyes."

"It does really get to you sometimes. I had a 16 year old in yesterday. Child deaths are the worst. Suicide's on the rise. You don't want to go into work and see that – it gets you down. And then there's the old guys, that hang themselves. Had two of those today, and no one to release the body to. That kind of loneliness. It takes a certain kind of person to be able to deal with it."

Chloe takes her hand.

"I can understand that, Lara. I don't know how you cope with it. I guess I'll have to learn to toughen up a bit when I qualify."

"Mostly you don't have time to worry. We get through a thousand PMs a year - all the bodies South of the river. Infectious diseases. Maternal stillbirth. You dread a big pileup, or a train derailing. Everyone has to stay at work until it's all over; all the bodies brought in. Some of the casualties don't make it through the first 24 hours. They're quick to process – cause of death is usually pretty obvious - but it's a lot to take in all at once."

I've zoned out of the conversation but Chloe is lapping it up. Lara and Zoe are swapping anecdotes like ping-pong balls, and I've heard most of them before. I've got too much on my mind to relax. I'm worried about Doc. I should have mentioned the latest case to him today, rather than waiting until tomorrow. I tried to call him again earlier, and went straight to voicemail. No reply to yesterday's email either. It's not like him. Normally he's an open door. I'm only across the road from the hospital; it would be easy enough to pop back, and he's very likely still in his office.

At least it's not open-plan. I picture the office interior with many papers stuck to the glass walls, layered on top of each other. Random mess? Or carefully arranged to conceal what goes on inside? It feels strange to be thinking about Doc this way. He hasn't seemed quite himself since I came back – not the Doc I remember from before the hand incident.

Don't be silly Charlie. Leave it for now. After all, it's not like he ever goes anywhere, is it? Go and see him in the morning, just like you planned. It will be too weird barging into his office and asking him about that.

"Anyway you lot, I'm off. No rest for the wicked. Seems like Doc needs his laptop sorting."

"Aren't you off-shift?"

"He's taken to working late recently. I don't mind - it's not like I've got anything better to do."

"OK, well when you see him, tell Doc to answer my emails!"

Laurence seems like a man with something on his mind, and I can't help wondering if there's something else he wants to say. I keep my eyes on him as he hurries away.

Following

Most people don't know, or don't care about the amount of data an Android phone (or any phone, but it's more insidious and easy to hack on some systems than others) collects about them, and how easy it is to take this data and form a picture of every moment of their waking days – especially in London, where you're never more than a few feet from a phone mast. Getting Eva's number off Charlie's phone was tricky, but once he had that, it was a piece of cake to track her location.

Now Eva's pin was located at the Imperial War Museum – en route to his flat from the Annie Nightingale. He decided to check out what she was up to. It was just a few minutes walk, and on his way home. He spotted her immediately, There she was, sitting on a bench near the main gate, seemingly deep in conversation with a man he'd never seen before. They made quite a contrast: Eva, zipped up in tight black leggings, with long leather boots and a tailored jacket; the man bundled in a shapeless overcoat that looked as if it had once fit well, before age withered him. He had a shock of white hair and was balancing an old-fashioned hat on his knees.

He wondered what had brought them together. As if Eva felt someone watching, she scanned around, and Laurence concealed himself behind a wall. When the view was clear again, Eva and the stranger were already disappearing up Kennington road. He followed them as far as Walnut Tree Walk, where they turned off the main road and vanished into a block of flats.

She would probably be there for a while. His best approach was probably to retreat to the Tankard, and wait for her next move. As he nursed a diet Coke and kept a watch on the door, he tried to fit this latest information into his mental dossier. Keeping tabs on Eva was taking a lot of time. Her file had grown so unwieldy he had to create a new database schema to hold all the bits of her. Even then it felt like she had a way of slipping between the cracks, as if she could become mist, and vanish.

Laurence wasn't the man to be afraid of a challenge. The more impenetrable Eva was, the more he wanted to peer into every part of her. As yet, he didn't know what he would do with the information he found, but in Laurence's world, information was currency, and like a miser, he couldn't help gathering it up.

Now he had the tools to create a timeline.

But he still didn't know why.

All hands on deck

My desk phone rings at 3:40 pm, whilst I'm busy writing up PM reports and updating the rota. I consider sending it voicemail, so I can get my paperwork finished and get the hell out of here, but I'm soon glad I didn't. There's been an incident at Parliament. Some guy hijacked a London Tour bus, which careered along the busy pavements of Westminster Bridge and Parliament Square, crushing an unknown number of pedestrians. He was taken out by a police marksman, but not before stabbing an MP on his way out of Commons, and several bystanders.

The Met have put Parliament Square in lockdown. So far two dead, maybe more and at least one person jumped off Westminster Bridge as the tourist bus zigzagged past. The coastguard are combing the river for bodies. Generally the victims would be shared between different hospitals, depending on the nature of their injuries, but as it happened right across the river, they're all coming here.

Time to clear the decks. Even in the windowless mortuary, through layers of building and soundproofing, I can hear the buzz of helicopters. The hospital itself seems, if anything, quieter than normal; things are still fluid. Anyone who can move is probably pressed up against the north and west-facing windows of the hospital, watching the situation unfold on the bridge.

I get another call – this time from Laurence, who tells me that some clown in Operations decided to email all@ to warn them about the emergency, and remind them to keep calm, and use procedure - and the resultant million plus emails has just about taken the rest of his systems down. It will probably take a couple of days to clear the backlog. Never rains, eh?

I go through to the PM room, where there's drum and

bass on the stereo, and each of my technicians are bent over a client, in various stages of autopsy.

"Folks."

I clap my hands and wait for them to stop and look at me.

"Sorry to cut in. A major situation is unfolding and we've been asked to stand by and deal with any fallout. So far we have one stabbing, and multiple injuries due to a bus running into a crowd of pedestrians. I'll need to put the whole staff on standby. No one is allowed to leave until the situation stabilizes. We need to potentially make space for....Well, I'm afraid we're looking at a possible twenty."

Lara pulls down her mask and puts a blood stained glove up to her mouth.

"I've requested backup, and porters. Each of you work with a porter, and we'll start getting them shifted around. Fran – can you update the charts?"

"Of course Boss."

"Let's get to work."

* * *

The phone rings again. Damn. I'd better take this one.

"Hi Mother – are you calling to check I'm OK?"

"Well yes, generally – checking you haven't had any axe-wielding maniacs rampaging about the hospital, that sort of thing."

"No Mother. There's been nothing like that. But there are some very definitely dead people, and more on the critical list – so if you don't mind, I'd better get on."

"So, you don't know when you'll get off?"

I sigh, and explain as patiently as possible.

"Probably not for several days at this rate. Look, I'll call you when I get a breather. Everything's fine, alright?"

You could say I have a complicated relationship with Mum. After Dad left, it was just the two of us. Those were our closest times – I barely remember us as a family of three. It was just me and Mum from 6 to 12. But then Dad got a new girlfriend, and wanted more contact. I was going through my teens, and at first resisted it tooth and nail – I didn't trust him as far as I could throw him. But actually his new partner wasn't so bad, and Mum had started having boyfriends of her own, which brought it's own complications. As if to compensate, got much more strict, wanting to know what I was up to day and night. By then of course, she'd already lost me to the streets of Brixton, running with a crew. By 14 I'd started going clubbing, selling a few class A's here and there to pay my way. I've known from the earliest age, as soon as I could dress myself, that I wasn't a girly girl. Soon after came the understanding that I didn't like boys – something Mum has never been able to get her head around. Dad was more laid-back, and Dad's house, and his girlfriend Naila provided a welcome respite from Mother's surveillance, Naila would always cover for me if I wanted to spend the night 'at a mates' house', and there was always a spliff round there too – another thing Mum didn't approve of. My absences from home became more frequent, as did the arguments on those occasions when I returned. Sometimes Mum would get tired of arguing, and resort to fists. The one thing that didn't suffer was my schoolwork. When everything else was falling apart, that was one area where I was able to keep up standards. Even if I'd been out all night clubbing I'd be up with the lark and at school bright and early. It was my way out.

Now that I'm older, I realise that Mum was trying to protect me – but the scars of our many arguments remain. I'm not sure we'll ever be able to build that trust up again. Mum tries, and I know our distance makes her sad – but not enough make me want to let her into my life again.

Not the time Charlie. Definitely not the time. And best not be caught conversing with yourself either...People will talk!

Another call. What is it with the phone today? Mostly people don't call me at work. This time it's Eva, and I tap the 'I'll call you back later' option to send a message. The last thing I need now is to get into conversation. It will probably have consequences – ignoring Eva usually does – but that's low priority right now - there's just too much to do.

It could be said that Eva comes with a lot of baggage – for someone who seems to travel through life so light, she's dragging something heavy behind her. Her past is like a trawl net – mostly underwater, with an unknown catch, some of which would probably be impossible to identify. I don't even know if she has any family – she could even be an orphan for all I know. She hates talking about her past, but she often has nightmares, and talks in her sleep. Nothing that makes sense. She wakes up screaming and clutching me like a drowning woman. Then it takes a long while to gentle her back to sleep. She doesn't want to make love, just to be held. There are definitely easier people to have a relationship with, if I'm being entirely honest with myself. Not that I've ever been that great at stable relationships. Maybe I'm as much to blame as Eva.

I step through to the prep area, and start the complicated process of suiting up.

The path not taken

On the 159, Eva tried Charlie's phone again. For the third time it went straight to Charlie's cheery voicemail without even ringing. The traffic was backed up all the way to the Imperial War Museum, and she'd been gazing at it for twenty minutes now. She glanced at the time. Five after four. Charlie didn't usually screen her calls unless things were crazy, especially as she'd normally finished for the day by 4 pm, and they'd arranged to meet after work. Whatever was holding them up must be massive – and possibly involve Charlie.

Her phone chimed – a message, but not from Charlie. It was a new client. He had passed the 'pervert test' by not asking if she was wearing kinky boots the first time they spoke on the phone, and none of his messages since had set off her warning sense. He knew the rules. No touching. No kissing. She replied, agreeing to meet him at her studio two days hence. Eva had travelled all over the world, learning her craft, but had found her home in London. There was a curiously formal etiquette to the BDSM scene here that was a welcome contrast to the extreme sadism and humiliation of the German and Japanese scenes. Everywhere a different style, but the intertwining of pain, pleasure and sexual power universal. Eva was there not just to cause pain, but to help them transcend it.

Abruptly the lights inside the bus blinked on and off, and the driver turned the engine off. Around her the other passengers sighed and tutted, and started to gather up their belongings. It seemed the road ahead was closed. The driver made an announcement.

"It doesn't look like we'll be going anywhere for a while, so if you want to get off now and seek alternative transport to your destinations, I'd advise that you do that now. The bus will be terminating here."

There was a swift rush for the doors, and Eva found herself on the pavement opposite the Imperial War Museum.

She considered and discarded the thought of going into the museum. She had never been a fan of war. Madness interested her more – the many lunatics held there over 150 years. And the sobering thought that had she been alive at that time she would have been one of them. She decided to go into the gardens and sit for a while. She could always walk to the hospital from here if she got a message from Charlie.

Meanwhile she could make good use of the time by planning what she would do with her new client. Ever since she had become an independent she had felt a deep sense of ownership of her clients – and a deep understanding of why each of them came to kneel and be hurt by her. It wasn't just the fee - the tribute - that gave her power. Nor the look in their eyes as she expertly applied nipple clamps, slotted hooks into the fascia of their skin, hung weights from their testicles, until they cried mercy. She always said to them 'You must say mercy for both our sakes', and she meant it. She's not an abuser; they agreed the rules and she provided the service.

Was it worth trying Charlie again? Probably not. She would know everything in time. Meanwhile, if there had been some kind of major incident there was every chance that she would have the next three to four days to herself. Charlie would be flat out doing overtime, and too knackered in between to want to socialise.

Inside the gardens were quiet, insulated from the road by soaring London plane trees, just now coming into leaf. Above her she heard the harsh ascending call of a magpie. Where? Amidst the mostly bare branches, lightly dusted with green, she spotted flashes of black and white plumage.

Of course they would be here. She looked around. There, on a lone bench, she saw an older man with a neatly folded newspaper on his knees. She looked away, and then, furtively, back again. He looked like someone else – a guy she'd met here a couple of times before he had invited her back to his flat near the Tankard. He had proved a most willing subject, and perhaps she'd been neglecting him whilst other matters claimed her attention. Were they sending her a reminder?

The scene was just a game she played – it would never be enough for them. It never would be. Soon they must have not just blood, but life. And what did she get? Youth. Health. Luck. Escape. Once it had been worth it...

She peered up through the branches, trying to make out how many there were, trying to separate their clacking chatter into the voices of individual birds. And then there was a flash of black and white feathers swooping over her head and they were gone. Still, the message seemed clear, and she had time to kill. He would almost certainly be at home. There was a bakery across the road that did half-decent pastries. She wouldn't want to arrive empty-handed.

A teabag

Victor opened the tea caddy to check, even though he knew already that there would be nothing but dust inside. He'd already re-used the last teabag three times, and thought wistfully of those days when he had been so profligate as to make himself pots of tea, with two and three bags. Imagine! Maybe he should switch to leaves. Maybe he should be better at economizing – but economy would only go so far with prices rising all the time. Nothing ever gets any cheaper. At least now the newspapers are free, even if most of the news seems unbelievable. Funny how you never think it will go that way – at 20, at 30, at 40 you never imagine that one day, in your seventies, you'll find yourself counting teabags and ruing pennies spent.

Actually, as a student in digs, those many decades ago, he had been poor. But it was a different kind of poverty – the camaraderie of the set meant they could throw their few shillings together for a drink or two, and live on soup and beans. Now who was there? Everyone was dead, or had moved on. His parents had passed away. They'd never been a very large family, nor particularly close. How had it happened that he knew not a single person from whom to beg a teabag? Of course the neighbours were out of the question. They'd just see him as a charity case, and the last thing he needed was their pity.

He should have found something more to fill up his later years, He'd been an ad copywriter in his time. He flattered himself that he could still turn a sentence. From time to time he'd kept a journal, but for a long time now it didn't seem as though there was anything worth recording. Maybe he should take it up again – if only to have where to direct his thoughts.

After all, a journal was a kind of conversation – even if only with yourself.

His life had not always been so lonely. There had been Tom, and their weekly games of chess - every last Tuesday night of the month for nigh on 23 years. It was like a metronome, ticking off the years...and then, a dozen or so games later, he was gone. Victor had played him in the hospice; he remembered that last game like it was yesterday.

"Check"

Tom winced.

"You didn't need to say that."

"Tom, are you feeling OK?"

"Kind of. It doesn't hurt any more. Actually, the drugs are very effective. Mate in six though. How things have changed."

They had worked together for 25 years. Tom was a family man, but he'd always made time for Victor. The monthly chess games became more sporadic when children arrived, but never lapsed completely – and then as Tom's marriage faltered, they had resumed their earlier regularity. It was always just chess though. All surface, no interior, and now Victor regretted not delving more deeply.

And then Tom was gone. Another funeral. In fact, thinking about it, that was the last funeral he'd been to in a long time, apart from a distant cousin. And really, they hadn't talked much when he was alive, but at least it had been a real, long friendship.

You couldn't really blame the government, not as a pensioner. Every day you read stories of food banks, bedroom tax, child poverty. There are riots in the streets. 1% have all the wealth; everyone else has 1% of nothing. The news is always dire. But still the pension comes through, regular as the junk mail on the doorstep.

"Victor, do you really need a cup of tea? With no teabags, there's milk to spare. Nice hot milk's probably a better idea, don't you think?"

His voice sounded loud in the small kitchen. Doesn't do to start talking to yourself; who knows where that might lead? The next thing you know you're answering yourself back, and what if an argument ensued? No, not hot milk first thing in the morning. The thought of it! A man needed a decent cup of tea.

And why do I still get up, punctually, at 8.30 each morning? The same dull round of it, as if I can't bear to miss even one moment of this world. What changes? That a teabag could be the tipping point. The very idea!

"Victor. Get a hold of yourself. One day teabags, the next day everything!"

That was all very well, but the fact remained. He did not have the readies to purchase a teabag. He could not borrow a teabag. Of tea there was none.

Wool-gathering again. Is that what they mean by a fugue state? You're suddenly there, in the moment, and you've no clue how much time has passed, in that daze. He awakes, finds himself clutching an empty tea caddy at the kitchen sink, gazing out the window without seeing what is there.

Winter had stripped the trees of their leaves, leaving them skeletal, the spring foliage not yet grown in, and there was nowhere for the birds to hide. There, in the fork of a tree, was a magpie – and he could swear it was looking back at him.

I don't know Victor. One minute you're talking to yourself – and the next it's magpies. Male or female? How do you tell the difference? The magpie spread its wings and settled again. Victor stepped to the side, and the head tracked him. It was watching him! Well, they were known to be thieves.

Victor's kitchen window was on the ground floor of his housing association flat in Bermondsey. In an effort to make the environs less grim, at some point the council had put in some trees, which had grown in a spindly way to about twenty feet tall now. He realised that the magpie was not alone. There were several others in the trees, and they too seemed to be watching him. Could it be possible? He liked being able to watch people walking past from the kitchen window. He never felt overlooked – it made him feel less lonely in fact. But now, under the gaze of a gulp of magpies, a mischief of magpies, a charm, a mystic, a murder of magpies (what was the term?) he felt uneasy, and wished the window were equipped with a blind.

Victor, you need to get out more if four birds in a tree worry you that much.

It wouldn't do.

I need to get out for a walk. Fresh air – that will sort it. Walking is free at least. And it's a while since I've been to the river. That's what I'll do.

It was a while since he'd seen a magpie at rest; they were such handsome birds. The contrast of black and white feathers; the lustre of their iridescent tails. The magpie flitted to join its fellow, but still, didn't take flight. Well and all. I should wrap up warm and go for a walk. Go and look at all the new developments past Tower Bridge, where the mayor's headquarters squatted like a great spaceship tethered to the edge of the Thames. There were still free things to be had in this great city, if he could make the distance. It didn't look like rain.

Victor put down the tea caddy and went to fetch his coat. Worn now. The shoulders dropped and shiny from years of use, it still retained its ability to keep him warm. Had it always been so heavy? He changed his slippers for his best outdoor shoes and wrapped a scarf tightly around his neck. He would do. Spectacles, testicles, wallet and watch. Wallet in the inside pocket – thick with bus tickets and receipts and coupons and cuttings it made a comforting bulge. Umbrella? You never knew, and it could double as a walking stick – not that he needed one of course.

Another little lie you tell yourself, eh?

All ready now. He locked the door behind him and crossed the empty vestibule to the street door. Mid-morning, and the estate was peaceful, although in the distance he could hear traffic, the blare of a siren. He heard the raucous cry of a bird above him and looked up. The magpies, it seemed, were still watching him. He set off through the estate.

It wasn't too long until he hit the high street, and followed it along until he had reached Tower Bridge. Even though he had been that way barely months before he was shocked at the changes a short time had wrought. Then it had been swathed in scaffolding; pedestrian routes dark passageways through the mass of construction. Now new buildings had sprouted, like mushrooms – blocks of colourful modernist flats replacing the office blocks that had been thrown up in the seventies. The old police station, the warehouses that had once lined the river – gone. Around the Lord Mayor's HQ a grid of wind-tunnels inadequately humanised by stone benches and water features with aspirational words laser-cut into their sides blocked his view of the river from Tooley Street. At ground level were all kinds of new-style eateries, where a cup of coffee cost a week's food budget. Busy-looking people crouched on tall stools and pecked away on laptops. What trees there were looked out of place in all this vastness – a careless scribble against the acres of glass that reflected the emptiness back in an infinite tunnel. Victor began to regret his impulse to take a walk. This new London was no place for him. Perhaps further on he would find buildings on a more human scale.

Hays Galleria was still there, an elegant Georgian interpretation of the golden section, but filled now with tourist-friendly gift shops and cafes – and everywhere people spending, grazing, wandering with bulging branded shopping bags. Victor arrived at a large sculpture – a work inspired by Jules Verne, marvellous in its steam-punk madness, intricate and beautiful. Here he could rest a little while, on a wrought-iron bench, painted green, with familiar wooden armrests, which wrapped its way around a column. The sculpture took the form of a ship, half harpoon, half giant fish, all wrought in bronze. Rigging and masts festooned with chains, it soared up into the light cast by building's atrium, eight funnels reaching like an organ about to give song. The walk so far had been about half a mile, but already Victor was more tired than he cared to admit – and onwards to Tate Modern would be another mile, through the melee of London Bridge. But Oh! Southwark Cathedral also lay that way. He would continue.

Now he was glad he'd brought his stout umbrella along. He levered himself to his feet and made his way back onto Tooley Street. As he neared London Bridge station he looked up and was unexpectedly aware of the bulk of the Shard towering over him. He had seen it of course in the distance, from Borough – another spike in an increasingly unfamiliar London skyline. But never from this angle. Never this massive! He paused, where Tooley Street met Duke Hill, and considered his best route forward. The new street layout, over two levels, was confusing. Victor decided to stick to the ground and crossed the busy road to Montague place. The cathedral at least had not changed much, and it was open. Inside, the high naves muted the buzz of tourists that filled it. Victor took a seat in one of the chairs that had replaced the old pews. Vaulted arches soared above him, and again he reflected that he'd probably walked far enough today. He didn't belong in this London of people who didn't do eye-contact, who sealed off the outside world with earphones, who seemed to be constantly glued to the screens of electronic devices. Here in this familiar and unchanging place he didn't feel so lost, but he was still conscious of his solitude, and a weariness that was deeper than the pleasant stiffness of overused muscles.

* * *

Eva wandered aimlessly along the South Bank. She was worried about Charlie. There was nothing she could do until she heard from her, She needed to go somewhere to clear her head. Southwark Cathedral would do. There were people to watch and she wouldn't have to buy a coffee. Mostly tourists, but also troubled souls pausing a moment on their journey. Despite the fact that there had been a church there for over a thousand years, it had never felt like a particularly religious place – those windows too bright and too tall, the ceiling too high. It didn't bring back the claustrophobic feelings of the dark chapel she remembered as a child; thick stone walls, tiny windows – built for defence. Priest boxes, and shadows, and a tall pulpit with a secret room. Flickering candlelight, and the Stations of the Cross; the last agonies of the Christ. Hard hands in her knickers.

Next to the cathedral was a sunken garden – a hidden jewel tucked between the railway bridges and viaducts – where a few trees grew. Even before her eyes searched for them her ears had detected the raucous calls of magpies. She knew they'd be there, and they were. How many this time? One...two...three...was that all? Right above her: a fourth. Why here? Was it a warning? Or a reminder to look out for something? Sometimes she looked to the Tarot for clues. Four for the Emperor. Hermetic Order of the Golden Dawn. The principle of order, and control. It didn't tell her anything right now. There stood the door over the cathedral, open, but she dared not go in. It must be a warning, or why would there be so many?

Long unthought of her parents' faces flashed on her inner eye. Features set in hard slabs. Disapproval. Disappointment.

They were farming stock. You followed the almanac. The phases of the moon. Egg moon was for planting; Grain moon for reaping; Harvest moon for gathering. Cold moon, when everything slept, and ice gripped the land.

She had found a way to make every moon a harvest.

Tomorrow's energy today. And as she got better at harvesting that energy, concentrating tomorrows, her power grew.

With greater power came a greater need for renewal; the crash was harder each time. That was what drove her out to seek another one – drove her out like a starving villager in the depths of Winter to look for caches of food that had somehow escaped the rapacious appetite of the community. The whole must be protected at the expense of the individual.

The magpies set up a chorus of chattering, throwing their calls back and forth until she found her eyes flashing from tree to tree. Were they trying to tell her something or to distract her? Eva couldn't be sure. She paused. Took stock of the people passing in and out of the entrance ahead of her. Beyond the double doors she could see an expanse of parquet floor, but that was all. A few chairs were visible, empty. She realised she must look strange, peering in the door. At least inside the magpies couldn't watch her any more. She went in.

The air was cooler inside than out, despite the fact it was winter. Sound, muffled, interior full of echoes bouncing off the intricately carved stone pillars up to the vaulted ceiling above. Eva took a seat near the back of the rows of chairs, tucked her handbag by her feet and looked around discretely.

Most of the seats were empty, with a few occupied by people whose heads were bent in prayer. The tourists tended not to sit down when visiting the cathedral – they drifted around the edges, looking at the paintings and statues, and admiring the stained-glass windows. Eva's eye lit upon an old man who, like her, was gazing around him, people-watching too. She realised their eyes were about to meet and quickly dropped her head to avoid contact. He looked too well dressed and clean to be homeless, and yet she got the feeling that he wasn't there to pray.

As if he could feel her looking at him, he turned his head and she glimpsed his face before she dropped her eyes. She sensed a powerful blast of loneliness from that brief contact. It caught her by surprise. How could you feel someone else's loneliness? And what could you do with that...power? Don't be ridiculous Eva. But were the magpies normal? Maybe it was all part of the same story. Maybe if she could feel loneliness from twenty feet away she would start to understand them better. In fact, it all made sense. That's why there had been four magpies outside the church: one for sorrow, two for joy, three for a girl...but there were never three.

Why did they always point her at the men, making of her a succubus to steal away their souls?

Victor meanwhile had been holding a conversation with himself. Of course he had noticed the exceptionally tall and elegant woman, whose eye he had almost caught before she looked away. It was good to rest and lose himself in the presence of the cathedral, to let his mind and his eyes wander, with no sense of urgency. Just...sometimes he would like to have someone to talk to – to share the glories of that splendid architecture; discuss the changes wrought in London by modernity. He imagined his voice rusty from disuse: the only interaction when he bought a pint of milk or a loaf of bread. And even that was rapidly being replaced by self-checkouts; unexpected human in the bagging area.

You're still staring at her. Victor! – So I am. Look up at the ceiling – that's safe.

He was still looking at her. Eva could feel his gaze, but disconnected, a thousand-yard stare, his real attention elsewhere. And then he wasn't, and she risked another look at him. He was gazing upwards. There was something vulnerable about him, throat exposed, old skin hanging down in wrinkles from his skinny neck, and again: that powerful sensation of loneliness.

Eva kept her eyes on him and took in the rest, the details that had escaped her first quick glance. He looked healthy for his age, despite the liver-spotted hands, the wrinkles. His eyes were clear, and he didn't have that jaundiced look common to the very old. He didn't look like a drinker – the swollen nose, the burst veins were missing. He was wrapped up warm against the chill, with a scarf peeping out from the collar of his coat. He carried an umbrella with a curved handle, but no newspaper. He was skinny to the point of emaciation. He gave the impression of someone who was often hungry.

Eva checked her watch. Half an hour until she had to meet her client – twenty minutes if she left herself ten to get there. She could of course be late, and in fact that was one weapon in her arsenal, but it still didn't leave much time. She decided to act quickly.

"Hello, I'm Anna. I couldn't help noticing you looking at me earlier."

Victor was surprised to discover that the woman he had spotted earlier had moved to the seat next to him. He had been lost in a fugue state, gazing up at the ceiling above. How many minutes had he lost this time? What must he look like, gazing vacantly at the heavens? Oh well – at least a church was one of the few places he could get away with such behaviour. It was acceptable to look lost in thought.

And now here he was, staring gape-mouthed at her, and she awaiting an answer.

"Oh I'm sorry. I didn't mean to be rude. I'm Victor."

"It's a beautiful cathedral. I often come here when I've got a bit of time to spare. It's so peaceful, don't you think?"

Victor was thrown. There he was, wishing he had someone to talk to, and, as if by magic a beautiful lady had approached him. He was momentarily tongue-tied. Eva pressed on.

"There's been so many changes around here, don't you think? It's good to have a constant."

"Yes." Victor managed. "It has changed rather a lot."

"So, what brings you to Southwark Cathedral today?"

What had brought him here? A teabag? But he could hardly tell her that. She'd think he was mad.

"Oh, I come here from time to time. I was just taking a walk and it's a good place to stop. No one bothers you. I mean....of course you're not bothering me...that's not what I meant to say at all!"

This was going to be a lot easier than she had expected.

"I'm glad about that. Sadly, I have to go soon – but I could meet you here tomorrow if you're free? I'd love to continue our conversation. What do you say?"

"Sure, yes, I mean, of course – I'd love to. I could meet you tomorrow at..."

Victor checked his watch and Eva wondered if it was the kind that had once been given on retirement for faithful service.

"I'll meet you here at noon. Will that be OK?"

"Yes Anna – that will be wonderful. I'll look forward to it."

"Bye for now."

He watched her walk away and reflected that it was probably time for him to go too. Who cared about a teabag when you had a date with a beautiful lady? Victor set off for home.

From the bridge above, Eva watched him go. There was a spring in his step that belied his age. She heard wings, fluttering. A magpie had landed a little further along the bridge. It watched her, flicking its tail up and down. She nodded at it, and as if they'd made a compact the magpie nodded back, and then took flight.

Coming home

I haven't stopped for 10 hours straight. The death toll from the attack was thankfully lower than feared, but we still have a lot to do, reconstructing the victims so that family members can view their loved ones.

What's it all for, eh Charlie?

I blink to clear the sweat from my eyes. As usual the air-con is fucked, the temperature is in the high 20s. Bundled up in surgery scrubs, wellingtons, mask and cap I'm struggling to focus.

After yet another incident / terror attack (depending on whether you were reading the right- or left-wing press) I'm ready to call time on nutters with knives, rented vehicles, homemade nail-bombs that leave a shattered mess for my staff to piece together, and no answers for their relatives. Behind the supposed motive of religion or ideology lies a deeper rage, a deeper alienation of those that know they'll never be part of the 1% that seem to grow inexorably richer no matter how shit the world is for everyone else. Idiots! As if killing innocent people can fix disaster capitalism?

I've seen many dreadful things in my twelve years in the NHS – but the pace has rarely felt so relentless. It seems that every other day there's a new atrocity. And with ever increasing cuts to core services as austerity bites, my team is taking on more and more.

I clean up quickly and soon I'm sitting on a Brixton-bound bus.

I never know if Eva will be there when I get home.

Could there be someone else? It's possible. We never promised fidelity, although for some reason I assumed she wasn't seeing anyone else. When you love someone you don't look outside the garden.

She's probably at work. Thursdays are one of her busiest nights, and she often goes back to her place after a late shift.

I once asked Eva if she knew her flat-mates well. The answer came, laconically, back.

"We don't really mix. Keep our own business."

She has a flat-share in an anonymous block on the Tashbrook Estate where the kitchen is cramped and the bathroom is always curiously cold. Her bedroom isn't much bigger, and packed with many, many, clothes, with a single bed squeezed in between a wardrobe and chest of drawers. I've only been there once – it was not a place to go back to.

That's why she's started doing my laundry. She says she enjoys a bit of domesticity, and I'm certainly not going to complain if she's up for removing the lollipop sticks and cigarette filters that I always forget to take out of my pockets when I do it myself. All that home-cooked food is a welcome change from my usual picnic approach to dinner, consisting of slices of ham straight from the packet, and a bit of coleslaw on the side, and I'm even feeling healthier for it.

It feels nice to be looked after. My upbringing was chaotic, I don't remember anyone washing my clothes. I started doing my own laundry when I was eight, and couldn't bear to be filthy any more.

Do I love Eva any more?

How can you love someone you don't know? And I have to admit even after almost a year together, I don't feel like I do know her. Not really. Often she is withdrawn and silent, or picks a fight and we go to sleep with our backs to each other, far enough apart so that no part of us touches. Increasingly, I wake alone.

I find myself thinking about Chloe and remembering the easy way we hung out together; that cheeky grin. Wouldn't that be so much less complicated than Eva?

What about that Goldie gig coming up – drum'n'bass

royalty – normally I'd be booking tickets asap for me and Eva...but now... Do I even want to go with her?

I don't have Chloe's number, but that doesn't necessarily mean I can't track her down if I want to. Maybe she'll be up for a bit of Goldie? Leave it for now - it's a small world. Sure I'll bump into her soon enough.

Goldie though. I might as well see if anyone else is up for going...Shukes, Alice, Luce?

-- anyone fancy this next Friday? Need something to look forward to on a dark night. ;(...Goldie at the Academy anyone? Bueller?

Idly I flip through my feed. Death...austerity...election... blah blah blah. I turn off the phone and close my eyes. I'm so tired that the journey home passes in a blur, and I nearly miss my stop.

It's already gone two when I unlock the front door, and Thug is not happy about it. He stalks the small studio scolding me. I spend a few minutes making a fuss of him and filling up his dishes.

Going through from the kitchen, I find Eva curled up on the couch – waiting up for me? She stirs, and opens her eyes.

"You're back! I wasn't sure when you'd be done. You must be exhausted."

"More like wired - that was a pretty intense shift."

I sit down on the bed to and start taking off my boots. Eva unfolds herself from the couch.

"Let me do that for you darling."

She kneels and loosens my laces, easing the boots off my feet, before moving onto the rest of my clothes. I close my eyes and submit to her ministrations. I'm knackered but I also need to unwind or I'll never be able to sleep, and tomorrow will be just as busy, what with the paperwork and the clients we've had to put on hold. I stand as she unbuttons my trousers, slides them and my pants down.

"What about pyjamas, Charlie?"

"No need. Wouldn't we be more comfortable under the duvet?"

She arches an eyebrow.

"I think we might."

She stands up and starts to undo her buttons. One. By. One.

"Let me do that for you."

I unfasten the remaining buttons swiftly, and slip her dress off one shoulder, and then the other, until I'm left with a puddle of silk in my hands, and smooth bare skin within kissing distance of my lips. Eva seeks out my lips, hungrily, as though that's all she's wanted all night. We drag off the rest of our clothes in a fury, and collapse onto the bed, still entwined, hands seeking out the sensitive places, lips every-where. Before long I get the release I need, soon followed by a dreamless sleep.

Part 2

'Why, this is hell, nor am I out of it.'
Mephistophilis, Doctor Faustus, Act 1 Sc. IV

Temper, temper

From outside, the building in Flatiron Square looked derelict. Once upon a time it had been a set-building workshop, and then had lain empty for years, until Eva had discovered it and rented it as her studio.

The buzzer went and Eva checked the camera discretely positioned above the street door, before pressing the enter button. She was waiting, as she always did for new clients, at the top of a dark staircase in a pure white room, furnished with a simple desk and two chairs. Light streamed in through a paper window, and illuminated the water jug and two glasses that sat in readiness. She could hear his heavy tread on the stairs, and kept her voice crisp as she called out 'come' in response to his diffident knock on the door.

She told him to take a seat and asked him about his expectations, his limits. Does he have any health conditions? What had made him choose her? Many of the questions had already been answered on the phone, but she liked to watch them tell her about themselves. They were inevitably nervous. As well they should be. This was a man she would be hurting, and binding. She needed to know if he would be physically robust enough for the scene. Dead clients are hard to explain.

How would he like to play today?

Maybe she should use her Shibaru skills, suspending him upside down in a web of red hempen ropes?

A gloved fist shoved up his anus?

Head harness or not?

Is he the kind that likes to be gagged? Whipped?

Cut?

Now that she had established the ground rules and gained his trust they were ready to move on. She pointed to a door in the wall behind her, and told him to go through to the other room, remove his clothes and wait on his knees until she was ready for him. Half an hour or so in the black-walled room, lined with shackles, ropes and wicked-looking hooks should put him in the right frame of mind.

The door closed behind him, and Eva spent the next half an hour thinking about what she would do to this apparently well-versed masochist. She's used to the type. It was like a drug for them. He probably had a wife and kids at home who were completely unaware of Daddy's dark side. And in a way, wasn't he just like a junkie, visiting her for his fix? A superficial pleasure that soon wore off, leaving in its place even greater pain, despair, and need. She knew Doms that claimed that the scene was about trust, mutual respect, kinky games, theatre and play. Their customers were not just clients, but friends. Eva knew better. The tribute was a transaction, after all. The game was, at the end of the day, about money and power. There was nothing intimate about it.

After this she would go straight to Charlie's place and hang out until she got home. At least she could keep herself busy tidying up the flat, and making it nice for when Charlie finished work. Clear up the piles of clutter on the coffee table – rolling papers, flyers, tickets, old tobacco packets. Do the laundry. Maybe even do some ironing for her. Be part of her world. The small things they know about each other. The way Charlie's pockets are always full of lollipop sticks. Eva tried to remember the first time she had thought of unrolling them, of writing messages on them. She rolled them back into tight tubes, tied with brightly coloured bits of string, and left them in the garden for the magpies to find. And if the cat got one, all the better. A small revenge.

Charlie hadn't mentioned the cuts. She had to know. She didn't talk about her work much, but Eva knew she had done a post-mortem on at least one of them. Their deaths were on her patch. Hiding so much becomes exhausting after a while. And how did the magpies know which notes were intended for which people? They never failed. She was just as constrained as the clients who called her Madam – the only difference being that it was a game that they had chosen to play; a straight transaction: cash for pain.

Don't question how those notes are delivered – to Ronald, to Vincent, to George, to Freddie, to Frank, to Tommy, to Tony; all those broken men. And especially don't question how the notes are written, in a daze where she feels woven into the warp and weft of a great game, the pen in her hand an extension of another's will. Change the subject. Time to start the game. He's probably in the right frame of mind by now.

Seven for a secret

"All right Charlie – what can I do for you today?"

It's Ben – a friendly guy, who keeps the pub running pretty well, despite the heavy nutters they get through the door.

"Pint of Strongbow, please Ben. - Oi Kerwin – add me on to the next round of Killer, alright?"

I hang out at the bar as Ben pulls my pint.

What a day. Three babies, a heart attack, two strokes, ligature case - another old man with those same marks, and then, as if that's not enough, two more ligatures, and a TB case that required a full suit up and scrub down.

Old men taking their own lives spooks me. Do they just get to the age of seventy odd and think 'that's it – it's time to hang myself?' Sod the pension. Winter deaths make more sense, but why kill yourself in the summer?

"Here you go Charlie – one pint of our finest cider. Enjoy!"

I take a long drink, and feel waves of tension leaving me.

Then I notice Chloe with a bunch of medical students. Do they always run in packs? Well, Chloe's alright. Maybe they won't be too bad. I'm about to give her a wave when I hear Kerwin bellowing my name in his Jamaican lilt.

"Charlie – it's Killer time. And you'd better give these guys a whoppin' ya know. I'm relying on you now."

* * *

Afterwards Eva caught a bus to Brixton and watched Borough High Street inch by with the first beats of Goldie's Ring of Saturn already insulating her from the world around her. On the bus she repaired the damage to her makeup. On her cheekbone a spot of his blood. H was a big guy, and she'd built up quite a sweat tying him up. MAC to the rescue. Base coat, foundation, powder.

At least he hadn't turned rough on her; they went like that sometimes. One minute it was all 'Mummy, I'm sorry – punish me Mummy', and then in an eye-blink she'd be faced with six foot of angry man. Over time she's got better at spotting the fast-food Johns – the ones who give false names, enter the dungeon with shifty eyes, and leave still fastening their trousers. Sometimes she wonders if being freelance is worth it. There is something to be said for having someone to complain to. Out with the mascara – touch up with the clear stuff. A dab of perfume, and finally, on with the lips. A quick pout into the mirror – she'd do.

Around her the other passengers were lost in their devices. Some wore headphones; still others stared into space. All those lives lived. These days more than ever she felt as though she were looking at the world through a dark mirror – one-way glass. Their glances told her otherwise. She wasn't invisible to the red-haired lady in the green jacket, or the restless man with a can in his hand and a jiggling knee. Eyes met, dropped. That was how it worked in London – you looked away. She didn't care – it made what she had to do easier.

Four more stops. Eva fidgeted in her seat. As the bus hit the gridlock around Elephant and Castle and ground to a complete stop for first one minute, and then five, Eva realised that she couldn't bear to be stationary. She needed to be in motion. She ran down the stairs and hit the emergency exit button. The driver turned to speak to her, to ask her what the hell she was doing, but she was already gone.

She threaded her way through the lanes of traffic into the dark maw of the underground. Down the escalator like a bird in flight, onto the tube.

/ *Temper temper, temper temper; think you've had your fun.* /
On the platform a southbound train awaited her, rushed her through the tunnels to Stockwell, paused, and then rocked its

way to Brixton.

/ seven eight nine /

She joined the throng of commuters heading home from an honest day's work; running the gauntlet of ticket touts, buskers, beggars and street preachers, insulated by beats still playing through her earbuds.

/ You don't have to worry. What's done is done /

How she wished that were true.

VANITY, VANITY – ALL IS VANITY.

Outside on the pavement another Brixton preacher is bearing witness. It's the same sermon every day, and perhaps he's right. She had long thought Christians were vain, if it came to it: a religion based on shame, not honour, not self-reliance. A culture ruled by men.

Don't fool yourself – you're still ruled by men.

Every time Eva put on her make-up, her battle-paint, prepared herself for another 'date' with a stranger, she reaffirmed their hold over her. How could they be expected to respect a woman they had paid for? Chattel; her life in their hands.

HOLD ON LOOSELY TO THE THINGS THAT ARE OF THIS WORLD. HOLD ON TIGHTLY TO THE SPIRIT. ETERNAL LIFE WILL BE YOURS IF YOU SUBMIT TO HIS WILL.

He holds himself erect. His skin is ebony; his clothes immaculate. Charlie said he had once been a famous boxer. He is courteous; she's seen him pause his preaching for a sleeping baby.

THE ROAD TO HELL IS WIDE. THE ROAD TO HEAVEN IS NARROW, AND TAKES MANY TWISTS. YET, TAKE YE THE NARROW PATH, FOR IT LEADS TO RIGHTEOUSNESS. ONLY THE RIGHTEOUS ARE PURE.

If he knew what I was he would label me Jezebel. There's no room in his liturgy for me, or the likes of me. It's not vanity, it is power; taking back control. I will not surrender to a vengeful God. I choose to send these souls to Satan. A small service...

/*fucking temper*/

By the time Eva reached Coldharbour Lane she couldn't hear the preacher any more; his words drowned out by the traffic, the shouts of other preachers.

Instinctively avoiding Rush Common, with its colonies of magpies, she decided to take the slightly longer route down Effra Road, which also happened to pass the Hoot. It wasn't that she didn't trust Charlie, exactly, but the memory of the way she had been with that girl lingered. The easiness between them. Maybe she should drop in after all. It wasn't an evening to spend alone. She'd rather endure the Hootananny regulars than be at the mercy of those thoughts.

She was wary of magpies. She knew they were almost certainly watching her. Trees lined the road on both sides; in the gardens set back from the road; in front of the business park; in the pub gardens. Maybe she would have been better off taking the lattice of streets that wended their way behind the Effra to meet at Brixton Water Lane: Rattray; Kellett; Saltoun. Beneath her feet she felt the Effra flow; its trapped bulk surging through the pipes that had been laid to constrain it. Her feet were dowsing rods, her arms pendulums, divining the current of the city. If not through the magpies, it could find another way to instruct her. She could not run from it. She could only delay the inevitable by losing herself in the crowds.

From the corner of her eye she caught a flutter of motion, almost out of range. She turned her head, tracking it, and spied the magpie as it perched on the cast iron railings across the road. It returned her gaze steadily, head cocked, then hopped down off the railings and sidled along the pavement, still watching her, shadowing her on the other side of the street, fluttering from perch to perch until she was halfway down the road, where it flew up to the rooftops, the better to get an angle on her movements.

The magpie was in the North quarter, associated with air, and signifying sleep, death, winter. She waited to see if it would land. 'If you come left-wise, and it calls before you, he is a doomed man on whom it calls thus.'

They were like yarrow sticks. You could read volumes from a flick of tail. Back home they signified death. If you saw one on a house it was considered very unlucky.

Eva quickened her pace. She didn't want to think what it might portend; what she might be required to do next. She kept her head down, avoiding eye-contact with the other pedestrians. It would soon be time to start another round of the game. Focus on now. She was almost at the Hootananny. There was a good chance Charlie was in there. She scanned the garden. No sign. She continued to the street door and peered inside. Charlie had her back to her, poised for a shot, and in the background she could see the usual suspects. Eva could see the soft nape of her neck; could almost feel the roundness of her small buttocks in her hands. Charlie let fly, and as she stepped back to admire the effects of her shot, Eva realised with a shock that she was playing that girl.

Eva ducked back out of the doorway, and out of sight of anyone in the pub. She felt the anger rising within her; the tenderness she had felt moments before replaced by rage. Maybe it was a chance meeting and Charlie hadn't known that she would be there. She certainly hadn't mentioned it. Eva tried hard not to jump to the obvious conclusion. Anyway, there was no point making a scene. That would almost certainly backfire. She was not unaware of how hard she had been to live with recently; the sacrifices that Charlie had made on her behalf.

What should she do now? Maybe the only thing to do was to brazen it out. After all Charlie was her girl, and it wouldn't do any harm to stake a claim. Eva turned back and pushed open the door to the pub, her features already rearranging themselves into a smile.

* * *

I'm halfway through a tense third round of Killer, down to my last life, when I look up and see Eva coming in by the garden door. I wave and call out to her.

"Alright darling – just in the middle of a killer round. The boys will get shirty with me if I keep them waiting."

"Of course, Charlie. Can I get you a drink?"

"Cider and black would go down a treat darling. Ta!"

I give Eva a quick hug, and turn back to the table, but the interruption has killed my flow. I missed the shot, and abruptly I'm out. Well, it's probably for the best. I make a great show of being prostrate with grief as my name is rubbed from the board, and go to join Eva at the bar.

Eva is waiting at the bar for service, standing out from the usual clientele of the pub in her white silk shirt and a flared skirt. Usually my taste runs more to tattoos and piercings, but once again I find myself appreciating the height of her; the way the skin glows on her cheekbones. She is angular, but soft in the right places, and as I reach her I slip a hand under the back of her shirt and stroke the smooth warm skin beneath. Eva leans back a little into my touch, and I lose myself for a moment in the sensation of her silken back cupped in my hand. Then Everton shouts out "Oi you two – get a room!", and breaks the spell. Eva winces and scowls in his direction.

"Do you mind if we go home instead my darling? I'm not sure I can take the pub today?"

I take a wistful look at the pool table, but it never works to mix. And we really do need to talk.

"Of course love. Let's hit the road."

* * *

Eva traces her finger down my arm, distracting me with tenderness.

"Charlie – since how long did you have the flowers?"

"Hmm?"

My eyes are closed, blissed out.

"Do they have a story?"

I open my eyes, meet Eva's, looking down at me.

"You have so many tattoos, and more since I've met you. Like you're gradually covering yourself with ink. I feel like if I know why they are there, then I will know you better. I can touch the outside, but the tattoos can maybe tell me more of what is on the inside. They remind me of the Tarot. Stars scattered on your arms – you are the whole universe. I want to lose myself in you."

She is intent, eyes inches from my skin, fingers following them along the delicate ridges that mark the edges of the ink. 'Made in Brixton' curls around my shaved nape.

"Here is the wheel of life. Here are the Stars, and the Sun, and the Moon. But what do they mean to you? That is what I cannot read. Your story, the book of you."

She traces their outlines with her fingertips, following the passionflower vines that wind around my belly button. Over the slopes of my hipbones, her palms make a well of my stomach.

"It's more of a fanzine. I suppose they do have stories behind them. Different artists. Different times and people in my life. See this one?"

I crook my little finger, where along the outside joint, in curly cursive script is inscribed 'time for tea?'

"Cherry Cakemix, departed and sadly missed. There's five people with these tattoos. It's a way of remembering her, always. This one?"

I raise my arm. 'If you're not living on the edge you're taking up too much space' carved into my forearm.

"This one's a comment on my misspent youth. I wouldn't read too much into them. Really. The stars are a good way of covering youthful...indiscretions. Some early ink that wasn't who I am now."

I don't know anything about Eva's past, but I know something isn't quite right. Seems like a good time to fix that. I start to dig a little.

I run my finger lightly down the inside of her arm; her pale firm skin, with barely a hint of veins beneath it. I stop when I reach the only tattoo on Eva's body. It looks like some kind of rune; 6 short black lines cross-hatched into the skin of her wrist, the size of a fingernail, like three sevens intertwined. I tap the spot gently.

"And what about this one? You never got the urge to get more ink?"

"No."

Eva drops her head to my shoulder and traces a line of kisses along my collarbone. I wrap my arms around her; pull her close and kiss the crown of her head.

"So, is there a story behind it?"

Eva jerks. Stiffens…

"I didn't mean to stress you out, Eva."

Silence. Eventually she replies.

"It's OK. We were talking about it, anyway. It's natural for you to ask. I'm just not used to sharing."

"We don't have to talk about it if it makes you unhappy?"

Eva is quiet for so long this time that I start to drift off, the long day catching up with me. I'm on the cusp of sleep when a whisper cuts through the gathering dreams.

"It means I belong to them."

I'm still wondering if I heard her right when sleep overtakes me.

Finding the way

Beside her, Charlie's breathing is deep and regular. Eva can't sleep. She had so wanted to open up to Charlie, but she felt paralysed.

Things had happened, at home, in the old country. She felt hollowed out, made absurd by the actions of those men, lent authority by the vestments of a religion that promised kindness. Those things were coming out now, but in those days they were never spoken of.

There was that moment, with an old man's hands in her knickers, when with an almost audible click, she let go of who she was and donned a mask. There was a disconnect, between what seemed and what was. There was no going back from that.

She remembered the old plays – you didn't see them any more, but she remembered them from springtime visits to country relatives. The actors were terrifying, with wooden masks that leered and twisted in the flickering light of uncertain electricity, playing out old stories full of death, and pain – and yet at the end the masks came off to reveal people that she knew – dancing, smiling, laughing, as they washed down mountains of *pierogi*, sausage, bread, with glasses of home-brewed *samogon*.

Eva is not her real name. Names don't matter.

She thinks of the countless roles she has played to get by; all the masks she's worn; all those stories she's been part of. She's never been free. Every single story was preordained, one scene following another with the inevitability of day and night. Any time she felt doubt or uncertainty as to what she was meant to do a magpie, would appear, like a well-trained prompt, to give her the next cue.

The first time she met Charlie she plucked the name 'Eva'

out of thin air, and that's how she's been known ever since. No one needs to know her date of birth. Bar jobs and dates pay cash. She keeps her money in a safe place.

Her mother had always spoken of the devil – how she must protect herself from His temptations. She said Eva was sinful and would come to a wicked end. Her father was a remote and terrifying figure, who beat her, at her mother's instigation, until she learnt to endure in silence. They thought they had cured her of her wickedness, of the temptations of Lucifer.

Lucifer was the light bringer? She began to doubt their word.

She would not be part of any creed whose servants abused her so. She would make a pact, with blood and chanting, and dedicate herself to him.

It was about a week after she had made this decision that she saw the seven magpies – and she remembered the old superstitions. They were Satan's servants, come to remind the nearly-departed of the debts they owed. A magpie on the house was always a terrible omen.

As she watched the birds began to strut, tails spread, in a complicated dance. It seemed like there should be some pattern, or message. If there was, she couldn't fathom it.

And then it came to her that the magpie were just vessels; that there was some other consciousness controlling them, looking out through their eyes. Something immeasurably older. The Old one, they called him. There was no going back now. Six of the magpies took flight – she broke that gaze for a moment as they swirled, and her eyes were filled with the royal blue flashes of their wingtips: the letters of a dark compact coalescing out of the shape of their wings. Like an M...Mine. But there must be blood to seal the deal. That was how it worked when you made over your life to him.

She looked back at the seventh magpie, and saw it was

still watching her. As their eyes met it hopped to the side and scratched the ground with its foot. There was a glint there – something shining – a shard of glass. The magpie scratched at it again and hopped away, as if to say 'come and take it'.

She would need to cut herself. It wanted her to cut herself, or if not the magpie, whatever, whoever was behind those eyes.

She stepped forward and stooped to pick up the shard. It was ten centimetres or so across – perhaps a fragment of a bottle, with one wickedly sharp edge and two blunter ones. It felt right in her hand. - But where? And what?

And as the magpie watched her steadily the knowledge came into her mind. The sign of the magpie, of the fellow-hood. Of her servitude. With a steady hand she cut six interlocking lines into the skin of her forearm, and watched as the ruby blood welled and began to drip on the ground. The magpie nodded its head as if to say 'the compact is made', and then, dozens of them were there, surrounding her, scolding in their loud voices. Her legs gave way beneath her and she fell to her knees, and then, knew nothing.

* * *

After that she never got sick. When she hit eighteen she seemed to stop there, stayed fresh as a daisy, ever on the cusp of losing her innocence even after she left the village, then the city, and finally the country – and worked, hustled, lied, bribed, and slept her way around the world honing her skills. During those years she had begun to research more about the lost magic of the witches: the spells of binding, of repulsion; of good luck and misfortune. With access to the Internet it became easier to find information – ethnographic studies, stories patiently collected by scholars, dispassionately described. They couldn't take her to the heart of it. 25 years ago now, and she was still doing his work.

She had found the building some years back, tucked away

off Union Street, just a few steps from Bankside. Almost all of the windows had been bricked up; the deeply recessed door around the side in Flatiron Square secured by a roller blind, with a large padlock apparently rusted shut. For two pounds Eva checked the land registry, which told her it was long disused. She bought a set of bolt cutters and a high-viz jacket from Screwfix, and snipped the lock off the shutter as bold as you please at 5 am in the morning.

The shutter was stiff and rolled up with a groan. Eva raised it to waist level and slipped inside. She didn't plan to be here for more than five minutes, but she rolled the shutter down anyway.

Inside it was pitch black. Eva pulled out a torch and shone it around. At one time it might have been a factory. The floor was covered in dusty lino and ahead of her large swing doors gave access to the main part of the building, whilst to her right stairs led up to what could have been offices. She pushed open one of the swing doors and peered in, her small torch barely piercing the gloom. A large double-height room. Bolts on the floor, where machinery had been removed; it would have been bright when the windows were open. In the cavernous darkness it was hard to get a sense of the space. She retreated back through the door and retraced her steps to the hallway. In the narrow confines of the stairway the light reached all the corners, which were festooned with dusty spider webs. Droppings crunched beneath her feet – mice or rats? No matter. She reached the first floor, and a small landing with five doors, all ajar. They opened onto empty rooms, stripped even of their carpets. In the torchlight she could see bare floorboards, patches on the walls where pictures or notices had hung. She stopped and stilled her breathing. Outside, she knew, Southwark was gradu-ally awakening – Southwark Bridge road only a couple of hundred metres away; but here was silence. She waited a few moments more, and felt the rumbling that signalled a train nearby. She stepped out of the room and crossed the landing to the side that backed onto the railway line.

As she pushed the door fully open, Eva caught a glint of light. She crossed to the window and looked out, to find herself at eye-level with the tracks, but separated from them by a small yard and a high wall. No direct view of this window for the train passengers then. It will do.

Eva went back out onto the landing. The last door opened onto a steep set of stairs which must lead to the roof. At the top was another door that was bolted from the inside, but not locked. She opened it, and found herself on a large flat roof, surrounded by a low railing. Looking down into the yard she could see another disused building hugging the lee of the railway line. The empty window-frames were set with thick black bars.

There used to be so many abandoned buildings in London, but over time they vanished; been converted into flats or furnished with live-in guardians. Eva lived in a series of squats when she first arrived in London. She'd learned a lot about how to get into properties; what constituted breaking and entering; how not to advertise your presence. It was a lot harder now, but it could be done. You wore dark clothes; smart casual. You never covered your face. You came and went at unsocial hours. It was easy to become invisible if you knew how.

Some of those rules had changed in the era of ever-tightening housing laws; ever-diminishing supply. Nevertheless, she could still list properties that were easy to access, discrete, and most of all, empty.

It was starting to get light. Eva locked the door and descended to the ground floor. In the torchlight she could see her footsteps in the dust; it was clear she had been the first visitor in a long time. She crossed to the shutter, and rolling it up a little, peered out. Flatiron Square was deserted. From her bag she pulled an equally rusty padlock, visually identical to the first. The only difference was that she had the key to this one. She had bolted the shutter behind her and casually walked away.

* * *

She remembered the day that they met.

She was walking through Soho, those familiar streets, that always, unexpectedly, feel like a safe space. Soho's tiny gridlocked streets lack trees, birds. They are the ultimate expression of urban life. Cards by the doorbells; uneasy bedfellows. Massage, tailors, literary agents. In a window, amaryllis blooming obscenely – so many red bursting blossoms spilling unashamed from their vase. Tiny clubs. Gradually being lost forever to Crossrail, but Eva doesn't care about that. There's always somewhere new to go.

Where was she? Trying to get make sense of everything. It's hard. She's so closed – even to herself; the facets of her mind hard, jewel-like; even she can't look inside. She might get trapped in the shut-box mirror-looking version of herself that is all that others see. Pause....How old is Eva? Much, much older than she appears. How many years had she lived to make her way to this place?

More than she cared to think of now. A fly, preserved in aspic. Forever young.

For a long time now she had thought she got the worse end of the bargain.

Pause. Stop. Turn off the internal dialogue. It's uncomfortable – a post-communist exercise of self-criticism. Stop it now.

This is not our place. There are the buildings; the rooftops hide us, and anyway – why should we need to touch the ground? We are of the sky. We are we. One of we watches her. There must always be one of we watching that human.

Hair wing-dark sweeping over huge dark eyes. She must

be cold, so bare. Where are the feathers to warm her?...Shut them out. Mad? Or wicked? No need to hear their thoughts. Not now.

A winter's day. Dark, Cold. Barely lit by yellow street lights that jaundiced everything they touched. She was walking down Wardour Street after meeting a client when a magpie flew down towards her, startling her, and landed on the pavement at her feet. She stepped back, involuntarily, and the magpie flicked its tail. It wouldn't meet her eye. It walked a few steps towards her, with the awkward high-stepping gait of one who is more comfortable in the air. She took two more steps back, and found herself in a doorway, which was open behind her. She turned back towards the magpie, but in the moment her attention had been distracted, it had disappeared.

Eva stared at the spot where the magpie had been. There was something on the pavement. A tiny, pastel-coloured, scrunched piece of paper, where she hadn't remembered seeing one before. She bent to pick it up, and unfurled the crumpled sheet. It appeared to be a post-it note, with a few scrawled words on it 'Zoe, don't' forget to do fridge 4', and it was signed 'Charlie'. She wondered what it could mean. Just then there was a whir of feathers, and she looked up just in time to fend off the magpie before it dashed itself against her. She took two more steps back and realised that she had crossed the threshold of the door behind her.

She found herself inside a gaudy bar with a light-up floor. Some kind of game seemed to be going on, and from the all-female clientele, featuring many tattoos, rainbow accessories, short hair and piercings she guessed it was probably a lesbian bar. Only in Soho. Five girls inked up and raucous were taking part in what appeared to be a game of bingo. A sixth was at the bar, and as she looked towards her, she heard her shout back to her friends 'What was it you wanted Charlie? Cider and black?'

"That would go down a treat Zoe!"

In her fist she still had the crumpled sticky note, light enough to be carried in a magpie's talons.

Charlie. Zoe.

She knew what she had to do.

Raking over the past

Luke's a typical slab-man - I can spot his work a mile off. Shit stitching, unnecessary cuts, and a sloppy finisher. Yet again I've had to draft in another technician to ensure the body is fit for the family to collect. In fact, since some of the cases in progress had to be moved to the longer stay fridges, to accommodate the attack I've noticed several sloppy PM's that have slipped through my usually vigilant net.

There's nothing for it but to check them all over. It won't take long to get them out and do a quick recce. I might as well make a start now. I check the rota, and grab my notes. Number 4 bay is free. In the changing room I suit up and grab a camera from the shelf. There's a spare gurney already waiting by the fridges. I square my shoulders and pull out the first drawer.

It slides out silently and I get a quick visual on the tag to confirm it's him before slipping the shroud back into place. As I wheel the gurney through to the PM room Lara looks up in surprise.

"Thought you were up to your eyes in paperwork?"

"Quality control."

"Luke's are they?"

"You know the score. As you were crew!"

"Of course boss. To hear is to obey."

I wheel the gurney to bay 4 and slot it into place. I pull the shroud back. Ronald, Caucasian male, 76, looks in pretty good nick, and has been stitched up neater than I'd expect by Luke. He's done a messy Y incision for the internal examination, rather than the neater T incision that leaves fewer marks, but that was probably so that he could examine the neck muscles better. I do a quick review of the various incisions. And then I see it.

That strange mark on his inner thigh – left leg.

I place one hand under his knee and the other beneath his ankle and part his legs so I can get a clear view. There it is – that series of four strokes. I bend closer and peer at the marks. The way they join at the tips and cross in the middle. So precise. I pick up a magnifying glass from the station next to me and examine each stroke minutely. The scar lines are slightly different from each other – the fourth stroke wider, and therefore possibly fresher than the third, which is a little darker than the second, and the first the faintest of all. It looks as though they haven't been made all at once, but over time. That could explain the neatness of them. There's no blood obscuring the start point. And perhaps, over time, the cutting became more confident, more certain.

I stare at the mark, my brain working overtime. I can feel Lara looking at me.

"What is it? That one's already been done hasn't he?"

I consider bringing her into the investigation. But for now, the less people who know about it, the better.

"Yep. Haven't you got a few PMs to be doing or something?"

My raised eyebrow is enough to make Lara blush and bend her head again to her work. As a trainee APT she's under continuous assessment. We're mates in the pub but it's a different story during working hours.

I focus carefully on the scars, using the small tripod and a ruler in the frame for scale to get a super close-up shot. Then I rearrange Ronald, cover him up and wheel him back to his fridge.

The next two bodies are clean; nothing out of the ordinary about them. They too go back into the fridge.

George, male, 82, white, of Vauxhall Grove isn't as well-preserved as Ronald. He wasn't found for a while. 5'8", running to fat, with varicose veins in his legs and his flesh hanging from his bones in stiff folds. Again the cuts.

They are not as neat as Ronald's, but again tell-tale signs suggested they have not all been made at the same time. Very odd. I take a few more shots, return him to the fridge, and go to find the next on my list. Numbers 5 and 6 are clear – in reasonable shape, and all the right checks noted on the exam form. And then there is Freddy. Male, white, aged 73 at the time of his death, and a resident of Camberwell Green. Freddy is obviously a big fan of tattoos. Names and portraits surrounded by garlands of roses writhe up his arms and cover his chest. He has letters stencilled on his knuckles, and, there on his inner forearm I find the now familiar symbol, between a depiction of a bird in flight (ex-felon?) and an anchor (a stretch in the navy perhaps?).

Freddie's mark is tidy, and much fresher than the other two. The final line has barely had time to heal and still looks angry, like it got infected. More photographs. I have everything I need for now. Freddy goes back in the fridge. I can tell that Zoe and Lara are curious as hell as to what I've been up to for the last hour or so, but they know better than to ask. I'll tell them when I'm ready and able.

I go back to the changing room and put my scrubs in the laundry. I didn't need to do any cutting, but good hygiene gets to be a habit. Then I go back to my office. I download the pics from the camera onto my secure drive and delete them from the camera. Then I open them side-by-side on my screen and sit back, fingers templed, and ponder what they might mean.

It's not unusual to see the marks of self-harm on patients – you see it all the time on younger victims. And it would fit with the apparent suicide motive. The cause of death is identical in each case: asphyxiation and strangulation caused by a ligature. But any kind of self-harm on a man of this age is very, very, unusual. Typical of a slab man not to bring it to my attention. They don't like complications.

The 2004 human tissue act made it illegal to share or broadcast a photograph of a dead person, or any part of their body, unless you have specific clearance – and for some reason that I can't quite fathom I'm reluctant to draw attention to this yet by putting in a request.

Something definitely doesn't seem right.

Is it their age?

I consult my notes. All in their seventies and eighties.

Or the location of their deaths? All South-Londoners.

Are there similar markings to be found on bodies in other mortuaries across London?

Circling my mind is a thought that gives me an uncomfortable feeling.

These strange marks are symbols. There's a word for these kinds of cuts, cicatrise, but aboriginal marks on old men? Old white men?

Gang markings on the bodies of victims of stabbing are commonplace. Each crew has their own iconography – often just a crude letter, or a teardrop, roughly tattooed with a pin; very occasionally done with a blade.

Wounds on the bodies of teenagers, ladders of scars, speak of lonely angry hours. I've seen scarification, on the faces of Ghanaians, Congolese, Eritreans. Yoruba encourage keloid scars by rubbing ashes and grease into the fresh cuts.

Were they all in some kind of club?

I pick up my desk phone and dial Doc's extension one last time. After a few rings his answering machine kicks in, and I put the phone down.

There's no way I'm leaving him voicemail.

It's time to go to the police.

I'd rather it wasn't me, but somebody has to.

More of the same old

I unwrap a lolly and shove it into my mouth, My favourites are the cheapest kind – real teeth breakers in day-glo colours, that came with a paper stick that I pick up by the fistful at 6am from the corner shop, where they tease me and tell me that my lovely white teeth will turn yellow. I savour the sickly taste of chemical cherry as I scan the list of PMs upcoming.

The rota is looking extra challenging. Twenty-five cases a week is normal. At least half of those are infants: stillbirths, sudden death syndrome; infanticide, hangings, drownings, asphyxiations. Some weeks a tide of suicides wash up on the doorstep of the mortuary like flotsam from the Thames lapping at the riverbank.

Other weeks it's ligatures. These are the most common form of suicide. One of the most compelling arguments for gun control my mind: hanging is so much neater.

This week is no exception. Seven cases, five men, two women. Seems like there's always more men – most of them fifty plus. They kill themselves throughout the year, but it peaks in December, January and February. A couple of times a week there's a jumper – some poor sod whose last action was to delay the journeys of thousands of people across the train network.

Bridge suicides are less frequent. Is that because people worry that jumping from a height might not be guaranteed fatal, or that there won't be enough witnesses if they kill themselves that way?

Such questions are academic – a matter for statisticians and psychologists. Not something that I usually have time to ponder when I'm flat out, trying to keep ahead of the backlog.

The new locum doesn't seem promising – he's called in sick again, and it probably won't be too long until the doctor signs him off. Stress. It gets some people like that: death day in, day out; the full spread of human wickedness and weakness; the physical reality of death. So I'm down a pair of hands already. The vice is off too – annual leave. Joy. Fingers crossed there aren't any major incidents, or we'll be fucked. Comprehensively.

I look down the list again, wondering if there's anyone else I can pull in. My senior, Zoe, is off half the week for training.

Bloody brilliant.

I start assigning cases, giving myself the most complex, and making sure I balance the infants and the adults. There's nothing worse than a whole day of babies, and few people have the mental fortitude to handle more than one infant abuse case a week. It's best to get these over early in the day, and follow them with a couple of the more...academic jobs.

And then there's Doc.

It's been too long now, and I'm not sure how to bring it up. It's not like we've not spoken to each other. We've had several chats, and he's been in to consult on one of my more abstruse and complex cases, but I haven't seen any evidence that he's followed up on my notes, and I haven't been able to locate the PM sheet for that day, which has never happened on my watch before. There is no record of that first chat with him, that night in the mortuary, at a time when, strictly speaking, he shouldn't have been there. Now I'm beginning to feel a bit dumb for ignoring that at the time. I was so intent on telling him about what I'd found. I'm starting to wonder if I made a mistake. Maybe I should have involved the police when I found the first mark. It didn't seem much to go on, then.

I've had plenty of opportunities to mention it; I'm in regular contact with the police – referrals from forensic pathology, coroners reports, and trauma reports – but this feels different. Normally I'm tasked with trying to find evidence of a pattern someone else has spotted. Now it looks like it's all on me.

I still have no evidence except some almost invisible cuts and a collection of scraps of paper in a file. There has to be a connection between them.

They are all men. Elderly men. But that's not enough in itself to build a pattern: why these few, amongst the two hundred people a year that die alone, with no one to arrange their funerals, or treasure their effects?

They all lived in South London.

All are suicides, not that common a cause of death, and all with the same CoD, strangulation by hanging. The ligatures are still in storage and they are all different: a tie; a belt; some electrical cables.

I finish the first lollipop and tuck the stick in my pocket, mechanically cursing the directive that had removed waste paper bins from every office in the hospital to 'reduce waste'.

I reach for the file that contains the scraps of paper I wrote the codes on. Body tags. On the reverse side: name, date of birth, vital statistics. Old, male and white. How do the marks fit together? What is the pattern? If I can find the key, then perhaps it will begin to make sense.

I reach for another lollipop and start planning my report.

Always start with a list.

In the left column, the victim's vitals – Name, age, gender. Cause of death. Then next to that 'P' for possible, '?' for maybe and 'x' for no connection/clean. I'm going to have to go back over the cases I've already cleared, those that are still in the fridges, awaiting proper disposal; satisfy myself that I haven't missed any clues.

There must be a pattern.

Were the marks self-inflicted? Had someone else made

them? Why were they all the same? Some of the bodies had more than one set of marks on them...so there must be a 'who' and a 'when'. Could it be some kind of calling card? Left by someone who doesn't like old men?

A lot of questions. I'm used to answering questions – 'What was the exact cause of death'. I spend my days piecing together bits of the human jigsaw, which sometimes takes considerable pathological detective work, not to mention a wide understanding of human nature and habits. Usually the detective work starts and ends in the mortuary: the real crimes handed over to forensic pathology; the investigation managed by the police.

Again I come back to the 'how'.

Hypothesis one: the cuts were inflicted immediately post-death: unlikely due to lack of blood / local trauma. The cuts are too fine, and sometimes suicide victims aren't found for days...

OK within 24 hours of death; maybe they stuck around to commune with the body for some reason.

What if the marks appeared after the body was trans-ferred to the hospital? Access to tools...Access to a range of bodies to add marks to. And why? Maybe it's some kind of tagging system. A series of messages? Or warnings? Not a murderer, but a subtle way of linking a series of deaths as if to say 'investigate me please' - and only likely to be noticed by me, or Zoe, who would tell me immediately if she found something unusual. Could it be some kind of ritual marking?

There's no point looking for camera footage. No CCTV. Fingerprints?

That kind of stuff lives in books, and anyway the whole place gets a regular top-to-bottom steam-clean, with daily scrub-downs of all the work areas.

Maybe the 'how' would answer the 'who'. How could someone get access to the remains? The mortuary shifts run from seven to four normally – anything after four is overtime, and the mortuary is pretty much guaranteed to be unstaffed... when...night time? Of course it's locked at night, but that wouldn't stop someone with the right level of access. Maybe if I can cross-reference the date the bodies in question were admitted with the night-shift rotas. With literally hundreds of staff on that could be like looking for a needle in the proverbial. Or maybe not. Someone must have access to the notes for each patient – then be able to match those to which fridge they were stored in. Someone therefore has access to computer records.

Someone who knows their way around the mortuary – who's at least been here before. Someone connected to me?

Could it be Doc? Could he be making the marks? What about that case with the transplant surgeon who left his initials on his patient's organs not so long ago? Stranger things have happened Charlie.

There's a beep from my computer: new message.

Hi Charlie...yes, I'm still waiting for that software PO. There's always one, isn't there? ;) – Laurence

p.s. Cheese night?

Shit. Laurence. He could fit the bill...access, knowledge... but what motive? Why would Laurence want to send me messages that way? Hypothesis 2 is feeling like a tottering edifice of shite. When you've ruled out the possible...

Time's a-wasting Charlie. Autopsies won't do themselves.

I shut down my computer and go through to get suited up for the first case of the day.

***

Up in his office on the ninth floor, Doc sat, pensive, thinking about the implications of his night-time activities.

Allograft – the business of recycling dead humans – has grown so large over the last decade that you can buy stock in publicly traded companies that rely on corpses for their raw materials.

Human tissue is used for wrinkle fillers, penis enlargements, burn victims. Recycled tissue use is more common than you might think. Bladder slings; surgical screws; plastic surgery materials – nose and breast reconstruction; bone grafts.

Human tissue samples are categorised into three levels. Category three comprises whole organs or 'significant' body parts. Category two comprises samples of human tissue which are not a significant part of the body - small tissue samples, blocks slides etcetera. Category one, includes scrapings, fingernails, hair, stomach contents – which would not generally be considered part of the human body. Some, like the pineal gland, involved in the production of hormones, saliva glands, could be considered organs – but they're so small they would be unlikely to be missed.

Notably the police themselves didn't bother listing any materials below category three when they carried out their human tissue audit.

When the artist Anthony Noel-Kelly stole body parts to use as moulds for sculptures in an exhibition, he spent a mere nine months in prison. Dick Van Helsen, who retained thousands of children's organs, including the head of the child stored in a jar, spent less than three years in prison and had his license to practice medicine suspended.

Once the biological material has been removed from the donor, the recipient acquires the right to possession and use; regardless of whether he or she is also the owner. Obviously in this case you'd have to prove there was no donation.

In order to accuse someone of theft, you need to recognise that body parts can be owned, and as a consultant pathologist, Doc had the ultimate plausible deniability. Cord blood, platelets, stem cells…are all category one. No one would bat an eye over a pathologist keeping some of these for study…

The dark net closes

Doc got another text message – this one more threatening than the last somehow, although the language was deceptively mild; surprisingly so, given the perilous state of his affairs.

- Your account is £96,452.26 in the RED. Talk to us if you're having problems managing your risk. We can help.

Could they? Really?

Speculating on International Finance had been a game at first. He didn't need the money – consultant pathologists were some of the few who were generously provided for by the NHS. But Doc suffered from hubris; the overweening delusion of his own intelligence. He had everything under control. He read the papers, synthesised the available facts, and invariably invested the right way, inexorably, it seemed, parlaying his original modest stake into a dizzying sum. How swiftly things change. One bad deal and abruptly his safely hedged position was looking a lot more precarious. Too many market fluctuations in the wrong part of the world. Too much complexity. He'd revelled in controlling the system, and now he was at the mercy of an algorithm.

His small glass-walled office was stuffed to the rafters with books and papers; his desk a mound of documentation. Rows of drawers held clinical samples. He didn't merit a river view; glass walls opaque from halfway down, clear above, gave anyone a view of his space. He'd made use of every surface with enigmatic charts, clippings, musings, taped to the glass, like a crazy collage of his mind, with sticky notes charting a hazardous path through the twisted forests of his research. Usually he loved it this way – it made it feel more private. Now though, he worried that there might be someone standing just outside the door. His cosy cubicle began to feel claustrophobic

He decided to go for a walk on Hampstead Heath. These days he lived in a nice mansion flat in Maida Vale, and drove his car to work, but when he first came to London, as a student, he had been in a lodging house near Hampstead Heath, and then, memorably, homeless for seven months when he had found himself unable to pay the rent. He had always had a gambling problem if he was honest with himself.

He found out that were ways to support yourself on the Heath; you could forage, if you were desperate. He watched the young Poles, who seemed to know the best things to pick and tried to copy them.

Sometimes, scavenging for mushrooms, he had ingested the wrong variety, and wandered the heath for many hours in the grip of delusions, so that as dusk approached he couldn't tell whether the stationary figures in the trees were statues, some men waiting for a hookup, and some mere figments of his imagination brought on by his painful experiments with the edible. You could exchange sex for money. Don't think about that. That was then. And now? What had changed? Nowadays he wore the trappings of a successful man, drove a Jag; had earned the right to precede his name with Professor; had built up a debt of nearly £200,000, and he had no idea how he would ever pay it. At the root of it he was the same man; his hunger would never be satisfied and he knew himself well enough to know how low he would stoop once he was backed into a corner.

So he came here, to walk it off, taking pleasure in the feel of his feet striking the ground; the satisfying burn of muscles under-used whilst he led the sedentary life of a hospital consultant.

He had passed the bathing pools now, on a route that took him past Viaduct Pond to where the paths became more overhung with trees, like green corridors insulating him from the sound of the city. The ground was firm and dry beneath his feet, unpaved but lightly graveled, so he could hear the crunch of his footsteps. He decided to cut across the woodland. Here the trees were widely spaced, old and massive – remnants of ancient forest. The dirt path disappeared under a carpet of fallen leaves, sunlight dappling the branches above his head. For a while he enjoyed childishly kicking the leaves as he walked, and then he paused for breath, and quieted himself. He had an uneasy feeling, a sense of foreboding that didn't match the bright afternoon, the woodland. He was no longer alone.

Doc looked around him. Perhaps it was his imagination. He waited another moment, silently, and then he heard it – the crack of a branch as though someone had shifted from one foot to another. And what were they doing here, in this hidden away area, far from the usual cottaging spots? Surely it was nothing to do with him. He was getting paranoid.

Doc crossed the clearing, heading towards the path that led up over Parliament Hill. In front of him two men materialised, silently, from behind the trees.

They had dark hair cut short – one bearded, the other clean-shaven – and looked to be in their thirties. Fit, with a slightly military air. They didn't look as though they meant him any good. And was that a blade? Doc made a break for it, and the bearded one stepped to block his path, putting out a hand and resting it on his chest. The other stepped behind Doc. He felt something sharp in the general area of his kidneys, maybe a knife. He should have been paying attention, but he suspected the men were well practiced in keeping silent.

And still they didn't speak.

Doc tried to put some confidence into his voice.

"Who are you? Do you want my wallet? Is that what this is about?"

The bearded man smiled. It wasn't a warm smile. He moved one hand towards his jacket pocket, and Doc felt his heart stop, the pulse hammering in his throat and his bladder suddenly gave way. When his hand reappeared he was holding an envelope, rather than the expected gun. He offered it to Doc, who took it reluctantly. With a blade at his back he had little choice.

He stood there, not knowing what to do next, holding the note in his hand. The bearded man nodded to his accomplice, turned his back, and disappeared into the trees. A bag was pulled over his head, pulled tight at the throat, the point still digging into his back. He put both hands up to his throat, fumbling for the tie to ease the pressure. When he finally managed to remove it he was once again alone in the clearing. Or so it seemed. The envelope lay at his feet.

He looked around once again, and then bent down to pick it up. The outside was blank, and it was sealed. He hesitated, and then tore it open. Inside were several folded sheets of A4 – standard office type paper, and a typewritten note on the top sheet:

We have contacted you several times about the money you owe to International Finance, but you have failed to respond to any messages. Do not think that you can avoid surveillance. We are watching you all the time. We will send you further instructions soon.

So, it was connected to International Finance, and the debt he owed to them. He should have realised that immediately. He'd been ignoring it, as though it might go away.

And then he turned over the next sheet.

--transcript starts

PRCMAX 02.26 03.56am: Our client is looking for samples of brain tissue from multiple ethnicities. We will pay GBP 20,000 for each sample.

. . . .

DRW 02.27 07.40am: Have access to samples. Payment terms?

. . . . . .

PRCMAX 02.27 08:23am: PO BOX 1256, WC1 4AX. Bank transfer on confirmation of delivery or cash post restante.

. . . . . .

DRW 02.27 08:31am: Terms accepted. Cash best for me. PO Box to follow.

. . . . . .

DRW 02.28 11.22am: PO BOX 3345, SW4 3YV.

. . . . . .

PRCMAX 02.28 11:31am: You will need to supply a phone number. Further communication will be via messenger.

. . . . . .

DRW 02.28 11.22am: Fine. 07654 424 453.

That was just the first of several pages – covering the whole of his interactions with the 'Chinese' biochemists. There were the Darknet messages, which is where he had first seen the message that seemed to hold the answer to his problems, and then all the following messages, listing the samples required; confirming the payments received. Payments that he hadn't used to settle the debt owed to International Finance...he had lost that money too, on other online gambling sites.

It dawned on him that he'd been played all down the line. It's not just the debt, it's the realisation that the people he owes the debt to are not a nice, regulated trading company, but a much more sinister organization. International Finance was just a cover – the public face of a vast money-laundering network. What was the purpose of that scam? He sensed it wasn't really about the money. Was it about the hospital? Maybe they needed someone on the inside that they could control?

Doc shoved the letter in a pocket and took off at a run for the tube station, taking the shortest route, homewards, to the places where he was known.

Four for a boy

Laurence was at work, thinking about Charlie. Odd for Charlie to ask him whether he's seen Doc recently. Maybe Doc hasn't been answering her messages? Charlie's email is far more trivial to hack than Eva's, as Laurence has already got a backdoor to the hospital system. He feels just a bit guilty going through her messages, but that soon passes. Charlie's work mails are perfectly business-like, so it doesn't feel like a personal invasion.

A few emails from Charlie to Doc asking him to answer her calls. No replies from him. For weeks! No mention of any odd PMs. Could it have been something she'd mention to him in passing, rather than an email? No paper trail?

Might not mean anything.

Another weirdness, that might explain the lack of responses. Doc's been accessing the system via VPN for several weeks – logging in from outside the hospital. Obviously that's what the VPN was for, so there's nothing particularly suspicious about this, but it's unusual enough for Doc, who had barely used VPN before that. In fact, he was so clueless about IT he'd asked Laurence to help him set up a webmail account, and he called him pretty much every time he needed to print something. By this point Doc had basically given him a back door, and Laurence used it now, logging into Maps with Doc's ID and looking at his location history. He hadn't been to work for a while. In fact, apart from a trip to Hampstead Heath a couple of days before, it didn't look like he'd left his house for days.

Now that Laurence came to think of it, he'd been too distracted by his obsession with Eva to pay attention to what was going on with Charlie for a while. Had she been unusually quiet at the pub? He'd been so wrapped up in his own thoughts, but he had the feeling she was worried about something. Come to think of it, why would she ask him about Doc's movements? She could just pick up the phone and call him up. Maybe he'd been focussing on the wrong person. Caught up in Eva's life, he'd taken his eye off the ball. Or Charlie, more to the point.

Anyway, Eva wasn't going anywhere. He needed to get eyes on Doc.

Holed up

Doc hadn't left his flat for days. You could get away with that now; have anything delivered. It probably wouldn't stop them. Even supermarket deliveries were a calculated risk, but at least he could use the vidcom to see who was outside. Would they send the same guys back again? Unlikely. For all he knew they'd bugged his flat. They were probably quite capable of entering whenever they liked, and he couldn't stay awake all of the time. He had to sleep – sometimes. He wasn't sleeping much. He was too scared. The knife had been a warning. He didn't like to think of what they would do next. At least he didn't have any dependants for them to use as leverage. There was truly no one who would miss him. Apart from maybe Charlie...he wondered what she would think when she found out what he had been doing. What would she make of his actions? Doc suspected she would feel betrayed. Speaking of which, he should probably update his out-of-office. It wasn't so unusual for him not to be around for a couple of weeks – he regularly attended conferences – but he'd been avoiding his computer in case there were any more messages from them. He couldn't go on like this. He was going to have to do something.

He fired up his laptop and logged into the hospital network. It never got any faster. The IT guy, Laurence, had been able to speed it up a bit last time Doc had asked him to look at it, but that had been some time ago, and meanwhile it had slowed down to a crawl again. Eventually he was into Outlook, only to find a large number of unread mails in his inbox. There were several from Charlie. He hesitated and then opened the most recent.

From: C Tuesday, Head APT
Subject: Radio silence

Dear Doc,

Don't suppose you've had time to file a report on the marks yet? I found a few more. Actually several more. We need to get the proper authorities to look into this pronto. Did you get my voicemails? I haven't seen you around the hospital lately. Are you at conference? Anyway, let me know where you're at, and if you haven't had time yet due to workload, I'll be more than happy to get on it for you. Is everything OK? It's not like you to blank my emails. If I haven't heard back from you by tomorrow, I'm going to have to go ahead and file the report. Sorry if that makes things a bit sticky, but I don't really have a choice at this point. Hope everything's alright.

All the best,

Charlie

The other messages were in a similar vein and there was nothing he could do about it. He probably should have let her report it when she'd first mentioned it to him. He'd had other things on his mind though. Plus there had been only one set of marks. Perhaps he hoped it would just go away. Now it was going to look as though there had been some attempt at a cover up, which wouldn't reflect well on Charlie, She didn't deserve that, and he was already in so much trouble there was no point throwing her career under a bus just to keep the cops off his back. It was just like Charlie to keep on with it. Nothing crooked would ever be allowed to occur on her watch.

He would have liked to know where they came from himself. He'd been so wrapped up in his own worries he'd not spent any time thinking about it. Well, there wasn't any point worrying about it now.

He opened the mail settings, and looked for the out of office section. There was a conference in Iceland that would do nicely as cover – it was a two-week symposium that he'd attended before. He was going to have to disappear. Now: how do you do that these days?

The first challenge

Eva breathed in the warm summer air of a perfect day. The sun had come into its full promise and everything around was fairly bursting with growth; the sun a gentle benediction; waxing crescent moon sharp against a cornflower sky. Everything shone. Eva wished she could rewind to those early days with Charlie; off to Brighton for a day by the seaside. She'd been better at separating the parts of herself before, swept along by Charlie's joyful sun-worshipping. How she longed to be that carefree now. They were always watching her.

Their cover was perfect amongst the leafy boughs, but the ki-ki-kik gave them away, always scolding. One, two, three... four at least. The game of spotting them. One on a chimney pot. Two in a tree. Over there on a sickly looking sapling,, the foliage failed to conceal another. Four. And a fifth? She could hear it, but not see it. Chak-chak-chak-chak-chak chak chak – like rifle fire.

And was that a sixth? What was the message? No matter. She knew what she was here to do.

She rang the bell softly. From far inside she heard the click of his front door, and then, closer, the sound of him shuffling through the front hall. She knew, from observing his habits, when he left the house. Consequently, she hadn't warned him of her visit. This was one of her favourite tactics to keep them off balance.

The door opened a crack, and she could see an eye, surmounted by heavy whiskery brows.

"Oh! Hello Anna – how very wonderful to see you. But I haven't got anything in."

"Dear Victor – Do not worry yourself. At a whim I decided to visit on my way past. I bring you cakes!"

"Oh, that's so very kind of you. Do come in. Excuse the state of the place. I get so few visitors nowadays."

He opened the door wide to let her through, and then scurried past to hold the inner door. Inside, a long threadbare corridor connected the few rooms of his flat. A couple of coats and a hat were hung on the wall, and a single pair of shoes was neatly lined up below them. Like the hall, these were rather threadbare. But why would he need new clothes? He had reached the age where they were likely to outlast him – cast aside or given to charity on his no-doubt solitary demise.

"Come in, come in."

Victor edged past her and opened the door at the end of the corridor.

"Have a seat in here whilst I get some tea on."

He looked questioningly, almost lovingly, at the cake box dangling from Eva's wrist.

"Of course." Eva smiled, "The cakes! Here they are."

Not all of them were ordinary cakes. She handed them to Victor. Inside a beautifully wrapped box there were three: a tiny lemon tart, and two fresh cream mille-feuille pastries.

"What a lovely box. I'll be there in a minute."

Eva wandered through to his sitting room. It had the feel of a space that rarely changed – ornaments a little dusty, yellowed papers on the mantel over the gas fire, 1970's push button telephone. There was little on the walls to suggest the owner's personality, and the whole room had that slightly awkward quality of the elderly bachelor's den. There was a single comfortable chair, with a footstool, and two high-backed wooden chairs that saw little use, judging from their dusty seats. She pulled one closer to Victor's and sat down to wait.

From the kitchen she could hear the sounds of a tray being assembled. The clatter of cups on saucers. The tinkle of the teapot lid. Apart from that, the flat was silent – astonishingly so for London. The blind was down, and the room in semi-gloom, but out there in the bright April day she knew that the magpies were roosting. Three this time. She had seen them on the way, but sometimes it was best to pretend you hadn't noticed. Anyway, she was doing what they wanted.

Victor came in with the tray and Eva jumped up to clear a space on his cluttered table. He had been doing the crossword and a large magnifying glass lay atop it.

"Just throw those on the chair. Here we go. And just in time for tea. Would you like to be mother?"

It took a moment for Eva to understand that he'd asked her to pour the tea, rather than giving her an SM role to play.

"Of course. How do you like it?"

"Milk and one sugar please. These cakes look terribly nice. So very kind of you."

"It is nothing. Which one would you like?"

"That one, please. I must confess, I have a weakness for cream cakes."

Eva laughed and passed him one of the mille-feuilles, and then handed him a cup of tea.

"I could not have guessed."

Sitting down with her own cup she watched him over the rim. It was obvious, from the way he approached the unexpected treat, that he was hungry. He was far too proud to admit it of course. He cut the pastry into four neat sections and ate them one by one. Eva picked crumbs off a small lemon tart, and sipped the very weak tea.

"So, have you been out much? The weather's so much better now. Any more walks to London Bridge?"

"Not since we last met, actually. I hadn't realised quite how far it is. I've been leading a quiet sort of life. And what about you? I hope you don't mind me asking, but what would a lady like you want with an old fart like me?"

Eva was waiting for that question, although she was surprised that Victor had been so direct. Of course he wasn't the first to ask it. It meant that they'd reached a crucial point. She wondered if she'd primed him enough. She'd made the mistake of moving too fast before, and messing up everything. She felt like a fisherman, who having hooked her prey must play the line; so easy for the bait to slip.

"Well Victor, the truth is I am not short of material assets, but sometimes my life feels a little...empty. I'd like to give a bit more back. I feel like we live in a world where all the people are wrapped in their own selves. They don't look around them. They don't make time for other people. And these people get left behind."

There were a number of ways to broach the subject of the game, as she'd learned by trial and error. She'd lost a couple of them at this point. Choosing the right approach was as important as the timing. The magpies had told her that Victor was ready; they had as good as marked him. The opening gambit was up to her.

Sometimes she used sex, sometimes fear, and at others loneliness. It wasn't so very dissimilar from her paid work – but the key difference was agency. The men she met through work were engaged in a transaction that provided a framework, and that gave them power. In this context she had to build the framework herself, painfully, stick by stick, with stolen materials, to construct an untidy nest. It was a balancing act that felt precipitous, but when it worked, the rewards could be very great. On the other hand, failure would cost her life.

She can feel an almost tidal tug at her sense of self; she's running to stand still. She was careful not to betray her sudden fear.

"Well that's very good of you. And I certainly shan't complain if a lovely young lady chooses to visit me. As you probably guessed, I don't get a lot of visitors. You're really very lovely Anna. Please don't take that the wrong way. It's a treat for these old eyes."

So, it looked as though the special cake was having an effect. It was subtle, a slight reduction in his defences, but enough for her purposes.

"Look as much as you like, Victor. I'm lucky to have this face, this body. I should share them with those that deserve it."

Eva sat silently and let his eyes roam. She had dressed conservatively, planning the 'lonely pensioner' gambit, but it seemed that the rules had changed. A different approach would be called for.

Victor's breath was coming faster. His hands had been resting loosely on his lap, but now she could see that his fingers had begun to entwine themselves as if of their own volition.

"Do you like what you see, Victor? I don't mind if you look a little more."

Victor's voice came back a little rougher than before, and so quiet she could barely hear him.

"I like it very much."

"I'm glad, Victor. You can look as much as you like – so long as you don't touch. Are you OK with that Victor?"

"Yes, of course! I wouldn't dream..."

"Of course not Victor. I felt that the first time we met. And that you were a little lonely. I'm so happy I could help Victor. Would you like to see my breasts, Victor?"

The reply, when it came, was even more strained.

"Yes, yes I would."

"And so you shall, Victor. But first, you must promise me something else. We're going to play a little game – and every time you win, and go on to the next round, I'll show you a little more. But it must be just between the two of us. Can you do that for me Victor?"

She didn't think he had anyone to confide in, but it was best to be sure with these things. And complicity created a bond.

"Yes Anna – of course. Who would I tell?"

"That's wonderful Victor. OK, let's start. Here's how the game works."

My girl lollipop

Doc's office on the 9th floor is deserted, and the piles of correspondence in his cubbyhole suggests he hasn't been there for a while.

This strikes me as very odd.

Doc occasionally attends a conference that keeps him away for several days at a time, but I can't remember the last time he took a holiday, and he normally lets me know if he's going to be away. What else have I missed? As I take the stairs two at a time back down to the basement I'm mulling over my next move. I can't put it off any longer: I'm going to have to contact the police myself – and explain why I didn't inform them earlier. It will definitely be awkward, but it has to be done. Doc's been stonewalling me too long now.

Back at my desk I hesitate and then pick up my office phone. It's 101 for non-emergencies, isn't it? I dial the number and get through immediately, which is a surprise. Which service? Police. No, it's not urgent. Yes, they can call back. Please use the number for the Mortuary – I'm reporting in my professional capacity.

Moments later I get a call back from a DC Smith, who asks if they can come and take a statement this afternoon. I don't need to check the roster to know that the afternoon will likely have a bit of flex in it. I give him a quick outline of the situation – finding the first marks; realising that there were more of them, and that there seemed to be some kind of pattern. I gloss over the fact that Doc seemed keen to avoid any kind of investigation, and now he is missing – and DC Owen doesn't push it. I promise to send him through my notes, and agree a time for them to come and do an interview later this afternoon. Then I put the whole thing out of my mind and change into my scrubs.

* * *

I'm washing up when Zoe pops her head around the door.

"There's two cops here. Say they've got an appointment with you?"

I can tell she's curious to know what they're here for, but I don't have time to explain it now. I continue methodically scrubbing between my fingers.

"Thanks Zoe. Can you ask them to wait in the office? I'll be right through."

"Alright Boss."

I dry my hands and strip off my overalls, which go in the hamper, and my boots, which I stow neatly in the rack. I give myself a quick once-over in the mirror, and run my fingers through my short hair straightening the sharp fringe that half-obscures my face. I'll do.

When I get to my office there's two cops there, shoehorned uncomfortably into the tiny, cluttered space. The taller one introduces himself as PC Owen. He has close-cropped thick dark hair and a Welsh accent.

I ask them to sit down. One on my desk chair (the desk, of course, free of extraneous papers); and the other on a stool I keep for visitors. I remain standing. Always keep the advantage of height whenever possible when dealing with the pigs. That was one thing my dad taught me.

It would be easy for me to slip up with him, because he seems so cool. That would be a rookie error though. Not going to happen. I've got nothing to hide, but Dad taught me young never to trust the cops. Now I'm in a position of responsibility, that sometimes seems a bit dated, but old habits die hard.

"Thanks for taking the time to speak to us this afternoon – we know you're busy. The report you sent through for us was very thorough, but we'd like to ask you a few questions, just to clarify a few points, if that's OK?"

"No problem - although I'm not sure what I'll be able to add to what I've already told you..."

I pull a lollipop out of my pocket and unwrap it carefully, before popping it in my mouth, and giving them both a level stare.

DC Owen has his notebook out, pen at the ready.

"Just start at the beginning."

So I do. I tell them about being off work, coming back after six weeks (though I leave out the part about why); about finding the first set of marks.

DC Owen stops me there.

"Are you able to show us an example of these marks? Are any of the bodies still on the premises?"

"Of course! Until we know what's going on, those bodies are evidence. They stay in the mortuary until we get some answers."

DC Owen smiles at my enthusiasm.

"Well, that's very helpful. So, can we see them now?"

"Sure. Right this way, gentlemen."

I lead them through to the cold storage area. The stainless steel walls gleam dully in the strip-lights. The two cops file through behind me, and stand looking at the numbered drawers, with their utilitarian handles.

I pull a scrap of paper out of my pocket; I've made a note of which fridges Freddie, George, and Ronald are in.

"Ronald was the first one I found, so let's start with him. Fridge 7."

The drawer slides easily and silently out on well-oiled runners.

"I told you I came across a couple more - they could have been earlier. They'd come in with an previous batch, but then got shunted down the rota after the Westminster attack."

Ronald has been wrapped from head to ankles in a shroud. As I pull aside the stiff folds, he comes swimming up out of the frost. I'm not expecting a reaction; a cadaver isn't nearly as gruesome as a murder victim, and I do like to leave my clients nice and neat when I've done with them. Ronald looks perfectly composed, if a bit frosty, after nearly four months in the freezer.

I've been pretty neat with my scalpel, but the T incision stands out clearly on his chest; shocking to look at against the white of his skin, marbled with blue veins; from collar to sternum. I can feel the way their eyes are drawn to them. But that's not what they are here to look at.

"The mark is on the left inside thigh. It's only visible with his legs parted, and even then, it's hard to spot."

I grasp his ankle and knee and carefully part his legs. Ronald's thighs are those of an old man, and on top of that his flesh has sagged once the rigor mortis wore off. Still, there are the cuts, surely made by a razor, and in the shape of an 'M'. DC Owen pulls out a small camera.

"Do you mind?"

"Of course not, but I have to ask you not to share the images in public form without written permission."

"Noted."

DC Owen leans in, craning his head over the marks, his ear almost touching Ronald's shrivelled groin. He's probably well used to dead bodies.

DC Owen is already putting his camera away. He's not quite so casual now.

"Are the others all like this?"

"They're pretty much identical – and in the same place too. There's a vanishingly small chance of them not being connected. Hence my calling you."

"Ok, well, I think we've seen enough for now. Can we go back to your office and take down a few more details?"

"Sure."

I wrap Ronald back up and slide the drawer back in.

"Don't any of these drawers lock? "

DC Owen's partner speaks for the first time. Actually, now that I come to think of it he never introduced himself. In fact, he hasn't said a word up to now. I look at him properly for the first time. He even shorter than PC Owen, and a classic ginger, with deep-set eyes spaced close together over mashed looking nose. There's something about the way he holds himself that's combative; more your archetypal copper, always probing, looking to trip the suspect up. In this sense they're the classic good cop / bad cop combo, but something more complicated is going on.

"No – there's always someone here, and when there's not, the mortuary is locked up tight."

Ginger looks meaningfully at his partner, and DC Owen makes a note in his book. I can tell they're drawing some conclusions, and maybe not helpful ones, but there's no point worrying about that now.

"What about after hours? Is there anyone ever here?"

"Almost never – unless there's a major incident."

"And then who's here?"

"Usually just us APTs. Maybe the odd consultant."

"Ms Tuesday, if you don't mind me saying, what made you call this in? It's pretty unusual to get this kind of call from staff. It's usually a consultant or the coroner. Have you talked to your boss about this?"

Shit! Marian. No. It hadn't even occurred to me. I never tell her anything. Mutual ignore seems the best way to conduct our respective business.

"She's more focussed on the administrative side, and it seemed a weird enough pattern to bring to someone's attention."

"You said that you'd noticed the marks a while ago. What made you wait until now before saying anything?"

The million dollar question. I was kind of hoping that he

wouldn't ask that. Note to self: don't underestimate the cops. Don't sweat it Charlie. You've got nothing to hide.

"I did mention it to Dr Barnard. He told me he'd call it in; not to worry about it."

"But he didn't? What made you decide to do it yourself?"

"We covered that. When I found the second, and the third. They were so close together."

"No, I don't think we did cover it."

His voice is flat. It's like he's reading all the misgivings I've had about Doc; I've got to hand it to him – he's gone straight for the irregularity and he's worrying it like a dog with a bone. I stall for time.

"I beg your pardon?"

"Well – did you talk to him again?"

"No. Not directly. I did send him some emails."

"In a typical week, how often do you interact?"

"Sorry?"

"Meetings? Lunch? Watercooler?"

"Oh – I guess normally…he'd come and look over the cases that had come in most days."

"Normally?"

DC Owen is scribbling away. He seems to be writing an awful lot considering how short my answers are. It occurs to me that I should probably be a bit more forthcoming.

"Actually, I haven't seen him for a while. We haven't had a chance to talk about it."

"Do you think he had a reason for not reporting the marks? Didn't you think it was odd that he fobbed you off?"

"Not really. He's a busy man. Maybe he just ran out of time. As have I. Is there anything else I can help you gentlemen with?"

I put all the authority I can behind it. I run the mortuary after all.

I can tell Ginger knows he'll not get anything else out of me today.

"I haven't got any more questions for now. If it's OK, my colleague will take care of the paperwork, and then we'll be out of your hair."

"Sure."

Back in the office, they go through the motions, and take my particulars again. They give me their business cards, promise to be in touch soon, and leave.

Making the pact

She had taken his clothes, one by one, as he removed them, folding them meticulously, and laying them in a neat pile on his recliner. He felt like he was delivering himself into her hands; a delicious vulnerability, and at the same time a mounting tension. First came slippers, spectacles, jumper. He unclipped his braces, unbuttoned his trousers, and sliding them down, sat down to remove them. His movements were slow. He handed the trousers to Eva, and started to undo his tie. The buttons of his shirt followed.

His fingers were sure and never stumbled – not on the collar button, not on the other ten. Even the cuff buttons yielded easily. Yet he was not calm, anything but. It seemed a peculiar contradiction.

"Are you worried, Victor?"

His eyes are resting on the cuff. He looks up. Eva's gaze is candid. It seems no smile lurks there. Her eyes are open very wide. She looks so young. She should seem vulnerable, but somehow isn't.

"No Eva, no, I'm not worried."

"That's good. You're doing well."

She holds her hands out, and Victor remembers the shirt and tie, and hands them to her. He is down to his underwear now. Long undershorts. Vest. Eva's eyes are on him. He sits up straighter. He had never run to fat. He has no reason to be ashamed of what she sees.

"Do I need to take everything off?"

"We both do, Victor. We need to trust each other completely."

"Well," - Victor tries for lightness - "at least it's not too cold. We shan't freeze."

Victor takes off his vest. He leans down and removes his

socks. Standing up, he quickly removes his undershorts, and sits down again. Now he can't look at her. It's been years since he's been naked in front of a woman.

"Pass me those, and relax please Victor. It's my turn now."

The chair seat is unexpectedly rough against his bare shanks. He keeps his eyes averted; afraid that she'll be put off by his gaze. He can hear zips unfastening. The rustle of fabric. The creak of the other chair as she sits down. He stares hard at his hands, the liver spots, the moles. That crepe-like skin.

"We're ready now Victor. Can you look at me, Victor?"

They are the hands of an old man, and he knows how his body must look. He longs for the confidence he felt moments before. Spindle shanks.

Her voice comes again.

"Victor. This is all about trust. We are the same. We are naked as the day we were born."

He looks at the floor. There are her shoes, neatly lined up next to his house-slippers. There are the clothes, folded in two piles. Not touching. His gaze slides back along the floor. Rests on her feet. Her toenails are red, with some kind of shiny finish. Her toes are straight. Her feet have high arches. Her ankles curve into slim calves. With glowing, golden, unblemished, hairless skin. She has her legs crossed at the knee. He tries to relax. Think of it like a life-drawing class. A lifetime ago. It feels like she's holding a pose, one wrist resting gently on the other. Her stomach is flat, with, he is surprised to discover, a jewel winking from her navel.

And now, there are her breasts. He sweeps past them, furtively, feeling somehow dirty, until he meets her eyes. She watches him steadily enough, but still...was there something desperate there, beneath the light veneer?

She smiles brightly, but it still doesn't reach those big eyes. She lets them travel along his body in turn, and he becomes newly conscious of his wattled neck, his ribs, shoulders turned in to a chest gone concave; the sinews around which his pale fresh is draped. And on, and down. He notices afresh how his thighbones have become bowed, barely knit to his bony hips. His own nakedness precludes even the possibility of any sexual thoughts. He watches the top of her head – the hair neat and shining.

Again, she looks him in the eye.

"Breathe, Victor. It might help you to relax. Can you do that? Can you breathe with me?"

He realises he has been holding his breath, and slumps, with an explosive sigh into the chair.

"I'm going to breathe in for the count of five, hold for three, and breathe out for seven. We'll do that a few times. Let's start now. OK?"

She starts to tap her hand gently on the side of her chair, and Victor silently counts along in his head. It does seem to help – at least it normalizes the situation. He feels heavy, and very light.

Eva has been watching for this moment, when his clenched hands gradually uncurl, palms up, to show his fingertips.

"I can see you're feeling a bit better now. How are you doing, Victor?"

"I feel...I feel a bit strange. I don't feel like I want to touch you. I'm not used to...Seeing a woman in the light. Old-fashioned of me I suppose."

He is silent. He wants to ask 'And what about you?' – but is it even his place? She seems so sure, mistress of the situation. She must have done this before. But he knows he can't ask that either.

"You're doing fine, Victor. You passed the first test. From now on we will always be like this together. We can trust each other now. Naked as the day we were born. Naked of sin."

They look at each other for a while, and then Eva starts
to dress, slowly. Victor isn't sure what to do, and waits for a
signal. She watches him as she fastens her clothes. Pulls on
her shoes. And then she bends and takes something out if her
back. It is a polaroid camera. She focuses and takes a picture
of Victor, and then hands him the camera, which is already
spitting out a photo, already darkening and resolving into an
image.

"This is for you Victor. You look like you know how
to handle a camera. It has a film in it already – with 22
exposures. I've just used the first one. From now on, every
time we play a round in the game I want you to document it
by taking a picture. That way you'll have nothing to worry
about, because everything will be recorded."

Victor was confused.

"What do you mean I'll have nothing to worry about?
Why do we need to record it?"

"Sometimes, just so that I know you've completed the
task. Sometimes, the challenge will be to go somewhere, or
to find something. The camera will help you document that."

She was pulling on her clothes, adjusting her cuffs,
bending to fasten her shoes.

"I've got to go now – but we can meet next week if you
like? In between I'd like you to start keeping a diary for
me. I want you to take a walk every day, and if you see any
magpies, I want you to take note of it – how many, where
you saw them. At which phase of the moon."

"Magpies? What has any of this got to do with magpies?"

"You'll come to understand, Victor. The magpies have
messages for us if we only know how to read them. Augury
is an ancient art – even the Romans would never make a
decree until they had consulted with the Augur and read
the movements of the birds. It's something that I've been
studying for a long time. I can teach it to you too. We are all
part of a web – a web driven by fate, being and necessity. But

we don't have to be at fate's mercy. That is what the game is about. You need to give yourself to it, before you become a player. Are you with me Victor?"

Eva sensed that she was losing him, and worried that she might have gone too far, too fast. Victor shook his head, as if in denial, and she took his hand in hers.

"I don't want you to worry Victor. It's all part of the game. It's in the rules. You trust me don't you, Victor?"

Victor looked at the smooth hand clasping his. Never to hold that hand again. He pulled himself together and looked her straight in the eye.

"I do trust you, Eva. Sorry to doubt you. Of course, I trust you completely."

Five for silver

The note was written on a tiny scroll that unrolled to a small square of paper, perhaps three inches wide. He wouldn't have noticed it, except that a piece of red thread was tied around it, which caught his eye. It was on the windowsill, outside his kitchen. Leaning out to pick it up he could see there was something written on it, but not what. He took it inside to find his reading glasses.

As usual they sat atop the crossword on the table in the sitting room. He settled them on his nose and peered at the tiny letters written on the scrap of paper. V.i..c...t... It was his own name. He slid the red thread off and unrolled it carefully to avoid ripping the paper. Inside it was a note in her hand, those distinctly back-sloping letters with their florid curls.

"Dear Victor,

Today I want you to go and count magpies in Green Park. You must speak to no one.

Imagine you are a monk, who has taken a vow of silence."

He deliberated over the note all morning, but much as he tried to distract himself, he couldn't deny the pressure that was building up within him. He even put the note in the bin, before changing his mind, and fishing it back out. A few tea leaves had stained one corner, and he smoothed it out and brushed them off. After all, he had agreed to play the game. There must be a reason that she wanted him to go there and count magpies.

She was right: when Victor arrived at the park, there were five magpies there, having some kind of meeting or congress. It was mid-summer, and plenty of deck chairs were out. He watched idly as a lady in a 1950s tea dress accompanied by a frock-coated gentleman were served cucumber sandwiches and cups of tea by a waiter from Dukes. Storm clouds massed. He hoped it wouldn't ruin their picnic.

Why had he never noticed before how monochrome this park was? Green of course. 100 feet away a fence separated the park from the growl of Piccadilly – there was verdant nature, the trees dripping shadows upon the green grass. Still the magpies massed. He hadn't quite appreciated how communicative they were. You could watch them and it was like watching semaphore – but without a codebook. Their tails were the flags that wagged up and down, the high contrast of their black and white stripes against the green, the contrapuntal positioning of their heads.

"Victor?"

Was she there? Or just a memory of her?

"Victor – you have something important to do. Remember this. Remember: five for silver."

But...that was how many there were now, and he remembered the camera. He was supposed to capture this. They were so shy – it wouldn't be easy.

Slowly, he eased it out of his pocket. They were in the trees, on the grass, in the time that he'd been watching, they spread out over a fairly large area. The magpies continued that odd dance. It might speak volumes if he knew how to read it. Five...There were five. And there, not ten feet away. a strange installation. Statue? A plain monolith with round holes cut so you could see through, bisecting the view with glimpses of more green. Six feet tall and fashioned from brushed steel, it made a good cover. He positioned the camera behind one of the holes and peered through, only then noticing small silver buttons recessed into the holes. Pressing one, he was rewarded with a trickle of water. It was a drinking fountain.

"Victor – it's come to something when you're sitting here wondering what a bunch of magpies are saying. Still though, it's not every day you see that."

He must stop talking to himself this way. It didn't look

good.

She knew. That was why she'd sent him here. He remembered the camera needed to be wound on for the next shot. At the sound the magpies rose in a flurry, and he inwardly cursed at the thought he'd lost them, vainly tried to see where they had gone.

They landed again, closer together this time, as if grouping against a common threat. He squinted into the viewfinder, twisting the focus dial to fit them all in shot. Click; again they took flight, and wheeled away, but he was fairly sure he had caught them. That would have to be enough for now. Time to head home.

A place of safety

I finish the rota at ten to four and push my chair back from my desk. About bloody time – for the first time this week it looks like I might not have to do any overtime. It feels good to come up for air. Obviously. I'm still on call, but with everything seemingly under control, hopefully I won't have to drag my arse into work for three glorious days. Compassionate leave apparently. Mustn't grumble.

OK. Breathing space. First thing on the agenda is Eva.

- Can I see you 2nite?

Almost immediately the message status updates so I know she's read it. The seconds tick by with no response. She can text like lightning when she wants to. More moments pass. Looks I'm being ignored. I thumb out another message.

- Sorry to ignore you, but I've had a lot on my plate. Been hell at work all week.

- Barely a moment to wipe my arse let alone message people.

It's little enough. Obviously not enough. More read receipts. Still no answer.

- Babe, I get you're pissed off and said I'm sorry. Heading home now. Maybe hook up there?

Again, the message is read immediately. Maybe I don't need to explain myself any more – at a certain point you expect them to understand. Isn't that what relationships are for?

* * *

Eva sat in the white room and reread the messages from Charlie again. She was still covered from neck to toe in black latex, but had removed her mask and shaken out her hair. She began to brush it out with long strokes whilst she thought about how to reply.

Dissimulate. She mustn't know about Flatiron Square. About any of it.

Actually she'd barely spared a thought for Charlie since they'd not managed to meet on Monday. She'd been too busy. With an effort of will she pulled her mind out of the session she'd just finished, still bathing in the pleasurable feeling of power that came after a scene played out well.

'Real' life was so much more complicated; the rules so much harder to fathom. And she still didn't quite understand what the magpies wanted with Charlie. Why had they linked the two of them up?

Recently it had become harder to focus on their relationship. Eva felt herself drifting away. It became harder and harder to keep track of the lies. What did Charlie know? What did she suspect?

There must have been a reason. Perhaps they needed her to be more human to do their work. Maybe she should call her up now. End it. Stop pretending, and embrace the darkness completely. Wouldn't it be kinder to protect her?

Eva stood up and went through to the black room. Instruments and harnesses were still scattered around and she began to gather them up. The floor would need washing. She needn't worry it about it now – she didn't have any more sessions booked for a few days. Ahead of her, the hours stretched, empty and solitary, except for the work she must do for them. She thought of the nights that Charlie had gentled her to sleep, kept the nightmares at bay.

Who was doing the protecting?

Eva made up her mind and pressed call.

* * *

I've just got in the door when my phone rings. I dump my bag on the couch, throw myself onto the cushions, and dig it out of my pocket.

"Hi darling – I hope it's not a bad time?"

It's Eva. I wonder why she called instead of texting?

"No, it's perfect. I just got home from work this minute."

"Good to hear it. We haven't seen each other in so many days I wanted to hear your voice. How was your day?"

Her voice is warm and I wonder how much to tell her about the day. I consider mentioning the old white guys, the marks, meeting the cops. Probably best not over the phone.

"Pretty hellish actually. We're still working through the backlog from Monday. Plus on top of that, I've been dealing with some pretty weird shit at work. I'm sorry I've been incommunicado all week. How has everything been with you babe? I hope you haven't been too lonely?"

"Of course I've missed you, but please don't apologise my darling – your work is important. I'm sorry you've had so much on. "

A pause. There's a crackle on the line and I wonder if I've lost her, but then she speaks again.

"Actually I've been very busy at work too. Back to back shifts at the bar. Good for my bank balance anyway, but maybe not so good for my girlfriend. I should have been here to look after you."

I think wryly of the laundry and hot meals. The flat is in a bit of a mess if I'm honest. I'm not nearly such a good housekeeper as Eva.

"And it shows darling. The place is a right state, and both me and Thug could both do with your loving ministrations. Where are you now?"

Another pause. Thug jumps up onto my lap and starts kneading my chest, whilst I try and bat away his claws. Why do I get the feeling she's also mentally editing out things I don't need to know right now?

"I'm going home – I just got finished from the bar ten

minutes ago. Actually I'm dead on my feet. They ran me ragged today – it was so busy. All I want to do is kick off my heels and take a shower."

She's never said much about her bar job. What kind of bar job requires you to wear heels? Maybe not the time Charlie. I picture the cold little bathroom in her flat. Is she trying to tell me that she doesn't want to see me tonight? Is that why she called? Or maybe she just wants me to try a little harder.

"Well, I'm not going anywhere for the foreseeable. And I don't care if you're a bit stinky. Why don't you hop in a cab and come and shower with me? I reckon I could even stretch to a foot-rub..."

From down the end of the line I hear her throaty chuckle.

"Oh darling, that is so very tempting. At least let me change out of my uniform and into something a little more comfortable. I'll be home soon anyway. Then I'll jump into a cab and be with you in no time."

That wasn't so hard. Maybe I shouldn't be so paranoid.

"Excellent. And I'll do my best not to be asleep when you get here. Don't be too long."

"I'll be as quick as I can darling. See you soon. Kisses!"

Eva hangs up, and I give Thug's head a scratch, whilst he arches it beneath my hand to get a better angle. I look around at the chaos of a week of overtime and too many on-calls. Maybe I'd better straighten up a bit before she arrives.

* * *

Eva put the phone gently on the desk in front of her and unzipped the front of her latex catsuit. She'd worked up enough of a sweat during her last session that most of the talc had been absorbed and the suit wouldn't slide off easily. She'd have to use lube next time. Once she was completely naked she walked over to a door concealed in the white wall, and clicked it open to reveal a cupboard. She cleaned up the remaining streaks of talc with wipes and hung the suit on the rack with her other costumes. Then she took out her street clothes and dressed methodically. Within twenty minutes she was ready to leave.

Night time warning

It seemed an age since she'd set Victor the first challenge. Not because she'd been idle – the devil makes work for idle hands and Eva's had been more than full, with clients almost every day.

And of course Victor wasn't the only recruit to the game. Ronald was coming on nicely now, and Fred had nearly reached the end. But there was something about Victor... maybe it was the trust that he obviously had in her; the way he had refused to look at her body that first time. She wasn't used to men who tried to rule their passions, who had respect. And it had made her delay setting him the next challenge; moving him onto the next stage in the game. She realised she would miss him. What would happen if she stopped it here?

So she distracted herself from Victor by throwing herself into her work. She took every job that was offered, and in between shuttled between her old men, upping the game for those that were nearing the end. She put off the rituals that were due, and tried to avoid the sense of mounting pressure. She knew what it was waiting for.

To save questions she'd told Charlie she had back-to-back shifts at work, so she was staying at her own flat. It was easier that way. Charlie didn't ask her much about her work, and she thought she knew why. It wasn't because Charlie didn't want to know, but too many times it had caused arguments. Eva keeps odd hours; she doesn't seem to have any friends but she's always out, and she gets a lot of calls. There are too many numbers on her phone and Charlie's not interested in an open relationship. They've been fighting, and some of the fights have turned physical. There was the broken hand, of course, but that wasn't the only time. In the last three weeks alone Charlie has gone to work with black eyes, with scratches on her face. They're not good for each other, but there's something addictive about her.

There was so much unsaid. Eva didn't really know where to start, so often, they didn't speak, but let their bodies communicate. Closeness. Spooning. Hand in hand. A careless finger on her nipple, an arm about her waist. It was enough to have that incidental, affectionate, careless love. It was more than she'd ever had before.

Maybe, later, much later, she would speak. Of what had gone before. But for now, the insouciant trust of her was enough.

So, Eva was away. What she actually was, was...well exhausted. Not emotionally drained...it didn't feel like she had enough left for that. It was dark. 3–4 am? Just enough chill in the air to remind you of the small, cold, bitter isle you'd made your own – but ostensibly June, and an unseasonably warm one.

She had been with H at Quo Vadis, where he had booked a private room, and spent the evening pleasurably torturing him with distance, unavailability and scorn. It was easy – not only did he remind her of a toad, he rarely had anything interesting to say, and his medical fetish was so infantile, so clearly the result of low self-esteem, that the scorn was hardly an act. He wore his usual t-shirt, sweats, designer sunglasses, at odds with his overweight frame, the sagging chins. He smelt. She had worn a heavy perfume, a cloying musk that was redolent of a deathly sense of decay. H was rich of course – they all were – and wore the trappings of success, but there was a hole inside him; a lack that would never be remedied.

It didn't manifest itself in ways obvious to most people, but Eva had become expert at spotting weakness, like a carrion bird who spots the tiniest stumble in the gait of a beast wandering far below. Once identified she would exploit any flaws ruthlessly, until she had brought them down as low as it was possible for them to go. There was always a chink to be found if you searched long enough.

At 1 am he suggested going back to his place. She hesitated. It felt like giving him the upper hand; that could be dangerous. He was also a generous tipper. Against her better judgement she agreed.

She should have known better.

Everything changed once he shut the door behind him; the balance shifting as though the closing door had been a fulcrum, as if he were emboldened by being on home territory. He wanted to put his hands on her. That was not part of the deal. She tried her usual tricks; used her matron voice, cursed him, and when that had the opposite effect to that intended, and he still kept coming at her, she got scared and raked her nails down his face.

That was not part of the deal either. No limo ride back for her.

And here she was walking back from Surrey Docks in her limousine shoes. She could have got a cab, but her phone was dead. Maybe she was losing her touch. She had always been able to exert absolute control. The clients; the game. In the final analysis they were both the same thing. She controlled the pattern, and they followed it. Until she didn't. She couldn't afford to lose any more clients. She wished she could give up all her clients. Give up everything. Be free. Give up Charlie?

Maybe it was time to stop? She could just stop. Oh, how she wished she could just stop. It's not as simple as that. There was too much at stake – she couldn't afford to give up now. It would be too easy for her to become the sacrifice. Every night now she dreamed of flying; more of her human-ity was leached away. They needed blood. She needed it not to be hers. Maybe it was just nerves. She always got this way near the end. It had never been this bad though. She had always been able to keep the two sides separate up until now. Actually that wasn't quite it. The magpies had given her power, over all those men. Just so long as she fulfilled her side of the bargain.

The streets were dead quiet. In the distance she could hear the drone of traffic. No birds sang. She passed housing developments, lights off. Every ten feet a pool of light around a lamppost. Spiky shadows told of landscaping, an entirely made environment.

And then, there, where there shouldn't have been any... there all around her was a murder, a fright, a warning of magpies. She had never seen so many. She didn't think they came out at night.

In the lamplight their markings seemed more garish, and they were still landing, 5, 6, 7, still swooping in, 8, 9, 10, 11, until she was surrounded. Turning around she realised she was entirely encircled. Each bird, turned, just so, side on to fix her with a single eye.

The pavement here was wide. And where could she run? And why would she run. Eva forced calm. Clenched her hands. Felt her feet upon the ground. Centred her balance. And still they watched her, motionless but for the occasional random tail flick.

Or was it...was that the third, the fifth, the ninth, and then the third again?

And then a pause...

....and more tail-flicking.

She would go mad with this. Not the same again...again the stop. And Eva was still, as still as she could be...

Stop. Pause.

She realised she was standing there, at 3 am, in the street in South East London, surrounded by magpies...

And then in a body they flew at her; she felt the surprising slap of their wings; felt claws scrabbling; threw her hands up uselessly to her face and they banked, and were gone. Eva lifted her hands to her face, and felt the marks of their claws; dozens of tiny scratches covered her chin, her cheekbones. She could feel a slick of blood already starting to form.

She would be marked, as H had been marked. Their protection was contingent on her cooperation. The message was clear – and anyway she wouldn't be able to work until the cuts had healed.

She knew they wouldn't let her put it off any longer.

* * *

Victor found another note on his windowsill, tied once again with a brightly coloured length of string.

'I need you to go to Brockley Cemetery. Find a hollow tree, past the allotments. There will be a package in there for you. Trust me. Don't fail me.'

Another message? How did they get onto his windowsill? Had she left it there, or had someone bring it? Why was it so tiny? And why hadn't it been left in his letterbox? So many strangenesses he didn't know where to start. As he stood, turning the note over in his hands, he heard a scrabbling at the window. He looked, and there, bold as brass, was a magpie, looking back. It cocked it's head, hopped a couple of steps to the side, and tapped on the window with it's beak. He looked down at the note in his hand, so light, so tightly wrapped. Small enough to be carried in a magpie's claws?

That's crazy, Victor.

As if satisfied its job was complete, the magpie flicked its tail, and was gone.

The investigation stalls

I'm in the PM room when I get the message that PC Owen and DC Smith are in my office. By the time I've scrubbed up and made it there they've already made themselves comfortable. I'm glad I keep an empty desk. They get straight to the point and are noticeably less friendly this time.

"Good afternoon Ms Tuesday. I know you weren't expecting us, but as we were in the neighbourhood, we decided to pop in and see if you had any more marks to report?"

"None this week."

"We've been trying to track down anyone that the deceased may have been in contact with before their deaths – but we've run into a bit of a brick wall. It seems like they all had one thing in common: a lack of known associates. And therefore, a lack of evidence. We haven't been able to identify a single person who recalls having seen them recently or noticed that they'd not been around."

I'm still processing this again, and he's onto the next point already.

"In a couple of cases the bodies had been in an advanced state of decomposition; they hadn't been found for days after their apparent suicides. Although it formed an intriguing pattern, and possibly strengthened the link between them, it wasn't much use in advancing the investigation.

We've got one piece of potential evidence – a note, with traces of saliva. It's written on the kind of paper that's used for making lollipop sticks. In fact just like the one you're sucking on now. Seems a bit of a surprising coincidence.

"You said that some of the bodies hadn't been found for a while, and that they were all ligature cases. Is there anything else in your mind that might connect them? Any other detail that you've recalled since our first meeting?"

I shake my head. Nothing.

"I put everything into the first report – of course I would have let you know if there had been anything since."

We move onto Doc, who's away at a conference somewhere overseas. Do I know when he'll be back? Any idea why he hasn't filed the report?

"No. It's not like him at all. Normally he's all over the paperwork."

"In your opinion, could the marks have been made by him? It wouldn't be the first time; surgeons have been known to 'sign' their patients' organs, like the recent case with the kidney transplant guy..."

Typical. Thousands of operations performed every year, and the only ones the public remembers are the ones that get into the paper. I shake my head impatiently.

"With respect, that's the kind of thing you read in the tabloids. Doc's not that guy."

"It's a line of enquiry that we'll be pursuing."

"Well it doesn't seem very likely to me. Those marks were clearly inflicted over an extended period, possibly weeks before the time of death. That's in the report too."

"Nevertheless, Ms Tuesday, we would like to review the CCTV, to get a feel for anyone who might have been hanging around when they shouldn't be."

"That would be Laurence's department – he's the IT manager. Few caveats though. There's no cameras in the Mortuary, so if you hope to see people sneaking around desecrating the bodies you're in for a disappointment."

"And where will we find Laurence?"

I'm shocked to realise that the focus of their investigation has shifted. Having found no background material on the victims, they seem to have decided that the link is via the hospital. Or are at least entertaining the possibility. What a time for Doc to be away. I think fast.

"I'll call Laurence for you – but I'm not sure if he's on site now. He often works the late shift."

I dial Laurence's number, which rings four times and goes through to voicemail. As I expected. Laurence loves the night shift, and it's barely 2 pm.

I put the phone down without leaving a message and turn to PC Owen.

"Well – it looks like he's not on shift. Should I call back and leave a message, or would you prefer to do it yourselves?"

If PC Owen is disappointed it doesn't show.

"Don't worry about it. I'll take down his number and we can follow up ourselves. I think we've taken up enough of your time for now."

"Sure thing."

I jot down Laurence's number on a post-it and hand it to PC Owen, who rises to his full height and sticks out his hand.

"Thanks for your cooperation. We'll be in touch. Please let us know immediately if there's any developments."

"Will do. I'll see you out gentlemen."

"No need – we can find our own way out."

Once they have left, I sit at my desk thinking about what has just transpired. It doesn't look good. In fact, I don't like the direction events have taken at all. There isn't much I can do about it though. I'd better let Laurence know that the police might be in touch, before he gets a call from them out of the blue. How much is he going to need to know?

Damn! Where is Doc?

Dover crossing

Doc woke up with a stiff neck, and a momentary sense of disorientation. Then he remembered where he was – a fleapit hotel in Dover that he'd chosen because it was cheap and near the port, whilst he worked out the stealthiest way to leave the country. Not the kind of place he would ever normally stay, which might throw them off the scent. It seemed like a sound plan. Ferry to Calais, then either overland by train or bus, or a cheap flight to somewhere economical he could lay low for a little while. Shame he couldn't call on a yacht-owning friend to get him out of the country, but he didn't want to put anyone else at risk. He lay in the uncomfortable bed and considered the thought of a cup of tea. The room could stretch to that at least, and someone had thoughtfully left a ferry timetable by the bed.

At length he sat up and started dressing in the rumpled clothes he'd discarded at the foot of the bed the night before. He'd packed as light as possible, hoping to make it look as though he'd just left his flat for a stroll, not for the foreseeable future – squeezing a spare pair of trousers, some socks and pants into the leather satchel that was almost a part of him. He'd had to leave his beloved mandolin behind. Then he set about making a cup of tea; boiling the small kettle; wringing the last few drops out of the minute plastic pots of milk that were all that was provided.

As he drank it, he considered his next move. The cheap hotel on Athol terrace had an unlovely view, looking out over the great davits that moored the ferries, and attended day and night by the clanking of chains, the growl of engines revving and idling. He could smell diesel fumes through the crack of his opened window; but for his purposes it was perfect. He could see the ships arriving, and time his approach so that he could walk on as a foot passenger without booking first. Not that they were likely to be monitoring all entrances and exits to the country, but the police certainly would, and it never hurt to be careful.

Who are you fooling? You're not cut out for this cloak and dagger stuff.

It looked as though his intended ferry was about to start boarding foot passengers; the lanes were almost empty of lorries and cars, all of the coaches already loaded. He finished his tea, grabbed his satchel, and gave the room a quick once over to ensure he hadn't left anything behind.

Downstairs he dropped his key in the deposit box at reception. A uniformed attendant was doing something with his back to the counter, but as he heard the clink of keys he turned around.

"Doctor. I hope you had a pleasant night?"

Doc felt his hands go numb, and a band of pain gripped his chest. It was one of them – the two men he had encountered on Hampstead Heath.

As he saw Doc's eyes widen with recognition and fear, the man smiled, revealing white, unnatural teeth.

"I wonder, are you considering a trip overseas today? I wouldn't recommend it. I've heard sea voyages are very bad for your health – and you don't look like a well man."

Doc looked around anxiously. Perhaps he could still make it. Where was the other one?

"You're looking for my friend? He's not far away. He's waiting for you by the ticket office. You didn't think we'd lose track of you that easily, did you? Our employers would be most upset if that happened. You're going to be very useful to them."

His expression was lazy and contemptuous, his smile the fixed rictus of a cat with a mouse at it's mercy. Well, damn them. He would not be a mouse.

Doc took a deep breath, and felt the band loosen a little.

He focused on calming his racing heart. He lifted his chin, and thrust his chest out, unconsciously assuming a fighting stance...fight or flight warring in his brain; but what was needed now was calm. Calm. By now he felt he could trust himself to speak without a quiver in his voice.

"Hem. Hello. I suppose I really should have known I'd run into you here. I'd be interested to know more about your methods. They're most impressive."

He was proud of how that came out. The man chuckled, and then his expression hardened.

"So, what's it going to be?"

His hands rested by his side, but Doc could see their rhythmic clenching and unclenching; the play of muscles beneath the overly tight uniform. He momentarily wondered where the rightful owner was.

Just then a party of four came noisily down the stairs, chatting amongst themselves, to check out. Doc stepped back towards the door as they headed for reception, blocking his view of the man behind the desk. He took advantage of the moment to slip out of the hotel and onto the street. Where could he go? He had a few seconds' start at least. He ran along the street, and down East cliff. It was quiet and empty of people, but halfway along on the right he could see a sign for 'the last pub in the civilised world', which turned out to be a backpacker's hostel. He slipped inside. He could do with some breakfast, and he had an idea he would be safer with other people around.

Mortuary tour

I'm deep in paperwork when I hear a knock at the door. I spin my chair around, expecting and half-hoping it will be Doc, but to my surprise Chloe is standing there.

"Hello you! What brings you to these parts?"

"I've been seconded to Histology as part of my third year curriculum. I thought I'd pop in and see if I could get you to give me that tour you promised. That is if you're not too busy?"

She glances at the small pile of papers on my desk, and then clocks the many photos adorning my wall– a selection of memes printed out from buzzfeed alternating with comedy shots of the mortuary crew dressed up in hazmat gear, and pulling silly poses. She steps into the office and leans in for a closer look.

"These are hilarious! Just too funny. And how cute is that cat! Well, how about it? Care to show me your domain?"

I close the folder I've been working from.

"Sure. There's no PMs going on now though – everyone's finished for the day. I'm just finishing up a bit of admin. Nothing that won't keep."

In the small office Chloe is distractingly near. I brush past her on the way to the door.

"Follow me."

I've done this tour many times before, but usually for colleagues, not someone I fancy. I keep my tone neutral as we continue past the various rooms that lead off the main corridor to the PM room.

"That's the family room – that's where people wait whilst we get the bodies ready. No one there now of course. That takes us through to the fridge room."

I wave around the steel-clad doors that line the space.

"Babies; long term storage; high-risk. These are the fridges with the clients that are ready to go out, and those ones, nearest the PM room, have the new clients, ready for PMs tomorrow. I suspect you're more interested in the PM room. I'm guessing you've covered dissection already on your course."

"Yeah – most of year one and two was anatomy - and of course more rats, rabbits and frogs than I can count doing biology at school. We didn't get access to 'fresh' cadavers though - most of them were prosections or plastinated specimens of donated bodies. The supply of bodies left to medical schools isn't large enough to risk students on 'virgin' corpses. This is something else."

We reach the PM room. Chloe pauses and takes in the view. I have to admit it does look pretty impressive. Six PM bays fill the centre of the large room whose central column features large whiteboards, listing the data that needs to be collected for each autopsy: name, age, weight, height; brain, heart, lungs right and left, spleen, kidneys, thyroid and renal levels. Usually when I give the tour I have to explain the abbreviations, but Chloe is already there.

"And the numbers down the right – those are the levels right? I guess it's easier to write up here on the board, rather than messing about with a laptop whilst you're doing a dissection."

I smile at her, already feeling we can talk in a way that isn't accessible with Eva. It's not just that she's interested, she also has an insight into the problems I deal with on a daily basis.

"Exactly. The prosected samples you work on as students don't get too messy – they've already been treated to prevent decay. Some of the bodies we get in here are already in an advanced state of decomposition. You definitely don't want that shit all over your computer. Here's my station."

"You'd never tell from looking around this place. It's spotless. I've used some of these tools before, but what on earth is that?"

I guess that she's not had the opportunity or need to remove the top of someone's cranium before.

"It's a skull saw. We have them in two sizes – infant and adult I thought you covered that kind of thing in first year anatomy?"

As usual, all is present and correct. Instruments laid out with millimetre precision.

"Everything is so organised!"

"Well, I do like to keep a tidy mortuary – people work more efficiently that way. And you never know when you might have an inspection. And what about you? Have you decided what area you want to specialise in when you qualify?"

"So, I'm really into Pathology. Apparently I have a flair for it according to my tutor. There's just something amazing about the way the human body works; ingenious and precise – like a fine timepiece. Understanding the workings of the human body – and what the consequences are when something goes wrong with it. I don't fancy general practice. Live humans are so much more problematic."

You could say that again. I think ruefully of Eva, wondering what's going on with her, and why she doesn't sleep at my apartment any more. It feels like we've drifted apart over the last few weeks; and that is very noticeable after the previous intensity. I have to say it's almost a relief. There's too much going on for me to be distracted…And Chloe is certainly distracting. I'd like to flirt with her, but it doesn't feel appropriate here at work. I keep my tone light and professional.

"I hear you. We deal with our fair share of live humans too - relatives and friends of the deceased; the police. Sometimes I don't get into the PM room at all."

"That must be frustrating for you. I never really got people, but I get anatomy. It just makes sense to me – like slotting lego blocks together. Emotions are so messy compared to science. I'd rather cut up a dead person than talk to a live one."

"It is! When we're busy it feels like there's not enough hours in the day; the last thing you need is an hour with a relative who doesn't get that you can't just rock up to the mortuary and collect a corpse. Not that you ever let them see your impatience of course. Would you like to see the fridges next?"

"Definitely, if you've got the time. I don't want to hold you up?"

I'm more than happy to spend more time in Chloe's company – and enjoying finding out more about her. She's someone I'd like to get to know a lot better.

"It's alright. Anything other than the dreaded paperwork – and it won't take long."

We leave the PM room and go through the dressing room, with its rows of rubber boots and shelves of gloves, masks and hazmat suits. I start with the long-term fridges, opening each door so that Chloe can see the bodies stored on the shelves inside, ice-rimed feet protruding from the shrouds within which each was wrapped.

"These guys have been here for a while, for various reasons. Either they're waiting for a coroner's report, or there's no one to release them to."

I slide one tray out and gently unwrap the body, careful not to choose one of the ones with the strange marks on. I don't want to get into that with Chloe. A dark skinned woman in her late 70s is revealed. Chloe is silent as she gazes at the figure before her. What's going through her head?

At length she speaks. Her voice is hushed, awed.

"This is nothing like the bodies that we worked with in Anatomy class. You knew that the spirit was long fled from those cells; a mere model of a human being; all the questions already answered by an earlier inquisitor. The t's crossed, the i's dotted; nothing else to learn. What you do is totally different – inherently more interesting, with questions to be answered every day. The starkness of it. Visceral. Raw. Bones, sinews, bloodless flesh. That would make me want to get up in the morning. The chance to satisfy my sheer fucking curiosity everyday. There's nothing I want to do more."

Obviously we share the same need to know how human bodies work.

"Sometimes you can't satisfy your curiosity. There's people cremated every year on the NHS who will never be identified, cause of death unknown."

"Well – that's not too different to real life is it? What do we ever know about anyone? Even my parents were a mystery to me. Words were a weapon in my family. Mutual infidelity kept them too busy during my childhood to have any time for me; and when they finally, acrimoniously split, it was to move in with respective lovers, leaving me out in the cold. Of course, that was a place I'd got used to inhabiting, and one which arguably I created for myself once it became clear there was no room in their lives for me. At least science is incontrovertible."

"Sounds like my mum, with her many boyfriends. Well I say mum, but I actually had two; one of them wasn't strictly my blood mother – she was my dad's girlfriend, but even after they split she still looked out for me. What about school? That was a place I always felt safe. Like a way out you know?"

"Not really. I was bullied at school but did well anyway and went into medicine as a fuck you to my parents because I knew it would cost a fortune, and that they would pay for it...Thus, also, the tattoos, and body mods. And more...I was a very naughty girl indeed. You must think I'm so shit - poor privileged only child whose parents didn't get on. I didn't lack material things, but I was lonely; I spent far too much time on digital devices."

A phone starts ringing in the distance. I gently rewrap the sheet and slide the body back into its compartment.

"That's coming from my office – I'd better go and see who it is."

Chloe follows me to the office, and waits at the door as I race in and grab the handset.

"Hello, Mortuary, Charlie speaking?"

PC Owen is on the other end of the line.

"Just a minute please."

I put my hand over the mouthpiece of the receiver and turn to Chloe.

"I have to take this one, sorry. Can you let yourself out? Let's catch up at the Walrus soon."

Lunch with Mother

Sooner than expected, it's time for my monthly lunch with Mother. It's a ritual that's been going on for years, and despite the fact that hanging out with Mother never fails to wind me up, it does salve my conscience – at least once a month I get a visual on the old dear, and ensure she's still alive. She always insists on meeting when the moon is full. She says it shows her in her best light. Or maybe she's just trying to annoy me. She's always been a mug for anything esoteric.

Eva turns up just as we're sitting down. I give her a significant look, but I don't want to open a whole can of worms by mentioning the situation with Doc in front of Mother, or that I've been trying to get hold of her for days. Mother has got used to me being gay, but she's been very vocal about her disapproval of previous girlfriends. She approves of Eva because she is beautiful, and dresses well. Yes, she really is that shallow. Still, it makes a change from the usual litany of complaints.

We always go for a family roast in the Social – or the nu-conservative club as we've taken to calling it. It was once the actual Conservative club, but the eighties and nineties whittled the original clientele away until it couldn't support itself anymore, and an achingly hip pub chain snapped it up, re-opening with all its kitsch décor intact, formica tables, portrait of Maggie Thatcher and all. We eat in the main room of the pub, watched over by a portrait of the young Queen Elizabeth, defaced at some point in the transition from down-at-heel social club to shabby chic gastropub. How Brixton has changed.

Mother makes most of the conversation. She doesn't notice that I'm not taking part. There's a man strumming a guitar for the diners a couple of tables along. She's perfectly happy to hold forth about the songs he's playing; the memories of youth that they trigger; in her head she's still inhabiting those heady times when she was a beauty; reliving the parties, the drug-taking; uppers and downers and watching dawn over the bridge. As she talks about it a touch of that faded glamour returns, puts a sparkle in her eye. To hear her, it was all rock stars and limousines, but my memories are very different. Waterloo Sunset triggers a long and rambling monologue about London in the sixties that I've heard a million times before. I let it wash over me whilst I concentrate on working my way through Yorkshires, roast potatoes, chicken, red cabbage and parsnips. They do a fine roast here. As usual Eva eats like a bird, picking at a sliver of chicken breast. Although there's only the width of a table separating us she seems as distant as the moon; the sharp planes of her face set in hard slabs.

In the background the song changes to Marley's 'Is this love?' And am I feeling it? If I'm honest, no. I feel like someone who has forgotten tenderness; who looks at the woman opposite me and sees a stranger, not a lover. There's only so much you can give to someone who gives back so little of herself.

I look at Eva dispassionately, like she's a client waiting to be worked on. Her bones stand out like wings from her back; vertebrae visible on her spine; her hips emphasise the hollow-ness of her belly. When did she make the transition from thin to skeletal? That indefinable air of sophistication that I was initially attracted to has been tainted, as if she's been let out of the Priory for the weekend. Are her eyes and skin a little yellowed, her complexion less fresh? Why does she look so much older?

A dead-eyed zombie gazes at me – dark eyes that swallow love, kindness, everything.

I get it. She's an emotional vampire. Energy sucker. Maybe I've been avoiding Eva because I feel so knackered after we've been together. Way more colds and sniffles than usual and I haven't even been hitting the marching powder. Working too hard I suppose.

And then the waiter's here, asking if we enjoyed our food, and Mother Dear is flirting with him, of course. The state of her. Nearly seventy, in a low-cut dress and heels. Her lipstick is perfect. My tom-boy style has always been a bone of contention between us. It was all 'Why can't you be more feminine?' Why does she always do that? Of course she'll flirt with the waiter, and the guy with a guitar and a smooth voice, and a copper pot left on his table, for tips. There'll be no money coming his way from Mother Dear – just a smile and a wink. Doesn't she realise it's creepy, from a 70-year-old woman? She thinks it's part of her charm. It annoys the hell out of me.

Remembering my childhood, and how I had to learn to protect myself from the men in my mother's life, who checked in, for a little while, like bees sucking nectar, before they moved on, leaving her broken. And she fell for it every time, always that desperate need for approval. It's something that I've never needed. What I crave is a deeper relationship. I can see straight through the other kind. Is that the kind of relationship I want with Eva?

And would Chloe be any different? I can't quite figure her out. On the surface she just another privileged girl from the home counties, born to succeed, from the tips of her finely turned toes to the ends of her shining hair. Still, that's not all there is to her. It feels as though there's something more she wants to share with me. She has her own demons. No one normal has that much ink on their body. I should know about ink; each mark signifies a road hard-travelled. Chloe must have her own reasons for the designs that cover most of her body from neck to ankles, but so far I haven't had the opportunity to explore them. I shouldn't even be thinking about this. I don't do infidelity – it makes everything too complicated and I hate lying. This doesn't feel quite like a normal relationship. Take the bracelet that Eva's wearing now, for example. It appeared last week – a crystal set in a ring of gold, on a slender chain that hugs Eva's wrist as though it was made for her. And Eva has changed. She's lost her sleekness. She seems pared down; her skin rough; her lips chafed. She reminds me of Coldharbour Lil. Unexplained – that bracelet. When I asked where it came from, Eva told me that a magpie gave it to her. These things make me realise that I'm dealing with a damaged person. There are too many loose ends. I've been there before. It is time to disengage. The best I can hope for at this stage is to limit my exposure. Maybe Mother Dear can help with that. She's been drinking steadily throughout the meal, but at least she's in a good mood today.

"Well that was tasty once again. I don't know about you, but I couldn't manage another bite. Assuming no one wants dessert? Another G & T, Mother?"

As she looks at me I see her sway a little. Her eyes are glazed. It doesn't look as though she needs another drink now. I turn to Eva, who gazes at me mutely, as though she's been reading my thoughts, and is just now processing them.

"Eva? No? Looks like we're done here then."

I stand up and stretch, before walking around the table to where Mother is sitting. I give her a dutiful peck on the cheek.

"Bill's all settled, so you've nothing to worry about – I paid when I ordered our roast. I'm going to pop next door for a couple of games of pool at the Hoot...you're welcome to join me of course?"

I know what the answer will be. Mummy hates the Hootananny even more than Eva does. She actually shudders.

"No dear – I'll not set foot in that awful place. I don't know what you see in it – full of drunks, and filthy."

I'm saved from replying as Eva cuts in.

"I'll take Carole home if you like Charlie. Maybe we can

see each other later?"

"Thanks Eva – although I'm sure she can make it home by herself. She's a big girl. I've got an early PM tomorrow, so I'll be hitting the 159 at 5 am. Maybe take a rain check till tomorrow night if that's OK with you?"

I keep my tone light, but I can see in Eva's eyes that she knows it's the beginning of the end. And it's there in the dullness of her voice as she answers.

"Sure, Charlie. Whatever you want. Just let me know when you've got time to see me."

She leans in, and kisses me on both cheeks, European style, rather than the kiss on the lips that usually precedes our partings. Then she holds out an arm for Mother and they leave the bar together. As I watch them go I compare my small and slight mother with Eva's tall and slender form. Although they seem so different, there is one thing that's similar about both of them. They both have a whiff of damaged goods. Maybe that's what attracted me to Eva. She reminds me of mother, and a part of me instinctively wants to help.

Brockley Cemetery

Victor took the train to Crofton Park, and walked
down the small high street towards Brockley and Ladywell
cemetery. The first gate he came to was locked, so he
continued on, keeping the cemetery railings to his right until
he came to the main entrance, the gates ajar in invitation.
Entering, he was presented with a choice – to take the left or
the right path. The right path was broad, and well cared-for.
The path on the left was narrow, and overgrown, studded
with ancient graves leaning in towards his feet, all entwined
with ivy and brambles and bindweed. A blind angel, features
worn with time and breast speckled with lichen, turned her
head away in grief. Ahead of him the narrow path stretched
out into a darkening vista, trees grown overhead to form
a tunnel of green that obscured the sky. If there was any
writing on the stones they were too worn to read; names,
dates and epitaphs alike consigned to the dustbin of history...
or the hungry fingers of Mother Nature.

Victor paused for breath. Of course he had brought the
notebook with him. He kept it on him all the time now. He
had come to enjoy the ritual of recording. Mingled with his
notes on the movements and behaviour of magpies were
other jottings. He kept a log of his journeys, following the
points of the map. He had come to realise there was a pattern
to the places that she sent him to, and that it was connected
to the strange symbol, and the cutting. He kept a note of
everything connected to the game, but he was careful never
to mention her by name. There were oblique references here
and there, but certainly never her name. It didn't feel right.

Highgate cemetery. Bunhill Fields. Walthamstow, West
Norwood. Old Barnes. Camberwell. Brockley and Ladywell.
What was her purpose in sending him to these places?
Cemeteries all – to the East, the West, the South, the North

of this great city. He had forgotten the scale of it until he had started making these journeys. The thousands upon millions of dwellings. The way the train cuttings bisected the denseness of it. The many and varied people that formed villages and tribes within the vastness of the city that was never still. But here, in amidst the graves where they came to their final sleep – or rotted, and were eaten by worms, depending on what you believed...here, there was some peace.

He came to a bench and decided to sit awhile. After all, he was a kind of bird spotter, and had an idea that you never spotted them on the move. Birdwatchers hide in the shadows and keep still and silent. Not a soul was around.

A light breeze rustled the leaves above his head. A squirrel ran down a tree trunk and across the path, never glancing at him. He made himself even more still. Sunlight dappled down through the leaves and played tricks with his eyes. He closed them. Felt the cemetery around him. Felt the warm air brushing his cheeks. Felt the timeworn wood of the bench beneath his fingertips. Wondered what he was doing there.

And then he heard it. The scold of a magpie. The sound was unmistakable. He opened his eyes and they were there. Perched on the tilted stones. Astride the path. One almost at his feet. Six of them. Six is hell. Their voices so harsh, that according to legend they had to ride on the roof of Noah's ark.

A feather glinted on the ground and Victor bent to pick it up. As he turned it over in his fingers a strip of iridescent plumes at the edge of the feather caught the light; further along a patch was precisely delineated in white. There could be no doubt that the feather came from a magpie. Victor held it for a moment longer, pondering, and then placed it carefully in his pocket. He would transfer it to his notebook later.

She had told him to look for a hollow tree in the new part of the cemetery, next to the allotments. It seemed a very public place to hide a secret – in plain view of both people visiting the graves of loved ones, and gardeners digging over their potatoes. He supposed that they must have other things on their minds. His own parents were buried far away – he hadn't visited them for many years. They had passed away within a short time of each other, as if they couldn't bear to be apart, and he was left alone.

He came to the end of the old part of the cemetery, and found the playing fields, edged with a thin strip of playground fenced off and inhabited by shrieking children. Here the grass was shorn and the graves marched cheek by jowl up the slope, the most recent not yet capped with stones. A single giant weeping willow broke the monotony.

Victor stopped to rest. He looked around for a bench, but there were none – just a low haha running along the edge of the burial plots – and he couldn't quite bring himself to sit there. He paused awhile and leant on his stick. He could see another big tree up ahead and as he approached it a gap opened up in the fence to his left, through which he could see the allotments she had mentioned. That must be the one. There was the trunk, and within it a dark shaded hollow. Reaching it, he could see that time, woodworm or rot had eaten the whole inside out. He peered down inside, but couldn't see into the shadowed depths. There was nothing for it but to reach his hand in. As he felt around inside he discovered a section where the rot had left a kind of shelf, and on it, his questing fingers touched a package.

He felt his heart contract, and looked around to see if anyone was watching. A lone woman stood before a grave several hundred feet away, her back to him, in an attitude of grief. His fingers clenched around the package. Without looking at it, he slipped it into his inside pocket and continued on.

* * *

Victor did the whole journey home, on foot, by bus, by overground train, with his hand in his pocket – clutching the small package to ensure it would not be lost. Eventually he made it back. He opened the front door and removed his outdoor shoes, placing them methodically below the coat hooks, and shrugged on his slippers. He removed the jacket that had weighed him down on a warm June day, and arranged it carefully on its hook. He walked through to the kitchen and placed the package on the counter. A cup of tea first. He had a feeling he would need it.

The kettle boiled and he treated himself to a fresh teabag; extra sugar. Hot sweet tea. Shame he didn't have anything stronger to put in it. The package filled him with a nameless dread. But he also knew how easy it would be, had seen it in himself how the drink crept in like a thief if you weren't paying attention. He never kept it in the house now. Not that he could afford it any more.

He took the tea through to the sitting room, and went back for the package. It was too thick to be just paper, and he could not think what it contained. It was securely taped. He would need a knife to open it. He brought them back to the sitting room, and lowered himself gratefully into his recliner; put off that moment with a sip of tea. Regarded the package.

"You know there's nothing good inside that package, Victor. You know that, don't you? So why are you going to open it anyway?"

Maybe he should leave it till later. Maybe he shouldn't open it at all. Maybe, the next time she came calling, he should refuse to answer the door.

But he knew it didn't work like that.

"What are you going to do, Victor?"

It was he who had spoken, talking to himself again, but it felt like her voice.

And he had promised to trust her, here, in this very spot, when they had both been naked. 'Naked of sin' as she had put it. It couldn't be so very bad, could it?

Do it Victor.

He picked up the package, and the knife, and began to cut through the tight wrapping. Inside he found a note, and another package. There was also a feather – a magpie's feather from the way the light caught the dark plumage and threw out flashes of blue and green. The note was written in black ink, a curiously crabbed but neat script that was tiny and impossible for Victor to read unaided. He reached for his magnifying glass, and squinted at the small letters. The note was not signed, but he knew it was from her. He began to read.

'Now you have completed another level in our game, it is time to move onto the next challenge.

I can't promise it will be easy – nothing worthwhile ever is. It will however be necessary.

Open the small packet before you read the rest of this note.'

Victor put down the magnifying glass and picked up the package. It had been wrapped around several times with tape, and he searched for an end in vain. Finally he settled for slicing carefully through one end and cutting off the top, envelope style. Inside was a white plastic bag, folded around its contents. He traced the outline of something coiled inside with his fingers. He placed the bag on the table and turned back to the note.

'I hope you have followed my instructions. It is very important that you follow them exactly. Today you visited Brockley and Ladywell. It is a beautiful and mysterious place, and I know you will have encountered some of our friends there. I hope you have been keeping a note of some of these encounters. These are the first steps on your journey. Think of them as the stations of the cross; steps in your redemption. When the time comes you will understand all; the magpies will guide you.'

Victor couldn't read any more. The paper fell from his shaking hands and he had sat motionless for many moments. He did not know how much time had passed. When, finally, he had come to himself again, he noticed his tea had gone cold. He took it through to the kitchen and poured it into a small saucepan to reheat. He thought about what she had said. Was about to say. He had the feeling that if he read to the end he would be entering into a contract.

You're not being honest with yourself Victor. You know it started the first time you let her into your house. You invited her in. A lonely old man; a pretty lady. Who are you trying to fool, Victor?

Again he had the feeling he was channelling her voice... and she? Who or what was she channelling?

You know you've got to open that package, Victor. You have to.

The tea was boiling furiously. He turned off the gas and added a bit more sugar, before pouring it back into the cup. He'd have to watch the sugar, or he'd be drinking bitter tea when it ran out. He'd often thought that the perfect cup of tea was like the Trinity: milk, tea, sugar. Only when they were present and in ideal union could you have a perfect cup of tea.

What a thought! Shades of a catholic there, Victor.

It was a long time since he'd bothered with religion; not since he'd nodded through mass during one year at a Catholic primary school at the age of 9. What had it been called? St Lukes? Sixty-two years ago! Sometimes it frightened him. So long ago. He had been alive for so very long now, and the years flipping by in an eye-blink, so it seemed that he napped and Christmas fled past, and yawned, and it was Spring, and opened his eyes and Summer had arrived again, faster and faster, like one of those flipbooks he had made as a child.

And now this. He dared not go back into the sitting room. The note sat where he had left it, the pact unmade. It was only 8.30, and the summer days were long...the night would be longer. He picked up his tea and went through to his bedroom instead.

Part 3

The city is never silent,
the young are never pure,
and even the innocent are guilty
of something...

Sav

When had Doc stopped telling me the truth?

He's always been straight down the line. One of the good guys. Always treated me like an equal, unlike some of the consultant pathologists, who look down on us mere technicians. And yet, the police showed me his notebooks, where he keeps tabs on his transactions with the Chinese, and his online account, which shows him hundreds of thousands of pounds in the red. He's definitely been up to something, but I'm not convinced he's responsible for the marks. As far as the police are concerned, it's cut and dried. Motive. Opportunity. Evidence.

Then there's Chloe. Swapping messages is fun, but hard to maintain what with all the other stuff going on. And of course, the small matter of one of London's busiest mortuaries to run. It's safe to say that I'm a pretty stressed bunny. I look at the clock - 4:30 pm – and round at my office. Everything shipshape for now. Oh well, when in doubt, hit the boozer.

* * *

High summer in the Hoot Garden generally means football. I take a seat and consider my next move. I'm feeling pretty shit, can't see the wood for the trees. I'm wondering how the fuck Doc ended up like this. Worrying about what's going on with Eva. Fretting about how to tell her that it's probably over between us. About how Eva might react. A voice breaks into my thoughts, South-London, with more than a hint of Cyprus.

"Whassa matter girl?"

I look up to see Sav, a first-generation Cypriot who's been coming to the pub for years, notable for his large collection of hats.

"All good mate - just a little tired is all."

"Bullshit. Listen. I know you. You're not usually like this. What's bugging ya?"

I think about whether I want to say anything or not. Sav's alright. We're not too close, but I've known him forever. He's a good guy. What the hell. Maybe he'll actually be able to help.

"I'm in a spot of bother at work. The one guy I thought was totally trustworthy turns out to be a crim, and my girlfriend is lying to me. No one's quite what they seem."

"Start with the girl. If she's not making you happy, everything else will seem shit anyway."

"She needs me. She's had a lot of shit in her life. I can't just ditch her. "

"Don't think about that. You're too kind. You're so busy giving all the love to everyone - and you're not giving no love to yourself. What do you need? It's your life. You can't live somebody else's."

"True dat. At the moment I just need to be me. And I need to figure out the weird shit that's been happening at work."

"I can't help with that. All those dead bodies give me the right willies."

"I can't really talk about it anyway..,"

True to form, Sav swiftly changes the subject to football.

"What about that save yesterday though, Rodolfo? I thought Senegal had it for sure."

Yesterday's football. Who was playing? Of course – Senegal v. Peru. For the first time since I can remember I've not been paying attention to the beautiful game. Normally I'd be in a couple of sweepstakes, glued to every match. Sav sees my blank expression and looks briefly worried again.

"That's not like you Charlie. You really do have a lot on your mind. What are you drinking?"

"A Red Stripe mate – but finances are a bit strained. I can't get you one back."

"Don't you worry about that darling – what comes around goes around. I'll be right back."

Sav disappears inside to get the drinks, and I lean back against the wall, which is still warm with the afternoon's sunshine. I close my eyes and cover my face with my hands. I still don't have any answers. I keep coming back to Doc. To Eva. To Laurence. Everything is connected, but I can't see how. Or how it could be. The sun beats down from above, warming my hands, and creating a glow through my clenched fingers. Then I get self-conscious, and open them, looking around to see who's there. No one's paying any attention, and I can see Sav coming back with our pints. With no football on, the beer garden is almost deserted.

"At least they're quick at the bar today."

"Thanks Sav – very much appreciated. I don't get paid until next week. I'll get you one back then."

"I told you – don't worry about it. You always share when you 'ave a few quid." He takes a deep draft. "Ah...that's good. At least it's cold and wet anyways."

He raises his glass to me, but I'm not paying attention. I've just clocked Chloe coming out of the public bar. Any minute now she'll spot me. It was a close thing, last time, between leaving her and taking her home. In the end I chose the path of honour, but we haven't had a chance to discuss it since. Sav notices me looking, and follows my glance.

"You like that girl, don't you?

I drag my eyes off Chloe and focus them on Sav.

"She seems nice enough."

I keep my tone level, but Sav isn't fooled for a minute.

"Don't try it on with me – I weren't born yesterday. I can tell you like her. It doesn't take a genius to work it out. Anyway – you can tell Sav. I won't tell no one. I won't tell that girlfriend of yours neither. So that's why you were looking so down in the mouth eh?"

I open my baccy and start rolling one up. Chloe still hasn't seen me. It will definitely not look cool to be chatting about her if she does rock up to the table; ideally I need to shut this conversation down now. Just then Chloe clocks me, and waves. I turn to face Sav.

"She's coming over. Probably best not to talk about it now, if you don't mind. As I said there's a lot of stuff going on. I do appreciate the concern though."

"Don't stress Charlie – I get it. Listen – I've got to get off. People to see! Catch you later. Keep your pecker up!"

I consider heading home – my drink is nearly finished – but I can't just split. It would make a weird situation even weirder. I wave back, and watch Chloe as she approaches.

Damn you Charlie...you're too long in the tooth to let your cunt do the thinking for you.

"Mind if I join you?"

"Of course not – make yourself at home. It's been a while..."

Now what did you have to go and say that for Charlie?

Chloe raises an eyebrow, as she considers which side of the bench to choose.

"I should have known I'd see you here of course. How's things with the girlfriend?"

"Not so great at the moment actually. I'd rather not dwell on it if you don't mind."

Chloe's expression immediately softens.

"I'm sorry Charlie. Would you rather I left?"

"No, it's not you. It's this place, and shit going on at work. You'll be a nice distraction from all the other shit going on. I think I'd rather be somewhere else though. Too many eyes and loose lips here, if you catch my drift."

"I'm alright with that. Did you have somewhere else in mind?"

"Maybe we could go to your place?"

I keep my tone light, as if it's the most natural thing in the world to invite myself round.

"Sure – I can't guarantee we'll have the place to ourselves..."

"No matter. At least we won't have half the nutters in the Hoot on our case. Let's go then."

***

Chloe's room is tidy, and the walls are bare, apart from a couple of framed prints whose details I can't make out in the gloom. Things feel a little awkward. It's one thing flirting in the pub and swapping cheeky winks at work, but now both of us know that only one thing can happen next. There's no going back from this.

"Sit anywhere you like – not that there's much choice."

I look at the beanbag in the corner – obviously a solo reading spot, and the bed that dominates the rest of the small room, and raise an eyebrow.

"I think I'll sit here if you don't mind."

As I settle myself on the bed, Chloe asks me if I fancy a drink. I wonder if she's stalling for time.

"Sure – anything's fine. I'm not fussy."

"There should be a couple of beers in the fridge, assuming my housemates haven't tea-leafed them. I'll be right back."

Whilst she's gone I wander around the room examining the prints on the wall. Old medical illustrations, dark etchings of the human form, all sinew, bone and muscle. An anatomical drawing of a two-headed baby. In the corner by the beanbag is a small stack of medical textbooks, with a plain black A5 notebook on top. Perhaps a journal? I resist the urge to look inside. Rude...

And then Chloe is back in the room, clutching a couple of bottles in one hand and an opener in the other. I make space for her on the bed, and take the bottles from her. She's about to say something, but I stop her lips with one hand and start to unbutton her shirt with the other. She shuts her eyes and lets me undress her, passive as a child.

Beneath her clothes I discover a lot of ink. She's covered in tattoos that could be based on the anatomical drawings that adorn her walls. She has one over her heart, ventricles and aorta, and branched veins scrolling over the curve of her breast; ribs picked out with the major organs peeping between them. Over her belly the outline of her uterus and fallopian tubes. They are like windows into different parts of her body, framing the sinews and muscles of her arms and legs.

And what about the windows into Chloe's mind? I know even less about this girl than Eva, but I have a feeling that she'll be far easier to discover.

Eva more often than not wants it hard and frantic. Sex with her involves toys, fisting. Anal penetration. She can be incredibly tender, but I always get the feeling that she wants to be punished. Chloe spent the first half hour just stroking my nipples, tracing her fingertips up and down my thighs, until I was gasping and spreading my legs. Then she went in for the clit. Slowly building things up as she massaged me in ever decreasing circles, replacing fingers with tongue, drinking at the core of me. Finally I could take no more and I pulled her up, bodily, until we were both grinding together, slick with sweat, and I could tell she was coming too, because I could feel our cores expanding and contracting to the same rhythm.

The next go was lazier, and more intimate - just learning each other's bodies. This time it was Chloe's turn to be explored, and I ran my tongue and fingers over every inch of her before I went inside, feeling the core strength of her, until we were both sated and fell asleep.

We never drink the beer. When I wake up, through sheer habit, at 5am for work, the bottles are still stacked next to the bed, and Chloe is sleeping deeply. I quietly gather my clothes together and make my exit without disturbing her at all.

Cutting

Victor had been surprised to note how many magpies there were when you started looking. He hadn't ever paid much attention to birds – apart from to enjoy their song on a spring afternoon. The magpies, he learned, were not songbirds. Their cries were harsh and scolding. He wondered why she wanted him to observe them, but maybe it would become clear in time.

Each evening, he'd taken to looking back over the notes he'd made on that day's walk. It was actually curiously satisfying, keeping a journal. He hadn't kept a diary of any kind since he was at school, and then it was just a brief period during his mid-teens. He still didn't understand exactly what the magpies had to do with anything, but he had come to enjoy holding a written dialogue with himself. He wasn't sure if he was ready to share it with her. It felt as though she had already stripped him bare, and there was a part of himself that he wanted to keep secret.

So he added to his notes, and tried not to worry about what she might make of them.

At the end of the week she arrived again, all smiles and bearing cakes. Once more she was unannounced, but Victor was prepared this time. He had plenty of tea. They went through the ritual of brewing, pouring, sipping. She never took her eyes off him. It was hypnotic and unnerving. Victor pretended not to notice. He cleared the tea things away.

"Victor – you've been watching the magpies. Have you noticed any patterns?"

Victor thought for a while. He wondered if he should mention the notebook. He had left it next to his bed. As he looked back at her he expected her to challenge him; it felt as though his lie was written clearly on his face. Maybe she misinterpreted his silence as reflection.

'Nothing?"

He looked down at his hands, the backs speckled with liver spots. The same hands that had cramped up as they'd rediscovered the muscles required to wield a pen.

She sighed.

"No matter. Maybe later the patterns will become apparent to you too. Aren't you going to undress, Victor? Don't you remember our promise?"

"Yes, of course. It had sort of slipped my mind. I'll do that now, shall I?"

She returned to studying him, whilst Victor removed his clothes. He didn't feel so self-conscious this time – she was so matter-of-fact about it. In a short time he was as naked as Eva, and sat down opposite her.

"How do you feel Victor? Are you ready for the next step? It's time for the next round of the game. I need to you to trust me"

Eva's features were chiselled; there was something blind and hard in her eyes, like the angels in the cemetery. He remembered the package, the coiled rope.

"I'm not sure."

Eva tutted, as though she was a head teacher, and he was a naughty little boy who needed to be disciplined, gently, until he came into line, but when she spoke again her voice was gentle, and she held out her hand to his. He hesitated and then took it. Her skin was smooth and cool as marble.

"Victor, did you go to the graveyard, as I asked?"

"Yes Eva."

"And?"

Victor wondered if his fear showed in his face, was apparent in the sweat that beaded his palm.

"Victor!"

Her voice was rougher now.

"I found the package that was in the tree."

"And did you open it?"

He dropped his gaze, unable to look her in the eye any longer. His voice was a mumble into his chest.

"Yes."

The hand holding his clenched.

"And did you read the note, Victor?"

He couldn't bring himself to answer. He remembered the cold fear that had gripped him as he had unwrapped the contents of the package. How could he explain his terror of blades? Why did she need blood from him?

"Victor. Will you bring the package to me please?"

From the depths of Victor's chest a whine rose, surprising him that he could make such a noise. It was as if his fear were a thing separate from himself, but he couldn't deny her power over him. Slowly he got to his feet, and only when he was standing did she loosen her grip on his hand. He turned and shuffled towards his bedroom, conscious afresh of his withered shanks.

When he reached the bedroom he hesitated. It was as if he came back to himself once he was out of her presence. His head cleared a little and the awful weight that had seemed to press on him receded. He stood and tried to gather himself. This had gone far enough. What had started as an erotic game had taken a darker turn than he could have imagined when she first invited herself into his house. He straightened his shoulders and told himself that he was going to march back into the other room and ask her to leave his house. There lay the package on the bedside table, hastily rewrapped in its packaging. He hadn't been able to touch it since. As he looked at it he sensed more than heard her presence behind him. When she spoke her voice was brisk, with a matronly air to it.

"Ah, there it is. I'm glad to see you've kept it safe."

She strode across the room seeming to glide, and Victor felt his defiance melting in the face of her power and beauty. It seemed unbelievable that he had doubted her. Did he really want things to return to the way they had been before? He had been going through the motions, surviving; but he had not really been alive. He tried to pull himself together, inject some lightness into his voice.

"I'm sorry – I was wool-gathering. It seems to happen more and more often these days...the old brain slowing down I suppose. I'll bring it through."

Eva smiled and spun around gracefully, seeming to pirouette on a single toe and dance out of the room. Victor was sure she knew the power of her body over him, and was using it. Although he was still afraid his desire for her was stronger than his apprehension about the future. He picked up the package gently,and followed her back down the hall.

Eva picked up the pen that had been sitting next to Victor's crossword, and quickly sketched a pattern on the margin of the paper:

She showed it to Victor.

"But what does it mean? I don't understand."

"It's a mark. I want you to inscribe it on your body. You already have the tools you need. They're in the package that you found in the cemetery. Can you give it to me please Victor?"

A part of Victor hoped that the contents had somehow been transmuted into something harmless and lovely, but he knew it was not to be. Inside were the bandages, the small bottle of iodine, and the package of razorblades that he remembered. The thought of cutting himself was horrifying. There was no way he'd be able to bring himself to do it. He gazed at her silently, knowing that she could read his face like a book. Maybe if she realised the sheer terror that the thought of cutting himself triggered she would back off, would let him skip this round. Perhaps she wouldn't make him do it in front of her. Maybe he could pretend somehow. Go along with it. But if he didn't, this might be the last time they could be together like this; he couldn't bring himself to disappoint her. She gazed at him with huge eyes, as if to say 'Look, how I make myself vulnerable before you.' She made herself look small, childlike, harmless. He wasn't fooled, but he allowed himself to go along with it for now. At least that's what he told himself. A part of him knew that it wasn't true. A small part, and hidden, he hoped, from her probing eyes.

She took both his hands in hers, and looked up at him.

"You promised when you started the game that you would trust me. You do trust me don't you Victor?"

Victor was amazed at how steady his voice was as he answered. He was learning to lie to her.

"Yes. I trust you completely."

Closing in

Laurence was working the Sunday shift at the hospital. Sunday was the same as any other day to him, with the added bonus of time and a half, and a nice quiet office to hang out in.

There was still no sign of Doc – maybe he had ditched the phone. Probably the most sensible thing to do in the circumstances, if a little frustrating for Laurence, since it meant he couldn't track him. Still, hopefully that meant International Finance couldn't either. Doc had always been perfectly civil to Laurence. He didn't begrudge his disappearance, but he was worried about the cops. Charlie hadn't said too much – just that they were following up on a case and wanted to review CCTV footage from the hospital. Oh, and by the way, had Doc been in touch or logged into his account recently? He'd had no contact from the cops in the week since she told him that the they had asked her for his number. What was keeping them? Were they're playing him? Waiting for him to give something away?

He'd been spending his time cross-referencing older messages with bodies; it's an incomplete record. Not all south of the river; some of the bodies have already been processed, and several were still in storage. The victims were usually lonely people, with no next of kin.

There's still too many gaps in the digital paper-trail. So. He was stuck. And he thought he probably knew where to find the answers. Undoubtedly locked up in one of Charlie's office drawers. She always did like to keep a tidy desk. She was always jotting stuff down by hand; a habit formed in the years before she had access to the office computer. The rotas and observation notes were written up by hand too; in fact Charlie's hatred of what she termed 'paperwork' – entering information on the computer - was a standing joke.

Laurence kept joining the dots. Eva got her kicks from playing sex games with old men who ended up in the mortuary. She's been round to see the latest guy, in Bermondsey, quite a few times now. Laurence has watched him shrink into himself; seen the dark rings grow around his eyes.

Eva targets the digitally dispossessed. He is blindfolded. Lost in pixels. He can't sit still. Back and forth. Why? Where is the digital footprint? Maybe it's time to act. He has to know. One last flick through the files. It doesn't take him long to find the report Charlie put together for the police, detailing the victims, and which fridges they're stored in. The mortuary is closed on Sunday, but there's always the possibility of an emergency case – a Jewish or Muslim family, where interment needs to happen within 24 hours. He has no plausible excuse if he's found in there. He spends a long time thinking about this. Is it a risk he's prepared to take? RFID fobs were no problem; he could just add access to that area to his door pass. Office and desk drawers didn't present much more of a challenge. They used basic 3-lever and tubular locks. It was pretty easy to make skeleton keys for those kinds of locks – you just file down all the teeth so only the end is left, which operates the inner lever. Or that was the theory. It took Lawrence a couple of days of experimentation until he was able to open his own office drawers with his homemade key. Once he'd cracked that making an office door key was easy.

The main door of the mortuary was a problem. That was a much more sophisticated 5-lever pin tumbler lock, far beyond his basic lock-picking abilities. He has no plausible excuse if he's discovered. So, he is going to have to find another way in.

He may not have keys to the mortuary, but ceiling cavities are no mystery to him. It's where all the cabling lives, and he's had plenty of practice crawling around looking for damaged wires. He can go in via one of the storage rooms on the same floor. That would be very, very noisy. In the films people were always crawling silently around ceiling cavities. In practice, any progress is accompanied by the booming of sheet metal surfaces, creaking ceiling supports, and showers of dust from disturbed ceiling tiles. It wasn't the kind of thing you could get away with stealthily if anyone else was around.

* * *

Once he's in there, he gets scared. The mortuary is a very different place when it's empty. There are no windows, and it's almost pitch black, apart from the glow of small lights that indicate the fridges are working. There's a dry, antiseptic smell in the air, and the faint hum of equipment. He has the number of the first fridge, but he hesitates.

He has to know.

He pulls himself together and pulls open the first drawer.

It slides out almost silently, with a whisper of well-oiled runners. The body is covered with a white cloth. He reaches forward to pull it back. It's an old man - a man that Laurence has seen before - but there's nothing human there now. His features are frosted, crystals sparkling on shaggy eyebrows. The flesh sags, but is frozen into place. When he leans forward to touch it, it's as hard as marble.

He pulls away more of the cloth. There, on the inner thigh, the mark that Charlie had described in her report. It looked like an M, but also a bird. Was that why Eva's eyes were constantly scanning – the trees, the sky – as though she were looking for something? Was she watching for birds?

* * *

Another week passes before he gets the call. DI Owen has a few questions; can Laurence assist with their enquiries? No need to come to the station - they'll pop in and visit the IT suite. His first reaction is terror. So far, he'd kept his mouth shut, but now it looked like maybe they were suspicious of foul play inside the hospital. Why else would they want to interview him? That was a different story.

He's nervous. He says more than he meant to. About Doc. About how the mortuary was run. And they were kind of friends – at least since Laurence had become a cheese night regular. Just how had that happened again?

He knows too much and his methods are questionable. He shouldn't know about the samples; the messages from International Finance. He shouldn't have been downloading Doc's email; seen the statements – initially remittances, and then ever-larger bills, for more than he could earn in five years. This is information that the police should probably have, but he can't tell them. He would certainly be out of a job if anyone knew the full extent of his misuse of the hospital IT systems. That, and the fact that he's got previous. He had just escaped a caution, when the victim decided they couldn't deal with the court process any more. Institutional green walls. Black rubbberised top on the table that's bolted to the linoleum floor. It's like he's back there in that interview room; that same sense of claustrophobia grips him.

He'd been so caught up with Eva, with Doc that he'd forgotten what he should and shouldn't know. Shit. Maybe even that looked suspicious – that he hadn't asked what the interview was about. Maybe it made him look guilty.

Now they're coming here, to the Sanctum Sanctorum, at 4:30 pm tomorrow. Shit.

* * *

He doesn't sleep that night. He spends the next morning trying to get up the courage to go and see Charlie. He can see she's logged onto the network. Probably doing some admin. It's definitely time to come clean. The short walk from the IT suite to the Mortuary seems to take a long time.

He stands awkwardly by the door. It's the first time he's ever come there without a specific reason; a computer problem; even if the glitch was one he'd planted.

Charlie's obviously in the middle of something, hunched over her notes, pen in hand – but being Charlie instantly stops what she's doing and welcomes him in. And he realises he doesn't quite know where to start.

"Hi."

"Hi Laurence. What can I do you for today?"

"Umm...so...you know that message from the police?"

"Yeah – good cop bad cop? I wouldn't worry too much mate. Just give them what they want, and hopefully we can get them out of here sooner rather than later."

She gave him a bright smile that was endlessly patient, with a flick of the eyes that nevertheless communicated she still had work to be getting on with.

Laurence didn't feel this was quite enough to go on. He persisted.

"Oh...well...actually...umm...so...what is it exactly they want? They're coming at 4.30 tomorrow. I thought...well it seemed like a good idea to come and have a chat with you first."

Laurence realised that in fact Charlie didn't know too much about him. He knew she found him a bit unsettling, when he allowed himself to look at her for too long. She probably thought he was a nice guy. He could see her deciding to give him the lowdown – otherwise things had the potential to go very pear-shaped indeed. They both knew how the cops could make evidence out of the most tenuous of leads. He was still hovering by the door, and could feel himself starting to go twitchy.

It's a fine balance. He can see Charlie deciding how much to tell him. How much does he need to know to pull CCTV from the system?

"Take a seat Laurence. I think I probably need to give you a bit of context 'round about now. That is if you've got a few minutes?"

Laurence forced himself to process what she'd just said; he'd been lost in contemplation of her, forgetting for a moment that this was a meatspace encounter; that he wasn't watching her on a screen.

He took the offered chair.

"Of course. I'm off shift now. I just thought...you know... since they wanted to talk to me...I'd better check...just to see... if there's any....anything you think I might...need to say?"

Charlie smiled encouragingly.

"Laurence mate, that was a good call. You definitely did the right thing. Are you sitting comfortably?"

Laurence almost assured her that he was, and then realised that she was being rhetorical.

"Several months ago now I was doing a PM and I found some marks that seemed a little out of place. Doc had popped in, so I mentioned it to him – just to get his point of view. Generally we put it on file if something turns up that seems weird, but at the same time not directly attributable to Cause of Death. Anyway. Doc agreed it was a bit odd, and told me not to worry about it. I'd been working back to back shifts to catch up after the hand thing. He said he'd take care of the report."

She paused, looked across at Laurence, who was staring at his hands so he wouldn't be distracted from her words by looking at her.

"I didn't think anything of it – just assumed that the report had been filed – and then I found another set of marks, and then another – right around the time of the Westminster attack. That was a definite pattern. They were exactly the same."

"Are you with me so far?"

Laurence was busy fitting all these new pieces of information into the pattern he had been creating. Was it related to Eva, and her old men? He guessed that Charlie didn't know what had been going on with Doc, and the International Finance. How could he probe, without giving away the fact that he probably knew much more than Charlie. Focus on the marks. Stall.

"It turned out Doc hadn't got around to filing a report, and on top of that he wasn't answering my messages, which is not like him at all. Well...it's not the kind of thing you should ignore. I had to call it in myself."

"Actually I'm not sure I follow you. Were they some kind of tattoos? Was it some kind of gang thing?"

"No. These were old guys. Definitely not your average hoodies. Old white guys. Anyway, I probably shouldn't really be sharing this with you, but I think Doc's in some kind of trouble – and I think the cops suspect that the marks are somehow connected to the hospital. I've told them they were almost certainly inflicted long before they arrived on the premises – but you know that the pigs are like. That would be nice and neat – if someone at the mortuary was responsible. I know how these guys think. They can make evidence on the most tenuous of leads. Basically they're after footage of Doc's movements."

"There's no cameras in the mortuary – that means no footage?"

Charlie shook her head.

"Corridor shots. That's what they want – and, probably, to ask if you've seen anything 'suspicious'. Not that I want to impede their investigation. I just think they're barking up the wrong tree."

She looked expectantly at Laurence, who was still processing her reference to 'old white men'. How could she not know? Didn't she know anything about her girlfriend?

"Of course...I mean of course you're right. Umm...so... what should I say?"

"Just be honest. Give them the footage. I'm pretty sure it's some weird stalker thing – someone these guys all interacted with on a regular basis. Doc? It's just not his style. Anyway, that's neither here nor there. I'm rambling."

"Ok...well, I'll do my best."

"I know you will Laurence."

At that moment he would have done anything for her. For a brief second he considered telling her. Opening up about the files he had been keeping on Doc, on Eva. No. He couldn't bring himself to do it.

"So...umm...OK. I guess that's it then?"

"Yep! I'm sure you'll be fine. Anyway. I'd best get back to it. I'm behind on my paperwork."

Laurence stood up and made to leave, Charlie's attention had already switched to the papers on her desk. There was so much more he could have said – so much he could have told her about Eva; about the old men; about all the things he's seen; the messages he's intercepted. And Doc...maybe she was just being judicious with her info. Was the whole conversation a subtle warning not to tell them what he knew?

He felt a momentary pang of guilt that he'd hidden so much from Charlie, when she'd been so honest and open with him. There were too many parts of the puzzle missing. He didn't know how things stood between her and Eva. He just wasn't ready to have that conversation with her yet.

Ronald

She gave him a rope, coiled neatly in a white plastic bag. She told him he would know when to use it, and what to use it for; that the knowledge would come to him when he was ready to take the final step.

Ronald won't be missed by many. He'd become very standoffish with his neighbours as he got more involved with Eva's game. It changed the way he heard the world, saw the world. His eyes had sharpened until he could pick out tiny details blocks away, the smallest motion triggering his senses, lit by the giant moon: perigee approaching. His hearing had changed...high and low frequencies lost to him now. In compensation he found he could understand the calls of birds. The chatter and squawks of green parakeets became a vast conversation conducted at the level of the treetops. Wood pigeons cooing their love, threatening their rivals; songbirds warning of predatory ravens. And magpies... so many magpies...They called to him. Shackled to the heavy earth, he longed to fly. It was time to become one with the flock.

With his new vision he can see that the walkway is empty, can sense the deserted stairwells. He will not be interrupted. As he stands on the edge of the balcony, the rope looped loosely around his neck, it's almost as though the wind is gathering in his feathers. He can feel a weather front approaching. He is more magpie now than human. When he finally steps off the balcony it's more like taking flight than falling.

I am in blood stepped in so far

I wake before my alarm, Eva's shouting dragging me
struggling up out of sleep, from a dream that's already losing
its sharpness and turning fuzzy in my mind. She clings to me,
uneasily slumbering. I feel caged by her arms around me;
elbow in the ribs; knee in the groin; our once comfortable
embrace become a prison. There are dark shadows under
her eyes, and she looks haggard even in sleep. Her features
are drawn. She's clinging to me like we're in a shipwreck and
I can make out scattered words, jumbled together like she's
talking to someone else in her dreams, and holding both sides
of the conversation.

"I am old. Old. I must not be old. Not not...

He must fly soon...

Oh, why can I not be human. Please? Every night I
become more magpie. I dream of flying...flight!

The wind in my feathers! It is never dark in my dreams.
Please, I need to be human...

No! No! Take him. Is he not enough for now? There must
be another soon. There must be blood.

I will not be magpie!

Brittle. Dull. I hear with your eyes. I see the flock.

No! No!"

I consider waking her up. Should you wake someone
when they're having a nightmare?

"We are magpie. We feel the wind in our feathers."

"He will fly soon."

I make up my mind and cup her head in my hand.

"Eva wake up - you're having a bad dream."

Her eyes flick open, but all I can see is the whites. Is she
having some kind of fit? I stroke her hair and try again.

"Eva my love – wake up please. It's just a nightmare. You're going to be OK."

I'm not sure if that's true, but at least it makes me feel better. And it does seem to be working. She calms and her eyes close again. The muttering stops. Maybe she's dropped back into normal sleep? I glance at the clock. Almost 6.30, I need to be up for work soon anyway. Maybe I should just leave her sleeping.

As I gently untangle myself from her limbs and the knots that the bedclothes have got themselves into, Eva shudders and throws her head back, eyes still closed.

"Yaaaaaaaaaaaaaaaaaaaaaah!"

"Eva!"

I reach out towards her again, two handed, wanting to hold her, protect her. She doesn't react to my touch. She's gone again, somewhere else. Somewhere I can't follow. Either that or jacked up. But Eva doesn't do that – or anything habit-forming, as far as I'm am aware; just the odd recreational when we're on a night out. I pull back, not sure what to expect next, or what the hell is going on. I grab her shoulders; resist the urge to shake. It's far too early in the morning to be dealing with this kind of thing. Eva's head lolls forward, and she slumps into me. Has she passed out? What the hell is going on?

I lay her down and take her pulse. Her heart is hammering as though she's just done a flight of stairs at full pelt, but as I hold her wrist I can feel the rate slowing, gradually, until it's the unvarying thump, thump, thump of regular sleep. I smooth a hand over her forehead, wondering if I should call for help. Almost seven now, and I'm not even dressed yet.

Shit. Guess I'd better phone in sick...

I watch Eva sleeping for a little while, mulling over what to do. She seems to be resting peacefully. I might as well get dressed anyway.

As I reach for my jeans, I hear her stirring behind me. When I turn around she is smiling, awake. She seems to glow with energy, and as she cocks her head, I have the strangest impression – like there's a curious bird looking through her eyes, which glitter as she meets my gaze.

"Good morning darling. What's wrong? Why do you look so worried?"

"What the hell happened there? You freaked me right out!"

"It's nothing darling - just a bad dream. Maybe I burnt the candle too hard?"

I'm not convinced, which must be plain to see on my face, as Eva continues hurriedly.

"Please – can't you see I'm fine now?"

"You scared me. You were screaming in your sleep. What's going on, Eva? You were saying some crazy shit and then you passed out. That is definitely not OK. Has that happened to you before?"

"A couple of times. You don't need to worry about it. It doesn't happen very often."

"I think you need to get checked out. I can get you fast-tracked if you want to come to work with me?"

She jumps out of bed and takes my hands in hers, pulls me in for an embrace. Her skin is cool and soft, but for once she doesn't turn me on at all.

"No! I mean, there's nothing to be concerned about my love. I'm off today; I'll go and get a check-up, OK? Now, you'd better get to work. I don't want to be responsible for you being late. I'll text and let you know what happens."

* * *

Victor awoke from yet another nightmare. Normally he rarely dreamed, but these days it seemed that he had barely to close his eyes before dark clouds started to mass behind his lids. The wind whistled through sparse trees outside his window, and held the mocking notes of voices that spoke in a language he could almost understand. The dream clouds held messages - messages that teased him with their incipient legibility, as though if he just squinted hard enough, he could make them out. And then the clouds would seem to boil and thicken and darken until he realised that he was being slowly smothered, and he would wake, gasping for breath.

And then there were the voices he heard when he was awake. It happened at the oddest times – when he was making a cup of tea in the kitchen. When he thought 'What shall I do next?' – the answer would come back, from somewhere inside, 'Just kill yourself. Why struggle? Everything will be so much easier.'

That's when he began to be afraid that she wasn't quite what she seemed; that in making a pact with her he had cast himself at the mercy of unknown powers. He thought he would be able to keep a part of himself separate, that it was just a game he was playing; that he could turn the tables on her with his notebooks, and his secret thoughts. Now he was beginning to realise she was just a front for something much darker. He'd been a fool to think it was ever just a harmless game. And how was he to get out of it now? He'd an idea she wouldn't take too kindly to him quitting - and there might still be much to gain.

But how do I know she's wicked? Maybe we're both just mad?

Outside the window a huge moon threw the spindly trees into sharp relief. He never recalled seeing a moon so big. He had heard of supermoons. All that gravity. There would high tides and flooding in the newspaper tomorrow no doubt. Maybe that's what had given him nightmares. There was bound to be a logical explanation. As he stood watching it, shadows flitted amongst the branches, wings flapping and long tails jerking in a complicated semaphore. He could hear their chattering ricocheting off the glass and concrete of the apartment block.

Aka ak ak aka ka ka. Aka ak ak aka ka ka. aka ak ak aka ka ka

It was almost light – he wouldn't sleep again. He lay awake listening to them, and rubbed his fingers across the healing scars crosshatched on his thigh. Three of them now, and the latest was hot and itchy. He hoped it hadn't got infected. If he didn't react, maybe the magpies would leave.

What are you thinking, Victor? That this is about you? They're just birds. Maybe you really are going crazy.

And then it started: the scrabbling of claws against glass. Rat a tat tat. Tat tat; a bird or many birds.

Trying to get to me?

Victor pulled the blankets up over himself, hunkered down and covered his head with a pillow. He lay there for many minutes, willing them to go away. The bedclothes muffled the sounds but didn't mask them completely. When he couldn't bear it anymore, he got out of bed, averting his eyes from the window, and went through to the kitchen. He put the kettle on and turned the radio up as loud as it would go. Then he went looking for nails, a hammer, old towels, bedsheets, anything he could use to cover the windows, and didn't rest until he had obscured every single one.

A new arrival

It's already 7.45 when I arrive at the office to find Fran installed in her cubby hole. Normally I like to have a bit of time to settle in when I get to work, time to review yesterday's cases, and think about the plan for the day. A bit of peace and quiet before the shit hits the fan makes a big difference to how the day goes. Ah well. Not to be.

Fran looks up with a cheeky grin.

"Afternoon boss. I was just wondering if you were about to call in sick?"

"Very bloody funny. Water main leak on Kennington Road. I could have got here on foot faster. Still, at least I had plenty of time to peruse yesterday's paper somebody thoughtfully left on the seat next to me. I got to learn about the supermoon. I wondered why it was so massive last night."

Fran's into her astrology. I can see I've got her now.

"I can't believe I missed that. I love that kind of thing. When's the next one then?"

"Actually it turns out they come in clusters – it's to do with something called perigee – when the moon's closest to the earth. There's another one in three weeks. And get this – it's called a blood wolf moon."

"Well, I'm glad you made it in. It's looking pretty stacked today."

Typical. I sigh and drop into my office chair.

"When is it not? Alright Fran – so what are we looking at today?"

"Are you sure you don't want to grab a tea before we get into it?"

I look up at the clock. 7.52 am. Normally I've had my tea and have the rota done by now, ready for the technicians to start work at eight.

"Don't worry about me – we'd better get straight into it. I can cope without tea for now. Lay it on me."

Fran spins round and starts reading out case notes off her computer screen.

"Pretty much the usual selection. Two deaths in hospital, a couple of overdoses, and two infant mortality cases. The deaths in hospital will need to be done first thing - one's Jewish, the other Muslim. I was just about to assign them to Zoe, being as you weren't in."

I nod. Fran's on the money with that. Lara's keen, but as a fairly new trainee she's still not that fast, and the funeral directors will be keen to pick them up before lunch. Which means that they'll need to be ready for viewing by 11am. I make a note on my pad.

"Sure – she's pretty quick. Anything else?"

"Two stillbirths, unfortunately."

"OK – I'll take those."

I make another note. Looks like it will be a busy morning.

"Is that it?"

Fran scrolls down her screen, long nails tapping the wheel on her mouse, and her eyes flicking back and forth as she scans the new admissions.

"There's one external admission. Hanging. Nothing else that looks urgent."

I feel a jolt of apprehension hit me, and keep my voice casual.

"Vitals?"

"An 87-year-old male, by the name of Freddy. There's a lot more info on the Sudden Death form. I'm assuming you don't need it right now?"

Another hanging. For a moment I wonder if Fran's noticed a pattern. But then why would she?

"No. That's enough for the moment. OK – I'll take that one too. That should just about do it. Let's keep the afternoon clear just in case anything else comes in."

"Sure thing boss. At least no-one's called in sick today."

I finish my notes and hand them over to Fran.

"OK. I'm going to get that cup of tea now. Can you get onto the funeral directors and make arrangements for 11 and 12 am viewings? Looks like it's going to be a busy morning. One for you?"

Fran points at the cup on her desk.

"I'm all coffeed up for now. One more latté and I'll be climbing the walls. I'll get on with the rota."

As I wait for the tea to brew I think about the new case that's come in. The cops didn't tell me not to tell the mortuary staff, but it seems sensible to keep it under my hat until I have more of a clue what's going on. Probably best to find a quiet time to deal with it. I blow on the boiling hot tea, and take a long slurp. I wonder if I should call up the cops before or after the PM? Maybe I should have asked Fran to print out the notes after all, but then again, maybe there's no point drawing attention to it if it's just a routine hanging. I slurp a bit more of the hot tea and go back to the office.

"OK – better get on it. I'll be in the PM room if anyone needs me."

"Sure thing boss."

She smiles at me without a care in the world. Bless her. I attempt a smile in return, but it feels more like a grimace. I'm not used to hiding things from my staff. It doesn't sit well.

* * *

The morning flies by between two infant PMs, supporting the juniors with their autopsies, and managing the funeral directors and family visits. At 12.30 we're ready to wrap up. I'm writing up the vitals from each PM on the whiteboard. Zoe and Lara are already changing out of their aprons and putting on their shoes in the changing area. Zoe pops her head through the door.

"Are you coming to lunch boss?"

I'm pretty hungry, but if I want to get a look at Ronald without having to field unwanted questions now is probably the best time, and it won't take long to have a quick gander.

"Save me a seat – I've got a couple of bits of paperwork to deal with first. I won't be long."

Fran has left Ronald's notes ready for me, along with a plastic bag containing the ligature. A coil of white nylon rope. The much-used buff-coloured folder feels heavier than normal. Looks like the police have really done their homework on this one. I shake out the contents and read the cover report first. Name, address, date and place of birth. Clean medical history – no known substance abuse. Body found by a neighbour, hanging from the balcony outside his flat, and subsequently reported to the police via a 999 call. No next of kin. Several photos of the deceased before and after they had cut him free. He's wearing pyjamas, with a dark stain around the crotch, his head twisted at an unnatural angle, and his face obscured by hair that may once have been neatly combed over his bald spot. I turn back to the report.

It seems that the neighbour who called it in wasn't familiar with the deceased, and the police hadn't been able to get a positive ID on the last person to see him alive. No indication of whether they're treating the death as suspicious at this stage. Sadly, suicides by men of Ronald's age are far too common.

Best not to jump to conclusions Charlie.

Ronald is in the number 6 fridge. He's not been in there long enough to freeze, and would almost look as though he were sleeping, were it not for the tell-tale marks of asphyxiation: his forehead is covered with petechiae – red and purple spots caused by burst blood vessels. On his neck I can see the characteristic v-shaped lines that indicate death by hanging. It's my job to find out if there are any indications that wasn't the only cause of death, but I'm not proposing to get into that right now.

It doesn't take me long to find the mark. I guess I was expecting it. Everything else fits the pattern. It just had to be connected. Damn. Now I'm glad I told Fran to leave the afternoon free. I slide Ronald back into the fridge and latch the door. My stomach growls, reminding me I've not eaten in seven hours. The others are probably halfway through their lunch by now, which is just as well as I'm not sure I want company. Ronald will have to keep. This isn't something I want to get into with an empty belly.

* * *

When I get back from lunch it's almost two, and there's a message on my voicemail from DC Owen. There's been some new developments which they'd rather not discuss on the phone. They're coming over this way for a meeting this afternoon – can they pop into the Mortuary after two-thirty?

The cops are prompt, and I take them through to the PM room, where I've laid out Ronald. He's still shrouded, covered, except for his feet; pale flesh already drooping on the ball of the foot and the big toe. PC Owen barely blinks as the ligature mark is revealed. DC Smith is pulling out his camera, and I raise a hand.

"I'm sorry but I'm going to have to ask you to put that away for now. We need to get clearance from the Coroner in case it becomes evidence."

I see in his eyes he knows that; he's just chancing his arm.

"Sure. And of course, I'm sure you'll document anything you find as part of your report?"

I raise an eyebrow. What is he suggesting?

"Naturally."

"OK. As you were."

Cheeky git.

"Thank you."

I don't bother to keep the irony from my tone.

"So gentlemen, Ronald here only arrived this morning, so we haven't done a full autopsy on him yet. He would have been next on the agenda if you guys hadn't turned up. However, I did do a quick recce before lunch, and I suspect you'll be interested in what I found. I was about to call you when I got your message in fact."

DC Smith gives Owen a triumphant look.

"Here's the mark I found – it's on the inner part of his thigh."

I pull the shroud back so they can see the rough M cut into his pale flesh.

"I'm guessing this one was already on your radar then?"

I see DC Owen calculating whether to give something back, and then deciding that the knowledge gained outweighs the advantage lost. He pulls out a ziplock bag, containing an A6 black-and-red spiral pad, and a small package wrapped in brown paper.

"We found these in the top drawer of his bedside table. We've seen enough for now. Perhaps we could discuss it in your office?"

Fran's in the office, and I don't want her to get totally freaked out.

"Actually, we're probably best off in the family room. We're less likely to be disturbed there."

I wrap Ronald up and slide him back into the fridge. Then I walk over to the door that communicates with the family room and flip the room status to 'occupied'.

"This way gentlemen - no one will bother us now unless there's a genuine emergency."

We all sit down and PC Owen hands me the bag. I open the notebook first. The first few pages are full of shopping lists, budgets, doctor's appointments; the lonely minutiae of a pensioners' life.

I turn another leaf, to find a list neatly written down the left side of the page.

> 12 May: one (sorrow)
>
> 25 May: four (girl)
>
> 18 May: five (silver)
>
> 26 May: two (boy)

The list continues for three sheets, and then abruptly, ends in the middle of the page.

I turn another page, and then I see the sketch. Below, the words 'it is done.' I stare at it for a few moments, and then flip through the rest of the pages, but the remainder of the notebook appears to be empty.

"What do you make of it?"

I look up to find both of them watching me, as if they're gauging my reaction. I keep my tone neutral.

"To be honest I don't know what do make of it. Nothing immediately occurs. Do you think these random sentences are some how connected to the marks I've been finding?"

"Well, it's not beyond the bounds of probability. What do you make of the list before it? And what about the words in brackets? Do they remind you of anything in particular?"

I have the sense that PC Owen is leading me; that he's already made up his own mind. I read through them again.

"Sorrow...girl...silver...boy."

I wrack my brains; and then I remember something.

"Magpies. Maggot pies. There was a programme about them on the radio the other day. In the old days they were believed to survive on maggots. They were associated with the devil. People say 'good morning, Mr Magpie' to ward off bad luck. And there's that rhyme. One for sorrow. OK. I'm all out of magpie facts. What do you think it means? And how is it connected to the marks on the bodies?"

I use the Look on him as I ask the question. Few people

can withstand the Look. At the hospital, I'm known as the person you pick to fight the big boss in the last round of the game. When the chips are down, the Look is often the deciding factor.

PC Owen gives me the Look right back. Maybe he's that rare beast: a copper with a brain. I grudgingly up the respect level.

"It looks kind of like an 'M'. Would it be too simplistic to assume that it was 'M' for magpies? It fits. One for sorrow... two for joy...three for a girl...four for a boy. How does the rest of the rhyme go?"

DC Smith is already there.

"Five for silver, six for gold, and seven for a secret, never to be told."

The room is quiet. You can almost hear brains whirring.

I'm the first to break the silence.

"And the package?"

"Open it."

Inside I find a razorblade, some gauze; an empty bottle that smells as though it once contained iodine. DC Smith takes over the questioning.

"Do you think that blade was the same one used to make the marks?"

I turn it over in my gloved fingers.

"Could be. There's probably traces of blood on it if that's the case. Forensics are your best bet there."

Finally, a small piece of scuffed paper, folded into curl-edged quarters.

"May I?"

I pick it up.

"Be my guest."

I unfold it carefully.

-- You know what to do --

The handwriting is wobbly, and looks as though it has been done with the wrong hand.

"Do you recognise this handwriting?"

I spend some moments examining the note minutely.

"No. I can say that for sure."

I do recognise the type of paper it's written on. The edges are ragged and curled as though it was once tightly rolled into a paper stick. A lollipop stick? I finger the sweets in my pocket and decide there's no point mentioning this to the cops. It will only confuse them.

PC Owen gathers up the various pieces of evidence and puts them back in the bag. I wonder what's coming next. He seems in no hurry. His next question takes me by surprise.

"Doctor Bernard, do you mind me asking? Is he open about his sexuality?"

The question throws me. What's that got to do with anything? I've always been open about my own love life; in fact some would say I over share. Doc encourages me, and he's always been understanding, but it's definitely not a two-way street.

"We never discuss his sex life. It's not something I'd even consider discussing with him."

"And has there been any sign of Doc? Have you heard from him?"

"Not a thing."

"OK...well don't forget to contact us if he does turn up."

"You'll be the first to know. Now if there's nothing else, I do have a lot to do this afternoon – including getting on with the victim's PM."

I put some finality in my tone to indicate that as far as I am concerned, the meeting is over. DC Owen gets the hint.

"Well, thanks for your time. Do get in touch if you have any sudden insights. We'll see ourselves out."

Once they've left I sit for many minutes thinking about

what just happened, before going back through to the cold store.

I've a feeling Ronald's body won't have any more secrets to reveal than the others did, but I get to work anyway. He'll need a PM for the coroner's report.

Doc returns

Doc had plenty of time to think about his next move on the way back from Dover. Two and a half hours on an old train that smelt of stale hamburgers and urine, seats grimy with the effluence of uncounted commuters. He was sure he'd added some unwelcome visitors he'd probably picked up during his brief stay at the Last Inn Hostel. Plenty of time to come up with a plausible excuse for where he'd been since he'd been at the office.

The train pulled into Victoria. Doc considered going home from there, but it was a fairly short walk to the hospital, and perhaps he would be safer there. They had told him not to go to the police, but since the events in Dover he knew that he would never be safe. In his small office on the 7th floor he could plan just how he was going to explain to the police what had been going on. What about the blackmail material? The samples he'd taken from the hospital? Well, after all, it had only been a few cell sections, and the rest was just debt. It wasn't illegal to be in debt. It could be managed. How had he allowed himself to be controlled in the first place, over paltry money? He knew he'd been stupid to put his entire career at risk. He'd got greedy. He thought of the programs he'd listened to on the radio; the contempt he'd felt for some poor sucker, defrauded out of their life savings by their own avarice. Well, he'd been just as stupid but maybe it wasn't too late to make it right.

Once he'd left the immediate vicinity of the railway station the back streets were quiet. It took him just ten minutes to get to Lambeth Bridge, and with each step he felt more like he'd made the right decision. He would put himself into the hands of the law, having made sure he'd got all his ducks in a row at the hospital. As he arrived at Reception and waited for a lift to the seventh floor he looked around at the hospital with new eyes. It felt so long since he'd been there. As he watched the lift numbers slowly counting down, he heard a familiar voice behind him. He turned around and recognised a consultant histopathologist, Dr Singh.

"Ah, Doctor! How the devil are you? You owe me an email. I've been wondering what had become of you, and I'm not the only one. Have you been away?"

And what was it to be? A family situation? Well, it would probably come out in the end. Hospitals were terrible places for gossip.

"I had some personal business to take care of, unexpectedly, which kept me away from the office for a little while."

The beauty of the word 'personal' – Dr Singh would certainly be too polite to press further now. He even had the grace to look a little embarrassed.

"Ah well, of course. And you've no doubt got a mountain of correspondence to get through now that you're back. I'd better let you get on with it. Do keep an eye out for my message."

"I shall."

That part was a bare-faced lie; he didn't know if he'd get a chance to follow up on any of those unread emails. Meanwhile, the lift had arrived. He pressed the door open button, and turned back to Dr Singh.

"I'd better get on. I'll be in touch soon."

Cog in the machine

2:30 pm. Laurence hadn't been at work long. In fact he
hadn't been awake long. He'd stayed up long past dawn
exploring digital rabbit holes until his eyes were so bleary
he could barely see, and then snatched a couple of hours'
sleep before he had to leave for his shift. Consequently he
wasn't at his most alert when two cops appeared at his office
door. Ricardo, the other sysadmin was at his station and
Laurence didn't relish the thought of him earwigging their
whole conversation. He was about due to go off-shift anyway.
He looked at him meaningfully, suggesting he was fine to
clock off a few minutes early. Ricardo got the hint, although
his smirk suggested he was considering playing dumb, and
conscientiously doing a bit of free overtime.

Laurence wasn't used to having strangers in his office.
Two cops, in uniform, blocking his view of the banks of
monitors, was definitely an anomaly for him. One advantage
of the graveyard shift is that you rarely need to share an
office. Laurence was always happiest with his own company,
so that suits him fine. His palms were sweating. He scanned
the IT suite. Was there anything incriminating? He tried to
look through their eyes. He'd never been a cop. He couldn't
see anything that stuck out. His activities were confined to
the digital realm.

He'd no doubt they had forensic data analysts coming out
of their ears. How could he cover his tracks? What traces had
he left? Actually, maybe he was overthinking this. He read the
papers. The police were up against it, like everyone else. It
was unlikely they had the resources to bring to bear on this
project, with austerity and all that. Stay calm Laurence. He
could feel his cheeks burning; a gulp in his throat.

"Err...hello, officers."

The taller one took the lead.

"Laurence Kilpatrick?"

"Yes, that's me."

"I'm PC Owen. We spoke on the phone? And this is my colleague DC Smith. Would you prefer to talk somewhere a bit more private?"

"Err...well...Ricardo won't be back today. I don't exactly have my own office..."

He trailed off. He was already gabbling and he'd told himself not to do that.

PC Owen smiled encouragingly.

"Well, hopefully we won't need to take up too much of your time. Do you mind if we start by going back over what we discussed on the phone last time?"

He'd known they were coming, but not exactly when. He wondered how they'd known he was on shift? And why they hadn't called ahead to warn him they were on their way? He wouldn't expect them to turn up without any notice unless he was under suspicion. That was an uncomfortable thought. Best not to second-guess how much they knew; maybe he was in the frame. He thought guiltily back to his night-time incursion, two days ago.

DC Smith had his notebook out, and Laurence was painfully aware that he must tread carefully. He wished he'd recorded their earlier conversation; he'd been so freaked out the details had vanished from his head. He didn't dare contradict himself. He tried to swallow the invisible golf ball that had mysteriously become lodged in his throat.

"You'll have to remind me, I'm sorry. It's been so busy here lately I don't know whether I'm coming or going."

It sounded plausible, and since there was a grain of truth there, he hoped he'd get away with it.

"OK, well, let's start at the beginning then. We've already met with your colleague, Miss Tuesday, a couple of times. She mentioned to us that you have responsibility for managing the digital systems here. We're keen to review some CCTV covering specific date periods over the last three months, and potentially some email communications as well."

Here Laurence was on more familiar ground.

"Well, obviously I'll need written authorisation for that, what with data protection and all that. Can you be a bit more specific about what you need? This is a very large hospital, and we monitor literally hundreds of cameras scattered throughout the campus."

PC Owen was undeterred.

"But you do keep the footage?"

"Of course. We're required to by law."

"And can you retrieve time-stamped segments from particular locations?"

Laurence's professional pride was piqued by this.

"Certainly!"

He waved at the wall full of flat-screens, continuously cycling between different views.

"Each camera of course has a unique ID, and all footage is time-stamped. To retrieve specific segments I just specify which cameras I'm targeting, and a date-range, and save it out to a file from the raw data. I could have it for you in 24 hours...but of course, as mentioned, I'd need the correct authorisation to release it."

PC Owen nodded, and changed tack.

"Of course. And that's good to know. So, I've got a few more questions, if you don't mind?"

"Sure. I'm not sure how much use I'll be. I don't get out of the IT Suite much..."

Laurence could see DC Smith eyeing the doughy flesh of his arms, where they were visible beneath the sleeves of his t-shirt, and exchanging a glance with Owen. Too professional to smirk?

"Nevertheless, you work here. Do you have much contact with Doctor Bernard?"

"Not too much. I think I've only ever spoken to him maybe a couple of times? There's thousands of staff here. I don't exactly keep tabs on them. The squeaky wheel gets oiled, and all that."

"I see. And when was the last time you saw Doctor Bernard?"

Laurence tried to look as though he was wracking his memory. Was this about the blackmail messages? Well they didn't know what he knew. Best policy: play dumb.

"Oh, that would have been about six months ago. He had a problem with his computer."

PC Owen looked at him levelly. Did he think he was being played? He pressed on with his questioning.

"Which floor was that on?"

"The seventh."

"Was that your first visit?"

"Yes."

"And how long were you there?"

"I don't know. About 20 minutes? It turned out he had a hardware problem. I had to take the fan out."

"And what happened then?"

"I took his PC with me, swapped in a new fan, and dropped it back."

"And?"

"And that was it. He barely looked up - busy with his papers. To be honest I think he was just as happy without a computer."

"And have you had any contact with him since?"

"None."

"Dr Bernard hasn't been seen at work recently. Are you

able to tell me the last time he logged onto the hospital system? I'm assuming he was set up for remote access?"

"I do have access to that information, but I think maybe that comes under data protection too. I'd have to clear it with my manager...honestly, I'm not trying to be deliberately obstructive. Are you able to tell me why you need information about Dr Bernard's movements?"

"Sorry, we can't really discuss investigations in progress."

Of course not. As if they'd throw him a bone.

"I get it. And is there anything else I can help you gentlemen with?"

He was probably pushing it now. PC Owen did not seem happy. His next question was a complete change of tack.

"How well do you know the Chief APT, Miss Tuesday?"

"I've met her a couple of times. I wouldn't say I know her well."

"Interesting. Because it seems she's on first-name terms with you."

"Oh, everyone calls me Laurence. I'm not used to being referred to as Mr Kilpatrick. In fact when you called me that earlier, I almost looked around for my Dad."

PC Owen barely cracked a smile at this. His partner was still scribbling furiously. Now he looked up from his notebook and spoke for the first time.

"We have reason to believe that Dr Bernard has been making unscheduled visits to the mortuary. We're not making any allegations at the moment, but you are a person of interest, as is he. You're not required to speak with us, but we may be more...curious...if it feels like you're being less than candid with us..."

It was a not-so-veiled threat, and Laurence regretted his over-confidence minutes before. He put as much sincerity into his voice as he could.

"Of course! But there's genuinely not so much I can tell

you."

"But you are friends with Miss Tuesday?"

There was no point hiding their friendship. Charlie had probably told them as much.

"Yes, yes, I guess you could say that. I've been for drinks with the mortuary crew a couple of times. And everyone likes Charlie. She's just that kind of person."

"And how long have you been working here?"

"9 years."

They had stopped listening – leaning in to get a closer look at one of the screens behind him. He turned to see what they were looking at, and saw Doc waiting for the main reception lift, on Monitor 8. His eyes widened in shock, and DC Smith looked meaningfully at his partner. An unspoken agreement passed between them. DC Smith wrapped up, as PC Owen left the room. Had he gone to intercept Doc? Laurence could have told them they were barking up the wrong tree, but he had no particular reason to protect Doc.

"OK, that just about covers everything we need to ask you today. Thanks for your time Mr Kilpatrick. We'll follow up when we've got the paperwork. I hope you don't mind...I've just got one more question?"

Laurence couldn't imagine what that would be.

"Are you ever tempted to find out a bit more than you're meant to, given you've theoretically got access to everything?"

Laurence felt all the colour draining from his face. Why would he ask that?

"Of course not! That would be against the rules – not to mention a complete betrayal of trust. What makes you think I'd do that?"

"You wouldn't be the first insider to go crooked. And by your own admission, Doctor Bernard isn't the most IT savvy. We're wondering if he had help from a bad actor. "

"I wouldn't dream of abusing my position. This job

means everything to me."

DC Smith looked at him, a smirk tugging at the corner of his mouth, one eyebrow straining to raise. Laurence could tell he didn't believe him for a minute. They must know more than they're letting on. He couldn't afford to fuck up now. He concentrated on keeping his expression neutral. He knew DC Smith wouldn't miss any visual tells. He must have interviewed hundreds of perps.

"Of course you wouldn't."

His tone was heavily ironic.

"It's not like you've ever done anything like that before you joined the staff here."

Did he know about Laurence's history? Of course; he would have done his homework, and Laurence's previous contacts with the law would most certainly be a matter of record. DC Smith smiled unpleasantly. His radio emitted a burst of static, and he thumbed it off as he stood up.

"Well, I'll be off now."

Laurence got up to show him out, but DC Smith shrugged off his offer of help.

"It's fine. I'll find my own way out. You'll be hearing from us again soon. Maybe next time you'll be in a position to be a bit more...helpful."

Laurence didn't feel good about this at all.

* * *

Doc had only been in his office for five minutes when there was a knock at the door. Who could that be? And why now? Who knew he was back? Well, news travelled fast in the hospital. Maybe Dr Singh had spilled the beans.

He briefly regretted the papers that covered almost every square inch of the windows – it kept the outside world at bay, but also meant that he couldn't see what was coming, or who was coming. Whoever his visitor was, he was wearing dark trousers, and solid shoes. In fact, the kind of shoes Doc associated with the police.

He took a moment to compose himself, and steadied his voice.

"Come in, it's not locked."

The door opened, and suddenly the whole frame was filled with a uniformed policeman.

"Doctor Bernard?"

"Yes, that's me, otherwise I'd be asking questions about who's been using my office."

He tried for levity, but the officer's expression was so forbidding that his joke sounded weak even to his ears.

"Doctor Bernard, I am hereby placing you under arrest, on suspicion of the murder of George Frank, Ronald Wellesley and Frederick Spenser. You do not have to say anything. However, it may harm your defence if you do not mention when questioned something which you later rely on in court. Anything you do say may be given in evidence."

Behind him Doc could see a second police officer. He was shorter, and heavyset. He hadn't expected this. It took a moment to sink in. He was being charged with murder? The band of pain was back. He couldn't catch his breath. He staggered and sat down heavily on the chair behind him. Murder! It didn't make any sense! He struggled to get his raging heart under control.

"Are you OK Doctor Bernard? Do you need medical assistance? Water?"

Doc shook his head. After a few moments he trusted himself to speak.

"There must have been some mistake. You've mixed me up with someone else? I only removed a few samples. And I can explain why."

PC Owen was implacable.

"Dr Bernard we have reason to believe that you are

responsible for the murders of these men, and potentially others.

"I promise - I've never killed anyone in my life. And I've never even heard of these men."

"I'm afraid I'll need to cuff you. Can I have your wrists please?"

Doc fought to keep a rising note of panic out of his voice.

"I'm not planning on running!"

"I'm sorry sir, but it's standard procedure."

Doc turned around, reluctantly complying with his request. That would certainly set tongues wagging. It wasn't every day that consultant pathologists were led through the hospital in cuffs. He felt first one wrist and then the other enclosed in steel, and a click as the cuffs locked.

"Ok, we're going to take you down to the station."

"Which one?"

"It will be Charing Cross."

So, not too far away. Well, at least he'd be able to get legal representation once he'd been booked. He took a deep breath and tried to calm himself.

"I see. Well, it's not like I have a choice in the matter. Do you mind if we take the back lift? I'm assuming you've left your car in the basement car park? I wouldn't want to scare the patients."

"That's fine sir. You'll have the opportunity to let someone know where you are once we've got you booked in. OK. We're all done here. Lead the way DC Smith."

* * *

Almost before he knew what was happening Doc was being processed at the police station, and booked in with the Magistrate first thing the next morning. It's not how he imagined it. They take his phone, his belt, his shoelaces; the contents of his pockets. During 'processing' (fingerprints, photographs) he begins to question his decision to return to London. It was sheer bad luck they happened to be in the hospital when he'd gone into the office. Terrible timing. The law had seemed like a safe haven, but didn't feel like one, once he was in custody. He realised he wasn't mentally ready to go through with it.

Behind the booking desk, staff in civilian clothes were tapping computer keyboards. Doc sat patiently whilst PC Owen filled out the paperwork. He was still cuffed. Eventually PC Owen walked over to a printer and gathered the papers that were slowly being disgorged from its tray.

"This is your charge sheet. You are being charged with the offences set down below."

Doc stood up and reached out to take the flimsy sheets. The top sheet was divided in two, with demographic information in the header, followed by a list of charges.

[A] Louis Bernard, 62 (27.09.54), of Gayton Crescent, NW3 was charged with the murder of George Frank, 76, white male of Vauxhall Grove, SW8.

[B] Louis Bernard, 62 (27.09.54), of Gayton Crescent, NW3 was further charged with the murder of Ronald Wellesley, 76, white male of Pimlico, SW1.

[C] Louis Bernard, 62 (27.09.54), of Gayton Crescent, NW3 was further charged with the murder of Frederick Spencer, 73, white male of Camberwell Green, SE5.

"Do I get that phone call then?"

The answers sounded like they came by rote from the book.

"You have the right to tell someone where you are. You have the right to free legal advice."

Who could he ring? It would have to be Charlie. And he probably had a lot of explaining to do, but he had no choice. He had no one else to call.

* * *

I'm in the middle of a tricky PM when I get the message. Doc has been taken into custody, at Charing Cross police station. I barely stop to take off my gloves and mask. It's the last PM of the day, and I'll have to ask Zoe to take over. I have implicit faith in Zoe, but still, I hate to interrupt a job.

"Hi Charlie."

"What's going on Doc?"

"I was away on personal business."

That's a bit vague, given the fact he's been missing for weeks. I guess the call's being recorded. Still it pisses me right off. I deserve more honesty than that.

"And now you've been arrested? What's the charge? Did they give you a charge sheet?"

"Murder! It doesn't make any sense. They're saying I killed three men –but I've never even heard of them before. "

I don't know what to think. I used to think I knew Doc pretty well – but the last few months it feels like he's been a stranger. He's definitely been hiding something.

"Do you want me to come down?"

"I'm not sure they'll let you see me tonight. I can ask. They've booked me in with a magistrate tomorrow morning."

I consider this information. Could he really be responsible for the deaths of those old men? Was that why hadn't he filed the reports? It doesn't fit with the Doc I know, but how much do we really know about anyone?

"Charlie?"

"I'm still here Doc. There's not much I can immediately do. If I were you I'd make sure I got some legal representation pronto – and not any lawyer the police recommend!"

"I'll take that under advisement. OK Charlie, well I have to go now. Let's speak again tomorrow."

Doc handed the phone back to PC Owen and sat down again. He felt winded, out of control. PC Owen pulled him gently to his feet, and led him towards a heavy steel door.

On the other side of the door was a cell. A blue plastic mat to sleep on. Heavily varnished wooden bench. Dark lino floor. A single high window opposite the bed with a tight metal grille. Not that he was considering escape. He felt considerably safer in here. He hadn't expected to be taken into custody so fast – but from the police's point of view he hadn't been available for questioning up to now, and they obviously weren't taking any chances. And he definitely hadn't expected to be facing charges of murder. He'd been more focussed on his financial situation. Could the guys who had threatened him on the Heath have set him up? That didn't make any sense though. He was hardly going to be able to pay his debts from a prison cell.

Later on, a nice lady came around and offered him food, which was served on a plastic tray, like an airline dinner. It's many decades since Doc's been on the wrong side of the law; not since the 1980s – youthful support for the miners. The cell was surprisingly clean. He'd expected some kind of graffiti on the walls. There was no blanket, but it wasn't cold. By 10 pm the cells were relatively quiet, although that changed when they brought in a guy who spent a good half an hour kicking the door of his cell, shouting and swearing that he'd fucking have them. Doc kept quiet.

When the other prisoner eventually settled down all was quiet, but the lights blazed on. Doc pulled his jacket over his head to shut them out.

* * *

He was woken by the sound of footsteps on metal; doors clanging. Down the hall an early prisoner was being checked in. He walked over to the small glass window, set in the door of the cell, but he couldn't see much through it. He longed for a cup of tea.

No tea arrived.

After what seemed like forever he was put in a meat wagon, taken to the court, and put in a cell to await the Magistrate's decision. The police had applied for the right to keep the defendant in custody while they gathered evidence - having already absconded, he was considered a 'flight risk'.

Inside the almost empty courtroom was all pale wood and shiny white surfaces. It felt like a lecture theatre, the long desks equipped with microphones and legal pads. The magistrate sat behind a long wooden bench on a raised platform, flanked by a legal counsel and note taker, and listened impassively as the police officers made their case, before granting their request. Doc barely had time to take it all in before it was all over, and he was returned to his cell beneath the court, to await his transfer to prison on remand.

Ritual

Trees we can perch on, but they have no leaves. Now is the time of cold; the dark is falling. Before it was dark it was light. Many of us had congress together, making sounds with our beaks. She is there. She is here. I am here.

She let her guard down, and almost immediately their voices filled her, until there was no her; only we - just chatter - an endless, exhausting back and forth. Sometimes it's easier to let it flow. Step outside everything. She is not used to trusting; information is power to be used sparingly. Anonymity is the greatest power of all. Giving up herself feels like giving away part of herself. She held back the most important part from Charlie . She realised too late that was a mistake. It's the only way she can be saved.

We can feel the wrongness in her. She is not of the flock.

[Charlie!]

A handful of breast with a soft curve on it; the rail of a rib beneath, the nipple gently questing upwards.

I am not of the flock. I am I. I am I. I am not I.

We are she. What is she?

I am cold. I am the flock. I am more than I. I am We.

[I am lost. I am lost.]

We are voice. We are message. Murmuration; sound we can see and feel. We gather wisdom; integrate. Many flock; many call.

From our single throat the call comes; we see with sound; shape the picture of what will be and hold it against tomorrow. The path is set. She will give what is promised to us.

It should have been time for the harvest, but Victor was nowhere near ready. Eva felt herself weaken; felt the screens start to melt between the human self she projected to the world, and the bird self that needed to be renewed each full moon. For the first time in many years, it looked like she might miss the apogee. And then? It had never been necessary before. They had come so quietly she felt like a shepherd. With Victor, she needed to be a wolf. It was all she had. It would have to be enough.

She started with a pentagram, marking out her own satanic Eucharist in thick white lines that seemed to glow in the dark. It was an inversion of the Christian rituals of her youth, blending old traditions with hints gleaned from dark corners of HP Lovecraft books, the Necronomicon, Osman Spare's inferno, Yeats' automatic drawings - all woven into a spell of binding, of control. Would it be enough?

As Eva chalked in the final symbols the candles began to flicker, as if an unfelt breeze disturbed them. The walls became an abstract whirl of patterns, like pixels rearranging themselves on a screen. Gradually more regular patterns began to coalesce from the snow. There, on the yellowed paper, eyes took shape, and she felt herself pinned by their gaze whilst cold manacles settled around her wrists and ankles, the chill clasp of metal at her throat. She felt the invisible, intangible collar tighten until she was gasping for breath and fell to her knees.

Until this moment it had all been a game. She was always the mistress of the situation. When angry clients turned on her, she could walk away. No longer. The summoning had her. She could feel the hunger in it; sense its presence inside her as it rummaged through the contents of her mind. Sense how easily it could crush her, despite the pentangle, the wards, the candles, all the safeguards she had thought would allow her to bind and control it. They were as nothing in the face of this malevolence. There was a hint of the reptile, something that shone darkly in the dim light, something that slithered.

"What do you want of me?"

She forced out words, past the tight collar that constricted her windpipe, that even now she could not touch, but which she could feel, cold against her skin.

"What is it? What? I have already given you so many souls. Every time your servants called I harvested them for you. I seek to strike a bargain with you."

Somewhere she could sense the many creatures, which were all one creature, all manifestations of that great power, laughing. There was no mirth in it. There would be no bargaining with it either.

The pressure increased; as though the chains that held her bonds were tightened by some medieval torture machine she felt herself inexorably dragged downwards, until she was shackled, spread-eagled on the floor between the points of the pentangle; her refuge become a prison. Her world shrank. One by one the candles guttered out, and she was left in darkness. She began to be aware of a whispering sound, the fluttering of wings, the chitter of claws, many voices murmuring.

And then, in her mind's eye, impressions began to form – of the challenges, the sacrifices, the blood that it needed; the power that it needed. Why had she come without the sacrifice? The whispers intensified until they were an angry buzzing in her ears, became an agony that drove out all thought, until her mind could contain them no more.

* * *

Eva woke alone. The darkness had an everyday quality. The shackles had gone, but she could still feel the cold weight of the metal collar around her neck. She had hoped to harness the power of the magpies, to control them, to see what they saw. Instead she had unleashed something she could not control. There would be no reprieve for Victor.

Honesty is the best policy

Laurence sat in his office, in his usual chair, facing the bank of monitors that were his eyes on the hospital. For once he was oblivious to them. He was too busy worrying. He'd got through an entire pack of antacid already and he'd only been on shift for three hours. By now the news was all around the hospital. Doc had been arrested by the Metropolitan police. He had been seen, on his way out with two uniformed policemen, handcuffed no less!

Laurence was immediately all over the Met website. There it was, in the news section.

The police had charged Dr Bernard with murder. The previous day he had appeared in Westminster Magistrates Court, where he had been remanded in custody. Fuck. Shit got serious. He thought about his last conversation with Charlie, a couple of days previous, and about how he'd been less than candid with her about what he knew about her girlfriend's activities. Maybe that had been a mistake. He had been trying to save her feelings, but he was going to have to be honest with Charlie.

As soon as he had made up his mind he felt much better. He jumped up and headed downstairs to the mortuary before he lost his nerve.

Charlie was in her office, deep in paperwork. She looked up as he tapped on her open office door.

"Laurence! I was just thinking about you. So, obviously you've heard about Doc... Actually, where are my manners. Have a seat. Would you like some tea? I was just about to make some for myself before I sat down to tomorrow's rota and caught up with the admin. No rest for the wicked and all that..."

She was gabbling. That wasn't like Charlie. Laurence

wondered what had happened since their last chat that he'd not been party to. After the interview with the police he'd been properly spooked and dialled down his activities for a couple of days.

"Ummm... I'm alright. I don't really drink tea. I'm more into energy drinks – and I had one just a little while ago."

"Ok. In that case I'll hold out for a bit longer. What can I help you with? My computer is running like a dream, so I assume you're not here in your professional capacity?"

There was the look, and the raised eyebrow.

"No."

He looked down at his feet. He could feel Charlie looking at him and avoided her gaze. She sighed and continued.

"So, how did it go with the cops?"

Laurence was glad she'd broached the subject first. He lifted his head and started talking, fast.

"They asked a lot of questions about Doc. Had I seen him recently; when did I see him last; what we spoke about; when had he last accessed the hospital systems? Could I provide CCTV footage of his movements. That kind of thing."

"And?"

"Well...I gave them what I had. They wouldn't tell me why they were so interested, but...umm...actually they didn't really need to, because I already know."

Charlie's eyes widened and then narrowed. She looked at him speculatively.

"You do? How long have you known for?"

Laurence had to decide how specific to be...this was going to be tricky. Especially as he'd already had one opportunity to tell her that he knew far more than he should, when Charlie had mentioned the marks, and her concerns about Doc when they last spoke. Why hadn't he said anything then? Or to the police, during the interview? The little omissions had grown now into a great big lie, and he wasn't sure how to go around admitting it. Start with Doc.

"Well...I think so. Doc is in some kind of trouble...I kind of...saw some of his messages. He's got into debt with some kind of online gambling site...and they have been leaning on him to steal samples from the mortuary."

It took him a while to get the words out. Charlie was listening intently. He wondered what was going through her mind. He hadn't been specific about the 'messages' – maybe she would just assume that he'd been helping Doc access his email and seen them by accident.

"I can't really comment on what's going on with Doc I'm afraid. Let's just say I've spoken with the police, and they're looking into it. They've taken all his notes away, and I'm sure they're all over his messages and phone calls. They seem pretty thorough. I'm guessing you spoke with them too? They mentioned they were going to call you."

"Yes. I spoke to them yesterday."

"And did you tell them what you just told me? That you already knew about the messages? And the marks?"

"No."

"Hmm. I'm guessing you had your reasons for that. I'm not sure I agree with them. Honesty's the best policy in this kind of situation – otherwise you start to look guilty by association."

Charlie was telling him off, but at least she cared enough to give him a warning. He started at her, mutely. He knew he should tell her all of it. He knew if he didn't it wouldn't end well.

Her voice was gentle.

"Is there something else you want to talk about?"

Ok. Time to open up a bit more then. He had a feeling that she wasn't going to be so calm about the next revelation. Where to start? He looked down at his feet again, rubbing the toe of one trainer against the other as he tried to work out what to say.

"Umm..."

He ground to a halt. He couldn't do it. He couldn't admit to Charlie that he'd been stalking her girlfriend, reading her mail, and broken into her mortuary. Not only would she never trust him again, but he realised now that she would be honour bound to tell the police everything. That's just how she was. Even if it meant the end of her relationship with Eva, she would have to do the right thing and see justice done. And, he now realised, it would be the end of him. They'd never let him keep his job if they knew that not only had he been abusing his position; he'd also failed to blow the whistle on a serious offence.

"Laurence mate – I'm not going to bite you. You've obviously got something on your mind. What is it?"

"Seriously – don't worry about it – it's nothing. I need to get back now. I'll see you soon."

He could barely look at her as he turned to leave. He could feel her eyes drilling into his back, and his shoulders slumped even more than usual. He could sense he'd broken a bond of trust. It might have have worked out if he wasn't more focussed on the digital footprint than the human being. Humans have never been his forte. How would she feel if she knew all of it?

Losing the Midas touch

"Excuse me? Last time I checked you're meant to pay attention. Get down on your knees. Just in case you're in danger of forgetting, I brought you a little aide-memoire."

A thin leather collar dangles from his pasty hand.

Mr X was a long-term client, but now he wanted to change things up.

She had misgivings from the start. It's not quite right, because he wants her to switch. She can deal with that – normally it wouldn't be a problem. Eva usually played the Dom, but kept switching as part of her repertoire. It could be therapeutic to have an ego massage at the point of a whip.

Normally.

She's not in charge now.

Her edge is dulled by the drugs she's been taking to drown out their constant hectoring in her head.

The moon is waxing gibbous. One week until it's full.

One week until Victor reaches the end of the game.

If he finishes the game.

Until now Eva had always kept her drug-taking under control. Of course she played out with Charlie, but that was strictly a leisure activity. Now she began to zone out on Xanax, Valium. It helped to muffle the din of their speech, the constant conversation played out across the chimneys and treetops of London. Then a little coke upper before she had to meet a client started to become a breakfast ritual. She couldn't eat, but she didn't care. The coke stopped her feeling hungry. When she felt too jittery she brought herself down with alcohol – a nip of vodka, because it wouldn't smell. Until it became a constant loop of pill – line – sip; a kind of trinity that was self-perpetuating. Those were nights she couldn't bring herself to go to Charlie's. She didn't want her to see her like this. She didn't know what was worse: the constant din of magpie chatter in her head when she was awake, or the dreams of flying and wheeling with the flock that invaded her when she finally succeeded in drinking herself to sleep. Sounds lost at either end of the spectrum, colours washing out. Other senses are heightened. She starts to understand the language of birds, but human speech becomes babble.

Eva often had the sensation of being watched – had always assumed it was the magpies. Now she began to wonder. And then she saw him, and suddenly all of those half-remembered glimpses gelled into a certainty that he had been following her for a while.

She had noticed the way Laurence was with Charlie. Was that why? Was he trying to get something on her? He was just the type that would blackmail.

It had been a dull day, and night fell early. Along the Embankment patches of light from the street lamps only amplified the shadows in between. Along the balustrades mysterious creatures of the sea looked out across the Thames; their outlines uncertain and wavering in a mist that had sprung up as the dark mass of the river cooled and gave up its vapours. Long, low buildings swathed with ivy cast the path into gloom.

Eva had arranged to meet Mr X on the embankment, overlooking the Houses of Parliament, just along from the hospital. He wouldn't have far to come, and they had often met there, over the Summer months. Then it had felt like a playground, so deliciously close to Westminster, to the centres of power. She could tell it turned him on too. It was so close to the places where he was known. That was before that story broke. Really, it had been an error of judgement arranging to meet him there. And she could tell it had changed him too. Their liaison felt dangerous in a way it hadn't before.

With the dusk falling, and the Thames a great black mass

before her, and the dark trees lowering over the shadowed bank, she felt vulnerable. So many places for the magpies to hide. Tenuous glimpses in the corners of her eyes. They cannot conceal their cries – always strident – that cackle un-modulated – a harsh and ugly sound at odds with the elegance of their plumage. They are rumoured to steal songbird's eggs. Are they jealous of their music? Still she couldn't see them, but she knew something was watching her.

When he arrived, flustered, things immediately got off to a bad start. Normally she would have relished having him on the wrong foot, but that had been before –when she had everything under control. Perhaps he can feel the change in her; the cracks in the armour she's constructed to protect her from the world. Or maybe he's just irked that she's not paying attention. She's too busy trying to work out what's making her so uneasy to pay attention; to notice the moment that she loses him.

She has just spotted Laurence. What was he doing there? He looked furtive. This time it seems certain that he's there just to spy on her - but why? What could be his motivation? She doesn't have a good feeling about this. She needs to get out of this situation now.

She panics, runs, abandons the client in her haste to get away. She's wearing heels and turns them in a grate, falling awkwardly to the curb. Sprained wrist; twisted ankle; bruised face. The moon is only waxing gibbous. It would be a full week until Victor was ready to finish the game. If he was ready.

By now Eva is beginning to suspect that she's not in control of Victor any more. When did the balance shift? It's been a gradual process; the very act of keeping his own notes. The first time that he didn't mention the notebook to Eva. He's starting to weave his own patterns. It won't be long until he works out what's going on, and then he'll be free to make his own compact. Eva knows Victor is hiding something from her. She decides to deviate from the script.

She needs to bind him even closer to her. It hadn't been necessary with the others; the magpies had known which ones to pick, designed the game that bound them; ensuring that they would never question her mastery. She sensed he was hiding things from her. His eyes slid furtively to the side when they spoke; he had lost that quality of vulnerability that had initially marked him, become perceptibly harder.

She went back to the Atlantis Bookshop, in Bloomsbury, which specialised in the occult. The stuff in the window was mere dressing – books on self-help, Moore's Almanac, How to Eat Well, Feng Shui; reading runes and oghams; the lore of birds. Some of the material was more arcane. Eva had a feeling that the information she wanted wouldn't be on display. Who knew what rituals occurred on the first and second floor of the Georgian building, which had been occupied by the Atlantic bookshop since the 1920's? Eva browsed the bookshelves, apparently casual, whilst behind her she could feel the woman behind the counter sizing her up. Flame coloured hair – bottle applied, inexpertly. Something desperately sad about that flame-red hair; the lined face, doughy skin. Clinging to the occult in the hopes that it will help fill the gap inside. She needed a cover story. Research? Could she pass herself off as a scholar? Or maybe the direct approach would be better. Maybe it was the kind of place where they wouldn't turn a hair if you asked them for details of a binding ritual. If she knew enough of the dark arts to be useful, she'd probably see straight through any attempt at dissimulation.

Later, she was forced to admit defeat. Trying to find the information she wanted online had proved futile. There were thousands of results to her queries, but amidst the mass of information she was presented with, nothing leapt out as significant. She felt as though she was poised at the lip of an endless rabbit hole, one replete with twists and turns, dead-ends and cul-de-sacs. There were a few diagrams that caught her eye; symbols that felt as though she should be able to read them; motifs that recurred and nagged at her memory, like irritating threads she couldn't snip. These she saved, to the picture memory on her phone.

What must her search history look like by now? Who was monitoring all those billions of searches, other than the algorithms? They'd hardly be interested in someone like her, who kept below the radar, and never piqued the attention of the law...

A visit to the nick

Doc is being held on remand in Wandsworth prison. No trial date yet. I decide to visit. I need to hear from his own lips what's going on. It's not the first time I've been there; I know the drill. One hour max, in an open setting along with other visitors. First thing this morning I emailed my details to the prison, and this afternoon got a message back with three possible interview slots the next day, along with a bunch of information about what ID to bring and what to expect.

When I get there I sign in and get escorted to a large bright room. I take a seat, and look around, at the wide-spaced tables, each with a visit going on. Mostly women visiting men; the odd child. It feels rude to stare, so I look down at my hands.

I've not been waiting in the visitor's suite long when Doc is brought in. From the off I notice that there's something calm about him, like he has surrendered himself to the system. He's way more relaxed than I've ever seen him at work.

"Charlie. So lovely to see you. I'm sorry it can't be in more salubrious circumstances."

Still the same old charmer. I'm not quite sure what tone to take. Maybe I should just be straight up. I literally don't know where to start. Stealing samples from the mortuary? Really? It's like something out of a tabloid. It's not the kind of thing I'd ever expected to occur on my watch.

It's the kind of thing we'd take the piss out of on cheese night, after a few. I thought I knew him.

But I don't say that. I don't say anything. The seconds tick past. As he stares mutely at me I realise he too is embarrassed. We both look away. He breaks the silence first.

"How are things? How's it going with that girlfriend of yours?"

It completely throws me. I mean really. You've been charged with stealing body parts from the hospital, and you ask me about my love life?

"Eva is...well, I'm not sure how Eva is. I'm not even sure who Eva is any more. I'm starting to wonder if I ever knew her."

Or you, for that matter. But I don't say that aloud. Doc knows me so well I can see he's worked it out anyway. There's another silence.

Again, he breaks it.

"You must be wondering what you know about me too? I'd better come clean with you. It's true, I got myself into trouble with the International Finance. I thought I was clever. It wasn't very smart, taking those samples, although I see now, that was just for blackmailing purposes. I've been rather stupid. I definitely didn't kill anyone though. What would I want with old men? What possible motive could I have?"

Whilst he's talking I'm wondering what possible motive Eva could have? I know deep in my bones he's not the killer. I already have the answer to that question, now that I'm thinking about it. That chat about Eva's past. Her hatred of the church. The tyranny of old men. Hints of past abuse. Maybe I should level with him. Maybe it's the habit of years, but he's always given me good advice.

I lower my voice and lean in.

"Well, I'm beginning to wonder if maybe Eva did."

He hunches his long frame and rounds his shoulders against the rest of the room. I have his full attention now.

"Eva? Really? What makes you think that?"

I can see he is genuinely shocked. I continue, choosing my words carefully.

"A couple of things really. One, Laurence has been

following her around, for reasons I won't go into right now. He said he's seen her with several older gents, and there seemed to be something weird going on. And there was something she told me, a while ago. I think she was abused when she was quite young – by a priest. I wonder if she's somehow trying to get revenge for that? Some kind of payback?"

Doc's eyes narrow as he considers this information, and the implications for himself.

"I see. Well...that's rather circumstantial. You'd need more evidence. But of course you know her better than I do. And how do you feel about that?"

"I don't know Doc. As you say it's circumstantial. I think I need to ask her to her face, but I haven't been able to get hold of her. It just seems so crazy – but Laurence is convinced it's her, and that more people are at risk – some old guy in Borough, and another one in Kennington."

"Did you mention all of this to the police?"

"No! At least, I need to talk to her first..."

"Time's up!"

* * *

I'm sitting at a table on my own mulling over the visit to Doc, the marks. Too many similar deaths. I'm certain that Doc is innocent, but I have no proof beyond a feeling. I'm worried about where Eva is, what she's up to. I text Eva to see if she's planning on coming over to the flat, but there's no answer. My calls go straight to voicemail. I don't bother leaving any messages. Should I mention my suspicions to the police? Strictly speaking I should – not least because it would get Doc off the hook, but it's all so circumstantial. I really need to talk to Eva first.

"Mind if I join you?"

We haven't spoken since I gathered up my clothes and

sneaked out of her room at 6 am. Awkward? Just a bit. Never mind. Soldier on…I'm conflicted. Of course I've been thinking about her, but there's too many plates spinning for me to risk dropping any at the moment.

"Sorry, I was miles away. Sure – it's nice to see you."

"Hard day in the office?"

"You could say that. By the time I got back to work and wrapped up the admin on the day's cases it was beer o'clock. I don't normally drink alone, but I've got a lot on my mind."

"Must be tricky without Dr Barnard there to support you. I heard he got arrested?"

"I can't really go into that now - sorry."

"Of course. Anyway - it's none of my business. Do you want me to leave you in peace?"

She looks hurt. Damn. She doesn't deserve this.

"I'm sorry Chloe. I seem to mess up every time we see each other. I'm not always a dickhead, I promise."

"It's alright Charlie - I know you've got a lot going on."

"No excuse. Manners cost nothing! Anyway, now you're here, and it's just the two of us. Am I allowed to show you that I can also be nice?"

Good as gold

When Laurence finishes work at 8:30 pm the little red pin on Google Maps says Eva is at Southwark Bridge Road, which is only a 15 minute stroll from Tommy's. Laurence doesn't usually clock-watch, but he's been watching that little red pin all afternoon, and Eva's movements don't make any sense. It's a good thing she's not tech-savvy enough to turn off her location tracking. Looking back down her timeline, it seems like she's stayed put for most of the day, before taking this unscheduled wander. Maybe this is where she meets her clients?

He traces her to a building just off Southwark Bridge Road. It looks abandoned, with boarded up windows and graffiti on the shutters, but there's a new looking intercom by the door. He's sure she's inside. Alone? Or with a client? Time to watch and wait.

A tedious hour follows, as he goes over everything again and again in his mind. What is he missing? He's still feeling guilty about that unfinished chat with Charlie, and all the stuff he'd neglected to mention to her. He's close, but there's still too many gaps. He needs some evidence before that conversation can continue. And it needs to continue. People are dying.

If I don't do something, that's like, basically my fault.

It's not a nice thought. What is he doing here anyway, lurking outside a building in South London? It must look pretty dodgy. Maybe he should leave the detective work to professionals. Just the thought of that last chat with the plod was enough to keep him waiting there. He was so close.

★★★

Victor had found a note. He had followed her instructions

carefully. When had it begun to go weird? He sensed a wrongness in her.

Back up Victor. Let's start with this morning.

He had got up early, as he always did. Gone through to the kitchen to make tea. Noticed, on the way, a blank white envelope on the front mat. Inside was a note from Eva, written in ink in her neat hand.

"Victor – can you meet me at Number Six, Flatiron Square at 10 pm?"

The note was clipped to a printout of a map, with the address circled in red pen. It would be a longish walk from Victor's house - close to where he had first met her, but he thought he'd be able to manage it, if he left himself enough time.

He had left his house just before nine. It was a long time since he'd been out during the hours of darkness – he was usually tucked up in bed by then, and he wondered why she had asked him to meet her at night. Of course, she probably had another task for him, and young people were always night-owls. He remembered a time when nine hadn't seemed late at all.

The estate was quiet, but as soon as he hit the main road it was surprisingly busy. When this neighbourhood had been all factories and warehouses, there were rarely people around after work hours, except in the lone pub on Tanner Street, where workers went to drink their troubles away at the end of their shift.

As he turned onto Tooley Street it was brightly lit, lined with restaurants, their patrons spilling out onto the pavement. Victor looked at the throng and decided he couldn't face battling his way through them. He would use the bus instead. He might need to conserve his energy for what lay ahead.

Through sheer habit he had looked up Flatiron Square in his old A-Z – it wasn't far from Southwark Bridge Road. He could get a bus right here that would take him there. As he stood and waited for one to come along, he thought about the meaning of the note. How could he think that what he had with Eva was in any way a real relationship? The cutting? The power play? The endless strange tasks she set him in her mysterious 'game'? Why had he come?

At first it was just pleasantly erotic, made him warm with a desire that was intimate rather than lecherous; a sensuous feeling he hadn't experienced in years. Was he being honest with himself? Maybe he'd just been playing along to get access to that beautiful body. The thought made him uncomfortable. He didn't want to be that kind of man.

Still lying to yourself, Victor? Maybe you've always been that man, but you were too damn scared to do anything about it.

And now? Why did she seem ever less human to him? Was it the set of her head? The unconscious way she had of preening herself. Why did he keep dreaming of magpies?

He should have run a mile. Instead, he stayed there, waiting for a bus to take him into an unknown and possibly dangerous situation. Not for the first time he wondered when he had last been in charge of his own actions. If she was playing mind games with him it made sense that she would trick him into thinking it was his own idea and even rationalising it to himself.

She hadn't asked him to meet her anywhere before. In fact, since that day in Southwark Cathedral all their meetings had been at his house. Maybe Flatiron Square was where she lived? He'd never asked her, nor had she volunteered the information. And that was partly why he'd left so early – so he could arrive there, and have a look at the building, and the area around it, before he was expected. It was also why he had put on his dark, heavy overcoat, even though the evening wasn't cold enough to warrant it - it was barely October. It would help him to stay hidden in the shadows, he hoped.

The bus stop was equipped with one of those new-fangled

displays that told you what buses were due, and when. Everything was so easy nowadays – gone were the days when you never knew what would happen when. In two minutes, according to the display, the bus would be along. He perched on the uncomfortable sloping bench and watched the world passing by. The bus arrived and he waved his freedom pass at the driver, glad to be moving, but not without grave misgivings as to the wisdom of his journey.

Faster than he would have liked, the bus arrived at his stop. Victor found Southwark Bridge Road deserted. He couldn't decide whether that was a good thing or not. He had the feeling that it suited Eva's purpose perfectly. No matter, he told himself firmly; he wasn't going into this with his eyes closed.

He walked the few steps to Flatiron Square and positioned himself opposite the building where she had told him to meet her. Three floors, with ancient brickwork and graffiti across the top that read 'good as gold'...six for gold. Was it a coincidence? He suspected not. Most of the windows were boarded up, but he could see a faint flicker of light at the single window that was uncovered. It was only twenty past the hour. He settled himself into the shadows, never taking his eyes off the window. He pulled his coat more tightly around him and settled down to wait. Maybe it was the night; a trick of the atmosphere, but his ears felt sharper than they had in years. He could hear the rumble of trains, and the hiss of traffic. A plane pulling into City Airport. Trucks whispering across the bridge And, he could hear, unmistakably, amid the general din, the 'kak-kak-kak kak kat-kak' that meant a magpie was near. Watching him? Was it one of her spies? The building offered its silent face to the world.

★★★

Laurence wondered how long the other man had been there, fragile in a greatcoat he wore like a suit of armour. Not a client? Was he waiting to see Eva at the window too? Maybe one of her old men? It seemed too much of a coincidence to think he'd just appeared on cue. Time ticked past. He tried not to worry about all the things he couldn't control.

★★★

Ten o'clock arrived too quickly. There was Eva, beckoning from the doorway. Gone was the demure young woman with a neat French plait. She was wearing a flowing dark dress, her hair fastened with sparkling pins, dark kohl shadowing her eyes.

"Victor - so glad you made it. I hope the journey hasn't been too taxing."

Victor felt more composed than he had any right to be given the lateness of the hour and the strangeness of the situation. He took her hand with a smile that didn't reach his eyes.

"Everything is fine, Eva. I'm here aren't I? And haven't I done everything you've asked me to so far?"

It was almost as though he had split in two, and Victor the lonely pensioner watched from the hallway as a different man followed her up the stairs, his big bony hand clutching her small one.

Through the doorway he caught a glimpse of candles, a pentagram, a single chair, like a throne.

"Victor – I need to know you're OK before we continue."

"Should I sit in the middle?"

"Yes, Victor. The chair is for you."

"Very good."

He watched that other Victor take his seat, as Eva moved the final candles back into place so that the pattern was complete.

"Everything you have done so far has been in preparation, and now you are ready to open the final door. You have proven yourself a person who can be trusted to manage power. These words are a kind of oath, a promise. Are you ready to begin?"

"Yes Eva, I am ready."

Eva's voice became a harsh monotone.

"Yeshh....baar...aatoh....omé....moté...ghaat....ahaar... vesshta....niissh"

With each repetition, she turned to a different point, bowing to the four corners of the earth, to the North, the South, the East, the West; to the spirits that gathered, almost immanent, on the periphery of vision. The black room was leached of colour, and Victor was a shadow on the chair, his dark coat blending into the gloom. Eva circled him still chanting, the words coming faster and faster, increasingly oblivious to anything around her as the ritual caught her in its rhythms.

***

Many birds coming in to roost, all the same kind of bird? The fan tail - that shape was familiar. Were they Magpies? They lined the metal railings along the rooftops. He'd heard of pigeons roosting on buildings at night but he had always thought that magpies preferred trees. Hundreds of them.

The moon vanished behind a cloud as the flock swept from the roof and dove in formation into the front of the building. He heard glass shatter, wood splinter.

Laurence almost broke then. It was the silence that stopped him. Magpies were always noisy. Something else was going on here.

Wait.

***

Eva was oblivious to the gathering that filled the doorway, crowded the corners, drowned out her chanting with frenzied wing beats. As the first of the magpies flew at her, claws scrabbling for purchase, more and more of its fellows joined, concealing what happened next beneath a mound of dark feathers and the glint of beak and claw.

Victor felt their consciousness spreading and thinning, motes of awareness scattering across the facets of the room, a kaleidoscopic view that spun crazily through glimpses of fragments of information that don't join up; floor, symbols, Eva, walls, shards gradually scattering as he vanished through the cracks, whilst the simulacrum gathered strength, squatting on his chair in the centre of the circle.

As invisible bonds dragged Eva down, his dislocation was complete. The other Victor sat, watching; arms folded, face calm. He stood up, stepped over splintered wood and glass: a different man, remade, and better. He quietly left the room and let himself out of the building.

Marks in an almanac

The street door opened, and a man came out. Was it the same guy that he had seen go in earlier? He was pretty sure Eva had been alone. This man seemed taller, broader. He strode down the street with purpose, silver hair catching the light of a gibbous moon.

Laurence was puzzling this out when the door opened again. In the shadow of the doorway, he could just make out a dark silhouette, a stooping, broken-shouldered thing, dragging its feet. Could it be Eva? She stumbled down the road with her head hanging, without even bothering to lock the door behind her.

Laurence would never have another opportunity like this. He slipped into the building and climbed the narrow stairs to the first floor; through the white room, to find scuffed chalk marks on the floor, shards of glass and splinters; guttering candles; the corpses of many birds; scattered feathers: an empty theatre after the performance. Some kind of ritual had happened here.

He went back through to the first room. There wasn't much furniture – a desk, with a single drawer and two chairs. He opened the drawer to find a dog-eared copy of Moore's Almanac full of ads for sugar spells, money magnets; psychological techniques for increasing height, girth, intelligence; horoscopes; planting guides.

He came upon a slip of paper with rough sketches on it. Marking her place? It looked like it had been torn out of a notebook, and been much folded. There, in the centre, two columns of symbols. On the left: new moon, quarter, half and full. And on the right? A single line, then two, then three. The fourth like a bird in flight. Or an M. A magpie? And how were they connected to the moon?

The page she had marked listed lunar dates and times, with red dots next to several of them. January 10th, 2:21 pm – Wolf moon; February 9th – Snow moon. March 9th – Lenten moon; April 7th – Egg Moon. He'd never realised that they had names before. And the next moon? Hunters moon. It too was marked up with a red dot.

Four phases of the moon. Four sets of lines, gradually forming a rough M.

First cut...first quarter.

Half-moon, second cut...

Waxing gibbous, third cut.

Fourth cut – full moon. Time for the sacrifice.

After the first cut the die is set. They have less than a month to live. That's why the cuts hadn't been inflicted all at once. Charlie had all the pieces, but she lacked the key - and according to the almanac, Hunters moon was only eight days away.

He dithered over whether to take the almanac. Would Eva notice? Either way, if it were missing, she might panic and disappear.

In the end he decided to put the almanac back in the drawer, exactly as he had found it – but not before he had carefully photographed the cover, the moon chart, and both sides of the slip of paper he had found inside. He didn't want to tamper with the evidence, and Charlie really needed to know about this. It was almost 11:30. He couldn't call her now. Lost in thought, he barely noticed the walk home. As he fumbled for his keys, he was still undecided. She would probably be in bed. He should sleep on it, but he couldn't stop thinking about the magpies, gathering on the roof, and that room. Eight days till Hunters moon.

At 4:30 am he caved and started to compose a message to Charlie.

- We need to talk.

Should he send the photos that he took? No. They wouldn't make any sense out of context. Charlie would know what to do. Charlie would have estimates of the time of death for all of the victims. After all that was her job. If it was a calendar, the dates would match up, and she could go to the police with it. He'd barely need to be involved at all.

Sleep was not long coming after that.

* * *

After the ritual Eva went back to Charlie's house, looking for comfort, but Charlie wasn't there. No one was there, except Thug, who greeted her with raised hackles at the door and continued hissing and keening from under the couch until she left, ten minutes later, as if he could sense what she'd been in contact with. She was contaminated. She couldn't stay there. Eva had gone to Charlie like a homing pigeon. But it wasn't just the way Thug reacted to her that hinted she no longer belonged in that space. The sense of Charlie missing was more profound. Charlie was...elsewhere. But Charlie wasn't here now. There was barely enough human left in Eva to wonder why Charlie wasn't home by 11:30 pm on a school night.

The magpie part of her wanted to fly. She ricocheted around like a pinball, building up kinetic energy, that burnt her up inside instead of sustaining her. Like a vampire to a dive bar in King's Cross that was open all night, and where there were always a few bored, well-heeled and jaded guys who would buy you a cocktail for a smile. At least that was how it used to work, when she took the time with her appearance. These days she must look more like a street worker. What was worse...invisibility, or disdain?

Back to her small room in the shared flat. At least it was quiet. Trembling legs. The last of what was human inside her battled to feel worthwhile, tears silently leaking from her shuttered eyes. She couldn't bring herself to care about anything. Oppressive walls. She couldn't move. For the longest time she just sat, hugging her knees, head tucked in. Eventually she lay down, just there, where she was, still foetal, eyes unfocused, hair lank and tangled, limbs clenched.

Could anyone save her now? What made her want to keep living so much anyway? There was no ambiguity left – she was just desperate to survive. She was trapped there, with her back against the wall, trapped in the disconnect, constantly reliving that moment when she was first abused. She was still atoning for the blood she had found on her underwear and hid, shamefully, after her first 'confession'. Everything she'd done to stay alive, to become stronger had destroyed the human part of her. She'd gone too far; broken the compact.

The bird-self had become a safety net, but she was tired of migrating, trade winds ever shifting – once-safe perches dissolved into the sea. Charlie was her anchor to the human race, and she had been cut adrift – and the pull was so strong in the other direction, the burden of sin so heavy. And in the end, did she have the strength to stay earthbound? So much easier to loosen that fragile bond and float free. Shed the ballast. Shed the guilt that was part of her human self. She dragged her past behind her like a trawl net. She needed to fly.

Now she's curled up on her bed, too drained even to remove her shoes. Before, if she got to that point, Charlie would take them of,; ease her arms out of the sleeves; navigate the bends in her stiff joints. Oh, where was Charlie now? Where was anything that could save her? Eva had gone so far into herself that only Charlie's warm, breathing, living self could gentle her back into the human dimension. Lacking that she was lost in the wilderness inside her. She was wandering somewhere dark, a narrow path cut through the mist. A signpost loomed up, but she was moving too fast to read it. An impression of stark white letters on the four arms that promised choice. There was only ever one direction for Eva. Aloft, tail feathers spread to catch the wind, she left the failed world behind.

She slept at last, an arm thrown out, carelessly, the other pillowing her cheek. She slept for hours, dreamless, aloft in a high place, full of stars.

The calling bird

I wake up with a jolt, and untangle myself from Chloe, who is still fast asleep. Fuck. Stupid phone is out of juice. What time is it?

The curtains are closed, and barely any light leaks through the edges. I look around the room for a clock, but no joy. Chloe's phone is sitting on the bedside table, but I don't want to reach across her and activate the screen, in case she wakes up and it looks weird. Anyway, whatever time it is, I probably need to get to work pronto. I wasn't much use yesterday, what with all the distractions, and the team can only operate for so long on autopilot.

Then the screen of Chloe's phone lights up with a notification and I get to see the time. 5:05 am. So the old body clock still works at least. I've been getting up at stupid o'clock for so long now that it must be ingrained. I relax slightly. I can still be in time. At least I've had plenty of sleep. It's been a while, but I've been known to go straight to work after an all-nighter. I used to call the Monday morning bus the red eye.

Chloe still hasn't stirred. I debate whether or not to wake her. On the one hand I don't want to sneak off again. Once was forgivable, but twice would be sheer bad manners. On the other, it is barely five in the morning, and that's a savage time to wake anyone who doesn't have to get up. She looks so peaceful in sleep. In fact she'd been peaceful to sleep with, as we spent a few pleasant hours making love with the gentle fuzziness of tipsy people.

It's a nice memory, but time's a wasting Charlie. Need to get on it. I get dressed quietly and turn around for a final glimpse before closing the bedroom door behind me. I step across the hall, down the steps, and out of the house.

When I get to work there's no one else there. Just how I like it in the morning. I plug in my dead phone and make tea in the small kitchen. When I get back to my desk the phone has powered itself on. There's a message from Laurence.

- We need to talk

I get a sinking feeling. I've waited too long to deal with this. I text him straight back.

- What's happened?

The answer comes immediately.

- I found this.

The next message comes through with a photo attached. It looks like it's been scanned from a magazine. I zoom in and call him straight away. He answers after two rings.

"What am I meant to be looking at? Relevance?"

"It's a lunar calendar and someone has marked up a bunch of dates. The most recent was three weeks ago. Didn't you mention one of those weird deaths round about then?"

His voice sounds different. He has purpose. And looking closer, I can see that about half of the entries are marked up with those red dots. I go with it for now.

"Carry on."

I reach for my list of anomalies. It takes moments to check my notes and tally the moon phases against their estimated dates of death. I don't like where this is going at all.

"There was a death in March that matches the full moon on your list. July and August seem plausible too. Where did you find this?"

"Eva's place."

What were you doing at Eva's place? So many questions…

I hold my tongue. I don't want to stop him now. His words tumble over themselves, as though he can't get them out fast enough.

"It was in a book. Old Moore's Almanac. Most of it was rubbish – horoscopes, that kind of thing - but there was a piece of paper marking the page with the moon dates. It made me wonder if she's using them as some kind of calendar?"

"Stop. Laurence. Take a breath, mate. Start at the beginning. What is this about the moon? Why do you think it's connected to the marks? What's it got to do with Eva?"

"Because I also found this."

My phone pings again. I recognise the symbols as soon as I see the sketch. At least, I recognise the last one in the series. It's a set of lines crossing each other in the shape of an M – and the very same mark I've found on multiple bodies. And what about those dates that are still in the future? The thought gives me such a shock I feel physically winded, and it takes me a few seconds to catch my breath. Maybe Laurence has actually got something here. Fuck. Doc told me to look for something less circumstantial. Could Laurence have found it? It makes more sense than saying Doc's responsible for all of those deaths. I feel like I've just walked into a December sea; the shock of freezing water. Fuck.

OK Charlie. You can deal with this.

"Laurence – we need to talk properly. When are you coming in?"

He hesitates, and I can almost hear static, as if he's thinking furiously.

"Don't you think it's better if we talk somewhere else?"

"Are you at home?"

"Probably best if we don't meet at my house. It's...not really...suitable. I could meet you in the Cut? It's not too far from Tommy's. What about that Thai café - it's only five minutes away?

"OK – but I won't be able to get away till noon."

"That works."

He sounds so relieved I get a sudden insight into just how

scared he is.

"I'd better get on now, Laurence. See you later."

I cut the call. Now I really need to talk to Eva. I can't approve of his methods, but he makes a convincing case.

Should I try her again? I need to hear her voice. I know I need to take this to the cops, but I can't bring myself to make that call. I need to speak to her. I owe Eva that much. And then there's Chloe. I'm not the kind of person that just moves on. Shit timing. Fuck it. I shut the office door and call Eva, only to get her voicemail.

"I'm sorry, I'm otherwise engaged right now, Leave your details and I'll get back to you."

Strangely business-like. I never asked Laurence how he ended up at her place. Never mind. Shit to get on with anyway. Park it.

Damn hard to concentrate though.

I just need to keep her safe, protect her, give her space to get better. I've had enough clues that there's been abuse. She hasn't said as much, but I can tell she's traumatised by something. All those nightmares. I thumb out another message to Eva.

- All OK darling? Checking in. Give me a shout please

I press send and spend a few moments staring at the screen blankly until it powers off. Zoe's arrival breaks the spell.

"Morning Boss – how's tricks? Want a brew?"

I glance at my stone cold tea, and realise that I'd not even taken a sip - I'd been that distracted, and I don't want Zoe to clock how stressed I am. Too many questions.

"No - I'm good - ta love."

I power on my computer. Usually I leave it to warm up while I make tea, but everything's the wrong way round this morning. I barely know up from down.

No time for that Charlie. Take a deep breath. This too shall pass.

When I arrive at our meeting place, Laurence is already there, hunched over a table at the back in the far corner nursing a can of diet coke. Almost lunchtime. I order a Pad Thai from the counter at the front, and then thread my way through the tables.

"Alright mate? I figured I might as well grab some lunch whilst I'm here. Probably won't get a chance later. Anything for you?"

He looks up, briefly, and shakes his head, before going back to worrying at a cuticle with his teeth. There's no point rushing him. I'm painfully aware that Eva has been keeping secrets from me, but I force myself to wait until he's ready. He gives a last savage bite at his thumb and seems to come to a decision.

"OK. Here goes. I think Eva's...I think she's responsible for the deaths. The ones they've been asking about. It's not Doc. He's just doing his own thing. Not that he's any saint – he's got his own troubles. But it's Eva that's got a thing for old white men. Not Doc."

"And you know this because?"

Laurence looks miserable, and I feel bad for pressing him.

"Well, actually I've kind of been following her. And. Umm...I've read a few of her text messages. I didn't mean to... at first it was just a feeling that something wasn't right. I saw her outside the hospital, with this old man, and they had this weird vibe going on between them. And then the next week, I saw her again, with a different guy, and it just kind of started from there."

Clearly my poker face isn't working. Laurence rushes on.

"I'm sorry. Initially I was just curious. And I didn't like the thought that she was messing you around. I didn't like the fact that you didn't seem happy."

OK – I'm going to need a lot more info here. First off,

I'm not sure how I feel about the fact that Laurence has been accessing Eva's private information. Reading her text messages. Stalking her. What if he's been reading mine? I've been too distracted to put two and two together. I need to know what he knows, and questioning his methods probably isn't the most constructive way forward right now. I gentle my voice and lean in towards him.

"Well, I'm glad you decided to share this with me. Mind if I ask why now?"

"Well...It's mainly because the police are involved now – and I don't want them pointing the finger at you. I was trying to protect you Charlie."

He pauses, and I can tell he's not quite finished. There's something else on his mind. More fidgeting and nail biting.

"Is there something else you want to say Laurence? Something I need to know that you haven't told me?"

He looks at me, measuring, as if wondering how much more to tell me. I can feel myself starting to lose my temper. For fuck's sake. I force myself to remain calm. I can't afford to scare him off now.

"I think she's about to do another one. There's this old guy in Bermondsey she's been hanging out with. I just felt like I needed to tell someone before he ends up in the mortuary like the others. The cops were looking for the wrong person."

We're both quiet for a little while as I digest what he's just told me.

"I see. So, now what? I mean, I get why you wanted to share this with me, instead of the cops, but I think I need to hear from Eva too."

Part of me can't quite believe Laurence, but he does seem to know a lot, and it fits too well. I've had my own suspicions. I'm glad that Doc doesn't appear to have killed anyone. I'm not sure I'd ever truly believed it anyway, not really. And worryingly, I can believe it of Eva. Can I honestly say we've been good for each other? She became a part of my life so quickly - and not in a good way. Things haven't felt right between us for months; we've been drifting apart. What do I even know about her? Not much it seems.

Meanwhile Laurence just sits there, like an eager puppy, waiting for a pat on the head or some fucking thing. He has to have been reading my messages too. I'll have to see about that. Not now though. I need to get to the bottom of this. The mortuary will just have to get along without me for now.

"Where's this place of hers?"

"Just near Southwark Bridge – Flatiron Square. There's a graffed up building – 'Good as Gold' – that's where I found the almanac, and the other things. I left the lock on, but it's not fastened. I'm pretty sure she's not there now though. I don't know where she is. Her phone's off."

"OK – thanks Laurence. Don't worry about the cops – I'll handle them. Appreciate you coming to me with this first. You did the right thing."

Laurence's face brightens as though I've just handed him a present.

***

When I get to O'Meara street I walk right in through the unlocked door, and up the stairs. Eva's not there.

I see the white room first. The simplicity of it. Why? I compare it to my cluttered little bolt hole. There's the desk, and two chairs, just like he said. I open the drawer. There is the almanac, and inside, marking her page, the note.

The black room. The first visceral shock of those scuffed chalk symbols which I recognise from not-long-historic investigations into ritual abuse, for which my department was asked to submit evidence. But not quite the same...

Candles burnt out. A chair overturned in the centre of a circle; scuffed chalk marks; feathers - and are those corpses magpies? Why magpies? And this is Eva's place?

It all seems like hearsay until you realise that maybe, unexpectedly, it's actually all true?

I make one last attempt to call her and get the same message. Those clipped tones. I think of all the bodies that have passed through the mortuary this year. Each of those men might still be alive if they'd never encountered Eva.

What if she's just wicked, and others need protecting from her? Maybe she needs something that I'm not qualified to give her, and the only way to protect her is to make this call. I've so many people to shield, not least of all myself. Do the right thing.

DC Owen's number goes straight through to voicemail. Shit - I hate voicemail. I thumb out a message.

- Call me please.

***

Eva woke from a dead sleep to the sound of ringing. She reached across and stared at the backlit screen, tried to make sense of the black lines that wiggled across it, but there were so many distractions. Voices. Messages in her head. A conversation continued from her dreams.

We must have the sacrifice. You are the calling bird. Snare one to catch one. Victor can do our work now.

There was just a tiny bit of Eva left, watching this from a corner of her mind. Isn't that how the country folk catch magpies? How have they learned to use our tricks against us? Trapped like a bird in a snare, she knew she would have to pay.

Mechanically, fingers pale and malleable as putty, Eva tapped out their message:

- Meet me outside the War Museum at 2 pm tomorrow? E
Send.

A snare is set

I get back to find organised chaos. A fire in a factory off Black Prince Road has left five dead, ranging from smoke inhalation, to one poor soul who will have to be identified from dental records. They need to know pronto whether it was arson, or negligence whilst under the influence. Zoe's done a great job keeping on top of it – they've all been registered and put on ice - but I'm soon neck-deep in paperwork, seeing what else I can move to get the PMs done pronto.

When I finally get a breather I check my phone. There's a message from Eva.

- Meet me outside the War Museum at 2 pm tomorrow? E

Why the Imperial War Museum? Does she know it used to be a lunatic asylum, where they locked up lesbians? Lunacy... moon madness. Probably just a coincidence. Does the kind of person who uses a moon calendar believe in coincidence? Maybe not. And it's walking distance from work.

And why tomorrow? Why not right now? I'm torn between worry for Eva's safety and fear of seeing her. Now that I know what she's capable of. Do I even know what that is? None of the bodies showed any signs of violence – just the cuts and the ligature marks. Apparently self-inflicted hangings. Am I being hasty assuming she's somehow complicit in their deaths? I can't make sense of it. I'm glad that DC Owen's on the case. I close my eyes and see that room again. I'm comfortable in the mortuary; death doesn't frighten me. There's a science to what I do; answers to be found. This is something else again.

"Fancy a brew guvnor?"

Zoe's surprisingly perky considering the afternoon she's had. We're all looking at some serious overtime before we can call it a night, and she's been dealing with the brunt of it whilst I was out.

"I'll make them. You take a load off. One hobnob or two?"

She sits down with a sigh of pleasure.

"Thanks Charlie – better make it two. You're right. Don't think I've sat down since I got in! It never rains but it pours."

I grab her cup from the corner of her desk as I pass by. Zoe's already logging into her computer.

"I might as well get on with rescheduling the cases we were meant to get through this afternoon. One of them can't be moved to tomorrow – religious reasons."

"I'll get onto that one Zoe, if you can cover the paperwork for the others?"

"Gotcha. Luke can take up some of the slack too."

I'm waiting for the tea to brew when the call comes in from DC Owen. I watch it ring several times whilst I gather my thoughts. This is not going to be an easy conversation.

"Charlie. It's DC Owen from Kennington. Have I caught you at a bad time?"

Don't overshare Charlie. Just the facts. I inject my customary brio into my tone.

"DC Owen! Of course not. It's been pretty hectic today, but actually your timing's perfect. I take it you got my message?"

"I did. Sorry it took me a little while to get back. I was out on a case. So. You mentioned you found something you want me to take a look at? Shall I come down to the hospital?"

"Actually I'm pretty snowed under this afternoon – I've got to go straight into a PM after this. Doubt I'll get out of here before seven."

"OK. So, what was it you wanted to show me?"

"Actually It's not at the hospital - it's somewhere else. I found out someone else is connected to the hangings. Her name is Eva. I came across some notes at her….in a building she's using that seems like it matches the pattern of deaths. I thought you should probably know sooner rather than later."

"Eva. What's Eva's second name? Is she a connection of yours? Do you have any photos of her?"

"Actually, she's my…girlfriend. Although we're not exactly on at the moment. It's kind of complicated. Look. I haven't got time to go into the detail now, but I should be a bit clearer tomorrow. She wants me to meet her at 2 pm outside the war museum on Kennington Road. I thought you should know about what I found out first. She was in the building with an old man. It looks like they were doing some kind of ritual, and the place is a right mess - all kinds of weird stuff there. How about I give you the address and you go and check it out?"

DC Owen is silent, still processing what I just said. It must have come across a bit weird; there's this person that suddenly turns up out of the blue, and she happens to be my girlfriend.

"You know, this probably seems a bit sudden. It honestly never occurred to me that she might have anything to do with it. She has been a bit weird lately – I thought maybe she was seeing someone else. I've been so busy at work I didn't really put two and two together."

"And do you know where she is now?"

"No. I've not seen her since Sunday. I've been trying to hold of her, but she's not been answering the phone. We don't live together."

"Do you have her address?"

"I know where it is, but I don't know the postcode. I've only been there once. We mostly hang out at my place."

"We don't need the postcode."

"Fine. OK - She has a flat-share in a block near Aylesford Street – on the Tachbrook Estate. I think the block's called Wren House? Third floor. It was the second flat along from the stairs."

"OK – we'll send someone there to check it out. And

where did you say her studio was? I gather that's a different location?"

"Yep – near Southwark Bridge – Flatiron Square. There's a building with the words 'good as gold' painted on the top. It was in there. The door's not locked. Her place is on the first floor."

"We'll check that out too. We'll need a photo - preferably recent. Tell her you'll meet her tomorrow. We'll be on hand to make sure you're safe, and take it from there. Is that OK with you, Charlie?"

I feel uneasy. He had assumed control. What have I got into? It's not just down to me though. I promised Laurence. And whatever else he's done, Doc deserves to have his name cleared as regards the hangings. Regardless of whatever else he's done.

"Yes, sorry, didn't mean to leave you hanging. I was just wondering what will happen with Doc."

"Do you mean Doctor Bernard?"

"Well – surely he couldn't have killed all those people could he? I don't think the stuff with the samples is even connected. Yes, he was stealing category two samples – but it's not like he was harvesting organs. I would have noticed that. Remand seems a bit heavy for what's basically a minor crime. He wouldn't be the first pathologist to hang onto samples for longer than he should. He's been silly, but I'm pretty sure he's not a killer. And there were no body parts missing from the victims. What's the motive, if he was supposed to have been running a tissue bank?"

"You seem very keen to defend him."

"Well, I've known him since I was a junior. He's been a mentor to a lot of people here."

"How about we find out what's going on with your girlfriend first, and then we'll look into it. Anything else I should know? Anything you might have forgotten to tell me?"

"Nothing I can think of right now."

"Ok. We'll be in touch."

As I hang up I feel a sense of disquiet. Shit. The photo. Of course I've got one - a selfie of course - the two of us smiling in anticipation of the night to come, cuntettes in the background - taken that first night, when I snapped her pic to go with the telephone number I left on her phone. Smooth move. Can I really do this? How have things gone from nought to sixty without us even having time to talk about what's going on? Where the fuck has she gone? No time to get into that now. I'm back in that room.

It's gone too far. Send the photo Charlie. Done. Time to scrub up. PMs won't do themselves.

***

It's hours before we're finally ready to wrap up for the day. The urgent case had turned out to be a bastard. Actual cause of death in fact not the obvious, with a suspicion of foul play. We'd got through the rest by working in tandem, the four of us working every table; drum and bass booming in the background. As I send the blood samples off for analysis, I'm actually fucking proud of how well the team works together when the shit hits the fan.

Whilst I'm cleaning up, I remember Chloe. This morning feels like it was about a year ago. Did I even remember to send her a text message?

I'd got distracted by Laurence. What must she think of me, sneaking out again without so much as a note. Bad manners, Charlie. She doesn't deserve that.

Am I being evasive because I enjoyed it a bit too much? I won't lie. And it's not exactly great timing. I should call her, but it's awkward and I feel like I can't tell her why. It feels shit. I really care about hurting her feelings. Not burning bridges. It matters whether I see her again. My finger hovers over the call button. She picks up after six rings.

"Hi Chloe."

"Charlie! I was kind of wondering whether I'd hear from you again."

"Yeah. Sorry about that. You looked so peaceful I didn't want to wake you. It's been crazy here today. I've been running around like a blue-arsed fly."

"Hey – don't worry. You've got a lot on."

"Still doesn't excuse my behaviour. I had a really nice time with you last night."

"So did I. We seem to be making a habit of this…"

Is she asking about Eva?

"Anyway, I just wanted to say sorry for running out like that."

"No need. When will I see you again? Are you busy this evening?"

Just a bit - and I really shouldn't. Now is probably not the time to get distracted. I need to track Eva down, and I'm pretty sure I'll be hearing from DC Owen once he's had a gander at those photos from O'Meara Street.

"I shouldn't really…. I need to go home. Feed Thug. Get an early night. Tomorrow looks just as crazy as today was."

"Hey I get it. Well, how about we leave it for now?"

She sounds disappointed – the joy in her voice that was there at the beginning of our call suddenly gone.

"Look, I'd really love to see you, but I'd better not. It's not just work. A whole load of things are pretty crazy right now. I'll call you as soon as I've got them sorted out a bit."

"Of course. Well, you know where I am if you change your mind."

★★★

When I get home Thug is outside the door loudly demanding dinner. I feed him, put some laundry on and assemble myself a snack. Then I contemplate the long evening ahead. I have the curiously uncomfortable thought that I'm alone here, and Eva's got a set of my keys.

"Chloe? I changed my mind. Are you still up for a visit?"

★★★

And where is Eva? Still there, curled up in a ball, catatonic – a game piece, waiting to be deployed. Is there even a tiny bit of Eva left inside, peering out through the bars of her prison? There's only a couple of moves left before the die is set.

End game

We stay up till one am, getting to know each other. She's smart, down to earth. Funny. The kind of person I could spend a long time with. In fact, I can't see any downsides. We take it easy - spooning and chatting. She doesn't ask about Eva. I try not to think about her. It's hard, but Chloe's presence is like a balm, soothing the knot in the heart of me that I hadn't even realised was there till now. Our bodies fit together as well as our minds. I'm walking into work with a spring in my step when I get a text from DC Owen. Back to earth with a bump.

- Forensics are at Flatiron square and we have people watching her house. I'll be at the Mortuary by 1 pm to brief you. Then we'll shadow you to the meeting.

What should I tell Zoe? She'll not be too pleased to hear I need to take the afternoon off again. Well, she'll just have to deal with it. I sigh and get the kettle on for tea.

* * *

DC Owen turns up promptly at 1 pm. As usual he is accompanied by his ginger sidekick. I sign them in to the mortuary, and take them to the family room, which I've booked out. Not only is it more spacious than my office, but for obvious reasons I don't want to have this conversation there.

The first clue that this meeting will have a very different tone to our last comes as Ginger takes the lead.

"Miss Tuesday. I take it you haven't heard anything more from Eva?"

"You can call me Charlie if you like. I thought we were on first name terms?"

"Miss Tuesday, I need to caution you that this is an active

investigation. We've not got much time until your rendez-vous. I'd appreciate it if you kept on topic. Now, I'll ask you again, have you heard from her?"

I take a long look at him and then decide that he's just doing his job. Not everyone is blessed with my charm.

"Not since we last spoke."

"We've had people following up on the addresses you gave us. They both check out. We also found the documents you mentioned and other items, which are being reviewed by the forensics team right now. Another team has been keeping an eye on your girlfriend. She left her home address about ten minutes ago and appears to be making her way to your meeting place on foot. I have officers shadowing her right now, and they'll alert us when she gets there. Let's talk about what's going to happen at the meeting."

I'm not sure I like the direction this is taking. I look over at DC Owen, but he doesn't meet my eye. Interesting. Maybe I've underestimated Ginger. Maybe he's the senior. It feels like he's been biding his time until he's ready to make his move.

"We'll have people stationed nearby, ready to take her into custody. You won't be in any danger."

"It's not my safety that I'm worried about mate."

He raises an eyebrow, as if to suggest I shouldn't interrupt him again…

"As I was saying…"

"Sorry."

"As I was saying, we'll have people stationed nearby. You'll probably have to get fairly close to her but try not to block the line of fire in case we need to intervene for your safety."

"The line of fire? I beg your pardon? She needs looking after, not just taking down. Shouldn't there be some kind of medical team there too?"

"Don't worry about that. We'll have specialist officers on site who are trained to deal with mental health issues. We'll need you to get close to her for long enough for our people to approach her, and we'll take it from there."

He pauses for a moment, and shoots me a long look, as if daring me to heckle. I don't take the bait. I'm feeling mutinous, but decide to hold it for now. Satisfied, he continues.

"Let's talk logistics. Is this a regular meeting place for the two of you?"

"No – it's not the kind of place we normally frequent."

I'm trying for irony, but he doesn't give an inch.

"And how familiar are you with the area around the museum?"

"I don't know it at all. I see it from the front when I go past on the bus. I guess maybe I've looked at it for a bit longer if the bus gets stuck in traffic, but I don't think I've been inside since year five, when we went there on a school trip."

"And you haven't agreed a meeting place – somewhere she'd expect you to go?

"No."

"And you didn't think to ask her?"

"I've been pretty busy you know! It's not like I've had time to sit down and think about it. I've got a mortuary to run, just in case you didn't notice."

"So what exactly were you planning to do, when you got there?"

He's got me there. I genuinely hadn't thought about it.

"I guess I was just planning to arrive at the front gate and take it from there. I mean she asked me to meet her. She's bound to be waiting. She knows I'll be coming from the direction of Tommy's."

He gives me a withering glance that says 'civilian!' and spreads a street map on the table between us.

"OK. So, here's the plan. We'll have officers stationed around the grounds here, here, here, and here – and one on the entrance in case she decides she wants a tour of the museum."

As he speaks, he jabs a thick finger at various points on the map. I gaze at it, trying to fit the two-dimensional representation into the view from the top of the 159. I hadn't realised the museum stood in such big grounds. It feels like he's missing something, but I can't quite put my finger on it.

"OK, that seems fine so far. But what about this bit?"

I wave a finger in the general direction of the expanse of green behind the main building.

"We considered the possibility that she might be in the peace garden on the west corner of the site. I'll put an extra officer on that side. Anything else?"

I look down at the table again, but I'm not seeing the map. I'm seeing Eva the last time we were together. She hadn't looked well at all. All of these preparations seemed like overkill. In all our fights she'd never laid a finger on me. The feeling of my fist smashing into her socket; the unexpected jarring of brow bone against my knuckles.

Not now Charlie.

"I think you've thought of everything."

I look up at the clock. It's already 1:30.

"Shouldn't I get going soon? It's probably at least a fifteen minute walk from here."

"No need for that. We have a car. We'll drop you off around the corner and you can take it from there."

"Seems like you've thought of everything."

"Just doing my job."

There's a grim satisfaction in his tone that brings me up short. I'm considering a snappy reply when DC Owen speaks for the first time since they arrived.

"Suspect is approaching via Black Prince Road."

"Excellent. OK, Miss Tuesday, I suggest you wrap up whatever you need to for today. We'll be leaving in five minutes."

***

By the time Eva reaches the museum she is almost totally magpie; her eye as mindless as a bird; the only imperative flight. She cocks her head, listening. They are not far away. They wait for her, a madrigal of magpies – lost souls angrily questioning their damned status. The last vestiges of her humanity crumble in the face of their cries. She is ready to take her place; the bait is set.

***

Eva is there, sitting with her back to me at a picnic bench under a group of mature plane trees just inside the entrance. It's a dank kind of place for a picnic – damp tables green with moss. A place that never sees the sun. She hasn't seen me – at least she doesn't give any sign that she has.

"Eva?"

She doesn't look around. She gets to her feet unsteadily and disappears with disjointed hopping steps through a gap in the hedge. Following her, I see her disappearing down a narrow path, bounded on one side by a high brick wall overgrown with ivy, and on the other by a colonnade of trees.

I stop and look around, conscious of the plain-clothes police that DC Owen has stationed around the grounds. A woman wearing the overalls and hi-vis of a gardener sees me looking and tips her head in my direction. That must be one of them. I feel a little less tense. I look back at the path, to see Eva in the distance, almost out of sight, with a surprising turn of speed. I raise my voice.

"Eva!"

She doesn't even pause. I quicken my pace and try and catch her up, but when I reach the bend she is nowhere to be seen. The path ahead is empty. By this point the trees bordering it have thinned, and I can see the entrance to a building site; hear the shouts of scaffolders and the ring of metal as they work. A helicopter drones past overhead, momentarily drowning out everything else, and then it's gone, to be replaced by the screams of children in a nearby playground. I walk towards the sound and realise that I'm in the middle of an orchard – trees now bare of fruit, leaves yellowing and thinning. Funny I've worked around here for years, and I never suspected it was here. Once I'm in amongst the trees the sounds of the city are muffled and I can hear the bustle and calls of birds, the whisper of leaves rubbing together.

Through the trees I can see a bench, tucked in between two rosemary bushes, with a thick bay hedge behind it. And there is Eva, a tiny figure hunched on one end, almost concealed by the greenery around her.

She still doesn't look at me. She's collapsed in on herself like an umbrella that's lost its struts, discarded on a wet autumnal day. No. That's not it – like one of those seabirds you see stranded on an oil-slick beach.

She looks up at me, just as the heavens open. Fat drops fall from the sky and I am suddenly wet through; everything blurred through a curtain of rain.

I take another step forward. I've forgotten about the backup, the plain-clothes cops, DC Owen, Doc, all of it. She seems so vulnerable. I just want to take her home and tuck her up and gentle her until she's whole again.

I'm close enough to touch her. I reach out, and gently take her chin in my cupped hand; tilt her face up towards me. Her eyes are huge and dark and empty; rain painting long black streaks of mascara down her face, shocking against the pallor of her skin.

As I gaze into those blank eyes, I realise that all the kindness, stability, therapy, care, in the world won't save her. I'm looking straight into the void at the centre of her; a gaping maw that swallows love, hate, everything, and munches it up, and uses it as fuel to find more prey.

I back off, and look around for DC Owen's people, ready for them to step up and take it from there, but there's no one else in sight. It's just the two of us.

At least that's how it seems at first, until I hear the beat of many wings, and I become aware that we're not in fact alone. The trees around us are heavy with hundreds of black and white birds - a murder of magpies loudly congregating, protesting, massing. As if triggered by my glance they scatter swiftly in a great whirl of feathers and claws and swoop in formation close above us and I feel wings and claws striking me - but I am not the target, Eva is.

At last I see them rise, and bank and turn in a great wave and disappear above the rooftops and spires and trees, and look down to see what she has become. A small twist of body discarded on the ground like a broken toy. Two bloody holes that were her eyes.

That's it. Turn the page. Walk away.

Even for a woman schooled in gore, it's a hard sight.

Epilogue

The air is cold, and full of damp - no friendly thermals
to lift me amidst the cliffs and outcrops of the conurbation.
There, rising above the trees that surround it, the block I'm
aiming for; on an upper floor an open window beckons. The
note I carry is damp too, clamped tightly in my beak. I glide
up to the windowsill, tuck in my wings, and rest a moment.
Inside all is quiet and dark. I hop once, twice, towards
the window and then I am on the ledge. I cock my head,
listening. Silence. Behind me the sounds of the city, the hum
of traffic, the distant wail of a siren. I tune it out, listening
ever more intently. Now I can hear a faint but regular sound
of breathing, as of one asleep. Good. I hop once more and I
am inside. I drop the note, and with it a weight of obligation.
Of need.

I flick my feathers once, twice, and then I am gone, tail
spread to catch the breeze, back to the highest fork of a
London plane, where my nest is, and where I'll find shelter
from the incoming storm.

Acknowledgements

This book was researched all over London, including visits to the mortuary of a large central London hospital. The staff were generous with their time, and kind enough to fact-check what I'd written later. Big props to R, T, and the gang.

Appreciation is due to Terence Rusike, Daniel Jacobs, Martin Millar, Eun-Ji Moores-Kang and Jemima Kiss - excellent editors, who between them made sure my characters never get on a bus and off a train, and to Mike Bennett for art direction and design skillz.

Night Shift is a love letter to Brixton, and the eagle-eyed may recognise some local cameos. Thanks are due to Hootananny, Everton, Sav, Paul and Keith Smith, and the rest of our wonderful community.

Zelda Rhiando,
Brixton, November 2024

For information about this and other Ampersand Press titles, contact nospam@badzelda.com

About the author

Zelda Rhiando was born in Dublin in 1973 and read English Literature at Cambridge. She lives in South London with her husband, two daughters and four cats. Night Shift is her third novel.

Scared and Trapped in the Double-sided Mirror of Life
There Is a Way Out

Ingrid L. Sobers

PublishAmerica
Baltimore

Hardcover 978-1-4489-3310-5
Softcover 978-1-4489-3311-2
PUBLISHED BY PUBLISHAMERICA, LLLP
www.publishamerica.com
Baltimore

Printed in the United States of America

Table of Contents

THE SONG OF MY LIFE ANALOGUE 9
Introduction 12
Falling Down and Getting Up Again 14
The Easter Sunday Morning Service 32
The Best Flowers in the Garden 38
Scared in the Jaws of Death for the Second Time 44
Access Denied Because Mercy Said No 54
Let No Man Put Asunder 63
Depression Is Your Enemy 81
The Bones Shall Live 90
Demotion verses Promotion 97
Your Destination is Determined by 101
Your Path 101
Unspeakable Joy 107
The Anointing of the Holy Spirit makes
    the Difference 116
He's Coming Back as a Judge 127
Tithing and Offering is a Privilege accept
    Your Blessing 136
Trouble in the Storm 141
Holy Spirit 142

Dedication

There is therefore now no condemnation to them which are in Christ Jesus, who walk not after the flesh, but after the Spirit. Romans 8:1

I dedicate this book first to Mrs. Ingrid Lavette Erica Durrant/Sobers. Yes, after God it's all about me! Selfish! Selfish! Selfish! I love it!

To those who feel, or have felt trapped in a relationship, where you felt like there was no way out, and to those who are in adulterous relationships and fornications, and those who are being manipulated and guilt, please know that the maze is not as confusing as it seems. Remember to fear God who can destroy both body and soul, not a woman or man who can take you for child support.

When you seek God, all other things will be given to you, including your **own** husband or wife.

There is a way out.
God!

Acknowledgement

For I reckon that the sufferings of this present time are not worthy to be compared with the glory which shall be revealed in us. Romans 8:18

First, I want to thank my heavenly father who is the head of my life. **Jehovah Jireh** who provided for me in ways I cannot explain. **Jehovah Rohr,** for the way he led and directed my path. **Jehovah Rophe,** my physician (healer) for touching my body, mind and soul.

I would also like to take the time to thank my husband, Mr. Brian Sobers. Yes! I would not have been inspired to write this book, had it not been for him. What the devil intended for evil, God turned it around for good.

I would like to thank my dad and Pastor Cecil Durrant, and my mom Evangelist Charita Durrant, for always being there for me. They have been very good listeners, and never led me on the wrong path.

Thank you to my sister Lafleur Durrant, who encouraged me to never give up! Although I am the big sister, she stepped in and took my place on many occasions.

I would like to thank my big brothers: Pastor Uzmond Durrant for the hugs and smiles that went such a long way and Othneil (Jason) Durrant for letting me know how much he loves me, whether it's by telling me, a hug, or by a gift.

Thank you to my younger brother Conley Duurnat who is always interested about what is going on in my life, or with my husband, and letting me know I am special.

I want to thank my sisters-in-law: Shelly-Ann Durrant, Nickel Durrant, and Lisa Guy, as well as my brothers-in-law, Vincent Sobers, Simon Sobers and all other families' in-laws whose names were not mentioned.

7

Thank you to my niece, Shamequa Durrant, who always sends me a text or two to remind me that she loves me, and checks up on me. She is the first person to be by my side if I am sick.

To my other nieces and nephew: Tieysha Durrant, Renee Durrant, Dominique Durrant, and Christopher Durrant, I love you!

I would like to also thank all my aunts and uncles, special thanks to aunty Merle Barnum who prayed and lend a shoulder for me to cry on. I am not forgetting my extended family, Bethany Deliverance Church of God Inc., or my friends Maria Williams, Bernadette Henry, and Madeleine Freedom.

Finally, I want to thank Publish America for giving me a voice, when no one could hear me.

The Song of My Life Analogue

As a child I rose up early every Sunday morning
To the fresh smell of the ocean breeze
Listening to the voice of the sea singing
And hearing the trees clapping and rejoicing
The birds making melodic music with their singing
The aroma of dry Coco, roast banana and fried chee-chee
The village buses honking, farmers cursing, babies crying
The neighbors laughing and the children chatting;
The voices of the Rastafarian "Hail Sa Lassie I;
Jah lives! You bald heads"
As the scent of the ganja lagged behind
That's my village on a typical Sunday.
A barefooted child I went to school
With roasted banana and hot cocoa tea
Hip and hop on the hot black pitch.
My grandmother made quilts to keep us warm
She smoked her tobacco pipe on the long porch
Swinging back and forth on her rocking chair to keep her calm
The smoke of her tobacco stained her false teeth.
Her great words of wisdom she constantly repeated
If you lose a piece of jewelry it can always be replaced
But a stain on your family's name can never be erased.

Durrant is durable; strong is the name
Under much pressure, strength remains
Reaches others who are distressed, depressed and oppressed
Rich in all fragrance of love and all shades
Answered as angels sent from above
No one else ever stained the family name
Take charge my child never put our name to shame.

I watched Mammy do the cooking, while scrawling down important dates
    She even washed the cups and all the dinner plates
    She's like a big diamond sitting in a rock
    Her laughter is like the rainbow grazing in the sky
    Her hair is like silk and her skin as wool.
    She is the best of all mammies God alone knows.
    Papa sat in black by the window,
    And hum an old church hymnal "where could I go"
    My grandpa hands tainted from working the farm
    He smelled like burned charcoal even from a far.
    The sound of voices as they echoed in the village
    "Take up yo coco rain ah go come"
    I am thirty and two maybe much more
    Mixed with a little of every known race
    I have blonde, black and curly hair
    Dark brown eyes, peach colored skin, and a straight pointed
nose;
    I am neither black nor white
    Neither Christian nor Jew
    Neither bond nor free
    Just a lowly homemaker with no ethnicity attached to me.
    Ingrid has an irresistible charm
    No one knows the secret of her calm
    Gracious and graceful is her soul
    Reflection of her past made her a woman very composed
    Intelligence guided her as the bright sunshine day
    Devoted, she is to her family, friends and even foe.

Sobers is the surname given to her for show
Open-minded person that is a fact for sure
Braveness is her strong pursuit
Expression is in line for review
Righteousness is her only source
Sociable person, she can offer more.

I've crossed the Atlantic Ocean, bypassed the pacific sea
Born on the beautiful island of St. Vincent and the Grenadines
Located in the West Indies, The place my ancestors knew as the Gems of the Antilles.
The island of special spices such as cinnamon and nutmeg;
I migrated to the big apple, land of copious opportunities
People of different nations united as one;
Negro, Indian, Spanish and thieves;
Long hair, short hair, curly and straight;
Gathered together awaiting the snake
Young men, old men, women and all
Hear comes the message but it's a little too late
Keep your wallet in your inside pockets.
The mouth is closed as the snake crawls away in its hole.
I heard the sound of the paper as they silently turned.
The whispers of voices as they communicated more
"Buenas noches" ¿Cómo estás? Then back it came "bien, gracias.
Another voice in the corner yelled, "How de do todie, mam"
As the other echoed "wowrific"! Thank you, kind sir.

Introduction

Sometimes in all of our lives we are scared about something whether as a child or an adult, and often feel like we are being trapped. Some people are afraid of the dark, some are afraid of losing a loved one and others are just afraid to be alone. It's quite ok to be scared, as a matter of fact it's normal, but it is not normal to always feel trapped especially in your own skin.

The definition of being scared is an emotional experienced in anticipation of some specific pain or danger (usually accompanied by a desire to flee or fight).

I was mandated to looked in the mirror and was forced to see a woman who wasn't there before, a woman who was depressed, one who felt like a loser, and someone who had loss the true value of love and friendship and couldn't understand that life is also about loss. I was trapped in my own mirror, knocked down a few times and did not know how to get up and get out of my double sided mirror. I had lost my faith and did not have the strength in me to rekindle the fire that went dim.

I look back on my life and check the mirror and found out I did not liking the reflection that I saw. I then realized that I am still a long way off from achieving all of my dreams, but I am well on my way. As a child I recall hearing the fairy tale line *"mirror, mirror on the wall who is the fairest of them all"?* I knew I was the fairest in my head, but in my heart I felt a sense of insecurity. The mirror reminded me that I was a woman of purpose and was destined for great things. I need to be an example to other women and that I was fearfully and wonderfully made in God's image and likeness. As women we need to keep it real, too often we belittle ourselves and make ourselves feel less than we are worth.

I nurtured my pain and distress, and it grew more and more, as I watered and manured it. I was so unhappy with that person I was seeing; I built up a hatred for myself. The mirror reminded me on one particular day that I was special and that Jesus loved me and died for me, and if no one else loved me Jesus loved me unconditionally.

Most women think that without a man we are incomplete; yes, it's true that God created man, and then he realized, that man was alone and needed a companion so he created woman. As women, we are helpmates created to be by a man's side, not under his feet and not over him. The bible mentions that the man is the head of the wife and that marriage is honorable and the bed is undefiled. Sometimes we may look in our mirrors and realize that not all women are marriage material, and then we get ourselves in situations where we are trapped without a clear way out.

Falling Down and Getting Up Again

The steps of a good man are ordered by the LORD, And He delights in his way. Though he fall, he shall not be utterly cast down; For the LORD upholds him with His hand. (Psalms 37:23-24 NKJV)

For He shall give His angels charge over you, To keep you in all you ways. In their hands they shall bear you up, Lest you dash your foot against a stone. (Psalms 91:11-12 NKJV)

I want you to imagine the sun blazing off the black-pitched road, the rain making the mud all saggy and the banks as if washing away. As an adult there is only one thing that I would change if I have to live life over again. I guess you are waiting to hear what that one thing is, keep reading.

My family did not have money but we had something that was more precious than money and that's love for each other and the Creator. One would say, love cannot go in the pot, but money cannot buy you love. There are people with all the money in the world and yet they are unhappy because they have no one to share it with.

I always heard my grandmother said, "Poverty is a crime", but I never really understood what she meant. I am the first child of eight (five boys and three girls). Growing up in a large family was very challenging. We had very little money to survive on. With just one parent working and eight children going to school, it was hard.

I was born on August 9, 1968 to two loving parents in the village of Lowmans Windward. My parents later relocated to the village of Redemption Sharps, where I grew up with five brothers and one sister as one boy and one girl died. At the age of 11 years old my mom migrated to the United States of America in pursuit of a better life for her family, as my dad was the only breadwinner of the family.

I became a young lady about two months later and was so ashamed that I kept it from everyone for about a year and a half until one day I had an accident and a very close family friend discovered what had happened and demanded that I told my dad. I did not, so she went with me and then the lecture started that I should stay away from boys because I am going to get pregnant. Every month afterwards I had to go to him for money to buy sanitary pads or ask him for them.

As was mentioned earlier I attended the Bishop's College High School in St. Vincent and the Grenadines. As a high school student, I was not as privileged as most of my classmates. For example, I had one pair of shoe, which was worn to school and to Church, while my friends wore two or three different pairs of shoes to school each week. My sibling and I had no break or lunch money as our friends did. Instead we took roasted bananas, fried bakes or dumpling with limejuice for lunch everyday, except for Mondays. On Mondays, we got two dollars each to buy lunch and take a van to or from school. Even with the two dollars, the only things we bought were Mauby and butter bread or pudding, from Ms Robinson.

One of the values that were instilled in us was to "make do" or "be contented with what we had". My pop would also quote what one wise writer stated, "In whatever state you're in to be content, "thou shall not covet thy neighbors' goods". My dad is a Pastor and had been a Pastor for over fifteen years. He tried to bring us up according to his biblical belief. We tried to obey his teaching to the best of our ability until one Friday morning when dad told us he had no money to give us for lunch and that we should stay home from school. Being the problem solver that I tried to be, I told him not to worry we would be O.K. So we had breakfast (bush tea and Roast plantain) and left for school.

At our lunch break, I met my siblings at our usual lunch place. At that time I had to make an ethical decision. So, we left and went to a place that we called "Mackies Hill." It was just above my High School, where everyone hung out after having lunch and before the bell rang to get back to class. There were also two other high schools in the vicinity. I knew what I was about to do was morally and ethically wrong. I knew if we got caught I could have ended up in a detention hall or my dad would kill me (figurative), but I could not have disappointed my brothers and sister. My dad was a very strict disciplinary. Some people would say that he was abusive but in my country we did not know what the word abuse meant. We believed, and I personally still believe spare not the rod and spoil the child. We often allow our children to embarrass us and when the law takes over and start abusing because we choose not to discipline them we have a problem.

So my siblings and I started on our way although we all knew we were going against everything that our parents taught us and what the law of the country was, but that did not stop us from stealing. So we got under a big grafted mango tree that belonged to Mrs. Rose. I took off my shoes and climbed up the tree to get lunch for my brothers and sister, while they stayed on the ground under the tree. I threw down their lunch to them; they ate and then I got my lunch and ate it up in the tree.

On my way down from the tree, I saw my siblings running. As I looked down, Ms. Rose was under the tree with two dogs (a black one and a brown one). By that time, all my friends and by-standers were laughing and scorning. I jumped from the top of the tree to the ground and began to run. The dogs at the bottom of the tree began chasing after me. The big brown dog held onto my skirt and ripped it off. That made my friends laughed harder. I felt so mortified.

That was not all; it took the police about five minutes to get there. By that time I was half naked, my skirt was completely ripped off and half of my blouse was in the dog's mouth. The police took me home, where my dad was waiting with his castigation. My dad whipped me from my village to Ms. Rose's house, which is about one mile away, to apologize to her and get my school bag and shoes. I became the laughing stock of the village. Fortunately for me no charge was brought against me, but the humiliation of that day will always stay with me.

I never really understood what my grandmother meant by "poverty is a crime" or what my dad meant by "make do" with what you have; until that day of embarrassment. My interpretation of my grandmother and father's phrases was poverty is not a crime, but the things you do because of poverty are the crimes. And one should always be content or satisfied with whatever little one has, in order to avoid embarrassment. The questions that I try to ask myself before making ethical and moral decisions now, is what will be the outcome, the consequence, and can I live with the outcome and consequence. Did I mess up after that? Yes I did, Millions of times.

It doesn't matter what you think you've done and how bad the crime may have been. There's Forgiveness of sins for everyone, which is one of the element of justification. The forgiveness of sins was granted freely, readily and abundantly. God hates sin; He cannot stand to look at its ugliness. Therefore, un-confessed sin in our lives comes between us and damages our relationship with the Lord. Not only does un-forgiveness come between God and us, it also breaks our relationships with others. *(Isaiah. 43:25 NKJV) "I, even I, am he that blotted out thy transgressions for mine own sake, and will not remember thy sins."*

(And refused to obey, neither were mindful of thy wonders that thou didst among them; but hardened their necks, and in their rebellion appointed a captain to return to their bondage: but thou art a God ready to pardon, gracious and merciful, slow to anger, and of great kindness, and forsookest them not." Nehemiah 9:17 NKJV); ("For thou, Lord, art good, and ready to forgive; and plenteous in mercy unto all them that call upon thee". Psalms 86:5 NKJV) ("Let the wicked forsake his ways and the evil man his thoughts: And let him turn to the LORD, and he will have mercy on him, and to our God, for he will freely pardon." Isaiah 55:7NKJV); ("Moreover the law entered that the offense might abound. But where sin abounded, grace abounded much more, so that as sin reigned in death, even so grace might reign through righteousness to eternal life through Jesus Christ our Lord." (Romans 5:20 & 21 NKJV).

As was mentioned earlier that God hates sin and because he hates sin he paid a high price for the forgiveness of our sins.

There are several requirements for the forgiveness of our sins when we fall down:

✓ Sacrifice: God send his only begotten son Jesus Christ who knew no sin to die on the cross and paid the ultimate sacrifice for our sins and bought our forgiveness by dying a shameful death on the cross. In Hebrew 9 verse 22 says, *"And almost all things are by the law purged with blood; and without shedding of blood is no remission."*
" In whom we have redemption through his blood, the forgiveness of sins, according to the riches of his grace;" (Ephesians 1:7)

"For Christ died for sins once and for all, the righteous for the unrighteous, to bring you to God." (1 Peter 3:18)

✓ Confession of sins: John in his writing in 1 John 1:9 says, *"if we confess our sins, he is faithful and just to forgive us our sins, and to cleanse us from all unrighteousness"*. We must realize we are living in sin and admit our sins to God in order to have a relationship with him.

✓ Forgiveness of others: God has made forgiving others a requirement for receiving his forgiveness. *"Be kind and compassionate to one another, forgiving each other, just as in Christ, God forgave you."* (Ephesians 4:32 NIV) *"For if you forgive men when they sin against you, your heavenly Father will also forgive you. But if you do not forgive men their sins, your Father will not forgive your sins."* (Matthew 6:14,15 NIV)

✓ Repentance: *"Therefore thus saith the LORD, If thou return, then will I bring thee again, and thou shalt stand before me: and if thou take forth the precious from the vile, thou shalt be as my mouth: let them return unto thee; but return not thou unto them."* (Jeremiah 15:19 KJV) *"For thus the Lord God, the Holy One of Israel, has said, In repentance and rest you will be saved, in quietness and trust is your strength."* (Isaiah 30:15 NASB).
One thing we need to remember is, after we repent the scripture say *"There is therefore now no condemnation to them which are in Christ Jesus, who walk not after the flesh, but after the Spirit"*. (Romans 8:1 KJV)
Pardon is an act of a supreme God, in pure dominion, that grant a remission of a prison term due to sin, but do not seek

honor nor reward from the pardoned. Justification on the other hand, is the act of a judge, and not of a sovereign, and includes pardon, and at the same time, we are entitled to all the rewards and blessings promised in the covenant of life. God absolves the sinner from the denunciation of the law, and that on account of the work of Christ; he removes the guilt of sin, or the sinner's actual liability to eternal wrath on account of it. The Ten Commandments are a summary of the immutable moral law. The finger of God on two tables of stone first wrote these laws to the children of Israel when they were encamped at Sinai. And Moses broke the first tablets when he brought them down from the mount, which had been thrown to the ground by him. He was then commanded of God, to take two other tables back into the mountain where God wrote on them "the words that were on the first tables". The tablets were afterwards placed in the Ark of the Covenant. They are called "the covenant" (Deut. 4:13), and "the tables of the covenant" and "the testimony."

There are perceptibly "ten" covenant/commandment in number, but their division is not fixed.

The commandments are:

- *Thou shalt have no other gods before me.* (Exodus 20:3 KJV) God will not share his glory with no one. He's an all knowing, all-powerful God. He's unchangeable. He is a righteous and loving God. He's a holy God and expects Holiness from his people.

- *Thou shalt not make unto thee any graven image, or any likeness of any thing that is in heaven above, or that is in the earth beneath, or that is in the water under the earth. Thou shalt not bow down thyself to them, nor serve them: for I the LORD thy God am a jealous God, visiting the iniquity of the fathers upon the children unto the third and fourth generation of them that hate me; And showing mercy unto thousands of them that love me, and keep my commandments. (Exodus 20:4,5 & 6 KJV)*

■ *Thou shalt not take the name of the LORD thy God in vain; for the LORD will not hold him guiltless that taketh his name in vain. (Exodus 20:7 KJV)*

■ *Remember the Sabbath day, to keep it holy. Six days shalt thou labor, and do all thy work: But the seventh day is the Sabbath of the LORD thy God: in it thou shalt not do any work, thou, nor thy son, nor thy daughter, thy manservant, nor thy maidservant, nor thy cattle, nor thy stranger that is within thy gates: For in six days the LORD made heaven and earth, the sea, and all that in them is, and rested the seventh day: wherefore the LORD blessed the Sabbath day, and hallowed it. (Exodus 20:8-11 KJV)*

■ *Honor thy father and thy mother: that thy days may be long upon the land which the LORD thy God giveth thee. (Exodus 20:12 KJV)*

■ *Thou shalt not kill. (Exodus 20:13 KJV) We will argue the point that we never kill anyone, but Jesus interpret this commandment, He said if you've ever had hate or malice in your heart, or hated someone, you are guilty of breaking that commandment. You are guilty of murder.*

■ *Thou shalt not commit adultery. (Exodus 20:14 KJV) There are two types of adultery mentioned in the bible spiritual adultery and sexual adultery. Many of us know about sexual adultery but we bypass the spiritual adultery.*

21

SEXUAL ADULTERY: This is marital unfaithfulness. An adulterer is a man who had or is having sexual intercourse with a woman he was or is not married to, with a married woman or one who is engaged to be married. A woman is called an adulteress. Adultery is Fornication that is deliberate sexual intercourse between a man and woman who are not married to each other. The Bible regards adultery as a great sin and a huge common wrong. John 8 mentioned "this sin became very common during the era previous to the destruction of Jerusalem". So often we think that it's not possible to commit Adultery without sexual intercourse, but Jesus Christ warned, "You have heard that it was said to those of old, you shall not commit adultery. But I say to you that whosoever looks at a woman to lust after her has committed adultery already with her in his heart." As with the breaking of any of the Ten Commandments, those who are not washed in the blood of Jesus Christ will have to pay the penalty of hell damnation. The Punishment for transgression of this Commandment is the death penalty.

SPIRITUAL ADULTERY—According to the Apostle Paul in his writing we becomes "betrothed" to Christ when we accept him as our personal Savior. This relationship will be consummated fully at Christ's return, so we have entered into a permanent covenant relationship with him. He placed an engagement ring on our finger which is the most expensive ring in the entire world and that is in the form of the Holy Spirit.

Some of the fruits of spiritual adultery are:

➢ **Idolatry, which is the worship of a person or any image that was created by man.**
   There are a few forms of idolatry:

♦ *Covetousness: is the excessive desire and greed for gain, which is a sin. Money and possession is not a sin but when they take the place of God in your heart it becomes a snare or stumbling block to one's spiritual walk that may lead to spiritual destruction. (Eccl. 5:10 NIV) state "Whoever loves money never has money enough; whoever loves wealth is never satisfied with his income. This too is meaningless."*

"Take heed, and beware of covetousness: for a man's life consisteth not in the abundance of the things which he possesseth." (Luke 12:15 KJV) Covetousness leads to "many sorrows" (1 Timothy 6:10; James 5:1). Only God can give true, lasting satisfaction (Psalms 107:9; Isaiah 55:1-2 and joy that cannot be taken away (John 16:22).

♦ *Apostasy is spoken of as spiritual adultery in Jeremiah 3:6, 8, 9, where the Prophet wrote about Israel backsliding. He mentioned that she is gone up upon every high mountain and under every green tree, and hath played the harlot. And her sister Judah saw it, and after Israel adultery, and did not return they were given a bill of divorcement. This did not trouble Judah, so they went out and played a harlot also. So she defiled the land and committed adultery with the stones and with stocks.*

There are several Steps that can be taken to emancipation (freedom) from your spiritual adultery. James gives us some examples in getting free from spiritual adultery in James 4:4-17

The First step is:

- Apprehending the degree of God's grace: No matter how far away from him we have strayed, he is a loving God and is always willing to take us back so we can rebuild the relationship with him. God is well able to supply us with the resources to live faithfully to him in the world.

The parable of the PRODIGAL SON in Luke 15:11-32 is one of the amazing features of God's grace. I often imagine hearing the prodigal son singing the song on his way home:

"I've wandered far away from God, now I'm coming home;
The paths of sin too long I've trod, Lord, I'm coming home.
Coming home, coming home, Nevermore to roam,
Open wide Thine arms of love, Lord, I'm coming home.
I've wasted many precious years, now I'm coming home;
I now repent with bitter tears, Lord, I'm coming home.
I'm tired of sin and straying, Lord, Now I'm coming home;
I'll trust Thy love, believe Thy Word, Lord, I'm coming
home.
My soul is sick, my heart is sore, Now I'm coming home;
My strength renew, my hope restore, Lord, I'm coming
home.
My only hope, my only plea, now I'm coming home;
that Jesus died, and died for me. Lord, I'm coming home.
I need His cleansing blood, I know, Now I'm coming home;
O wash me whiter than the snow, Lord, I'm coming home".

- Like the prodigal son you need to acknowledge your infidelity and turn from it. Comparable to a marriage there can be no real reconciliation in a marriage, which has experienced adultery except the adulterer confess, take responsibility, ask for forgiveness, and clearly turn away from the adulterous relationship, there will be no reunion.
- THE GRACE GOD GIVES IN RESPONSE: "He will exalt you". God will lift you up and show you off as his prized possession! He will flood your heart with assurance of his forgiveness and delight in his commitment to you. That's a

lot of grace! To restore an adulterous marriage, there must be sincere repentance and forgiveness. The unfaithful one must believe he has been forgiven by his/her significant other and resume personal intimacy in the relationship— sharing your thoughts, showing affection, and expressing interest in each other interests. God never become distant from us, too busy for us; in a marriage we often distance ourselves. We are the ones who often wander away from God so he gave us *a free will* to return to him. The statement we often make, is, we feel so far from God, one writer asks the question "guess who moved". The answer to that is we are the one who always move without a forwarding address. I read a quote, *"Maintaining relational intimacy is the best ways to prevent adultery in the first place. Allowing personal intimacy to deteriorate almost always precedes adultery. I am least likely to be romantically attracted to another person when I am regularly initiating with and investing in and enjoying my spouse".*

I often tell my husband that I will never cheat on him because I will never put myself in the place to be vulnerable. His respond is that maybe you are Job. No I am not Job I am a child of the King who is sustaining my body, and I try to maintain personal intimacy with my husband, which blinds my eyes to another person.

- As a new liberated people from our spiritual adultery we should get involved in the ministry of God and be his servants. God's calling on our lives is for us to serve him in battle and to declare war on the devil. We are to seek God's direction and then go to war with our whole heart. We are to be able to endure whatever comes our way as soldiers. Paul in his writing to young Timothy in (2 Timothy 2:2-3 KJV) says, "*and the things that thou hast heard of me among many witnesses, the same commit thou to faithful men, who shall be able to teach others also. Thou therefore endure hardness, as a good soldier of Jesus Christ.*" Our role is to communicate God's love and truth to those who don't know him, and to encourage other Christians in their walk. There is no lasting liberation from spiritual adultery that does not include cultivating a "wartime" lifestyle. As long as we totally submit our lives to God, Satan has no authority over our lives and his bars are broken as we submit our ways to God. Satan will try to attack us in various ways and try to inflict chaos and destruction in our lives, but as long as we walk humbly before God and stay in contact with him God will sustain us.

The commandment continues:

- *Thou shalt not steal. (Exodus 20:15KJV) To steal is, to **"take"** and carry away anything capable of being stolen, the property of another. When we hear about stealing we only zoom in on stealing a tangible possession from someone. Stealing someone's life from them is also stealing; stealing someone's spouse is stealing too. Not paying your tithes is stealing.*
- *Thou shalt not bear false witness against thy neighbor. (Exodus 20:16KJV) This person robs his neighbor of his reputation and the confidence of his friend. The best way to stop a false witness is to bring the individual face to face.*
- *Thou shalt not covet thy neighbor's house; thou shalt not covet thy neighbor's wife, nor his manservant, nor his maidservant, nor his ox, nor his ass, nor any thing that is thy neighbor's. Exodus 20:17 KJV*

According to (Acts 5:31; 13:38; 1 John 1:6-9) All sins are forgiven freely. The sinner is by this act of grace forever freed from the guilt and penalty of his sins. This is the uncharacteristic sanction of God (Ps. 130:4; Mark 2:5). It is offered to all in the gospel.

There are several benefits of God's forgiveness. Yes, we are all offered a great benefit package, which is the result of our forgiveness.

✓ ***Blessing (happiness): Psalmist David in (Psalms 32:1 & 2 KJV) "Blessed is he whose transgression is forgiven, whose sin is covered. Blessed is the man unto whom the LORD imputeth not iniquity, and in whose spirit there is no guile."***

✓ ***Removal of sin: When God forgives us he removes our sins "as far as the east is from the west, so far hath he removed our transgressions from us." (Psalms 103:12 KJV) So he looks at us brand new because he forgave us.***

✓ ***Sins are not held against us: Jesus Christ shed his blood to cover our sins so he does not hold our sins against us. He destroys our record. Isaiah wrote in Isaiah 43:25 KJV " I, even I, am he that blotteth out thy transgressions for mine own sake, and will not remember thy sins."***

✓ ***Forgiving ourselves: One of the hardest things to do as human is forgiving ourselves. When God forgives us we can forgive ourselves and live a life above sin. Brethren, I count not myself to have apprehended: but this one thing I do, forgetting those things which are behind, and reaching forth unto those things which are before, I press toward the mark for the prize of the high calling of God in Christ Jesus. (Philippians 3:13-14 KJV)***

Often when we mess up, people tend to hold our sins against us; they like to remind us of who we were and not who we are. They tend to force/pressure us back in the mirror. It doesn't matter whether you were a murderer, thief, fornicator or adulterer/adulteress your sins have been forgiving.

The people that are more incline to judge you are the people that you had been involve with sexually, and don't know how to let go. And those people more tend to be women. My message to all sisters out there, when its over it's over; sex does not buy love and having child/children to trap someone would just make the man resent you. If God love you enough to forgive you he will provide someone that is going to love you unconditionally. We all fall down at times, but we need to get up, dust our clothes off and move on.

As a teenager I enjoyed reading, I finished a book in one day, growing up the books that were available was Nancy Drew. I remember coming home from school and finishing my chores would be in my room or on a big grafted mango tree in the back of the yard. It was on my 12 birthday I was in my room and a family member visited and I was sexually molested. The more I said no, the more he forced himself on me. For years I did not forgive myself I felt violated and yes, it set me back for a while, but I realized I did nothing wrong.

Everyone has something in particular that set us apart from each other. Paul admonished Timothy in (Timothy 4:12 KJV) says, *"Let no man despise thy youth; but be thou an example of the believers, in word, in conversation, in charity, in spirit, in faith, in purity."* Let's look at Paul's advice a little closer.

The Apostle Paul addressed Timothy, as *"My son in the faith"* (1Timothy 1:2)

11 Timothy 1:6-8, Paul exhorted Timothy to stir up the gift he had received, reminding him of the power and love which were his by the Spirit of God, and hence he was not to be ashamed of the testimony nor of Paul in his imprisonment. All these instructions were not put on record for the sake of Timothy alone. They are for the help and instruction of every Christian young man, and woman from that day to this generation. Paul wrote to Timothy in chapter 4 verses *12 "let no man despise thy youth."* He admonished as to how a young Christian should act, so that his/her youth should not be despise. We should be an example to the believers in word, in conversation, in charity, in spirit, in faith and in purity.

In Word— *"Let no corrupt communication proceed out of your mouth, but that which is good to the use of edifying, that it may minister grace unto the hearers."* (Ephesians 4:29 KJV) This would include profanity, evil speaking, or gossip. (Leviticus 19: 16 KJV) *"Thou shalt not go up and down as a talebearer among thy people: neither shalt thou stand against the blood of thy neighbor: I am the LORD."* Talebearing is condemned by the word of God.

In Conversation/Conduct-Our lives must be worthy of the Gospel. (1 Thessalonians 5:21 KJV) *"Prove all things; hold fast that which is good."* Abstain from all appearance of evil. Are we living like we have been born again into the family of God, or are we living like we are part of the world?

In Charity-1 Corinthians 13 describes the divine way love works. Love does not behave itself unseemingly. If we speak with the tongues of men and angels, and have not love it sounds like a brass and tinkling cymbals. We should demonstrate love for all, both friend and foe. And he said to him, *"You shall love* *the Lord your God with all your heart and with all your mind.*" This is the great and first commandment. And a second is like it: you shall love your neighbor as yourself.

In Spirit-We must be zealous for the Lord. 1 Corinthians 15:58 KJV (*Therefore, my beloved brethren, be ye steadfast, unmovable, always abounding in the work of the Lord, forasmuch as ye know that your labor is not in vain in the Lord.*" If any man have not the spirits, resulting in the fruit, of which Galatians 5:22, 23 speaks, being seen in our lives. It is well to remember what spirit we are of.

In Faith-The Apostle Paul was speaking to, old as well as young, when he bade every man, *"For I say, through the grace given unto me, to every man that is among you, not to think of himself more highly than he ought to think; but to think soberly, according as God hath dealt to every man the measure of faith.*" (Romans 12:3 KJV) Hebrews 11 is the great faith chapter of the bible, and it shows us that where there is faith there is works. The words "by Faith or through faith" are found eighteen (18) times in chapter 11 reminding us that faith is practical. Abraham looked for a city whose builder and maker is God; and Moses endured as seeing him who is invisible in natural light.

In purity-Matthew 5:8 KJV *"Blessed are the pure in heart: for they shall see God."* Matthew 5:*28KJV "But I say unto you, that whosoever looketh on a woman to lust after her hath committed adultery with her already in his heart."* The Apostle Paul exhorted Timothy to treat the younger women as sisters, with all purity. (1 Timothy 5:2 KJV) It is true for saints as well for sinner that, *"Be not deceived; God is not mocked: for* *whatsoever a man soweth, that shall he also reap. "* (Galatians 6:7 KJV)

Respect is something that is earned. It comes with integrity in our hearts so that the world can respect us. If we take heed to the six exhortations, we will be greatly respected in our local Church, in our community, and our youth will not be despised.

The Easter Sunday Morning Service
Isaiah 53:4-8 KJV

Surely he hath borne our griefs, and carried our sorrows: yet we did esteem him stricken, smitten of God, and afflicted. But he was wounded for our transgressions; he was bruised for our iniquities: the chastisement of our peace was upon him; and with his stripes we are healed. All we like sheep have gone astray; we have turned everyone to his own way; and the LORD hath laid on him the iniquity of us all. He was oppressed, and he was afflicted, yet he opened not his mouth: he is brought as a lamb to the slaughter, and as a sheep before her shearers is dumb, so he openeth not his mouth. He was taken from prison and from judgment: and who shall declare his generation? for he was cut off out of the land of the living: for the transgression of my people was he stricken.

Easter Sunday or Resurrection Sunday is the day that Christian set aside to celebrate the resurrection of Jesus Christ from the dead. Easter is an annual celebration of the Resurrection. Even in Churches that traditionally do not observe the other seasons of the year, Easter has taken an essential place as the high point of Christian worship. Easter is a variable feast it, does not have a fixed date, but is determined by a system based on lunar calendar adapted from a formula decided by the Council of Nicaea in AD 325. The date of Easter can range between March 22 and April 25 depending on the lunar cycle. The two major seasons in the Christian Church year is Christmas and Easter. These two seasons are expressions of the hope that God has given to the world through the birth, death and resurrection of Jesus Christ.

Christian's belief that Jesus Christ died and rose from the dead on the third day after his death on the cross. Through the death, burial and resurrection the penalty of our sins was paid by Jesus Christ, thus purchasing our sins that whosoever believe in him will gain eternal life.

It was a very mild and breezy day in April, on a Sunday morning I was, sitting in the front seat of the church, the minister was preaching about the crucifixion of the Lord and his coming back for the saints and he'll be coming to judge those that did not accept him as their personal Savior and Lord. Church was very crowded to overflowing and with all the body heat, inside the building was hot and humid and the air conditioning was out of order. Some of the latecomers stood at the back while others wearing high heel shoes headed straight to the front of the Church disturbing the service. Handheld fans were distributed and paper towels were circulating the audience as the members and visitors tried to wipe the perspiration from their faces. The water fountain was being refilled every thirty minutes with water, while some members went to the corner store to purchase their own water.

The Minister continued to preach, and as he looked at the congregation; It seemed that he was looking at a particular group of people "...He's coming back in the cloud of glory not as a loving Savior but as a frowning Judge. He held his hip and shouted "Hallelujah I can feel the spirit upon me, and I'm here to tell you that fire and brimstone, hail and fire, hell is your destination and much more if you don't..."

Suddenly, sitting in the seat on the right of me was a middle aged lady with a broad hat barring the person behind her shouting out "Glory and so shall it be" There after the Minister was up and down the aisle, "I feel it, I feel it." I was lost and trying to feel it, as my cousin said, "I did not catch a one"; I did not feel a thing. As the Minister continued, the Deacon was running behind him trying to wipe the sweat from his face, but could not keep up. In the mean time there was another outburst from a handsome young man sitting in the back; it was as if he was out of breath, jumping up and down in his seat, and repeating over and over, "Thank you Lord, Thank you Lord, Hallelujah you are worthy…"

The children became confused and some began crying, while others were just fidgety. A few ushers tried to calm the children down, while another young lady fell to the floor as if she was having ague. She began shaking and the Minister continued preaching; seeing people became affected by his message inspired him more, "…and the Lord will strike you as in the days of Ananias and Sapphira." Ananias was one of the members of the Church at Jerusalem, who conspired with his wife Sapphira to deceive the Christian brothers, and as a result fell down and immediately died after he had uttered the falsehood (Acts 5:5). "You need Jesus; today is the acceptable day of salvation, eternal life is offered unto you. Are you going to be trapped in the double-sided mirror of life? Will you choose everlasting damnation or are you going to spend eternity with the Lord?" The organist began playing very softly as the preacher continued, Where would you spend eternity? Eternity, eternity, where will you spend eternity? Finally he stopped and the first lady began singing:

"Were you there when they crucified my Lord?
Were you there when they crucified my Lord?
Oh!
Sometimes it causes me to tremble, tremble, tremble.
Were you there when they crucified my Lord?
Were you there when they nailed him to the tree?

Were you there when they nailed him to the tree?
Oh!
Sometimes it causes me to tremble, tremble, tremble.
Were you there when they nailed him to the tree?
Were you there when they pierced him in the side?
Were you there when they pierced him in the side?
Oh!
Sometimes it causes me to tremble, tremble, tremble.
Were you there when they pierced him in the side?
Were you there when they laid him in the tomb?
Were you there when they laid him in the tomb?
Oh!
Sometimes it causes me to tremble, tremble, tremble.
Were you there when they laid him in the tomb?"

By now the alter was filled with people, especially young people and they began to cry. Some were jumping and the ushers were running back and forth with sheets, covering the legs of those that were on the floor and wearing short skirts and short blouses. I sat there as a spectator and looked around realizing that I was the only one in my seat; as a bystander. I walked over to where everyone was standing, a few seconds after I felt a hand around my shoulder and a voice whispering, "Today is the day of salvation. God wants to visit you; I can feel his present upon you." At that point I became confused and I looked at the person as she continued, "Just open your mouth, raise your hands and say anything that comes to mind." I replied nothing is coming to my mind and she began speaking in another language, muttering something sounding like, "who say me tata to" then she tried interpreting what she said "you are God's vessel" At that point, I was really lost/confused.

In all the years I spent in Church nothing really interest me more than watching the women and men "speaking in tongues" and then hearing the young people trying to imitate what some

35

of the elders of the Church had done. I remember one particular young lady started speaking in another language, and when I said another language I mean another language. Everyone said that she was "filled with the holy spirit" she had the "gift" I do not speak Spanish, but I could have sworn that it was Spanish she was speaking. I placed all my attention toward her as she began speaking in staccato, cutting her expressions very short, and appeared to be in a state ecstasy. The Church and the entire congregation became silent as if the young lady was alone with the benches. She continued for about five (5) minutes, after which the ushers assisted her to a seat and the musicians began playing again as the Minister prayed for those who remained at the altar.

A few minutes later another voice echoed, in a different language this time, and in the back row another started to, and another across the room and by then it seemed that they were all arguing with each other while I stood there more confused than ever.

In school I studied a little religion and some of the professors believed that religion is nothing more than a philosophy of life. Everyone has their own belief about life with their own unique stories about creation; no matter how uncivilized or backward it may sound.

After the morning service ended, I headed toward the door heading for home. As I walked towards the exit the minister met me at the door and expanded on his sermon. He stated that, "God was going to use me for the building up of His kingdom, and to glorify him and he calls the young because they are strong and the word abides in them." I left for home I somehow felt different. I felt peaceful like nothing bothered me, and I convinced myself it was because of the prayer and commotion that took place in Church.

The next Sunday I arrived at Church extra early than usual and not as a spectator but a partaker; it really felt good. I remember closing my eyes and for a split second felt a tear or two running down my cheeks. I immediately opened my eyes, making sure no one was looking at me and proceeded to sit down, but it did not help. I wanted to just screamed, so to avoid that I got up and advanced to the restroom. I felt like I was flying and thought to myself…you've got to be kidding! Trying to escape, I continued towards the exit and heard a voice saying, "you can run, but you cannot hide." I stopped and looked around to see who had spoken; it was an unfamiliar voice, but there was no one. I continued the journey and the same voice called me by name Lavette Ingrid Erica Durrant. Remembering the story about Samuel that was taught in Sunday school; I convinced myself that it was impossible, it was just my imagination. It seemed like forever getting to the restroom, so I stopped and sat on a chair in the back and still heard the voice so, I did as Samuel and answered "Yes Lord thy servant heareth." Immediately tears began to flow and the things that were a mockery to me, I now could not controlled, from then on my life has never been the same.

I am in love with the Lord, yes I still don't speak in tongue or another language, but I ask God for the discerning of Spirit.

The Best Flowers in the Garden

1 Corinthians 15:55-57
O death, where is thy sting? O grave, where is thy victory?
The sting of death is sin; and the strength of sin is the law.
But thanks be to God, which giveth us the victory through
our Lord Jesus Christ.

There are times when we all like to stop, smell the sweet smelling aroma of flowers, and if given the opportunity to choose our own, we will pick the best flowers from the garden. There are times when it's ok to pick the best flowers, but there are times when I believe that the best flowers should be left in the garden for others to see and enjoy.

The days are always, hot in the island, but not humid.

This particular morning my family got up as usual and had devotion and we started our chores. One of my big brothers who were very talented in sports and charming to the ladies went outside. As my brother woke up he went out in the yard a health young man with not a care in the world. He was the partner of another big brother who in his own way was also talented and a "woman's man." His specialty was singing and music. They were like day and night in looks and talent. They were both unique in their own way and were both loved differently.

Worth-tee was very skilled in woodwork as was his brother, but I really don't think he was into it until later on in life after the tragedy of his brother.

The sun was up and the neighbors were on their way to work and I remember getting home and my brother was in a lot of pain.

Death, whether to a friend or family member is considered to be the most disturbing for any type of families and their friend/ associates. A death in the family can require major poignant and social changes whenever or however it occurs. The Death of my brother involved a sense of distress to the entire family and friends. It took me personally a while to come to terms with the loss of my big brother. My brother died at the age of 17 years after the doctors could not tell what the problem was.

It was Feb 17, 1986 I visited my brother where he was staying in Peninston Village and we laugh and had fun, just before leaving for home he asked me for some water he was thirsty; I got the water and he asked me to feed the water to him. I fed him the first glass of water and he asked for a second glass and then I kiss him good night. I left and went to get a van that was going to Kingstown and it was about 9:30 pm on February 17. I got a van about 10:30 and headed into Kingstown, when I got to the bus stop I met a friend who was waiting for me and he was sad, so I hugged him, and ask him what the problem was? He did not answer he said that my dad was waiting for me and he would explain. In the back of my head I thought I was in trouble for staying out so late and did not even call. So we then headed home and by the time I got to my village, the village street was full of people on the street and my entire family was on the porch/veranda. I then entered the yard and met my sister crying and for a moment it seemed that my heart stopped beating and my dad was sad, he tried covering it up, but he was not a very good actor. The first thing that came to mind was (oh my God!) my mom, as she was in the United States. My brother did not cross my mind as I had just left him looking healthy and stronger than he had been for months since he got sick. My dad then said to me that Worth-tee was dead. I froze for a while and then the tears just came rolling down my cheeks because I remember my brother asking me to give him his last drink of water before he went home to be with his heavenly father who wanted to spend sometime with him, and take good care of him.

I know that he's in a better place; I wondered why God had to pick the most beautiful flower in the garden, he was not as handsome as his other twin brother, but had a beautiful heart. His favorite song was:

"*Where He may lead me I will go,*
For I have learned to trust Him so;
And I remember 'twas for me
That He was slain on Calvary.
Refrain:
Jesus shall lead me night and day,
Jesus shall lead me all the way;
He is the truest friend to me,
For I remember Calvary.

O I delight in His command,
Love to be led by His dear hand;
His divine will is sweet to me, Hallowed by blood-stained Calvary.

Onward I go, nor doubt nor fear,
Happy with Christ, my Savior, near;
Trusting some day that I shall see
Jesus, my Friend of Calvary.

The funeral service was about two to three weeks later, as we awaited the arrival of our mom. It was a service with a different. Before my brother died he would always say, he did not want anyone to cry for him or over him. At the service there were no tears until his other half (twin brother) sang:

"*I'm kind of homesick for a country*

To which I've never been before
No sad goodbyes will there be spoken
For time won't matter anymore
Chorus:
Beulah Land, I'm longing for you
And someday on thee I'll stand
There my home will be eternal
Beulah Land, sweet Beulah Land

I'm looking out across the river
Where my faith will end in sight
There's just a few more days to labor
Then I will take my Heavenly flight

Immediately following that song my cousin who is physically blind sang another song,

"I'll singing glory, glory hallelujah 'I'll singing glory, glory hallelujah

I'll singing glory, glory hallelujah when I take my flight to my home on high,

There'll be no more sorrow there no more pain for the former things will be past away when I take my flight to my home on high. There'll be no more sickness no more burden's to bear no more pain no more parting over there, there'll be peace forevermore on that happy golden shore what a day glorious day that will be." Soon after that song the minister spoke for a few minutes and it was dynamic. He began by reading (1 Corinthians 15:54 KJV) *"So when this corruptible shall have put on incorruption, and this mortal shall have put on immortality, then shall be brought to pass the saying that is written, Death is swallowed up in victory."* He went on to say, "all the saints should not die, but all would be changed. Death never shall appear in the regions to which our Lord will bear his

41

risen saints. Therefore let us seek the full assurance of faith and hope, which in the midst of pain, and in the midst of death, we may think calmly on the horrors of the tomb; assured that our bodies will just be sleeping, and in the mean time our souls will be present with the Lord, Because of sin death gets all its hurtful power. The sting of death is sin, but Christ, by dying, has taken out this sting; he has made atonement for sin, he has obtained remission of it. Death may confiscate a believer, but it cannot hold him in its power." One writer wrote and I quote *"How many springs of joy to the saints, and of thanksgiving to God, are opened by the death and resurrection, the sufferings and conquests of the Redeemer!"*

We then started to the burial ground (cemetery) and on the way there we sang, and praise all the way there. It was as the Bible said, you should rejoice when someone died in Christ, which means they are in a better place. I know my brother has no more pain, no more sorrow and he has a purified body in modified clothing.

Death is something that's permanent for those of us who haven't tried it, know someone that has tried, if someone died out of Christ. It is a tragic situation when death comes knocking, especially when destiny shows up before time, we have to open up or he/she breaks the door down. It has no direction as to where the tide takes him/her. Death travels the world it's always on vacation, but yet never takes a vacation.

Death is as scary monsters that come alive for those that have not died or for those who have loved ones that died out of Christ.

My problem with my brother's death coincided with the death of my grandmothers. To me it was as if death was in season, it was one after the other. I thought about some of the things my brother said to me and at times I would feel sad, but not for long. And for a while it seemed I was losing him (his memory) and would think back. I would remember thinks that we went through together as kids. For example, One day a girl hit him and he hit her back, and she went and complaint to the teacher and my dad had to go to the school. When asked by the adults, why did you hit her? His reply was "I didn't latch she, she first latch me, and I latch she back."

A few days after we were on our way back from lunch, and he said I need to go to the bathroom. We began running to the school along with our other siblings. As we got a few yards from the school my brother stop running and I stopped and asked, why are you stopping? He turned to me and said, "It's too late!" I was a bit confused so I asked, too late? He replied, "yes it's too late, I'm finish." I was so mad, I had to take him behind a printing shop wash his pants and let him put it back on, as we headed up to school. If I have such memories I can't imagine how his other brother feels.

In our culture we believe that twins and triplets share more than regular siblings separated by age, we believe that they may genuinely feel what the other is feeling. The death of a twin or triplet whether an adult or a child, is also thought to have its own scrupulous distressing character. They lost not only a brother or sister, but also a part of themselves.

Scared in the Jaws of Death for the Second Time

"He holds victory in store for the upright, he is a shield to those whose walk is blameless, for he guards the course of the just and protects the way of his faithful ones."
(Pr 2:7-8 NIV)

A Soldier is someone that fights to defend. Their duties are to guard and protect everything within the limits. He/she is led by a commander in chief. In the United States, that would be the President. As Commander-in-Chief, the U.S. President outranks any military Officer and so has the inherent right to assume command on the battlefield. According to one writer the Soldier's creed is:

"I am an American Solider.

I am a Warrior and a member of a team.

I serve the people of the United States, and live the Army Values.

I will always place the mission first.

I will never accept defeat.

I will never quit.

I will never leave a fallen comrade.

I am disciplined, physically and mentally tough,

Trained and proficient in my warrior tasks and drills.

I always maintain my arms, my equipment and myself.

I am an expert and I am a professional.

I stand ready to deploy, engage, and destroy, the enemies of the United States of America in close combat.

I am a guardian of freedom and the American way of life.

I am an American Soldier."

As children of God we are soldiers in the army of the Lord and we are commanded by our commander-in-chief, which is the Holy Spirit to put on the whole armor of God that we may able to stand against the wiles of the devil, our number one enemy. Often, as children of God we fight our battle without the direct order from the commander-in-chief we fight in our own strength and we get hurt or killed in the process because we have no backup. The only way to be strong is in the Lord and in the power of his might. Our strength must come from the Lord, doing thing in our own strength we often set ourselves up to fail. When we fight in God's strength we are compensated for our own weaknesses. Philippians says, "I can do all things through Christ who strengthens me through danger that is seen and unseen." As soldiers' in the army of the Lord we are to take the whole armor of God that we may be able to withstand in the evil day, and having done all to stand. *"For we wrestle not against flesh and blood, but against principalities, against powers, against the rulers of the darkness of this world, against spiritual wickedness in high places."*

The battle we are fighting and about to fight for those who did not start fighting is a spiritual battle. The enemies' job is to try to knock us out of our spiritual walk, so that other soldiers would not have the opportunity to join the army of the Lord. There are spiritual and physical antagonisms that we must be willing to meet as soldiers of God. We must be fit and healthy for this spiritual battle, and the only way for us to stay fit is by studying the word of God, praying and fasting.

The pieces of clothing that the soldiers in God army needs are the belt, the breastplate, helmet, shoes, and the sword. The belt is use to hold the weapons together and keep the rest of the garment together for war. The belt is a symbol of truth according to Ephesians 6:14… "We art to fasten the belt of truth around our waist, and faithfulness the belt of his loins." 1 Kings 18:46 (NIV) *"The power of the Lord came upon Elijah and, tucking his cloak into his belt, he ran ahead of Ahab all the way to Jezreel. "* And we must remember that our commander-in-Chief is a spirit and we must worship him in spirit and truth.

The next piece of clothing that we should be wearing is the breastplate, which is righteousness. Isaiah 29:16-17 (NAS)…Then his own arm brought salvation to him, and his righteousness upheld him. He put on righteousness like a breastplate, and a helmet of salvation on his head…Pr 2:7-8 (NIV) *He holds victory in store for the upright, he is a shield to those whose walk is blameless, for he guards the course of the just and protects the way of his faithful ones.* Then you will understand what is right and just, and fair-every good path.

The next piece of clothing is the shoe. Some of us have soft feet we cannot stand the wear and tear of being without shoe. As a child I grew up with one pair of shoe that I had to wear to school, Church, and everywhere I go. I grew up in St.Vincent where it is hot and the pitch (street) will be scalding in the day, because of the wear and tear of the shoe there were holes at the bottom of the shoe, so I had to hip and hop all the way home. In the Christian walk we are prepared with a shoe for our feet that is fitted with the readiness that comes from the gospel of peace according to Ephesians 6:15. (Romans 10:15 KJV) described it perfectly *"And how shall they preach, except they be sent? as it is written, How beautiful are the feet of them that preach the gospel of peace, and bring glad tidings of good things!"* (Galatians 5:16-18 KJV) says *"This I say then, Walk in the Spirit, and ye shall not fulfill the lust of the flesh. For the flesh lusteth against the Spirit, and the Spirit against the flesh: and these are contrary the one to the other: so that ye cannot do the things that ye would. But if ye be led of the Spirit, ye are not under the law."*

Finally we have the helmet, which is salvation. The helmet protects the brain. It is our assurance of salvation that keeps our mind focused on Christ that when thoughts come that might discourage us we will be prepared to answer them with the sword, which is God's word. We should be so grounded in the word of God, that we would be able to stop the attack of the enemy when he strikes. (1 Thessalonians-Chapter 5:8 KJV) *states "but let us, who are of the day, be sober, putting on the breastplate of faith and love; and for a helmet, the hope of salvation."* (2 Corinthians 10:3-5 KJV) *"For though we walk in the flesh, we do not war after the flesh: (For the weapons of our warfare are not carnal, but mighty through God to the pulling down of strong holds ;) Casting down imaginations, and every high thing that exalteth itself against the knowledge of God, and bringing into captivity every thought to the obedience of Christ;"* (Ephesians 4:14-16 KJV)... *"That we henceforth be no more children, tossed to and fro, and carried about with every wind of doctrine, by the sleight of men, and cunning craftiness, whereby they lie in wait to deceive; But speaking the truth in love, may grow up into him in all things, which is the head, even Christ: From whom the whole body fitly joined together and compacted by that which every joint supplieth, according to the effectual working in the measure of every part, maketh increase of the body unto the edifying of itself in love."*

Now that we are dress we must carry the Sword of the Spirit and that is the word of God. (Isaiah 49:2 NIV) (*"He made my mouth like a sharpened sword, in the shadow of his hand he hid me; he made me into a polished arrow and concealed me in his quiver."* (Hebrews 4:12-13 KJV) *"For the word of God is quick, and powerful, and sharper than any twoedged sword, piercing even to the dividing asunder of soul and spirit, and of the joints and marrow, and is a discerner of the thoughts and intents of the heart. Neither is there any creature that is not manifest in his sight: but all things are naked and opened unto the eyes of him with whom we have to do." (P*salm 149:4-6 KJV) *"For the LORD taketh pleasure in his people: he will beautify the meek with salvation. Let the saints be joyful in glory: let them sing aloud upon their beds. Let the high praises of God be in their mouth, and a two-edged sword in their hand."* With the sword we need a Shield which is the shield of faith, Ephesians 6:16 encourages us that… *"above all, taking the shield of faith, wherewith ye shall be able to quench all the fiery darts of the wicked."* (Psalms 33:20 KJV) *"Our soul waiteth for the LORD: he is our help and our shield."*

I've mentioned how to be prepared for the war now I'm going to explain some of the darts that the enemy will be firing at you. Some of the fiery darts of the enemy at war is broken families, drugs, sex and emotional distress; lately these are the hot topics.

One of the darts that the devil use to get to God's people or to keep soldiers out of the army is the use of drugs:

It was in 1990 when I was faced with the situation of watching another sibling and not only another sibling, but also my one and only sister went through what my elder brother went through. I remembered her being locked away in the Intensive Care Unit (ICU) after being diagnosed with cancer. She was a drug addict and was far from God.

As mentioned earlier we were brought up in a Christian home, and our father every morning would faithfully have devotion with us and would give us an opportunity to share on the scriptures. Our parents both mother and father tried to bring us up to do the right things in life, but my sister refused to follow our parents rules.

She started smoking and clubbing, following the wrong crowd at twelve years old. She started to sleep on the street, and at friend's house. My father would talk and use the rod, but it went through one ear and out the other and as soon as the pain of the spanking wore off she would go again. My Dad got worried so many times and deep down I knew that he loved and still loves us all, but she just wanted to have her own way.

At the age of sixteen she became pregnant and now has a beautiful young lady, but it was not easy for her. In spite of the hardship she faced, that did not change her, instead it made her got worst; she committed one crime/sin after another. She started on drugs and fed her habit by stealing from all family members. The pawned shops were her home away from home. She would steal the family's jewelry and pawn them. One time she even stole my mom's rent money and knowing that it was all the money my mom had. I had my own room and I would leave for work and lock the door on evenings when I got home I would meet the door open, but was not broken into. My graduation rings a gold and a silver was missing, it took me about three (3) months to look for them only to realized later that they were pawned by my sister.

It is just God's mercy that she was not killed, I can remember many time she would just smoke and live her life like there's no tomorrow, I remember she would come home, after not seeing her for days and would just look up and say "God have mercy, don't let me die in my sin!" She knew if she died, where her eternity would be spent. I knew the memories of all of us childhood bible stories stayed in her heart as it stayed in mine. Sometimes the thought of suicide would cross her mind, but then I knew that she remembered there's a place call **HELL!**

Hell is defined as "a place of pain and turmoil where Satan abode and the forces of evil, and where sinners suffer eternal punishment." We often ask the question "is hell real?" We also ask if God is such a loving God, why would he create a place of torment call hell? Hell exists because some of us choose continually to do the wrong things, and need to be punished. God created us to have a freedom of choice, Life or death, hell or heaven, good or bad. When God made creation, there was no mention of hell until the devil tried to overthrow God in Matthew 25:41, it mentioned that hell was prepared for the devil and his angels it was not created for man. (2 Peter 3:9 KJV) tells us that *"The Lord is not slack concerning his promise, as some men count slackness; but is longsuffering to us-ward, not willing that any should perish, but that all should come to repentance."* There are over 162 references in the New Testament, which warns of hell. In (Matthew 25:41 KJV), Jesus says: *" Then shall he say also unto them on the left hand, Depart from me, ye cursed, into everlasting fire, prepared for the devil and his angels:"*

(Revelation 20:15 KJV) says, *"And whosoever was not found written in the book of life was cast into the **LAKE OF FIRE**."*

In (Matthew 13:42 KJV), Jesus says: *"And shall cast them into a **FURNACE OF FIRE**: there shall be wailing and gnashing of teeth."*

The man in (Luke 16:24 KJV) cries: *"…I am tormented in this **FLAME**."*

Luke 16 mentions a frightening picture of hell. The story was told about a rich man and Lazarus in their lifetime the rich man received good things and Lazarus had nothing, he was very poor. The rich man died, and was buried, and lifted up his eyes, being in torment, afar off, he saw Lazarus who also died was in Abraham's bosom. The rich man cried and asks Father Abraham to have mercy on him and to send Lazarus that he may dip the tip of his finger in water, to cool my tongue; for I am tormented in this flame. But father Abraham reminded the rich man that in his lifetime he had all good things, while Lazarus evil things; but now Lazarus is comforted, and thou art tormented. And beside all this, between us there is a great gulf fixed: so that they that would pass from hence to you cannot; neither can they pass to us that would come from thence. The rich man then begged to send Lazarus to his father's house: For he has five brethren; that he may testify unto them, lest they also come into this **place of torment.** (Luke 16:22-28)

Another question we often ask is "where is hell located?" The bible gives a clear location of hell. When Jesus Christ died on the cross, He descended into hell (To descend means to go down). (Acts 2:31 KJV) " *... Seeing this before spake of the resurrection of Christ that his soul was not left in **Hell** neither his flesh did see corruption.* "

(Matthew 12:40 KJV) mentions that *"For as Jonas were three days and three nights in the whale's belly: so shall the Son of man be three days and three nights in the **HEART OF THE EARTH.** "*

(Ephesians 4:9 KJV), states: *"Now that he ascended, what is it but that he also descended first into the **LOWER PARTS OF THE EARTH**. "*The Bible is clear—***Hell is inside the earth!***

So far according to scripture the present hell, is somewhere in the heart of the earth itself. It is also called "the pit" (Isa. 14:9, 15: Ezek. 32:18-21) and "the abyss" (Rev. 9:2)…

One day I know my sister was minding her own business forgetting there was a God and a hell as described only to find out that she was diagnosed with cancer. But somewhere in heaven, Jesus, the friend of all sinners, who came, that sinners would come to repentance, was looking down on her broken and contrived heart. In-spite of the condition she was in, she knew that she needed help, and sincerely wanted to do the right thing.

I remember being at home as I hated the hospital, much more the ICU and got a call from my dad. He stated that Lafleur was waking up and still in the ICU (Intensive Care Unit), and stated that she knew that she had to surrender her life totally to God. And that she wanted the peace and happiness that others had. If you wanted to know about heartache, pain, misery, anger and hatred, she can tell you or even write a book about it. Lafleur came out of the Hospital one Thanksgiving morning and went to Bethany Deliverance Church of God in Christ (Pentecostal) where our father is the pastor and knelt at the foot of the cross. I remember hearing her saying "Lord if you save me, my life belongs to you" then sang the song that I loved so much, *"Like a ship that was tossed and driven, led by a morning angry sea, when the storms of life are raging and the spirit falls on me, Lord I wonder what I've done to make this race so hard to run; but I say to my soul don't worry the Lord will make a way some how. Then I say to my soul take courage, the Lord will make a way somehow."* she surrendered and the Lord saved her and gave her an everlasting peace of mind and removed all pain, anger and misery. For days, she just went about just being thankful and trying to be a living testimony of what God's grace and mercy can do. After years of being on drugs she never went to rehab, and thank God for his healing power she is cancer free.

She had been forgiven by all of those that she have offended, but most of all by the one that can destroy both body and soul. God delivered her from all her sins and bad habits that had her bound over 8 years now she is set free. He took the shackles of chains that had her bound off her feet. Now she knows the power of *forgiveness.* If God did it for her, he will, do it for you, just give him a chance. If you should die today where would you spend your eternity? Are you going to the place that the rich man went, or are you going where Lazarus went?

Lafleur now have a singing ministry she brought out her first CD God did not deny me in October of 2009 and is launching her original CD in April 2010. God is blessing her and using her for the building up of his kingdom. When you have purpose it doesn't matter

where you run to or how far you may run God will bring you back.

Access Denied Because Mercy Said No

Though he slay me, yet will I trust in him: but I will maintain mine own ways before him. (Job 13:15 KJV)

Access Denied is a message displayed when unable to obtain access to a location that you have not been granted the proper access rights or do not have permission to access.

Mercy is kindness or forgiveness shown especially to someone a person has power over.

For those of us who are immigrant from another country we know that to gain entrance in the United States of America we needed a visa. Without a visa we will be denied entry into the country; and not only do we need to get a visa, but we need proper identification. The first thing immigration check for is for your identification and visa. To gain entry to the throne room of God we need to be identified as children of God and our identification is the seal of the blood of Jesus Christ. When we accept Jesus as our Lord and Savior we are sprinkled with his blood that was shed for us over two thousand years ago.

As human we often see signs that say **STOP! ....DANGER!** And we are more curious; instead of stopping we walk right into the danger.

I am one of the people who have the legal right to be angry. I've been put down, cast out and left to die, but thank God for his Grace and Mercy.

There was a man in the land of Uz whose name was Job; he was a man that was guiltless and honest, and one who feared God and turned away from evil. He had seven sons and three daughters. He possessed thousands of sheep, camels, yoke of oxen and female donkeys, and many servants; he was the greatest of all the people in the east. His sons would hold feast in the house of each other on his day, and they would send and invite their sisters to eat and drink with them. And when the days of the feast had finish, Job would send and sanctify them, and he would rise early in the morning and offer burnt offering according to the number of them all. Everywhere there is the Spirit of God there is the devil. The day that Job came to present himself before God, Satan was right there. The Lord said to Satan, "From where have you come?" Satan answered the LORD and said, "From going to and fro on the earth, and from walking up and down in it." And the Lord said to Satan, "Have you considered my servant Job, that there is none like him on the earth, a blameless and upright man, who fears God and turns away from evil?" Then Satan answered the LORD and said, "Does Job fear God for no reason? Have you not put a hedge around him and his house and all that he has, on every side? You have blessed the worked of his hands, and his possessions have increased in the land. But stretch out your hand and touch all that he has, and he will curse you to your face." And the LORD said to Satan, "Behold, all that he has is in your hand. Only against his soul do not stretch out your hand." So Satan went out from the presence of the LORD. There was a day when his sons and daughters were eating and drinking wine in their oldest brother's house, and there came a messenger to Job and said, "The oxen were plowing and the donkeys feeding beside them, and the Sabeans fell upon them and took them and struck down the servants with the edge of the sword, and I alone have escape to tell you." While he was yet speaking, there came another and said, "The fire of God fell from heaven and burned up the sheep and the servants and consumed them, and I alone have escaped to tell you." While he was yet speaking, there came another and said, "The Chaldeans formed three groups and made a raid on the camels, took them and struck down the servants with the edge of the sword, and I alone have escaped to tell you." While he was yet speaking there came another and said, "Your sons and daughters were eating and drinking wine in their oldest brother's house, behold, a great wind came across the wilderness and struck the four corners of the house, and it fell upon the young people, and they are dead, and I alone have escaped to tell you." Then Job arose, tore his robe, shaved his head, fell on the ground and worshipped. And he said, "Naked I came from my mother's womb, and naked shall I return. The LORD gave, and the LORD has taken away; blessed be the name of the LORD." In spite of Job mirror he did not sin or charge God with wrong.

Just when Job thought he was recovering from the shock of losing his wealth and his children, he was afflicted "with loathsome sores from the sole of his feet to the crown of his head. And he took a potsherd with which to scrap himself, and sat among the ashes." According to (Job 7:5 KJV) Job was covered with boil-like sores that opened, with puss (inflammation) and clogged with dirt, and infested with worms. Job's health failed, it proved to be too much for his wife. She had endured the loss of her children and wealth. But now with the health of her husband decaying, her impoverished, faith collapsed; then said his wife to him, "Do you still hold fast your integrity? Curse God, and die." But Job answered and said to her, *"You speak as one of the foolish women would speak; shall we receive good at the hand of God, and shall we not receive evil?"*

I don't know if you have ever been put in a position where all your earthly possession just seems to disappear in a moment. At time it might seem that you have a happy marriage; a good job, honest and obedient children and all of that just vanish overnight. And you start wondering what did I do? Did I sin? And you start questioning your salvation. As God bragged on Job, God is bragging on us. It took me a while to realize that, but I can see and hear in my mind eyes when Job was going through. Job was singing *"I can't even walk without you holding my hands the mountain is too high and my valley is too wide, down on my knees I've learn to stand, because I can't even walk without you holding my hand."*

Job friends soon arrived on the scene and tried to help Job figured out why his life fell apart; they began to articulate with Job. They said, "Obviously you've sinned. All these evils are God's punishment for things you've done. You must repent now, and quickly!" Job's friends failed to offer him the comfort he needed. Instead of ministering to Job in love, they judged him. After his friends' speeches, Job cried out in frustration and despair, I've heard this before; what miserable comforters you all are. How long will you torment me and crush me with words?"

They were both the betrayed and betrayer.

Can their friendship survive? Or will they live with the void?

Friendship is the allocation of laughter and/or sadness;
Friendship is leaning on each other when life's road is rough ahead; "One write said and I quote "lean on me when you're not strong and I'll be your friend I'll help you carry on."

> **Friendship** is taking the time to encourage each other along this journey that is the right path not to discourage and gossip
>
> > **Friendship** is finding a way to cope with new pains as they come Our way. When you are told, "I know that you have a problem with me sleeping out" and you are still there for that individual in spite of all the pain that's friendship.
> >
> > > **Friendship** is sharing love even when it seems hard to do.

Betrayal of a friend's feelings; be it premeditated or not, can destroy friendship and leave both individuals feeling empty. I once had a friend; no matter how hard we tried we'd always ended up in disagreements, but always managed to patch up and moved on. No matter how heated our arguments or disagreements were our friendship always managed to weather the storm. It wasn't until she hurt me so badly that the pain was too great for me to bear; it was then I realized that our friendship was like shooting stars briefly across the sky, which was a moment in time that I thought I would treasure forever, but it ended as a bombardment weapon. Maybe, with time, our friendship will grow and blossom again.

It was sometime in 1997 that I met this friend who was a friend of my fair prince. During the time of dating my fair prince I hardly, if I'm not mistaken, heard him spoke about that particular friend. We would be on the phone for hours and even when we were not he would always mention that he was by Mrs. Fee sister, so I thoughts that he was friend with the sister. It was not until we were about to get married that I was told by my fiancé then, that he wanted Mrs. Fee, who was Miss then, to be a bridesmaid at our wedding. I then went and bought the material for the bridesmaids and flower girl dresses only to learn a couple weeks later that she was pregnant and cannot take part in the wedding. Mrs. Fee helped out at the reception by helping to serve, we then got very close I would think, so we started talking and share things that I would think that true friends would share.

I did not lose sight that she was and still is my fair prince friend, but I thought she was the family friend and meant well. As in every marriage my fair prince and I had problems and he would go and tell her several things and she would come back and mentioned it to me or throw hints to get my reaction, and then when I respond accordingly, she would go back and tell my husband "your wife say' and the type of person my husband is, he would come home and start arguing and for days would not talk to me, but being a dim-witted I would continue to be sucked into the double sided mirror that was being set. We'd been friends for over 5 years, things happened that never should have and now we're no longer friends, but we are civil to each other. I'm still in shock why the friendship broke up, I was told that it was because I lied to my husband about being pregnant and then I was told that it was because I lied on her, saying that she called my house to ask for the Church address and mind you we spoke for years after that and there was no mentioned about it. Even after my husband and I had problems she would call and we would still chat. I knew everything about my husband through her when I heard anything and I ask her she would verify it, and some of the things I would just make up to get a response and I would know what I needed to know.

In my opinion the friendship dissolve when she became best friend with my husband concubine, and I really don't blame her because then she would have been in a spot, but the bottom line is, be a woman and accept your role and stop pointing fingers. She said to me that nothing like me or her husband can get between friendships for over 40 years; but the bible says forsaking all other and cleave only unto your spouse, and we two become one. Maybe I am judging, but something is not kosher.

In June 2006 the Church that Mrs. Fee attends had a street fair and I was not paying attention to that young woman and my landlord, as I worked at nights and slept all day, so they got there and began to discuss my life. The way I look at it, if the Landlord started a conversation, the womanly thing to do was, stop her in her track, and let her know that whatever happened or did not happen is not any of us business, but the business of Mr. and Mrs. Fair Prince; however, because she loves Malay (gossip) as we Vincentian would say she engaged in the gossip. The landlord came and told me of the conversation I went to my better half and upbraided him; and as I thought he would he went straight to her… That was not bad, she came to my house for which I paid rent and mind you, the Landlord husband was home, so she tried to take herself out and my so-called friend started to call me a lunatic I then lost it, and ask her if she want my husband, if she want to feel what I am feeling he's there. She called me ugly which did not bother me, because the good book says that I am beautifully and wonderfully made and marvelous is his work and to add insult to injury beauty is skin deep, once I had that no other woman my husband had or will ever have will possess that. She continued to say, "that if she wanted to give me competition I wouldn't have mouth to speak." I got really angry and wanted to tell her that if she can't keep her own husband how is she going to take mine; The advantage that I have over her or any other woman is it doesn't matter who my husband sleeps with he always come back home. He cannot eat gossip and it can't keep him warm at night because the other women including woman # 1 does not know how to feed him both ways... like I could. They maybe able to make him laugh by gossiping and when all is said and done he always come back home to mama. Many of us, think that Christianity means, sitting and taking crap from others. It is so ironic, that after the woman left my house she had the audacity to say my neighbors are not going to see her again, but they would be seeing you dressing up going to Church. I always say, you can fool most of the people most of the time; you can fool some of the people some of the time but you can't fool all the people all the time. Soon after she left my house, the neighbors inquired if that was the baby mother, and some of the people from the project were willing to stand up for me. And the bad thing was they wanted to know what grip she had on my husband knowing she's not the baby mother. She thought that I was going to look bad, but she was the one they were looking down on, making my husband look like a little boy, one who can't think for himself. Sad, but true my lover, and partner want me to let go, and move on for his sake. Should I respect his wishes, apologize again as I did over and over again and speak to her again? Or do I abide with my enemy while I'm in their way and when I'm not in their way move on as though we never met? I don't know.

When you lose something that you think is precious, when you don't know what to do, when you don't know what to say— but you still know how you feel, what should you do? Job said to his so-called friends, "How long will you torment me and crush me with words?" Job's friends thought they were helping with the wisdom they thought they had. But Job knew that the God he served didn't work the way his friends thought. Although Job felt as if God had turn his back on him, that God had abandoned him, Job still had a hope. In the depths of his pain, Job encouraged himself, *"As for me, I know that my Redeemer lives, And at the last He will take His stand on the earth. Even after my skin is destroyed, Yet from my flesh I shall see God;"* (Job 19:25 & 26 NASB) Shall not his Excellency make you afraid? And his dread falls upon you? Your remembrances are like unto ashes, your bodies to bodies of clay. Hold your peace, let me alone, that I may speak, and let come on me what will. Wherefore do I take my flesh in my teeth, and put my life in mine hand? Though he slay me, yet will I trust him: but as Job showed his so called friends that God's mercy is reserved for him and he comfort himself by remembering God's goodness.

When all is said and done in all this, Ms Fee was right, I did not get between my husband, and his friend, but his keeper got between him and her. I realize that I am something so I couldn't get between the friendships, but it seems "nothing" got between. Let go and let God and he will do the rest. My faith was tested during that period of my life, and the mirror was double-sided so it seems there was no way out, but I got the answer, on my knees.

Let No Man Put Asunder

"Marriage is honorable in all, and the bed undefiled; but whoremongers and adulterers God will judge." (Hebrews 13:4 KJV)

"Wherefore they are no more twain, but one flesh. What therefore God hath joined together, let not man put asunder". (Matthew 19:6KJV)

"Flee fornication. Every sin that a man doeth is without the body...

but he that committeth fornication sinneth against his own body.

What? Know ye not that your body is the temple of the Holy Ghost which is in you... which ye have of God, and ye are not your own? For ye are bought with a price: therefore glorify God in your body, and in your spirit, which are God's.

(1 Corinthians 6:18-20 KJV)

One hot summer day I sat alone in my room and was reevaluating my life. I kept sane by keeping busy with school, learning how to start and manage my own business. I attended Church and got involved in ministry. As a young adult, I thought that marriage was forever, and that the world should be a safe haven for all children. My dreams as I can remember, were to be a cop, and then a lawyer and move up to be a magistrate/judge. My dreams were shattered as a teenager, after being molested by the family member I trusted, and thought he would be one of the persons to keep me safe. I became very withdrawn, stayed in my room, read and watched TV after finishing my chores when I came from school. For years I would not trust anyone, and it was said that I was selfish and evil, but that did not bother me. I did open up to two persons and one of them was a neighbor of mine that was very spiritual. I then met a young man who also was a good friend of the family, he really helped me through my hurt; a few months later, I fell in love with him and I spent all of my teenage years with him. He reminded me that there are still good people around and its OK to have clean fun. A few years later, I migrated to the USA. I promised to send for him later, which I tried to get him a visa, and if that did not work I would spend a year and then return to St. Vincent, get married, and return to the states and file for him. He moved in with my dad two months after I came to the states, but before the plane could have landed properly at JFK airport, he started to have an affair, and it just brought back all the hurt that he worked so hard to heal. I did return to St. Vincent and the Grenadines one year after as planned and surprised him, as I did not tell no one I was coming, then I knew that the relationship was over.

I remembered two weeks later, as I sat on the porch and looking at our dog "Spot" taking care of his/its family, I told God and my dad that I needed a man that was going to love me forever, or I didn't need a husband, and would stay single. Spot and Betty were two unique animals; he would make sure she ate, and before he leave for the day, they would play and spend time with each other before he left or she had her boyfriends by the side too, but at the end of the day they knew who they had. I believed and still believe in having a close relationship with your family. If you want to call it family intimacy, then that's it. Sometimes our families may have issues that may be hard for us to get beyond, because we were deceived and wounded by the people that we love and trusted most. We have to remember that Jesus Christ forgave us even; when we didn't deserve it he still came and lay down his life for us. When he was on the cross we spat upon him, we crucified him, but he was still willing to say father forgive them for they know not what they've done.

God, when he created man, he realized that Adam was alone so he provided him with a helpmate.

One intense and luminous summer night the moon was full and the sky was blue. I walk the road of uncertainty, with a map that had no direction for me. I followed instructions and came to the bridge where I met mister fair prince.

I often look back and reflect with a smile that as outgoing and friendly as Mr. Fair Prince was and still thinks he is, I was the one who first spoke to him. We met at Church during construction work, but we did not speak. I remember one Spring Sunday morning after finishing worship I came outside with my jacket and was ask by Mr. Fair Prince to give my jacket to him and that was the first time he said anything to me. A few weeks later my friend brought me a bag with a teddy bear and flower that I still have and cherish after fourteen (14) years.

One afternoon I decided to call him after work and we sat on the phone for hours. It was then he worked up the courage and we will talk every evening for hours and sometimes fell asleep on the phone. As I often say he had a sweet mouth, like to speak things that he think will melt a woman heart or (whisper sweet nothing in your ears).

I was not looking for a romantic relationship because I spend most of my childhood in love with someone that hurt me real badly.

Sometimes, I often wonder if I was the problem, but looking back now I realized that some people cannot handle love, and they will always be looking for what they think is love, when love is right in front of them and they cannot see it.

To me when you love someone, your love should be unconditional. Love is something that should be cherished. (1 Corinthians 13 says KJV)

¹Though I speak with the tongues of men and of angels, and have not charity, I am become as sounding brass, or a tinkling cymbal.

²And though I have the gift of prophecy, and understand all mysteries, and all knowledge; and though I have all faith, so that I could remove mountains, and have not charity, I am nothing.

³And though I bestow all my goods to feed the poor, and though I give my body to be burned, and have not charity, it profiteth me nothing.

⁴Charity suffereth long, and is kind; charity envieth not; charity vaunteth not itself, is not puffed up,

⁵Doth not behave itself unseemly, seeketh not her own, is not easily provoked, thinketh no evil;

⁶Rejoiceth not in iniquity, but rejoiceth in the truth;

⁷Beareth all things, believeth all things, hopeth all things, endureth all things.

⁸Charity never faileth: but whether there be prophecies, they shall fail; whether there be tongues, they shall cease; whether there be knowledge, it shall vanish away.

⁹For we know in part, and we prophesy in part.

¹⁰But when that which is perfect is come, then that which is in part shall be done away.

¹¹When I was a child, I spake as a child, I understood as a child, I thought as a child: but when I became a man, I put away childish things.

¹²For now we see through a glass, darkly; but then face to face: now I know in part; but then shall I know even as also I am known.

¹³And now abideth faith, hope, charity, these three; but the greatest of these is charity.

As I mentioned before about my first love, hurting me by having an affair while I was waiting on him and had intentions of marrying him. He almost made me destroy my life with a married man. I am thanking God that he saved me just in time. I came to my senses before my life was destroyed or ended. There are times when we are faced with situations that seem to have no way out, but there is always a way out. God is able to take care of the impossible.

It was a couple years ago just when I was going through my situation, and its seems that I had committed the worse sin ever that some one sent me a paper and it read,

"Good Morning" "I am God. Today I will be handling all of your problems please remember that I do not need your help. If the devil happens to deliver a situation to you that you cannot handle, DO NOT attempt to resolve it. Kindly put it in the SFJTD (something for Jesus to do) box. It will be addressed in my time. Not Yours. Once the matter is placed into the box, do not hold on to it or attempt to remove it. Holding on or removal will delay the resolution of your problem. If it is a situation that you think your are: Capable of handling, Please consult me in prayer to be sure that it is the proper resolution.

Because I do not sleep nor do I slumber, there is no need for you to lose sleep. Rest my child. If you need to contact me, I am just a prayer away. As with all good things, please pass this on."

That is what took me through some of my hard times and it can take you through.

Mr. Fair Prince was my second true love; I loved him, and still love him with every fiber of my being. Some would say that, you can grow out of love or fall out of love, but if it was love in the first place, there is no falling into, and falling out of love.

I personally think that if you cannot love with everything, you should not love at all. It was a Saturday evening; we went out for the very first time after talking on the phone for hours. We hopped on the train to Coney Island in Brooklyn. On our way there he made me felt loved and wanted. We had a great time; after arriving at Coney Island, we went into Nathan's where we sat, and talked about things that we did not talk about over the phone; or when we saw each other at Church.

We spoke about my life before I met him, and he got so angry about my involvement with the married man although it was over before it even started; this was over almost 6 years before he came to the United States. I asked him about his family, what they were like, about his mother who passed away. He told me that they had a good relationship, and he wished she was alive for him to help her, and that his mother would have been living with him and his wife if she was alive. Personally I would have had no problem with that because I believe that family should be together.

It was on August 9th 1996 that Mr. Prince asked me to marry him and give me a ring for my birthday and engaged me at the same time. So we celebrated my birthday and engagement at home and then later that day we went out to dinner. The engagement was not a public one. I did not want it to be public until he asked my father for my hand in marriage, yes I am old fashion. My father was in St. Vincent and we kept it until he came to the United States. My mom knew and that was about it. The ring was not an expensive ring, but I loved it and wore it with pride. I am not a person that loves material things; it was not about what I can get from him, because he had nothing. I loved him.

The wedding was planned for May 31, 1997. My maid & matron of honor had a surprise bridal shower for me at 625

Bainbridge on May 10^{th,} 1997 I was not surprise they were having the shower, but was surprise to see some of my friends there which I did not know my other friends knew.

It's my Wedding Day, I got up about 6 am, bear in mind I said, got up, I could not sleep I toss all night. I am not sure if I was nervous or excited. My mom and aunt were in the kitchen cooking; the smell of curry was all over. I went to the hair salon, and had my hair done. I got back home about 11 am, and went into my room, and began to pray. I then took a shower, my matron, and maid of honor was late in getting to my house; when they got there I was almost ready, and the limousine was outside waiting.

I think I was the earliest bride when I got to the Church, two of the groomsmen was not there so I sat in the limo for a little while, then decided it was time to move on. We had two (2) ushers walk in the two bridesmaid, one of the usher was later, and the other never showed.

The weatherman predicted thunderstorm, but God smiled on us and gave us a wonderful day, it was not humid, and the rain did not come until we got home. The morning memories for me were tiredness, nervousness, frustration and excitement.

I wore a white traditional gown, very long train and a lot of beads. Headpiece was original; there was no makeup, white shoes, white stocking and a bouquet with the color of the bridesmaid, flower girls and matrons of honor colors. He was as handsome as ever in an all white suit fishtail jacket and a boutonnières.

The best man (Groomsman) wore black and white, the Ushers wore all white suit with green (teal) waist band and bow tie, the Junior bride were in all white, the flower girls were in lemon yellow, and the bridesmaids were in teal off shoulder dress, headpieces made from the same material, crunch hair style, white shoes and gloves. The bouquet was white with teal blended in, and there were two matrons of honor who wore hot pink with same color headpiece.

The organ prelude, the song, "you are so beautiful to me" began

The soloist sang, "Like a bridge over trouble water" the exchange of vows began

"You are flesh of my flesh and bone of my bone; I promise to love you as no other could

To cherish and care for you like no other would,

In sickness I'll bear your pain,

When the funds are low I'll be your gain,

Today I make you flesh of my flesh having chosen you apart from the rest."

Wow! You should have seen the smile on my face

Feel the pounding of my heart, and the tingling in my feet,

Love is phénoménal Still missing you my sweet dear

My past, my present and my future are the most important part of me.

I got married to a wonderful man, although a lot of people may not thing so and as I mentioned earlier, I believe in family intimacy. After few years in my marriage, I felt so disappointed, I thought, instead of getting what I asked for; all I got was another disappointment. This does not mean that my husband is a disappointment; the situation in my marriage was and still is the disappointment. I always wanted to get marry and travel with my husband, for two years we enjoyed each other, but things did not go as planned. I believed that in order to have a strong and healthy marriage or any relationship, fun should be a critical element in making that happens. When one get marry his/her best friend should be his/her spouse, you should want to be anywhere your significant other is and always want to hear their voice, to make sure they are happy. I honestly believe that couple should take at least 10-15 minutes here and there out of their busy schedule to have some fun together and fun does not mean sexual fun only. Laughter is a medicine, it's imperative for husband and wives to laugh together and not to take themselves too seriously. In a marriage, it's not easy to have a significant and lasting relationship without working hard towards one. To me, the word marriage should be change to compromise because that's what it is. The hardest thing in any relationship is, when one party is giving one hundred percent (100 %) and the other is giving about twenty percent (20%). Most of the time, the men are the one that fail to keep the covenant, for better or worse, richer or poorer, sickness or health. I got married May 31, 1997; we lived in a one-bedroom apartment for about 2 year. We moved to a three-bedroom apartment where we struggled with the mundaneness of our everyday life. I became so angry at times and many times I wondered why God put us on hold. It seemed like the walls were caving in on us. It was on August 9, 2003 on, the day of my birthday my fair prince pickup this lady and he had two (2) children with her.

Marriage is like a fire, that you can't leave unattended or like a bed of flower that you cannot leave without watering, while you decide to be running life all around town, and eating from the forbidden fruit expects the fire to be still kindled, the flowerbed to blooming or the marriage to be solid.

It is often believed that when the scripture speaks about whosoever God has joined together let no MAN put asunder (apart), that it means one partner having an affair. The scripture is speaking figurative when it mentions MAN, it is both men and women. From experience in-laws and friends are the main cause for tearing apart families.

I believe in the theory of "the one right person of marriage," my concept is that God had chosen me for my spouse and him for me. A lot of time we believe, that God make the decision of choosing our spouse, but God rarely directs us, but when we have made our decision and are married and we commit ourselves to each other he sanction the marriage and in turn we need to take our vows seriously. It is clear in the scripture that Jesus intended for us to stay together throughout our life. He says that husband should love their wife's as Christ loved the Church and gave himself for the Church, and in turn the wives should submit themselves to their own husbands. There are times when I felt that my husband was the "wrong" person for me, yet I pray that God would convert my choice? I am still committed to working things out, even when there were; presently I think I've made the wrong decision. Many of us view marriage as a contract instead of a covenant and in my view contracts can be broken, but covenant is a permanent commitment. If we learn to look in the mirror and see marriage as a covenant, one will get a sense of security and freedom. The covenant would allow me to get to know my husband, and he knows me we then would be bond as one. It allows us the challenge of growing old together in our marriage.

The Intimacy of my marriage was broken down, because after two years in the marriage no baby came. My husband became frustrated as his so-called friends teased him and made him felt less than a man. They rubbed it in his face that his sperm was weak. This caused a nervous tension on the marriage hence the relationship broke down. He began to be on the phone disrespecting me with them making statement, like, "I am going to look for a woman to give me a child." The worse part in all of this is, one-day we went on vacation, and in the house that we were staying, he slept with a young lady in the same house. I was devastated, but I honestly forgave him. Couple years later, I intern deceived him, by lying to him. The hardest thing is to do is to lie. You always have to tell another lie to cover up the previous one. I thought I was about to lose him, because I love him so much, I just could not see my life without him. A couple years later, he went and had a wonderful little daughter whom he thinks I hate. It took a year and a half for me to meet her; I am truly in love with her. At first I thought and still think that forgiveness is Unfair; there is something that's wrong with a person's reprehensible deeds going without punishment. I never believed in forgiveness until about thirty years ago. I lived a Moses law an eye for an eye and a tooth for a tooth. This is because as a child, someone that I trusted molested me as I mentioned before I had a closed mind from then on. After a couple years went by, and I got married, I learn to forgive completely, and move on, until 2004 when a so-called family friend showed she was nothing, but a snake in the grass, or, as one would say, "a razor blade that cut on both sides."

In life we tend to see the glass as half full, some of us see it as half empty. Relationships make us see the glass as half empty most of the time. What I realized, especially for the people who are supposed to be Christ-like, prefer to be followers rather than to be leaders. Society says it's ok if you have problems in your marriage to divorce, but the bible say the only cause for divorce should be adultery (fornication sad to say, the same concept is creeping into the Churches. The same bible that spoke about divorce mentioned that we should forgive seventy (70) times seven (7) a day, which is four hundred and ninety times a day. The scripture did not mentioned forgiveness from what sin. A marriage only works when the parties invest in their relationship.

Intimacy_ My husband and I have been married for over ten (10) years, and we continue to have a hard marriage. If the sole reason of our marriage was entirely to provide loving intimacy one would say that our marriage is pointless. There are times, when I really wondered why we, or should I say, I stayed in the marriage, as for me I was brought up to believe that marriage is for life. And I believe we really do love each other, if I can speak for my husband. It's just hard for us to transfer our love into happiness. This is just to prove that happiness is not the chief point of marriage. Marriage is a very important union to God for it teaches us what God's kingdom is like. It's all about love and it's natural that marriage should teach us about love. I think that in my marriage, its love that would not allow us to let go, passionate love and passionate tears did not allow me to accept defeat. My Marriage is a sign of something wonderful; it may not be happiness or peace, but its undeniably unwavering love.

Necessity-It is my belief that in every marriage a spouse should help the other to refuel when one is running on empty. In life, we all take on more than we can handle and we often need someone to keep us in check. I think that comfort; a place of solace, when one is discouraged coming from a mate, is a necessity in a marriage.

In every marriage its teamwork, God gives us unique individual gifts to enhance a marriage, not to destroy it. Most of the time in marriage, there are lots of strain because we tend to hold on to our own individuality, rather than considering ourselves as being one.

Value-The questions that a couple should ask is what is my worth? And what do I have to offer my spouse? In genesis when God created Adam, he realized that Adam was alone. He provided him a helpmate; Eve and Adam were so passionate that he said she is bone of my bone and flesh of my flesh, this is family.

Energy-So many people focus their energy on planning their wedding, instead of preparing for their marriage. When I got married my husband wanted simple if possible a courthouse wedding, but I wanted to feel like a queen for that day, because I knew that it was my first and only wedding. From then on I focus my energy on trying to make my husband happy. I am not saying that I succeed all the time, but I made sure that I did not give him any reason to go out and eat out, when I say eat out I'm talking about physical and emotional food. There were times when friends and others would think that I am stupid and I make all married women in America look bad, but my energy was focus on making my husband happy. He was the breadwinner of the family, so I was the homemaker and a very proud one too. One of the downfalls in my marriage was that we did not focus our energy as a couple building our relationship spiritually. We prayed separately, we just did not design our bond on God and his infinite affection.

Safe Harbor-As a family we should put emphasis in providing a safe harbor for each other whether children is involve or not. Our home should be a safe haven to unload our feelings, to laugh, to cry, to say how we feel and still feel loved and accepted. (Isaiah 32: 18 KJV) said, *"And my people shall dwell in a peaceable habitation, and in sure dwellings, and in quiet resting places."*

Trust-I believe that trust comes by having respect for your companion. Without respect it's hard to trust the one that you should and suppose to love. From my experience the more I respected my husband the more I trusted him; because I trusted him, the more he was free to be himself, therefore the cycle went on and on. We should be careful what we say to each other words are very powerful. As one writer said, and I Quote *"Faith-Filled words will put you over; Fear-filled words will put you under."*

We are living in a society where marriage is not respected any more. An affair "is a sexual relationship that lasts more than one night, when one of the lovers is publicly committed to someone else....Affairs are not one-night stand...

Neither is it a romance between two people who are both liberated from other ensnarement. The bible strongly spoke out against premarital relations. Sexual intercourse is to be confined to marriage. *"Marriage is honorable in all, and the bed undefiled; but whoremongers and adulterers God will judge"* (Hebrew 13:4 KJV). The physical intimacy in marriage is unsoiled and hearty. Those married under God's authorization must give all assiduousness (diligence) to see that their marriage bed remains undefiled. Marriage is honorable because God ordained it. It is not a mere convenient arrangement invented by evolutionary men. God created the man and the woman to fit into marriage according to Genesis 2:18-24; therefore Jesus Christ exalts marriage.

Some would say, various Affairs could be thrilling, stimulating, adoring and/or romantic; while others would argue that it could be damaging, destructive, cruel, painful, time wasting and demeaning. I personally choose the latter. Affairs often hurt all the parties involve especially the children. 99.999% of the time, an affair starts out as fun, but more and more one of the individuals involved began to want more from the relationship and then, the other partner feels entangled in such a relationship. I read an article that states, "If a married lover fails to make plans to leave home within the first three months of an affair, then he/she will never leave." The harsh reality is that even if a married lover does eventually leave his wife, or even if that wife actually dies, the man will usually get involve with someone else instead of marrying his mistress. I mentioned about the men affair, but women also have affairs, especially those that have a career, and the single men are hooked to such married women like glue.

Married people may fall out of love from their spouses, and fall in love with other people, be it single or married, that's a statement that is debatable. Some people have the philosophy that the wife is to make and care children, clean the house, wash the clothes, and when their lover is not available provide sex. Most married people that are looking for an affair outside the marriage is looking towards their lover to bring them compassion, understanding, great sex and a sense of soul connection, some people will include love, but love is often provided at home.

Although, by the corrupt ethical values of today's permissive society, we view premarital and extramarital sex acceptable and blameless in the eyes of man, nevertheless, the Word of God clearly declare that God (Who never changes— Malachi 3:6) consider it sin, so how could such a behavior be predestined? One of the things that I appreciate is that we have a freedom of choice.

One of the questions that people in affairs is face to ask is, who is more important, MAN or GOD, spouse or lover?

From my experience, affairs normally happen because of some misunderstanding between the couple. Sometimes one of the partners might think that the grass is greener on the other side, but most of the time there's more dry patches than green grass.

One thing we fail to realize when someone is married and they leave that marriage to start a new relationship or just have an affair weather its an extramarital affair or with a single individual; Extramarital affairs can last for years. If someone has emotional and physiological problems, thus causing their marriage to fall apart, they normally drag most of that baggage with them into the affair. Despondent married people often search for love with someone who may help them allocate the burdens of their lives. The affair may be gratifying, but marriage with the lover may not be possible.

When affairs happens most of the time, the keeper or concubine is the one that get hurts. And often a single person who is romantically involved with a married person often thinks that his or her lover will one day leave home. And they become desperate because another lonely year has past them by with just empty promises.

At some point in most, if not all… affairs never goes on for long and the one that is cheating always tries to end the relationship. Some affairs are done in secrets, others are just open; with emails and cell phone so widespread secret affairs are not easily exposed.

Some of the symptoms of a cheating spouse can be one of the under mentioned, but not limited to, there are several symptoms that you can look for.

❖ The use of prepaid cell phone is one of the main symptoms. The cell phone is purchase in addition to his/her monthly phone. With the prepaid phone there's no tracking. And if there is a monthly plan then the wife/husband cannot answer the phone. I had that experience, where for years my husband will tell me to answer the phone when he can't get to it, if I did not answer he will get upset. When the affairs started when I answer the phone I started to get yelled at, and was told that it was personal, and he does not touch my personal things.

❖ When on the phone with just a friend they yell, when they are with others they began to whisper. My husband have a big mouth when he is on the phone with his friends, you can stay in Manhattan and hear him in Brooklyn, but when its with a potential client or a client, you will be on the bed with him and do not hear anything that he says, then the oh and aha starts.

❖ Your intuition (most of the times is a woman intuition) tells you that something is wrong. This is dependant on the individual.

❖ Pick fight and then leave the house, and blame you for nagging and harassing. They are so uncomfortable around you, and easily moved to anger.

❖ The Internet or email is another way. With the high use of technology no one is the wiser who, when or what you are doing on the computer. They spend an excessive amount of time on the computer instead to coming to bed with you.

❖ The confiding in the spouse is broken. Your partner stops confiding in you if he/she use to.

❖ The one that gets me all the time, your partner never uses condoms for whatever reason. Maybe you are allergic to the rubber, or you are on the birth control pills, but he has condoms walking around with in his pocket or backpack.

❖ From experience, mutual friends start acting like you committed a crime. Most of the time it's because they are having the affair with your partner or they know that your partner is having an affair, and with whom and is condoning it.

❖ Spouses start accusing you of having an affair because of their own guilt.

❖ The spouse stops wearing wedding bands or conveniently lost it.

❖ Spouse suddenly wants to stop having sex with you as often as they use to, or in some cases wants to have sex more often than he/she use to, and wants to try out new and different sexual techniques.

❖ The smell on your spouse is foreign, the perfume or aftershave is not one that you know. And if it's a man there maybe lipstick on his shirts.

I personal experienced all of the above symptoms, that is why I choose to mention them; There maybe others, but those are what I know.

There are numerous dramas that can happen if one of the partners in the affair decides to end the relationship.

The main problem is, when one lover wants out, the other wants to continue to pursue the relationship and starts harassing the other person partner. Inter-reliant lovers normally have great difficulty letting go. Many lovers realize that something is missing, when the married lover is gone, and they end up dealing with great pain and havoc.

Being in a bad relationship and leaving any relationship that doesn't work often forces one to look in the mirror and evaluate their lives, work on our problems.

Depression Is Your Enemy

(1 Samuel 1:10 KJV) And she was in bitterness of soul, and prayed to the LORD and wept in anguish.

(Psalms 30:5 KJV) For His anger is but for a moment, His favor is for life; Weeping may endure for a night, But joy comes in the morning.

(Psalms 119:165 KJV) Great peace have they which love thy law: and nothing shall offend them.

(Psalms 42:6 KJV) O my God, my soul is cast down within me; Therefore I will remember You from the land of the Jordan, And from the heights of Hermon, From the Hill Mizar.

It's another day not sure what season, summer, spring, winter or fall,

I strain to see the sunlight as it tried to pierce through my glass stained window.

I then rolled over on my bed, which was facing the east and pulled the comforter over my head and tried to block out the sunlight. My eyes were blood shot as I looked at my wrist, with a sharp scissor, I entrenched the tip at the line where my palm and wrist met.

I imagined the blood spilling on the entire floor, as it smoothly spreads from my arm as the puddle stains the burgundy carpet.

I lay alone and thought it should be getting better, not worse, but everything seemed to be getting worse. Suddenly a calm smile came over me, but just a stare or word brought tears like a bad stormy day in September to my eyes. It seemed like the sun hadn't shone in my life since forever. Murky depressing cloaks seem to cloud my vision. My life had been taken over by aliens, time seemed to stand still, and taunted me; there was no way for me to keep up.

Depression was not new to me, it seemed like it was a way of life. The demons of depression settled comfortable in my mind, and would weigh heavily on my shoulder. They cover my eyes and lock my tongue so I cannot whine. They work over time stealing my joy, hiding my smile and taking my love. Desperation and desolation were disseminating, as they tends to play hide and seek in my mind. I tried to escape; I became withdrawn into despair.

The ghostly plain was dark and lonely. I was afraid and lonely felt trapped between the double-sided mirrors on the walls. The walls were wallpapered with a purple color flowerlike paper and smelled like ammonia; I screamed in agony. The pain in my head was unbearable, it seemed like blood was gushing from my brain. I cried out for pain, and I mentioned several times about the taste of blood, but was told it's all in your head; I went to doctor after doctor, but had the same diagnosis, brain waves are normal. All the CAT scan came back negative; I would constantly complaint and nagged.

My husband often says, "Oh it's a mind thing." I felt at one time that I was losing my mind, and I often said it, but was told that I am confessing it, and whatever I confessed I will possess.

It was in the summer of 2003 the pain was share torture, I cried out that I was scared but was not afraid. I wanted to run and started to, the nakedness of my womanhood exposed. My body was screaming for freedom and my mind was blaring out for help.

I lay in the dark wall papered room strap to the bed in Islip NY. I can hear the nurses whispering trying not to disturbed me, it seemed like they were screaming as I heard every word that they were saying.

The senior nurse on staff was saying, "He is a loser, why doesn't she move on with her life" as the other nurse mentioned, "it's easier said than done."

I escaped from that mirror, only to find another "If you ask me you are nasty" I was told on several occasion.

According to Encarta Dictionary depression is defined a state of unhappiness and hopelessness. It is a psychiatric disorder showing symptoms such as persistent feelings of hopeless, dejection, poor concentration, lack of energy, inability to sleep, and sometimes, suicidal tendencies.

What we need to realize is depression is a sickness that affects body and mind. It can be treated like every other illness as long as the symptoms and signs are recognized. We often think that depression just started in our generation, but according to the scriptures depression was from bible days.

Some of the signs of depression can be, but are not limited to:

❖ Feeling of hopelessness, glumness: Being the mother of my husband children was a dream I had more than anything else in my life, having someone else carrying his children was like losing everything else in the world. What made me more depressed were people telling me that I have option like adoption. I started to question God, and wondered if he cared, and if my needs mattered to him. Here I am serving you, doing what you wanted, and you said that adultery is a sin, and yet, you are allowing children to be born from adultery.

When there is a sense of hopelessness, we need to place our hope in God. There are times when it seems that our soul is disquieted. The psalmist wrote and I quote "Why are you cast down, O my soul? And why are you disquieted within me? Hope in God, for I shall praise him for the help of his countenance." 1 Peter 5:6&7 says "*Therefore humble yourselves under the mighty hand of God, that he may exalt you in due time; casting all your care upon him, for he cares for you.*" When we trust in the Lord with all our heart and lean not to our own understanding; and in all our ways we acknowledge him, he shall direct out paths. When I went through my period of depression lying on the hospital bed when it seems like I was all alone my favorite scripture reading that took me through the three days was (2 Corinthians: 8-9, vs. 16-18 NIV) "*We are hard-pressed on every side, yet not crushed; we are perplexed, but not in despair; persecuted, but not forsaken; struck down, but not destroyed.*"

Therefore we do not lose heart. Though outwardly we are wasting away, yet inwardly we are being renewed day by day. For our light and momentary troubles are achieving for us an eternal glory that far outweighs them all. So we fix our eyes not on what is seen, but on what is unseen. For what is seen is temporary, but what is unseen is eternal."

❖ Feelings of guilt, worthlessness, helplessness, in Genesis 4:6-7 Cain disobeyed God and his offering was not respected. Cain was very wroth, and his countenance had fallen. The Lord then said to Cain, "Why are thou wroth?

And why is thy countenance fallen? If thou doest well, shalt thou not be accepted? And if thou doest not well, sin lieth at the door. And unto thee shall be his desire, and thou shalt rule over him." David was a man of God own heart; he was the King of Israel after committing adultery with Bathsheba, the daughter of Eliam and the wife of Uriah the Hittite. He also used his power as King to be an accessory before the fact to kill her husband Uriah and later marries her. David became very depressed; it was not until he confessed his sins that he was released from his depression. He went to God and confessed his sins, and ask for forgiveness in Psalms 31 verses 22-24 *"For I said in my haste, I am cut off from before thine eyes: nevertheless thou heardest the voice of my supplications when I cried unto thee. O love the LORD, all ye his saints: for the LORD preserveth the faithful, and plentifully rewardeth the proud doer. Be of good courage, and he shall strengthen your heart, all ye that hope in the LORD."*

Blessed is he whose transgression is forgiven, whose sin is covered.

Blessed is the man to whom the Lord does not impute iniquity, and in whose spirit there is no deceit.

When I kept silent, my bones grew old through my groaning all the daylong. For day and night, Your hand was heavy upon me; My vitality was turned into the drought of summer. I acknowledged my sin to You, And my iniquity I have not hidden. I said, "I will confess my transgressions to the LORD," And you forgave the iniquity of my sin."

For many years my husband made me felt guilty. He said that I made him backslide, I made him went out and have children outside the marriage. It was not until June 22, 2009 that he admitted, that no one does anything that they don't want to do, that's when I was released. It's easier to blame someone else for your wrongs when guilt is eating away at you.

❖ Loss of interest or pleasure in hobbies and activities that were once enjoyed, including sex. Sex was my hobby. I remember I was the one that pursue my husband, but when the mirror came between us so there was no desire. I kept hoping the feeling would come back, but there was none. If he came home and wanted to have sex I will go through the motion, hoping that the feelings will come back, and that it will prevent him from sleeping around outside.

❖ Difficulty concentrating, remembering, making decisions:

❖ Having problem falling asleep or early morning awakening, or oversleeping.

❖ Loss of appetite and/or weight, or some overeating and weight gain. I went from a size 16 to a size 8 in one month.

❖ Thought of suicide or suicide attempts: A few years ago, I often wondered how people could think about taking their own lives. For me life was sweet, and it could never cross my mind of loosing it. It wasn't until I was trapped in the double-sided mirror of life that I realized that depression could make you want to commit or attempt to commit suicide. Some would say, such thought should be for the man who is not saved (non-Christian), but the question goes back to "aren't the Christian human? And also goes through depression?" When I went through my depression, my marriage just started to go down hill, and I had very low self-esteem. My husband was physiological abusing me, having several affairs. I just wanted to die, yes I taught about committing suicide. One day I was home and it darned upon me, that after I take my life and gone to a place of everlasting damnation, my husband is going to move on with his life, he have the chance to be forgiven for his sins; wherefore I took the focus off my marriage and I placed it on Christ. It was not easy; it's still not easy. From time to time I would feel depress, but the thought of suicide do not cross my mind anymore. I realized I am still loveable not withstanding my relationship is broken. The best way to keep depression under control is, study the word of God, or stay in the word. There will be times when you don't feel like it, but force yourself to be constant. Prayer is another way to alleviate depression; I tried searching the scripture for specific laws about suicide, but the bible says, "thou shall not kill" Killing is killing be it yourself, or others. The Lord had breathed life into us to do his work on Earth, our bodies are not ours to take; it belongs to God; He decides when we finish our purpose. Life turmoil's are only temporal, although it may seem like an eternity. "What? Know ye not that your body is the temple of the Holy Ghost which is in you, which ye have of God, and ye are not your own? For ye are brought with a price: therefore glorify God in your body, and in your spirit, which is God's."

❖ Physical symptoms such as headache, backache and all other body parts pain.

I've been battered
I've been bruise
Scorned and abuse
I felt alone and so confused
When Jesus rescued the accused

No more guilt
No more pain
No more sorrow
No more shame
Praise the Lord I'm free from blame

My faith was tested
My hope protested
My joy was stolen by Satan pimps
Praise the Lord I'm not ashamed
because Jesus took all my pain

I am stronger than I think
Every challenge life throw at me made me strong.
The problems that I encountered strengthen my mind, body and soul.
Every trouble I overcome increased my perceptive even more.

You taught me how to be a woman
Standing strong as a Leo Lion
You are my best friend and my lover
Let's keep on until the very end

Stick to your beliefs don't get pushed around
Is what you always taught
You wanted to be a family man so be a good example

My mind was full of confusion
My heart was full of pain and sorrow
Now you've started your own family
Remember that you need to be strong

I've tried to be a good wife, a virtuous and content one
And I've tried to be supportive to the children that's not mine
I hope they would grow up to be just fine
We've had many good times as well as bad
But my love for you is unconditional

You have to go I know it's time
I can't help but feeling sad and be twine
But I'll stay strong and never lie
So remember you need to be strong and stand tall with me in mine.

The Bones Shall Live

And when I beheld, lo, the sinews and the flesh came up upon them, and the skin covered them above: but there was no breathe in them. (Ezekiel 37:8 KJV)

There are times in our lives, when we question ourselves,
what's our purpose?
I have a purpose only to praise
I'm rejuvenated by God mercy and his grace
Prayer is the key that opens the door,
Operates by the guidance of his unchangeable grace.

I have a purpose
And I'm happy to share
Prove him
Understand him
Rejoice in him
Pay tribute to him
Open to him
Serve him
Enjoy him

And that's your purpose, for having purpose it's only to praise

I often questioned myself, what can I do as an individual in my Church and my community? In the site of God, one person can make a great impact on his/her community and world, while a Church can impact a generation; with God all things are possible. God took Ezekiel through a quest into a vision in the valley full of dry bones that was scattered abroad. The question that was asked is, can these bones live? As human of course the answer will be no, but Ezekiel knew that he's serving a God that is all powerful and that what is impossible with man is possible with God, Ezekiel answered and said God was the one who knowest. We are often trapped in situation that seems impossible and wonder what the outcome will be. In Ezekiel vision, God allowed him to be a part of the miracle, as we know, all God had to do was, speak the word and the bones would have come together, but he let Ezekiel, prophesy to the bones. I can imagine Ezekiel, in the valley of bones walking up, and down talking to the bones; I can picture him as being crazy. So it is, in our personal lives when we are faced with our circumstances, God allows us to be a part of the miracle, because we will appreciate our deliverance more. When God allows us to go through the test, he knows that we will have a testimony.

It was January 1, 2010 I attended Church and after Church decided to hangout with family and other brethren. I left the Church at about 4 am when I receive a text message, stating how barren I am, and I should leave the man (my husband) to be a family with his children, and went on to say I am a home-wrecker. For a moment, I forgot there was a God that can take care of all situations. That day I cried all day, and mind you, my husband did not care. He came home 10 am the morning, took a shower and called his concubine and left. I did not see him again until the Sunday. I remember about 11 pm Friday January 1st, 2010 I began to pray; I spoke to the dry bones in my life. I was released immediately, I remembered telling my mountains, this year is all about me! It was on Sunday January 3 my husband came to Church, the ministers prayed for him and told him that he belongs in Church. We got home from Church and he received a phone call and he told the person to take a cab. We went to bed, about 8 pm my husband was in pain the human side of me wanted to pay him no attention. It was about 11 pm when I said come let's pray; I took the olive oil and anointed him, and prayed; He then began to vomit.

I then called 911, went to the emergency room where we spend all night. I knew then that I was a true child of God; some people thought that I was a fool, but I felt good about myself after. It was about 1 pm when my husband phone rang it was his "keeper". I answered the phone and told her he was in the emergency room. She then proceeded to check up and what was surprising to me she knew that his wife was with him, but she still showed up at the hospital. I personally was uncomfortable, but was nice about it and kept the bones enacted and added sinews to the bones also.

I remember as a child, we sang in Sunday school this song, "them bones, them bones, them dry bones now hear the word of the Lord" Ezekiel began to call upon God to breathe life into the bones. When the prophet began to speak to the bones they came together every part in the right place to the rightful owner. The dry bones in the vision were identified as the nation of Israel that is cut off from God. In these last days the Church seems to be struggling to maintain its standard that God has destined for us. We often ask the question, what Jesus Christ had in mind when he said, "Upon this rock I will build my Church and the gates of hell shall not prevail against it."

God question to us, as his children in these times; is there anything too hard for, me to do? There is no problem that is too hard for God to fix. He can work it out for us he's the same God today as he was yesterday he never changes. We read the story in Genesis 18 with Abraham and Sarah his wife. Abraham and Sarah were old and the Lord said to Abraham… "Lo, Sarah thy wife shall have a son" those who were inside the tent, were listening to the conversation, overheard them and began to laugh. Sarah thought it was impossible because she was beyond the age of childbearing, and Abraham was too old to father a child. In verse 13 & 14 it states, "…Wherefore did Sarah laugh, saying, shall I of a surety bear a child, which am old? Is anything too hard for the Lord?" one of the things that we need to remember is … "The things which are impossible with men are possible with God" Luke 18:27. Maybe your situation that seems impossible is getting a job, could be your marriage, and could be your finance. It is easy for a person, who is not in your situation to tell you to "hold on, the Lord is able to bring you out."

Trust in the Lord with all thine heart and lean not to thine own understanding, in all thy ways acknowledge him and he shall direct thy path."

When you have a testimony of God's goodness and what he's done for you, and is still doing no tongue can tell.

In 2002 I started to feel a pressure on my heart, I ignored it until in 2003, when, the pressure of stress was too much for me I ended up in the hospital and the doctor said that my heart was bad and that I needed a pace maker. I refused because I could not see myself working with a battery. I still feel my heart tense up and feel like it's about to fall out of my chest. I take Bayer aspirin daily, and believe God is going to touch my heart and heal me. In 2005 I was re-diagnose with cancer; I have kept it a secret from everyone that I cared about me; I didn't need sympathy. I was advised by the doctor that if I waited too long to get pregnant, it's going to be a problem with the fetus, and if possible I should not try to get pregnant because of the toll it would have on my body.

I felt emptiness in my life that I cannot explain. I felt that the earth was caving in under me and there was no escape for me. At work there were times when I felt so stress, but I've been blessed with a job, which I needed the most. I never knew what it was like to be on my own, until I had to look in the mirror and saw reality. I lived with my parents until I got married, moved and lived with my husband. After we started having problem and the psychological abuse, even some physical abused started, I had enough, so the law was involved, he had two restraining orders against me and I called the police to see that he only walk with his clothing. I stopped participating in any Church activities and I took the back seat. My Christian life just went down hill, I felt so empty inside that there were times that I felt I was better off dead.

God had been so good to me during my hardship. He had been my provider I was out of work for a couple years, I was looking for work, but nothing was coming through for me. I remembered I began to question my belief about God that I had held since I was a child. I refused to see things rationally and was dealing on negative emotions, which were easy for me to do. After a few months, I was forced although I was not working, then after my husband moved out; I had to pay $ 900 a month. God did provide for me. I got a roommate who paid $350.00 monthly and as for the other $550 I honestly did not know how I made it, but it was taken care of without a penny from my husband. I remembered during my devotion one morning, and I open my bible randomly, and it was Isaiah 41:10 that caught my attention and it read; *"Fear thou not; for I am with thee: be not dismayed; for I am thy God: I will strengthen thee; yea, I will help thee; yea, I will uphold thee with the right hand of my righteousness."*

It was in 2007 one would have thought that I overcame the worse with my husband having a child. Hagar is the woman in the bible that Sarah gave Abraham to, after God told her she is going to have a baby. Abraham went into Hagar, and she was with child, Hagar became so high and mighty and called Sarah barren. Hagar began to take over. She would mention to others, and personally to me that I had eight years to have a child and did not, wherefore I am barren. The worse part of all this, my husband being there, hearing the entire conversation and did not defend me.

In October of 2007 I just cracked, depressed and I had no one to talk to. My husband was missing in action; he would spend all his time at this girl's house. The sad thing is I would pass by, his car would always be parked in front of her gate, hut would insist that he was not there, and I was judging her. I had a nervous break down, spend sometime in the hospital, but he did not care. The young lady still insists that they belong together ("they were destined to be") wherefore she is doing everything for me to divorce him. Since then, she got pregnant again, but I held on to my husband (my hands are tired, yet I am trying to hold on with my teeth). In an affair the people that get long time hurt are the keepers. Giving a man who is not "your own husband" two (2) and three (3) children do not mean he's going to leave his wife for you. In the long run a man who really loves you might come along, but because you have so many children with different men, he may not be able to have children of his own with you, so may decide to move on, or, if he decides to marry you might later go out and look for children with someone else. Children should be a heritage not a burden.

I was speaking to someone sometime ago, and I was telling them that people use the bible for there own convenience, and some people just don't understand. The bible speaks about husband loving their wives and wives submitting to their own husband. Then it mentioned that parents should train up their children that when they become old they will not depart from the training. Nowhere the bible it is mentioned to love your children like Christ loves the Church.

Sarah doubted God could fix the impossible, as Christians today; we likewise have a hard time believing his power. I've heard a lot of Christian couples that are having problem in their marriages who does not believe that God can save their relationship. I was there, and at times things seem hopeless; bitterness and resentment were built up over the years, but God can make the impossible, possible. We often try counseling, but unless we believe that God can fix our marriages, unless we put our faith to work, it's a waste of time and effort to go to counseling. It's so sad Christian marriages all over the world is ending up in divorce; even ministers are announcing their divorce. In my opinion any Christian couple that give up on their marriage without a fight, made up their mind to leave the relationship, but are just in the relationship to get someone else's approval for the direction they already took.

Demotion verses Promotion

" I returned, and saw under the sun, that the race is not to the swift, nor the battle to the strong, neither yet bread to the wise, nor yet riches to men of understanding, nor yet favour to men of skill; but time and chance happeneth to them all."
(Ecclesiastes 9:11 KJV.)

A **demotion** is the reduction of rank or position in an organizational hierarchy system. This is often caused by bad work habits or bad behavior.

Promotion is "the advancement of rank or position in an organizational hierarchy system." Promotion may be an employee's reward for good performance. Before a company promotes an employee to a particular position; it ensures that the person is trained to handle the added responsibilities. This is marked by job enrichment and various training activities. The first blessing of walking in the fresh anointing is promotion. I personally never met anyone who dislikes promotion. The bible says in Psalms 75 that *"promotion cometh neither from the east, nor from the west, nor from the south. But God is the judge: he putteth down one, and setteth up another."*

As children of God, we tend to seek promotion from man and bypass God's promotion. In life, there are often serious inequalities. Sometimes, the wicked seem to prosper, while the righteous is impecunious (needy); but its not so; there is no clear association between success and obedience to God, between prosperity and truth. As Solomon observed, *" The race is not to the swift or the battle to the strong, nor does food come to the wise or wealth to the brilliant or favour to the learned; but time and chance happen to them all."* **(Ecclesiastes 9:11 NIV).**

Often when we mess up, man tend to demote us from our position, be it spiritual or physical, but if we ask for forgiveness God promotes us, take us to a higher level, that man cannot fathom. Joseph Believed God plays a great role in our success or failure. He held his second born tightly in his arms and looking intently into his baby's eyes said, *"I'm going to call you Ephraim, because God has made me fruitful in the land of my suffering."*

I am where I am because God intervenes in human history. I am where I am because God helped me over life's rough spots. I am where I am because God gave me hope to believe His promises. That hope strengthened my will to choose to love rather than hate, laughter rather than tears, blessing over bitterness. Joseph believed the God of his fathers rather than the god's of the Nile. That choice empowered him to persevere rather than quit, to be a giver rather than a taker, to grow rather than rot, to act rather than procrastinate. Jesus chose to die on a cross, so that we could have infinitely more than the job of a life time. He chose the way of the cross so we could choose the way of life. I urge you to open your whole being up to God and you'll achieve much more than the job in a lifetime; you'll receive the gift of Eternal Life. I once heard of a story about "A super market that was giving children helium filled balloons, before walking outside the mother warned her son, "Hold the string tight or you'll lose your balloon." The son stumbled and inadvertently let go of his balloon. Up it floated, higher and higher into the clear blue sky. The mother expected a sudden outburst of tears, but no tears came. The child just stood there watching the dot in the sky get smaller and smaller. At last it disappeared and with a sense of excitement, he exclaimed to his mother, "Mummy, I didn't know my balloon could fly so high." Joseph had no idea his life would fly so high. Jesus chose you so you could choose Him, and knowing with Jesus there are no limits to how high you can fly." There were times in my life when I was down and out **(Psalm 75:6-7 KJV)** *"For promotion cometh neither from the east, nor from the west, nor from the south. But God is the judge: he putteth down one, and setteth up another."* shed a tear of regret over my situation, and hope for a better day. *"Humble yourselves in the sight of the Lord, and He shall in due time lift you up"* **James 4:10**. God's Word does not say when He will do this promoting, this lifting up. Abraham waited faithfully for years, dying in faith like so many others. Many of us will have to wait until the resurrection for God to finally exalt us, to lift us up with a real promotion. For years I looked for a human promotion, I wanted the approval of others. In the book of Ester, Haman was like that, he wanted tribute from other human beings, but was humiliated when Mordecai received honor, and not himself. When someone else is promoted, it is a natural human inclination to say to oneself, "What about me"? Human promotions are cheap and vain.

The business world is full of competition, politics and striving after the vanity of promotions. And the same type of behavior is creeping into the Churches (Ecclesia). I was reading a paper and came across this: "How many years have you striven for **God's Kingdom**"?

The ultimate promotion of all is to hear these words; I am pleased to announce the promotion of Ingrid Lavette Sobers to Queen and Evangelist in my Kingdom. Her promotion is effective immediately and she will report directly to me. Because she has overcome and kept my words faithfully to the end, I will give her power over the nations, she shall rule them with a rod of iron. I say to her, 'Well done, thou good and faithful servant, because thou hast been faithful in very little, have thou authority over ten cities. Enter into the joy of the

Lord!' Ingrid will assist me in the establishment of my kingdom. Holy angels and all the righteous ones, please join me in congratulating Ingrid, and supporting her in her new position."

It took me a very long time to realized, that when someone think of themselves very low, they try to make others feel the way they feel, but after realizing that I am royalty, those people need to come up to my standard, rather than I going down to theirs.

Some things that can help you keep that goal of spiritual promotion in mind are to:

- Recognizing that spiritual promotion will only be accomplished with God's hands not our own.
- Concentrate on the Lord's Prayer, "thy kingdom come thy will be done" as your daily prayer.
- The only way to be successful is to fail, learn from repeated failures, and keep trying. The more you fail and get up again, the more successful you will be. *"For a just man falleth seven times, and riseth up again: but the wicked shall fall into mischief"* (**Proverbs 24:16 KJV**).
- God has a way of intervening at the last moment, when it seems like all hope is lost, when all human efforts have proven unproductive, when in our helplessness we cry out to Him. It seems like we need these experiences to get rid of our human vanity. The Eternal says of us His people: *"I will go and return to my place, till they acknowledge their offense, and seek my face: in their affliction they will seek me early"* (**Hosea 5:15 KJV**.)
- No one can ever be able to say, "I deserve to be in God's kingdom. I am qualified." It is only by the grace of God that anyone will be there. Maybe we need to learn that promotion comes from God ALONE!

Your Destination is Determined by Your Path

"Trust in the Lord with all your heart. And do not lean to your own understanding. In all your ways acknowledge him, and he will make your path straight." (Proverbs 3:5 KJV)

Destination can be defined as the place to which someone or something is going or must go. Path is defined as a route along which something moves.

I am going to give you a crash course on driving, and for the drivers a refresher. First you will get into your car, you will adjust your seat and your mirrors, put on your seat belt, then you put your keys into the ignition (*a mechanism that determines when, where, and how a spark is delivered to an engine cylinder to ignite the fuel to start or run the engine*) make sure your right foot is covering the brakes before you attempt to start the car. You will then start the car and check your mirrors to make sure that nothing is coming in your direction, proceed to pull out with foot on gas lightly. I am sure before you do all this; you would have already determined your destination. God has given man so much wisdom, that man came up with a small device call the GPS (a worldwide navigation system that uses information received from orbiting satellites) all you have to do is. put in your destination and it will take you wherever you want to go. There are often obstacles in the way that can cause the GPS to give wrong direction, for example there could be construction that is going on and the road is close, or the signs can change, making it a one way. As Christians we have a GPS in the form of the Holy Spirit, He leads us into all truth. He is always with us, he never leaves us, if for some reason we tend to detour he is always there to get us back on track.

Christians sometimes find it difficult to determine God's destination for our lives when we are going through our situations. There are times when it seems as if we don't know how to find a clear path; we often become confused and frustrated. The scriptures tells us that God gave Moses the burning bush, he showed his will to Gideon with the fleece, and he spoke to Saul with thunder and lightening. When he does this for us, it's easy for us understand God's direction for our lives. To truly find God's purpose for our life, we must step out in faith which can be scary. We need to realize God is there beside us he will not allow us to stray if we trust in him as the Proverbs mentioned in 3:6." Psalms 37:23 tells us, *"The steps of a good man are ordered by the Lord...."* and Isaiah 30:21 informs us, *"Your ears shall hear a word behind you, saying, this is the way, walk in it, whenever you turn to the right hand or whenever you turn to the left."* God's word is plainly saying that God I will show you the way, how does he do it?

There are many people who are not God's people. That do not mean you are not the creation of God, it just simple mean you may not be born again, hence there is a difference. As born again Christians God guides us. Almost all of us if not all, have something or someone that we hold very dearly, we know when it's time to cut it loose; but we hold on for life. We all, at one time or another has something we know we need to get rid of, or one time had that situation in our lives. God desires are to give us total guidance in everything we do, including letting go of things, which as human may seem difficult to do; because some of us like to be in control. We like to hold on. I don't know about you, but I like to be in charge. God wants to usher us into a higher calling, we keep yelling out to him, Lord, but it's mine! You can't have it. The Psalmist says in Psalms 24 that *"the earth is the Lord's and the form is thereof the world and they that dwell therein,"* that means everything that we have is not ours. Everything we have is a loan to us. God is in charge of all our lives, if we belong to him. He owns everything that we have, that includes your wife, your husband, and your children. Some of us may say, well I wish he didn't have my children or my spouse, but he does. God owns everything in our lives and there is a direction, a specific direction that God wants to take us. Many of us who are parents, we hold on to our children for dear life. We often make the comment, they are our seed; but they belong to God, and God only loan them to us to train them up in the way that they should grow. The scripture reminds us, children are a heritage of God he never said that they are property of man. As for our spouses, he says we become one, wherefore if we are one, we all belong to God. Nobody is the property of another; we are God's property. God's target is, we should liberate our lives completely over to him, so that we can be fully guided by him. As previously mentioned some of us are such control freaks, we give God just enough. We never let go and say, God *"Take my life, and let it be consecrated, Lord, to thee; take my moments and my days, let them flow in ceaseless praise."* We tell him that *we are available to him; my will I give to you I would do what you say to, use me Lord to show someone the way and let me say my storage is empty and I am available to you.* Instead of telling God that, we tend to walk on the white line, so we can sway to either direction. I am a Christian, but don't mash my corn, I am holy, but every now and again, I have to put my sword aside for a few minutes, because I have to give someone a piece of my tongue. God wants a full commitment from us; just enough is not good enough. The beautiful thing with God is, you are never too old or to young, it doesn't matter what's your race. He says for as many as receive him to them he give the power to live holy. In order for God to direct our path, we must trust him completely; surrender everything to him, your mind, body and your soul. Lord take me and use me for your glory let my life be an example to my family first, then to my friends and neighbors. We often hinder ourselves from our blessing, we will whine and complaint that we are not seeing our headway, there is a reason, we are not following the recipe to prosperity. As Christian we tend to chase after money, but if we follow the formula for a good healthy life all other things, including money will be added to us. When we trust God, we ought to trust him in our situation. He is the same God in the valley, as on the mountaintop; he's God in the night and he's the same God in the day. We are still speaking about your direction. Peter trusted God when he stepped out of the boat, and began to walk towards the Lord on the rough water. It's a possibility that he was like me could not swim, but Jesus bid him come, he trusted God to direct his path, so he took the direction of the master. For a split second he began to take his eyes of the compass (GPS), and began to sink. He looked at the others in the boat and trust went up in smoke. We need to trust God with our finances, trust him with our relationships, and trust him with our marriages and he will guide and direct our path, we have to let go and let God. "**KILL SELF**."

Another thing we need to stop leaning on is our own understanding. We need to stop going on what you think. I don't know about you if I rely on my thinking I would be in serious trouble, everyone around me, especially those who offend me would know it. Many of us struggle with our

SCARED AND TRAPPED IN THE DOUBLE-SIDED MIRROR OF LIFE

Christian life; we are doing it alone, trying to make our own decisions. That's natural as all of us like our freedom. We often forget we are not our own when we fully surrender to Almighty God. A full surrender is a definite, deliberate, voluntary transfer of undivided possession, control, and use of our entire being-(body, soul, and spirit), to the Lord Jesus Christ to whom we rightfully belong.

As human we have issues, some different from others, and we perceive things out of our issues, I'm not talking about good things. We ought to have a mind like Christ, that's what Christianity is all about, being Christ-like. So we are not to have a mind of our own. Yes, we would not be able to perceive with our finite minds the infinite God, but the Psalmist David said in Psalms 8, *"Lord when I consider the sun, the moon and the stars in your handiwork, who am I that you are mindful of me and who am I that you send the son of man down for me"* so God desire for our lives is, trusting him and not to lean to our own understanding.

In all your ways acknowledge him and he shall direct your path. As children of God, everything we do we should acknowledge him, not only in our praise and worship but every waking moment, in our sleeping, while we are eating, in our conversations we should always acknowledge that our GPS is always with us. When we wake in the morning, we should thank him for being with us throughout the night. To acknowledge God is to learn about him, to get acquainted with him. Many of us acknowledge God because of what someone tell us about him, few of us really know who he is. To some of he's JEHOVAH_JIREH: "The Lord will provide." Gen 22:14 God always provides adequately when the times come. To others he's JEHOVAH-ROPHE: "The Lord who heals" Exodus 15:22-26. This implies spiritual, emotional as well as physical healing. (Jer.30:17, 3:33; Isa 61:1) God heals body, soul and spirit; that's the entire man. We are still talking about your destination. He's the JEHOVAH_ROHI, which is the great shepherd to others. Psalms 23 David said "the Lord is my shepherd," and because God was his shepherd, he lacked nothing, which meant he was also JEHOVAH_JIREH to David. JEHOVAH_JIREH led David in the path of righteousness; David relied on his GPS to direct him in the path of righteousness, when he went off root, God led him back. David mentioned in Psalms 23, "thou I walk through the valley of the shadow of death, I will fear no evil, for you are with him." JEHOVAH-SHAMMAH is there with him; others know him as the BEGINNING and the END, the FIRST and the LAST, I AM THAT I AM. Shepherds lead sheep, not follow them. A good shepherd knows where to take a sheep.

On the Christian journey most of us tends to fall off or some of us walk off the pathway, or change direction. We want to have our own way, thus falling away from God's direction. If we listen carefully or if we don't have our car in parked God push us back on track, and most of the time it's by any means necessary. We are still talking about him directing our path. God direct us in everything in our lives, when we trust, and we acknowledge him as Lord, and let him direct our path.

Unspeakable Joy

That the trial of your faith, being much more precious than of gold that perisheth, though it be tried with fire, might be found unto praise and honor and glory at the appearing of Jesus Christ: whom having not seen you love. Though now you so not see Him, yet believing, you rejoice with joy inexpressible and full of glory. 1 Peter 1:8 (New King James Version)

Joy is the knowledge of salvation that is personalized. It is a contribution to genuine Christian walk. There are many blessings that are available to the children of God, one of which is a very special kind of joy. Many of us had never and may never experience true joy in our lifetime. To me joy is more than laughter and rejoicing it's more than happiness to the heart. Unspeakable joy is a spiritual experience, which enables us as Christians to rejoice and leap. We have a hope, which gives us access to that unspeakable joy which is full of glory. The joy that I'm speaking about is so glorious that it's impossible to be express by words; it's like a fire shut up in ones bones. In 1 Peter 1:6-9 Peter spoke about this unspeakable joy. One writer mentioned there are three reasons for this rejoicing, which are past, present and future events.

The original ground for joy in the past, God have set us apart by the sanctifying of the Holy Spirit. The blood of Jesus has washed us, and we are born again to a new hope. When we have this Joy it make you shout, jump, sing and dance around like David. David danced before the LORD with all his might. The Lord had blessed the house of Oded-e-dom and all that pertaineth unto him, because the ark of God was returned. (2 Samuel 6). When a Christian accepts the joy, because we are set apart by God, it surpasses every delight, and gives us an experience that we never dream exist. (John 17:17 KJV) Jesus said, *"Sanctify them through thy truth: thy word is truth."* In other words what he was saying is, we are made pure and holy for his sacred use. When we are set apart by God, we will find ourselves pulling away from anything or anyone which will be a distraction to our Christian life. There are times when we will feel all alone, and, that we are forgotten. This is the time when we should spend quality time with God; he then will mold us and transform us into his image. There are different types of sanctification: Some of us are set apart for God purpose before we were born or save. God reminded Jeremiah *"Before I formed you in the belly, I knew you; and before you came forth out of the womb I sanctified you, and I ordained you as a prophet unto the nations."* In Genesis 25 verse 23, we are reminded how God set Jacob apart before he was born. *"And the LORD said unto her, Two nations are in thy womb, and two manner of people shall be separated from thy bowels; and the one people shall be stronger than the other people; and the elder shall serve the younger."* (KJV)

The Holy Spirit prepares the heart of his people to receive salvation, purpose and plan for our lives. There is also personal sanctification that is where you become more and more like Christ. This is where you began to grow and show your fruit. (Ephesians 4:13 KJV) mention… *"Till we all come to the unity and of the knowledge of the Son of God, to a perfect man, to the measure of the stature of the fullness of Christ;"* The Holy Spirit is the Christian teacher, who enlightens, cleanses, keeps and matures us. He also convicts us of sin and leads us back to the right path when we stray. The day will come when we will stand perfect in heaven with Christ.

The first step of being set apart is to answer to God calling is, saying yes Lord, and being obedient to his calling on your life. Samuel heard God calling him, Samuel was obedient, he listened, not only did he listened, he answered to God's calling. The second step of being set apart is to be dedicated. When we are dedicated to God, our hands, feet and entire body belongs to him. If we dedicate our lives wholly to God we will Go and Preach the Gospel. We are commissioned to *"go ye therefore and preach the gospel compelling the lost to Jesus Christ and that is at any cost."... "We are crucified; nevertheless I live yet it's not I that liveth but Christ that liveth in me."*

The present ground for our joy is, that we are God's elect. He said that we are Royal Priesthood; we are called out of darkness into his marvelous light. We are kept by God power through faith. Faith is the Substance of things hope for and the evidence of things not seen.

The future ground for joy is, we look forward to the hope that, one-day we will reign with him forever, and in the last day salvation will reveal to us. Unadulterated joy is that place in the heart where love, expectation, tolerance, reverence, answered prayer and perfect peace all unite to produce joy that is incomprehensible. Unspeakable can only be experience it cannot be earned.

The Psalmist says in Psalms 16:11: *"Thou wilt shew me the path of life: in thy presence is fullness of joy; and at thy right hand there are pleasures for evermore"* Nehemiah states, *"the joy of the LORD is your strength"* and that leads to the path of life. When we live in our own strength, when we lean to our own understanding according to Proverbs 3 we also soon fall in an empty desert of defeat. *"The LORD is my strength and song, and he is become my salvation: he is my God, and I will prepare him an habitation; my father's God, and I will exalt him."* (Exodus 15:2 KJV). Why is "the LORD....my strength," for each of us? Simply because it is his promise, given for the asking, if we will trust his Word: *"Hitherto have ye asked nothing in my name: ask, and ye shall receive, that your joy may be full"* (John 16:24 KJV), *"And this is the confidence that we have in him, that, if we ask any thing according to his will, he heareth us"* (1 John 5:14 KJV)

King David prayed in heartfelt repentance that the LORD would *"Restore unto him the joy of his salvation"* (Psalms 51:12). Though his salvation was secure, we know he was a man of God own heart, his joy was dissolute in the face of personal crimes against God. So that's why he prayed for restoration of his joy that is unspeakable. He looked to God alone who is the restorer of his soul that's why he wrote in (Psalms 23 KJV) *"The LORD is my shepherd; I shall not want. He maketh me to lie down in green pastures: he leadeth me beside the still waters. He restoreth my soul: he leadeth me in the paths of righteousness for his name's sake. Yea, though I walk through the valley of the shadow of death, I will fear no evil: for thou art with me; thy rod and thy staff they comfort me. Thou preparest the table before me in the presence of mine enemies: thou anointest my head with oil my cup runneth over. Surely goodness and mercy shall follow me all the days of my life: and I will dwell in the house of the LORD forever."*

Without that unspeakable joy our lives simply exist, no matter how many mountains we climb, no matter how many battles we win, or how many challenges we face and conquer. A victory without joy is like a tree without roots, which falls, the first wind that blows. (Joel 1:12 KJV) says," *The vine is dried up, and the fig tree of languisheth; the pomegranate tree, the palm tree also, and the apple trees, even all the trees of the field, are withered: because joy is withered away from the sons of men."* As human we do things that give us no self-satisfaction from the result and we remain empty in our achievement.

"Unspeakable Joy" is a vague "quality" which few people have found, although Jesus spoke about it, and is a presently attainable today: (John 15:11 KJV) says *"These things have I spoken unto you, that my joy might remain in you, and that your joy might be full."*

"And now come I to thee; and these things I speak in the world, that they might have my joy fulfilled in themselves" (John 17:13 KJV).

The apostle Paul in Philippians 2 wrote, *" Fulfill ye my joy that ye be likeminded, having the same love, being of one accord, of one mind"* likeminded and unity makes joy thrives.

Joy is embellished among the various kindred fruits of the spirit, just as it withers and dies amidst worldliness and works of the flesh. The Bible says, in (Galatians 5:22-23 KJV)*"But the fruit of the Spirit is love, joy, peace, longsuffering, gentleness, goodness, faith, meekness, temperance: against such there is no law."* As long as we have the unspeakable joy, which we are speaking about, it should be shared with, others or it can be lost. With joy, we learn to be kind and affectionate to one another with brotherly love, according to Romans 12 in honor preferring one another. Joy restores those that had fallen and restores relationships that are broken. We are still talking about unspeakable joy that tells us according to (Galatians 6:1 KJV), if a *"Brethren, if a man be overtaken in a fault, ye which is spiritual, restore such a one in the spirit of meekness; considering thyself, lest thou also be tempted."*

I have no greater joy than to hear that my children walk in truth" The apostle Paul teaches: *"But none of these things move me, neither count I my life dear unto myself, so that I might finish my course with joy, and the ministry, which I have received of the Lord Jesus, to testify the gospel of the grace of God"* (Acts 20:24 KJV).

We must remember that *"his anger endureth but a moment; in his favor is life: weeping may endure for a night, but joy cometh in the morning"* (Psalms 30:5 KJV).

The greatest time of joy will be when the Lord shall return for his bride the Church. Isaiah 51 vs. 11 *"Therefore the redeemed of the Lord shall return, and come with singing unto Zion; and everlasting joy shall be upon their head: they shall obtain gladness and joy; and sorrow and mourning shall flee away."* There will be no more sorrow or sadness for the former things shall past away, there will be unspeakable joy.

As children of God, joy flourishes when love is kind, it is exaggerated when there is peace, it is exalted during long suffering, and joy is revived through kindness and gentleness. With Unspeakable joy we are the light of the world, the scripture says we ought to let our light so shine before men, that they may see our good work and glory our father which is in heaven. We are to be the salt of the earth, without that joy we can lose our savor and cannot preserve that unspeakable joy. One writer wrote and I quote that joy *"focuses us on that high road leading to the kingdom. When discouragement pulls us down, joy lifts us high. When we are despised, joy is our friend. When we are cast down, joy revives our spirits. When we are persecuted for righteousness sake"*, *"the joy of the LORD is ...our strength"* (Neh.8: 10). *"And when death at last darkens our door, and our last breathe expires into eternity, we can say with the prophets and apostle:" "I will joy in the God of my salvation" (Isa.12: 2), "willing rather to be absent from this body, and to be present with the LORD" (2 Cor. 5:8).*

The joy I'm speaking about, enables us to rejoice in tribulation. *"My brethren, count it all joy when we fall into divers' temptations; knowing this, that the trying of our faith worketh patience. But let patience have her perfect work, that ye may be perfect and entire, wanting nothing."* James 1:4 KJV) Divers temptation comes in all colors, shapes and forms. Trial comes as a result of living for God. *"Blessed are they which are persecuted for righteousness sake: for theirs is the kingdom of heaven. Blessed are ye, when men shall revile you, and persecute you, and shall say all manner of evil against you falsely, for my sake. Rejoice, and be exceedingly glad: for great is your reward in heaven: for so persecuted they the prophets which were before you."* Mat 5:10-12 KJV)

There is always joy to match whatever temptation we may go through. In Acts chapter 5, the apostles were beaten, and were told, they should not speak the name of Jesus. Peter explained in 1 Peter 4 KJV from verses 12-14; *"Beloved, think it not strange concerning the fiery trial which is to try you, as though some strange thing happened unto you: But rejoice, inasmuch as ye are partakers of Christ's sufferings; that, when his glory shall be revealed, ye may be glad also with exceeding joy. If ye be reproached for the name of Christ, happy are ye; for the spirit of glory and of God resteth upon you: on their part he is evil spoken of, but on your part he is glorified."*

The only way for us as Christian to find unspeakable joy during our trials, and tribulation, we must understand the nature of our trial; (1 Peter 1:7 KJV) states *"That the trial of your faith, being much more precious than gold that perisheth, though it be tried with fire, might be found unto praise and honor and glory at the appearing of Jesus Christ:"* *"For our light affliction,, which is but a moment, worketh for us a far more exceeding and eternal weight of glory; While we look not at the things which are seen, but at the things which are not seen are eternal:" for the things which are seen are temporal; but the things which are not seen eternal."* (2 Corinthians 4:17-18 KJV) As children of God, when we rejoice in our afflictions of life, we can overcome victoriously knowing, what we are going through or went through is an opportunity for our faith, patience, love, and hope to be tested. If we are able to rejoice in the midst of such trial, surely we have a joy that is unspeakable and full of glory.

If you had never experienced and would like to experience this unspeakable joy there are some grounds you need to follow.

The first step is to accept the Lord who is the source for us being able to rejoice in all things. According to Philippians 4:4 *"rejoice in the Lord always: and again I say, rejoice." (John 14:23KJV)* says *"Jesus answered and said unto him, if a man loves me, he will keep my words: and my father will love him, and we will come unto him, and make our abode with him."* If Jesus is with us, we can receive that joy which is unspeakable! *"These things have I spoken unto you, that my joy might remain in you, and that your joy might be full."(John 15:11)* *"These things I have spoken unto you, that in me ye might have peace. In the world ye shall have tribulation: but be of good cheer; I have overcome the world."* (John 16:33)

The second step to receiving that joy is to believe in the Lord Jesus Christ, that we can rejoice with joy that is unspeakable and full of glory. Even if we cannot see him, yet believing….this is the element of faith and trust; which prompts us to be obedient to him with our whole heart. We can only receive that unspeakable joy when we truly love God with our entire being, but this blessing is only for those that truly believe and love Jesus Christ, and accept he was crucified, died, buried and is now seated at the right hand of God, making intercession for our sins. If we love him we would keep his commandment and live according to his precepts.

The Anointing of the Holy Spirit makes the Difference

1 John 2:19-20 (King James Version)

They went out from us, but they were not of us; for if they had been of us, they would no doubt have continued with us: but they went out, that they might be made manifest that they were not all of us.

But ye have an unction from the Holy One, and ye know all things

Anoint is define as:

❖ *Bless somebody with oil... To rub oil or ointment on a part of somebody's body usually the head or feet, as part of a religion ceremony, example in a Christian baptism.*

❖ *Ordain somebody...to install someone officially or ceremonially in a position of office.*

In Hebrew Mashyach is defined *as 'anointed one' one who is consecrated for a special office or function.* The anointing is the existence of the Holy Spirit being smeared over someone. It is the spilling over life of Jesus, which imparts our supernatural strength enabling us as individual to perform extraordinary mission, or role in an office in which we are called and/or appointed to. God *anoint* individuals to particular offices. For example, he chooses some and anoints them to the office of a prophet.

He chooses others and anoints them to the office of Priesthood and others in the office of kings. The scripture tells us, David was a man of God's own heart; God chose and anointed him as priest, king and prophet. When God rejected the foolish and corrupt Saul, Israel's first king, he sent Samuel to Bethlehem to anoint David as the successor (1 Samuel 16:1-13)....the Hebrew word for David is *daw-veed* meaning beloved. David returned to caring for the sheep, *but "the Spirit of the Lord came upon David from that day forward,"* (1 Samuel 16:14). David served King Saul from time to time as a musician and armor bearer (1 Samuel 16:21-23). It is quite certain that Saul did not yet know that his young harp player would soon take his place as king.

As Christians, we should have the heart of God. The anointing of the Holy Spirit is given through people to demonstrate God's love and power. Christ means the "Anointed One". Because Christ is in us, the same anointing he had on earth we also have in us. We know we have the anointing of God flowing through us when God's heart touches another person's heart through our heart. When we speak about the anointing of God, we are speaking about the Holy Ghost. He brings life to all that receive his touch. We gain God anointing, if we love him more than we love ourselves, love our neighbor as ourselves. When we grieve the Holy Ghost, the flowing of the anointing automatically stops. *Keep your heart with all diligence, for out of it spring the issues of life.* (Proverbs 4:23 NKJV)

Traditionally, married men and women share the same bed and same food. My husband and I have difference in opinion, we do not always see eye to eye, but we are one. So it is with the Holy Spirit, we are one, and I try to please him as best as I can he in turn should try to please me. I read this book a couple years ago "what would Jesus do?' from then, I would ask myself that question before I do certain things in my life. Yes, I'm human, at times we allow the flesh to take over, especially the tongue. When my husband went out and had two children outside the marriage, everyone thought I was foolish to be with him still. It's the anointing that makes the different, was it easy? Of course not! At one time, I forgot to think what Jesus would do, but the anointing kicked in, and Jesus said we should forgive seventy times seven a day. So the answer I came up with is to forgive and move on. My husband said, *"The only reason why I am doing what I'm doing is because, I want to hit my chest and say I win"* but as long as I have the anointing I am a winner, there is no loser in God kingdom, yes we fall down, but we get back up again.

Love is the foundation of oneness. The love chapter as it is often called is a chapter that all married couple should read, 1 Corinthians 13:4-7 in order to keep the oneness, and keep the flowing of the anointing in our lives. To grieve the Holy Spirit, we make the Holy Spirit our enemy. When one gives his/her body in intimate relations to another person then that's his/her legal partner, it causes grief, sorrow or sadness and separation when others come between.

Jesus was our best example when he walked on earth he walked with the anointing. When Jesus came to John the Baptist at the Jordan River to be baptized by him, the heavens opened to him and he saw the spirit of God descended in the form of a dove. He was led into the wilderness to be tempted by the devil, but he was victorious over the devil, and continued to minister with the anointing. It's only the anointing that can break the yoke of the enemy. Isaiah 10:27 says *"it shall come to pass in the day that his burden will be taken away from your shoulder, and his yoke from your neck, and the yoke will be destroyed because of the anointing oil."*

In the book of Mark, there is the mention of a certain woman who came into the house of Simon, the leper, where Jesus was in Jerusalem. This woman was in possession of a very precious ointment an alabaster thermos of spikenard. It is a very expensive and rare substance, extracted from a variety of bearded grass growing in India. This thermos of spikenard may have cost the woman over three hundred days labor. How many years this woman may have worked to save the money to buy it, maybe once a year? She bought some this year, some next year and so on. When the flask was filled, she sealed it and kept it to anoint her bridegroom, on the day of their wedding. But the bible says she broke the thermos, her life sacrifice, and poured the spikenard on the head of Jesus. She gave to Jesus, the most precious and valuable thing that a woman could posses, and reserve for her husband-to-be. For the perfume to be exuded, the flask had to be broken. We must be broken, to be God's anointed, remove pride that gets in the way of us being broken. As long as pride takes precedent over our lives, we will never be able to be taken to our highest potential.

God's anointing on us as born again believers is different. Some anointing is on the sand, some is in shallow waters and others are in the deep, and this is dependant on the amount of time one spends with the Holy Spirit. This is my opinion that the holders of the gift of the spirit are a threat to Satan's kingdom; therefore they will always carry the greater anointing. The Lord have anointed us for specific reasons: "the Spirit of the Lord is upon me, because he has anointed me **to preach the gospel to the poor; He has sent me to heal the**

brokenhearted, to proclaim liberty to the captives and **recovery to sight to the blind**. To set at liberty **those who are oppressed**; to proclaim the acceptable year the LORD." (Luke 4:18-19 NKJV)

(Matthew 5:3 NKJV) speaks about *"Blessed are the poor in spirit, for theirs is the kingdom of heaven.* The term poor can be an implication of being a beggar, when the bible speaks about the poor in spirit; a spiritual beggar which is hungry for the spirit of God. If you are hungry for a touch from the Holy Spirit, God's anointing can flow through you. The flowing of the Holy Spirit is up to the person who is hungry to receive him. (Luke 6:19-20 NKJV) and the whole multitude sought to touch him, for power went out from him and healed them all. Then he lifted up his eyes toward his disciples, and said: *"Blessed are the poor, for yours is the kingdom of God."* The bible spoke about some of the things that can hinder you from receiving the anointing, such as pride, bitterness, un-forgiveness and envy. Bitterness and un-forgiveness almost crippled me. It was in October 12, 2009, I went to upper Manhattan at 9 am for a childcare class to start a Day care, from there I met my sisters-in-law to go downtown to buy something for the baby shower. My husband came home after me, we were having fun when his phone rang, the person on the other end was trashing me, stating that child protective service was at their house, and said that I called them and said, he was sexually molesting the children. I work for the City of New York, I know first of all these people will never give out there source, secondly why would I set up my husband. The individual was upset because my husband sister was in America for two weeks, and did not want to see them or talk to them, I was accused that my sister-in-law and I call children service. I was bitter to the core. I've done a lot of things in my life, but as to put my husband in prison was the last thing I would do. I'm the one who have to do the running around and find bail money; I had to be dumb, stupid or drunk.

Talk about double-sided mirror that same week I was attacked by my Landlord. It was on Wednesday October 09, 2009 my Landlord called my husband told him, he should come and get me out of her house, because we were at each other's throat; mine you I hadn't seen that woman for weeks. Friday October 11ᵗʰ 2009 she heard the door open came out, and accused me with sleeping with her husband, and I should go and get my young men. The Saturday October 12ᵗʰ was accused of setting up my husband.

I thought the two individual was working together. The Double-sided mirror of my life comes in two's, never one problem at a time.

It took me a time to forgive but I was dying inside. (Matthew 10:31-14 NKJV) *"If the household is worthy, let your peace come upon it. "And whoever will not receive you nor hear your words, when you depart from that house or city, shake off the dust from your feet."*

Heal the broken hearted: "The word which God sent to the children of Isreal, preaching peace through Jesus Christ; He is Lord of all; "that word you know, which was proclaimed throughout all Judea, which began in Galilee after the baptism which John preached: "how God anointed Jesus of Nazareth with the Holy Spirit and power, went about doing good, healing all who were oppressed by the devil, for God was with him. (Acts 10:36-38 NKJV)

Some people think if a Christian gets sick and is not healed of all his diseases, this can be a lack of faith, or because he/she sinned; Others thinks healing was only for the apostolic age, when all diseases were healed automatically or instantly. What we need to realize is, God does not always heal all of our infirmities. Paul was afflicted by a "bodily ailment" while he was preaching to the Galatians according to Galatians 4:13-14. 2 Timothy 4:20 also mentioned that Trophimus was left in the town of Miletus because he was too sick to travel. Paul encouraged Timothy to manage his illness through medical means for his stomach ailment instead of praying. Some of us as Christian expect instantaneous healing when we pray but Mark 8 tells us, Jesus had to lay his hand on the blind man at Bethsaida twice before they was fully healed. God heals according to his will and purpose, its provisional on the will of God for our lives.

Sometimes God allows us to undergo sickness as a form of training in righteousness or as a form of discipline. Trials are often permitted by God for our sanctification, or because God brag on us. Job was a good example; he was afflicted with sore because Satan thought Job would give up on God if it seems, God had turn his back on him, but Job kept his integrity. Paul learned that when he prayed, God would remove from him an angel of Satan who was afflicting him: "And to keep me from being too elated by the abundance of revelations, a thorn was given me in the flesh, a messenger: of Satan, to harass me, to keep me from being too elated. Three times I besought the Lord about this, that it should leave me; but he said to me. *"My grace is sufficient for you, for my power is made perfect in weakness. I will all the more gladly boast of my weaknesses, that the power of Christ may rest upon me "* (2 Cor.12:7-9). We have to remember that God's grace is sufficient to sustain us when we are face with our infirmities in life. His grace includes physical and psychological health problem and financial problems.

God allows us to suffer to help others. Someone send me a thought and it *states "When life knocks you down to your knees, remember that you are in the perfect position to pray."* Paul became sick while on his first missionary journey and forced to stop traveling, is a good example, he was able to preach to the Galatians, for he told them: *"You know it was because of a bodily ailment that I preached the gospel to you at first"* Gal. 4:13. If he had not preached to the Galatians, he would not have later written the epistle, which appears in our New Testament. God used Paul's illness to bring salvation to the Galatians, and to bring us a work of scripture, through which we are still receiving benefits from God.

The anointing is also given to us to proclaim freedom to those that are in captivity by the devil. (2 Timothy 2:24-26 NKJV) And a servant of the Lord must not quarrel, but be gentle to all, able to teach, patient, in humility correcting those who are in opposition; if God perhaps will grant them repentance, so that they may know the truth, and that they may come to their senses and escape the snare of the devil, having been taken captive by him to do his will. Isaiah 10:27 NKJV) *"It shall come to pass in that day that his burden will be taken away from your shoulder and his yoke from your neck, and the yoke will be destroyed because of the anointing oil."*
"Therefore if the son makes you free, you shall be free indeed." (John 8:36 NKJV)

The anointing of the Holy Spirit is one of the greatest gifts from God. (John 7: 37-39 NKJV) On the last day, that great day of the feast, Jesus stood and cried out, saying, *"If anyone thirsts, let him come to Me and drink."* He who believes in Me, *as the Scripture has said, out of his heart will flow rivers of living water."* But this He spoke concerning the Spirit, of whom those believing in him would receive; for the Holy Spirit was, not yet given, because Jesus was not yet glorified.

For all the promises of God in him is yes, and in him Amen, to the glory of God through us. Now he who establishes us with you in Christ and has anointed us is God, who also has sealed us and given us the Spirit in our hearts as a guarantee.

(2 Corinthians 1:20-22 NKJV). If we want to be used by God and his anointing be poured on us, we must be willing to endure suffering. The experience of purification is not sweet, its bitter, but the end result has a sweet fragrance to the Holy Spirit. In Leviticus 26:31, *"I will not smell the fragrance of your sweet aromas. "Because of the obedience of Israel, whatever they were offering or doing for God's satisfaction was not pleasant to him. Whenever God's children are disobedient to him, He is not pleased with their prayers or whatever sacrifice they can offer to him. God cannot be bribed.*

Without being spiritually sensitive, we will not be able to hear the voice of God. Dwelling and listening in the presence of God will develop our spiritual understanding; but you have an anointing from the Holy One, and you know all things. (1 John 2:20 NKJV) The anointing which you have received from him abides in you, and you do not need anyone to teach you; as the same anointing teaches you concerning all things, which is true, and as he teach you, you will abide in him. (1 John 2:27 NKJV) Many are not hearing what the Holy Spirit is saying, it's only those who walk in the fresh anointing have good spiritual sensitivity and can hear the voice of God.

Another blessing of the anointing is; we would be fertile and produce fruit. In John 15, it mentions that those who do not produce fruit are cut off and those who produce are purged. (Isaiah 59:16-21 NKJV) *"he saw that there was no man, and wondered that there was no intercessor; therefore his own arm brought salvation as a breastplate, and a helmet of salvation on his head; He put on the garment of vengeance for clothing, and was clad with zeal as a cloak. According to their deeds, accordingly he will repay, fury to his adversaries, recompense to his enemies; the coastlands he will fully repay. So shall they fear the name of the Lord from the west, and his glory from the rising of the sun; when the enemy comes in like a flood, the spirit of the Lord will lift up a standard against him."*

The Redeemer will come to Zion, and to those who turn from transgression in Jacob," says the LORD. "As for me, says the Lord, *"this is my mouth, shall not depart from your mouth, nor from the mouth of your descendants,"* says the LORD, "from this time and forevermore." (Isaiah 60:1-2 NKJV) *"Arise; shine; for the light has come! And the glory of the Lord is risen upon you. For behold, the darkness shall cover the earth, and deep darkness the people; but the Lord will rise over you, and his glory will be seen upon you."*

The free flowing of God's love brings joy to God, and the person he flows through feels the joy. Love is the joy we get from God when we put his benefit, and the benefit of another person before our own. Paul wrote in Philippians 4 verses 4, *"Rejoice in the Lord always: again I say rejoice."* This was written while he was imprisoned. One would ask, how can you talk about joy and rejoicing in your situation? But the best type of joy is triumphant joy. It was because of the joy of the Lord that Paul was sustained in prison. Paul had communion with the

Holy Spirit. There was oneness between the Holy Spirit and Paul.

"Is this not the fast that I have chosen: To loose the bonds of wickedness, to undo the heavy burden, to let the oppressed go free, and that you break every yoke?" Is it not to share your bread with the hungry and that you bring to your house the poor who are cast out; when you see the naked, that you cover him, and not hide yourself from your own flesh? Then your light shall break forth like the morning, your healing shall spring forth speedily, and your righteousness shall go before you; the glory of the LORD shall be rear your guard. Then you shall call, and the LORD will answer; You shall cry, and he will say, 'Here I am' "If you take away the yoke from your midst, the pointing of the finger, and speaking wickedness, if you extend your soul to the hungry and satisfy the afflicted soul, then your light shall dawn in the darkness, and the darkness shall be as the noonday. The LORD will guide you continually, and satisfy your soul in drought and strengthen your bones; you shall be like a watered garden, and like a spring of water, whose waters do not fail. Those from among you shall build the old waste places; you shall raise up the foundations of many generations; and you shall be called the repairer of the Breach, the Restorer of streets to dwell in." (Isaiah 58:6-12) you will show me the path of life; in your presence is fullness of joy; at your right hand are pleasures forevermore. (Psalms 16:11).

He's Coming Back as a Judge

For the son of man is going to come in his father's glory with his angels, and then he will reward each person according to what he has done." (Matthew 16:27)

Isaiah says this of the DAY OF THE LORD. Isaiah 13:6 "Wail; for the Day of the LORD is at hand; it shall come as a destruction from the Almighty." (Isaiah 13:9 KJV) "Behold, the DAY OF THE LORD cometh, cruel both with wrath and fierce anger, to lay the land desolate; and he shall destroy the sinners out of it."

I'm sure you maybe wondering what his coming back have to do with being trapped in the double-sided mirror of life? You will learn that his coming give us the victory over the enemy.

As Christians, we have one hope that is the certainty of Christ return. One would ask, what is the proof that he's coming back; before his resurrection Jesus said, *"For the son of man is going to come in his father's glory with his angels, and then he will reward each person according to what he has done."* (Matthew 16:27 KJV)

After his resurrection: Jesus said, *"Only hold on to what you have until I come…I am coming soon. Hold on to what you have, so that no one will take your crown."* (Revelation 2:25 & 3:11 KJV). As a child I heard that Christ is coming back sooner than we think, it's been over forty (40) years, and he's still not here but he's forty (40) years nearer. 1 Thessalonians 4:15-17 says, "According to the Lord's own words, we who are still alive, who are left until the coming of the Lord, will not precede those who have fallen asleep. For the Lord himself will come down from heaven, with a loud command, with the voice of the

127

archangel, and with the trumpet call of God, and the dead in Christ will rise first. After that, we who are still alive and are remain will be caught up together with them in the clouds to meet the Lord in the air. And so we will be with the Lord forever." (Acts 1:11) "Men of Galilee," they said, "Why do you stand here looking into the sky? This same Jesus, who was taken from you into heaven, will come back in the same way you saw him go into heaven."

The importance of Christ's return signifies Victory over the enemies…in the Christian realm our greatest enemy is death. *"Then cometh the end, when he shall have delivered up the kingdom to God, even the Father; when he shall have put down all rule and all authority and power; For he must reign, till he hath put all enemies under his feet. The last enemy that shall be destroyed is death."* (1 Corinthians 15:24-26).

"Let us be glad and rejoice, and give honor to him: for the marriage Lamb is come, and his wife hath made himself ready. And to her was granted, that she should be arrayed in fine linen, clean and white: for the fine linen is the righteousness of saints. And he saith unto me, Write, blessed are they, which are called unto the marriage supper of the Lamb. And he saith unto me, these are true sayings of God." (Revelation19: 7-9)

"And I John saw the Holy City, New Jerusalem, coming down from God out of heaven, prepared as a bride adorned for her husband." Revelation 21:2.

"And there came unto me one of the seven angels which had the seven vials full of the seven last plagues, and talked with me, saying, come hither, I will shew thee the bride, the Lamb's wife." (Revelation 21:9 KJV)

Matthew 25 KJV: "Then shall the kingdom of heaven be likened unto ten virgins, which took their lamps, and went forth to meet the bridegroom. And five of them were wise and five were foolish. They that were foolish took their lamps, and took no oil with them: but the wise took oil in their vessels with their lamps. While the bridegroom tarried, they all slumbered and slept. And at midnight there was a cry made, Behold, the bridegroom cometh; go ye out to meet him. Then all those virgins arose, and trimmed their lamps. And the foolish said unto the wise, give us of your oil; for our lamps are gone out. But the wise answered, saying, Not so; lest there be not enough for us and you: but go ye rather to them that sell, and buy the bridegroom came; and they that were ready went in with him to the marriage: and the door was shut. Then came the other virgins, saying Lord, Lord, open to us. But he answered and said, Verily I say unto you, I know you not. Watch therefore, for ye know neither the day not the hour wherein the son of man cometh".

He came the first time as a babe to Bethlehem, but the bible teaches, and the Lord Jesus himself when he was upon the earth taught that: *"If I go, I will come again and receive you myself, that where I am there ye may be also."*

When the scripture speaks about virgin, it's about spiritual purity and the faithfulness of the saints of Christ. As children of God we should be faithful to God, we should crucified our mortal body and put on immortality. 1 Corinthians 15:54 *"So when this corruptible shall be brought to pass the saying that is written, Death is swallowed up in victory."*

We know that a virgin is defined as *"someone who has never had sexual intercourse or religiously a woman who have taken a vow of chastity for religious reasons."*

In the natural every man's fantasy is to meet and get married to a virgin. It is so sad, that, the society we live in, young people think it's a shame to be a virgin, the same apply to the spiritual realm. (Romans 12:1 KJV) says *"I beseech you brethrens by the mercies of God that you present your bodies as living sacrifice holy and acceptable and a reasonable service."* As Christians, we believe Jesus is the bridegroom, and is said he is coming back for the bride (Church). John 14:3 tells us *"And if I go and prepare a place for you. I will come again, and receive you unto myself; that where I am there ye may be also."*

As a child I heard that Jesus was coming again, and he's coming soon, it's over 40 years ago, it **"seems"** he's never coming back; What we need to realize is that his promise was over two thousand (2000) years ago, and surely he is coming back. The signs are all around. The people who do not believe in the Lord often mock and scoffer but 2 Peter from verse 3 tell us *"Knowing this first, that there shall come in the last days scoffers, walking after their own lusts, and saying, Where is the promise of his coming? For since the fathers fell asleep, all things continue as they were from the beginning of the creation.*

As the parable mentioned about the ten virgins sleeping while the bridegroom came so it is with the Church today, we are fast asleep.

The bridegroom cometh, the trumpet sound, but the Church is in a deep sleep. The Church awoke from its slumber with no oil in the lamp. Some of the bride had extra oil, but some just had enough for the wait; the bride that did not have extra oil with them was a result of having to carry around hatred, envy, malice, jealousy and pride. As for those who took extra oil, they were always praying and fasting and reading the word; they had the Holy Spirit to sustain them. Unlike the foolish virgin, they took humility, peace, faith, longsuffering, patience, temperance and truth. We often want to live our lives in sin, but when we fall into a situation, we want to borrow oil from our brother and sister; we have to realize, that brother/sister may just have enough for them. The Apostle Paul writes in (Ephesians 5:14-18 KJV) *"Wherefore he saith, Awake thou that sleepest, and arise from the dead, and Christ shall give thee light. See then that ye walk circumspectly, not as fools, but as wise, redeeming the time, because the days are evil. Wherefore be ye not unwise, but understanding what the will of the Lord is. And be not drunk with wine, wherein is excess; but be filled with the Spirit."*

My question to you is; Are you ready for the bridegroom to come? In school a lot of us like to procrastinate. I hated to work in groups, because, I would have finished my work weeks in advance, but having to wait for the other members of the team to complete their part, the day of the presentation is when we will be there trying to put everything together. When it comes to preparing for the bridegroom, now is not the time to delay preparation for the return of the messiah.

I read a passage sometime ago that made sense to me, there is no mention of the bride in scripture, the bible focus on the groom, yet in today society, the bride is the one who gets all the attention. I remember when I got married over twelve years ago, everyone eyes were on me, from the crown of my head to the sole of my feet. Who wasn't telling me to smile, was fixing my dress. One thing for certain, when the Lord shall appear all attention will be focusing on him, all eyes will be centered on him and him only. (Revelation 1:7 KJV) says, *Behold, He is coming with clouds, and every eye will see him…*

I don't know about you, but I will be caught up to meet him in the air. It will be a sad state for me if my bridegroom comes and I miss him. I will be going to a place where there will be no more tears to dim the eyes, I will be at peace forever, when my bridegroom I shall see. For the married couples, you know how excited it is when you are married and your husband comes home, it's an excited feeling to see them and spend some quality time with them.

Some of the signs of the bridegroom coming back:

(Matthew 24:32-35 KJV) "Now learn a parable of the fig tree; When his branch is yet tender, and putteth forth leaves, ye know that summer is nigh: So likewise ye, when ye shall see all these things, know that it is near, even at the doors. Verily I say into you, this generation shall not pass, till all these things be fulfilled."

❖ RUSSIA-RISE AND FALL: Ezekiel 38 and 39 tells us about Russia place in Prophecy. According to the chapters Russia did her deadliest work by invading the land of Palestine. Russia today is a great nation with the stage set for the fulfillment of prophesies. Ezekiel 38 verses 5 and 6 mentioned that Russia allies are Persia that is now known as Iran, Ethiopia, and Libya. A treaty was sign with Persia giving Russia access through the land to the Middle East and Palestine in the event of a war. Russia decision to invade Israel is in verses 10,11 & 16 of Ezekiel *"Thus saith the Lord God; It shall also come to pass, that at the time shall things come into thy mind, and thou shalt think an evil thought; and thou shalt say, I will go up to the land of the unwalled villages; I will go to them that are at rest, that dwell safely, all of them dwelling without walls, and having neither bars nor gates."* And thou shalt come up against my people of Israel, as a cloud to cover the land; it shall be in a latter days, and I will bring thee against my land, that the heathen may know me, when I shall be sanctified in thee, O Gog, before their eyes."

❖ THE RETURN OF ISREAL—THE FIG TREE IS BUDDING! The return of the Jews to Israel and Palestine as a nation is another sign of the Lord's return. God promised Israel to Abraham and his seed depending on obedience. The Babylonians and the Assyrians took the Jews into captivity because they disobeyed God. The enemies laugh at possessions of the land, but God promise that they will not keep possession. *"For I will take you from among the heathen, and gather you out of all countries, and will bring you into your own land."* Ezekiel 36:24
"Thus saith the Lord God; In the day that I shall have cleansed you from all your iniquities, I will also cause you to dwell in the cities, and the wastes shall be builded... And they shall say, this land that was desolate is become like the Garden of Eden...Then the heathen that are left round about you shall know that I the Lord build the ruined places, and plant that was desolate: I the Lord have spoken it, and I will do it" Ezekiel 36:33-36

❖ **TRAVEL:** I don't know how much you keep up with what's going on in the world today, but people are travelling all around the world and now everyone is going to the Holy Land. Daniel 12 vs 4 *"But thou, O Daniel, shut up the words, and seal the book, even to the time of the end: many shall run to and fro, and knowledge shall be increased."*

❖ **KNOWLEDGE: This is defined as information in mind:** "General awareness or possession of information, facts, idea, truth, or principles." This is another prophecy that Daniel prophesied. When you listen to or read the news, you hear that people in there eighty's and ninety's are going back to school. Satellites, telephone, television and computers are taking over. When you walk the streets, the youngest child has a cell phone. I have a ten year old nephew and he is so advance in the computer, that I have to be asking him certain questions, although I went to school for Business Administration. This is another sign that the coming of the Lord is near.

❖ **APOSTASY:** This is defined as "the renunciation (denial, abandonment, rejection) of a religion or political belief or allegiance." 1 Timothy 4:1 tells us "Now the Spirit speaketh expressly, that in THE LATTER TIMES some shall depart from the faith, giving heed to seducing spirits, and doctrines of devils. If you have spiritual eyes you will see that we are in a spiritual warfare the demon realm is taking over the world especially in the Churches. 2 Timothy 3:1-5 states…" *in the LAST DAYS perilous (dangerous) times shall come. For men shall be lovers of their own selves, covetous, boasters, proud, blasphemers, disobedient to parents, unthankful, unholy, without natural affection, trucebreakers, false accusers, incontinent, fierce, despisers of those that are good, traitors, heady, high-minded, lovers of pleasures more than lovers of God; having a form of godliness, but denying the power thereof; from such turn away."*

❖ **Counterfeiting the Gospel (2 Timothy 3:5, Matthew 15:9)**

❖ **Spirit to be poured out on all flesh (Joel 2:28)**

❖ **False prophets and false Christ (Matthew 24:24)**

❖ **Gospel to be preached to all the world (Matthew 24:14, Revelation 14:6-7)**

❖ **Earthquakes, Floods, Famines, Plagues and disease such as the world have never seen. (Matthew 24 and Luke 21)**

❖ **Wars and Rumors of Wars:** There are no longer rumors of wars there are wars.

Tithing and Offering is a Privilege accept Your Blessing

"Bring ye all the tithes into the storehouse, that there may be meat in mine house, and prove me herewith, saith the Lord of hosts, if I will not open you the windows of heaven, and pour you out a blessing that there shall not be room enough to receive it. And I will rebuke the devourer for your sakes, and he shall not destroy the fruits of your ground; neither shall your vine cast her fruit before the time in the field, saith the Lord of host." (Mal. 3:10-11 KJV)

I am including in my writing, the importance of tithing. I was out of a job for years and every time I receive any kind of money God received his tenth and my bills were paid and I am still marveled as to how, as I mentioned earlier. We lose out on our blessing and stay trapped because we refused to give back to God when he bless us.

Today as Christians there are a lot of controversies whether or not tithing is for the Old Testament people, or for us today. Jesus said, *"If Abraham were your father, you would do the works of Abraham."* The Scripture tells us that Abraham rendered tithes to Melchizedek. Abraham's children live as Abraham lived. Tithing was not simply a commandment that was given under the law. Abraham and Jacob lived hundreds of years before the law was given; they both offered their tithes to God. They did not need the Law of Moses; they were "a law unto themselves." Paul said it this way: "The Law was not made for a righteous man." (1 Timothy 1:9)

The tithe is the tenth of all the increase that God gives to you. What does "increase" include? Increase is, everything that increases the value of earthly possessions God places into your trust, be it earned income or unearned gifts. A tenth of everything "increase" to you belongs to God in the form of tithes. The tithes of your increase are not yours to give to God; it is God's for you to give, it's a privilege for us to have it to give to him. *"Bring ye all the tithes into the storehouse, that there may be meat in mine house, and prove me herewith, saith the Lord of hosts, if I will not open you the windows of heaven, and pour you out a blessing that there shall not be room enough to receive it. And I will rebuke the devourer for your sakes, and he shall not destroy the fruits of your ground; neither shall your vine cast her fruit before the time in the field, saith the Lord of hosts"* (Mal. 3:10-11)

Offerings on the other hand, are gifts brought to God beyond the tithes. God gave his people some discretion as to the amount or number of offerings to bring. Their financial situation in life and the depth of their zeal for God will be shown by their choices concerning offerings.

God instituted several offering in Israel for the people to bring to his servants. Just to name a few:

- There was the Offering of **"firstfruits"** which was a little offering taken from among the earliest of one's ripening crops. This offering was not in the form of money but in the form of crops. It was a required offering, but the amount of "firstfruits" brought to God was never precise, it was at the people's discretion as to the amount. The bible recorded that Cain brought some of the fruits of the soil, as an offering to the Lord.

- There was the offering of the **"Firstborn"** of your male animals. "All that openeth the matrix is mine; and every firstling among thy cattle, weather ox or sheep, that is male." Said the Lord (Exodus 34:19). There was the offering of the firstborn child in every family. The firstborn belonged to God, whether animal or human. Instead of bringing to the Lord's temple the firstborn child of every Israelite mother. The lord required Israel to offer a certain amount of money instead of the firstborn child.

Every male was required to offer a small offering of money with him, whenever God commanded the leaders of Israel to take a census. Exodus 30:14-15 states "everyone that passeth among them that are numbered, from twenty years old and above, shall give less than half a shekel, when they give an offering unto the LORD, to make atonement for your souls." A census was rarely taken in Israel, but when one was taken, each male had to make this offering to the Lord. Giving should be a joyous time in the lives of Christian. Exodus 36:5-7 tells us about the story of Moses, when he told the people of Israel that God had told him to collect an offering of materials for erecting a tabernacle, the people brought materials that Moses had to tell them to stop. After the tabernacle was built, God required an offering for the dedication of it, God specified how much of an offering was to be brought by each tribe. We no longer have to sacrifice an animal to God. One of the rules concerning animal sacrifice in the Old Testament was, the animal had to be without blemish. Leviticus1:2-4 states *"Speak unto the children of Israel, and say unto them, if anyone of you bring an offering of the cattle, even of the herd, and of the flock. If his offering be a burnt sacrifice of the herd, let him offer a male without blemish: he shall offer it of his own voluntary will at the door of the tabernacle of the congregation before the LORD. And he shall put his hand upon the head of the burnt offering: and it shall be accepted from him to make atonement for him."* Malachi 1:7-8 tells us, the Lord was angry when the people brought gift that was polluted. *"Ye offer polluted bread upon mine alter; and ye say, wherein have we polluted thee? In that ye say, The table of the Lord is Contemptible. And if ye offer the blind for sacrifice, is it not evil? And if ye offer the lame and sick, is it not evil? Offer it now unto the governor; will he be pleased with thee, or accept thy person? saith the Lord id hosts."*

The Lord loves a cheerful giver. Giving back to God that which belongs to him should not be a burden to us, it's not ours to begin with. The Lord wants us to give from our hearts; most of all he wants us to live a pure and holy life. We tend to substitute money for repentance. As ministers of God, we need to teach about tithing and offering, but we need to let the people know they need to present their bodies as a living sacrifice, holy and acceptable and perfect will of God. Some ministers are hireling, they know an individual is living in sin, but they are more concerned about the money rather than the souls of people. What the Pastors do not realize or maybe just don's care is, they are not helping the individuals who just send their tithes, or who "bribe" those pastors; they are killing them to satisfy their own selfish needs. Both the pastor and the people need to repent, especially the Pastor.

As children of God we are required or commanded by God to financially support our ministers, take care of his people. God people need to be educated about tithing. When the bible speaks about ten percent of our increase was his, and must be given to his servant, along with the offerings, he requires as well. Malachi to Israel asked, "Will a man rob God? Yet ye robbed me, Saith the Lord!" The question then and now is "How have we robbed God?" the answer to that question is, "In tithes and offering." A man cannot be trusted, if he can steal from God. If he can steal from God he can commit murder, there is nothing he cannot do to another human being.

Christian tends to doubt God; we do not put our faith at it works to bring him the tithes that he commanded. We often disobey God by refusing to give to him the tithes and offerings, so we give whatever to maintain appearance. It is better that we don't give anything at all, than to give just a potion of what is required. It seems, we are doing God a favor. We are not doing him any favor, we are just robbing ourselves from the blessing that God has for us. Tithing is a commandment and in order to obtain eternal life we must obey the commandments. One of the Ten Commandments is, "Thou shalt not steal," and robbing from God is stealing. Stealing is stealing, be it from mankind or from God.

Trouble in the Storm

Let not your heart be trouble
Is the motto I need to hear
Believe in the almighty and be not dismay
He guides your feet and closes your ear.

The sea may rage and the winds may blow
The tempest is strong
Thou the bellows roll

I've learned to surrender
And place my life in his hand
As I rend my heart and he direct my path.

Holy Spirit

He's alpha and omega the beginning and the end
    Operate with each other
        Lead by his Grace
            Yes To the possible

Spares the saints
    Punish the Sinners
        Ignite the light that shines within
          Reach the unreachable
            Immutable
              Transformable

CPSIA information can be obtained at www.ICGtesting.com
Printed in the USA
BVOW01s1009150514

353633BV00001B/81/P